© Beowulf Sheehan

DAVID MEANS, an internationally acclaimed fiction
writer, was born and raised in Michigan. His second collection of stories, *Assorted Fire Events*, won
the Los Angeles Times Book Prize for Fiction and
earned a National Book Critics Circle nomination.
His third book, *The Secret Goldfish*, received wide-
spread critical acclaim and was shortlisted for the
Frank O'Connor International Short Story prize.
His fourth book, *The Spot*, was selected as a *New
York Times Book Review* Notable Book of 2010
and won an O. Henry Prize. His books have been
translated into ten languages. His stories have appeared in *The New Yorker*, *Harper's*, *The Best
American Short Stories*, *The Best American Mystery Stories*, *The O. Henry Prize Stories*, and numer-
ous other publications. Recipient of a Guggenheim
Foundation Fellowship in 2013, Means lives in New
York and teaches at Vassar College.

Additional Praise for *Hystopia*

Named a Best of the Year Selection by *Kirkus Reviews*, the *San Francisco Chronicle*, *Commonweal* Magazine, and the Library of Michigan

"[*Hystopia* is] a meditation on war (not just Vietnam, Mr. Means suggests, but the continuum of combat that links veterans through history) and the toll it takes on soldiers and families and loved ones. It's also a portrait of a troubled America in the late 1960s and early '70s—an America reeling from unemployment and lost dreams, and seething with anger, and uncannily familiar, in many ways, to America today."
—Michiko Kakutani, *The New York Times*

"Supremely gonzo and supremely good . . . If Flannery O'Connor had written about Vietnam, Rake is the kind of character she would have created. . . . What is the relation between the chaos of lived experience and the coherence of narrative? How is trauma tied to the fracturing of narrative, to our inability to see the past as past, distinct from, yet leading to the present? Henry James once described the real as 'the things we cannot possibly not know.' *Hystopia* often reads, strange as it sounds, like a Jamesian investigation of knowledge, albeit one fueled by amphetamines."
—Anthony Domestico, *The Boston Globe*

"*Hystopia* quickly gains momentum and plausibility thanks to its richness of detail. Means is a writer of dazzling gifts: a challenging stylist and a keen observer whose senses seem, at times, pitched to a state of hyperawareness."
—Jay McInerney,
The New York Times Book Review

"*Hystopia*'s critique of Vietnam is Means's most realistic work to date, and its picture of social breakdown feels horribly believable, given the questions about civil rights, foreign wars and future leadership that Americans are asking today.

Ultimately, like all Means's work, this is about the human condition. How do we behave when our cultural and mental strength has been destroyed and replaced by a blundering government intent on doping us into submission? . . . Means takes a truer, harder look at the frailties and strengths of humanity than most authors dare, and in the young soldier's novel he has created a work of meta-fiction that crackles with life and menace." —Melissa Katsoulis, *The Times* (London)

"[A] wild, multilayered and deeply affecting novel . . . Means conjures a haunting, almost dreamlike aesthetic akin to that of Terrence Malick's 1973 film *Badlands*. His eye for detail is microscopic, and the natural world in particular is beautifully evoked. . . . This rich novel takes us far beyond Vietnam-era America; it is a potent examination of what makes, and keeps, us human."
—Francesca Wade, *Financial Times* (London)

"David Means's *Hystopia* is the boldest alternate history novel in years. . . . A debut novel that reinvents a genre . . . In his fidelity to a peculiarly American brokenness, Means's debut surpasses nearly all of his recent peers." —*Flavorwire*

"A drug-addled nightmare version of American history nodding in the direction of Philip K. Dick, Kurt Vonnegut, and Hunter S. Thompson. . . . *Hystopia*'s tale-swallowing meta-fiction ingeniously embodies the self-replicating mental prisons of war trauma." —Sam Sacks, *The Wall Street Journal*

"*Hystopia* by David Means is a fascinating novel within a novel. Complex without being confusing, the novel weaves Eugene's own battles with mental illness and his sister's disappearance into a beautiful, haunting tale of loss."
—Nancy Hightower, *The Washington Post*

"[*Hystopia*] is simultaneously heartbreaking, bitingly funny, realistic, and satirical; the hoops it asks readers to jump through regarding structure and authorial intent are a joy, not a burden. It successfully finds a fresh approach to war fiction." —Ian Swalwell, *The Kansas City Star*

"David Means, an excellent American short story writer, brings his exceptional talent to the fore in his first novel. . . . [*Hystopia*] is a profoundly important book. It demonstrates the futility of war for all who have taken part."
—Michael D. Langan, *The Buffalo News*

"[Means] has produced one of those rare, self-conscious books that operates on multiple levels, alluding to its own insufficiency while paradoxically becoming sufficient as a result. It works as a stylized reimagining of the Vietnam era, it works as an indirect revelation of the emotional truth of this same era, and it works as a subtle critique of the inability of stories and narratives to truly compensate when more than stories and narratives are needed."
—Simon Chandler, *Electric Literature*

"The very structure of *Hystopia*, his first novel, is a testament to Means's belief in the power of stories that demand to be told. . . . Some stories, Means suggests, are so explosive that they invite countless retelling, shedding new light—and darkness, too. In the real world, as in Means's novel, America has, of course, remained trapped in war. Means has a profound respect for the nation's actual explosive history; his plot gleefully alters details, but not the basic themes of the story, or their violent outcomes." —Amy Weiss-Meyer, *The Atlantic*

"The writing is beautiful and exuberant, moving and funny, and always one step ahead. The descriptions of getting stoned are as vivid as the landscapes. Means's characters live in a state of constant sensory attention that keeps them always attuned to the texture . . . the smell of lakes and trees, the taste of carbon." —Christine Smallwood, *Harper's*

"*Hystopia* . . . is powerful and expansive. . . . *Hystopia* gets at how storytelling is potentially therapeutic, alleviating the burden by sharing with others, but also fraught with outsider misunderstanding. Means's cleverly dovetailing layers of meditation, the meta-fictional framing, the sci-fi schema, the winking adaptation and reversal of expected plotlines all underscore the impossible slipperiness of a true war story.

—Chantal McStay, *BOMB*

"A compelling, imaginative alternative-history tale about memory and distress . . . By turns disturbing, hilarious, and absurd, Means's novel is also sharply penetrating in its depiction of an America all too willing to bury its past."

—*Booklist* (starred review)

"Means writes stunning prose and draws his characters with verve. . . . [*Hystopia*] reads like an acid flashback, complete with the paranoia, manic monologues, and violent visions, proving that some traumas never go away."

—*Publishers Weekly* (starred review)

"Means's first novel is a compelling portrait of an imagined counterhistory that feels entirely real."

—*Kirkus Reviews* (starred review)

"Terrifying and beautiful, *Hystopia* defies every evasion or sentimentality in its resolute evocation of a history our culture so readily avoids. Robert Stone would be proud."

—Christian G. Appy, professor of history
at University of Massachusetts, Amherst,
and author of *American Reckoning:
The Vietnam War and Our National Identity*

"A riveting, hypnotic dystopia of Vietnam combat veterans during the (fictional) second JFK administration. Amazing writing not for the faint of heart. Nuggets of beauty glowing in a pan of pain."

—Jonathan Shay, M.D., Ph.D., author of
Achilles in Vietnam and *Odysseus in America*

HYSTOPIA

DAVID MEANS

PICADOR   FARRAR, STRAUS AND GIROUX   NEW YORK

HYSTOPIA. Copyright © 2016 by David Means. All rights reserved. Printed in the United States of America. For information, address Picador, 175 Fifth Avenue, New York, N.Y. 10010.

picadorusa.com • picadorbookroom.tumblr.com
twitter.com/picadorusa • facebook.com/picadorusa

Picador® is a U.S. registered trademark and is used by Macmillan Publishing Group, LLC, under license from Pan Books Limited.

For book club information, please visit facebook.com/picadorbookclub or e-mail marketing@picadorusa.com.

Designed by Jonathan D. Lippincott

The Library of Congress has cataloged the Farrar, Straus and Giroux edition as follows:

Names: Means, David, 1961–
Title: Hystopia : a novel / David Means.
Description: First edition. | New York : Farrar, Straus and Giroux, 2016.
Identifiers: LCCN 2015035421 | ISBN 9780865479135 (hardcover) |
    ISBN 9780374714871 (e-book)
Subjects: LCSH: Nineteen seventies—Fiction. | United States—History—
    20th century—Fiction. | BISAC: FICTION / Literary. | GSAFD:
    Alternative histories (Fiction)
Classification: LCC PS3563.E195 H97 2016 | DDC 813'.54—dc23
LC record available at http://lccn.loc.gov/2015035421

Picador Paperback ISBN 978-1-250-11838-7

Our books may be purchased in bulk for promotional, educational, or business use. Please contact your local bookseller or the Macmillan Corporate and Premium Sales Department at 1-800-221-7945, extension 5442, or by e-mail at MacmillanSpecialMarkets@macmillan.com.

First published by Farrar, Straus and Giroux

First Picador Edition: April 2017

10 9 8 7 6 5 4 3 2 1

To my sister, Julie
and
To Max, Miranda, and Genève

Traumatic memory is not narrative. Rather, it is experience that reoccurs, either as full sensory replay of traumatic events in dreams or flashbacks, with all things seen, heard, smelled, and felt intact, or as disconnected fragments.
—Jonathan Shay, M.D., Ph.D., *Achilles in Vietnam*

So you people don't believe in God. So you're all big smart know-it-all Marxists and Freudians, hey? Why don't you come back in a million years and tell me all about it, angels?
—Jack Kerouac

HYSTOPIA

EDITOR'S NOTE

Certain historical facts have been twisted to fit Eugene Allen's fictive universe. The fires his text describes did consume most of Detroit and parts of Flint, and raged through the state to the north, but they did not, of course, burn the entire state from top to bottom. Details of the seventh assassination attempt made on John F. Kennedy, now known as the Genuine Assassination, have been changed slightly in Allen's narrative, which has it taking place on a mid-August afternoon in Galva, Illinois. As we know, Kennedy was killed a month later, on September 17, as he drove through the town of Springfield, Illinois, on one of his intimate wave-by tours, "throwing [his] fate to the whims of the nation," as he said so often in his later speeches.

That Kennedy deliberately endangered himself in public outings as a way to defy previous attempts made on his life is historical fact, and historians will be debating for years the effectiveness this gesture had in reducing, or increasing, the number of attempts on his life (six), and whether it helped to extend his physical life along with his political life. The great ash heaps—still smoldering as Allen worked on the novel—certainly could be seen from an apartment at 22 Main, in

Flint, in which Myron Singleton and Wendy Zapf had their first furtive lovemaking session. But the ash heap didn't stop—as Allen claims—at Bay City (which burned for three years) but extended all the way up into the thumb region before petering out. Another backdrop of Allen's narrative, the second great lumber boom, was simply a creation of his vivid imagination. Most of northern Michigan had remained reforested, with the exception of a few areas afflicted with white pine blister rust (even here, in most cases, the rust didn't kill the trees but damaged branches and reduced lumber value). The great second lumber boom (1975) didn't begin until shortly after the novel was finished. Certainly there were men like Hank (last name unknown), who stole into the state forests to poach lumber, acting as cruisers, locating the larger trees, and then going in at night (covertly) to cut. It is likely that Allen was inspired by his neighbor Ralph Sutton, a former lumberman who took him under his wing and taught him the intricacies of lumber poaching, even going so far as to take the boy on a few excursions, cutting trees from local parks.

EDITOR'S NOTE

On August 15, 1974, Allen was given a standard postmortem psychological examination, drawing upon the text of his manuscript and interviews with surviving family members, friends, and casual acquaintances. John Maudsley led the investigative team at the Michigan State Mental Facility. An excerpt from his extensive report, already considered a classic of the genre, is worth quoting:

> Eugene Allen had a tendency to self-isolate and was prone to bouts of Stiller's disease, a common condition

in the Middle West of the United States. Although the diagnosis is relatively new, still under study, symptoms include a desire to stand in attic windows for long stretches; a desire to wander back lots, abandoned fairgrounds, deserted alleys, and linger in sustained reveries; a propensity for crawling beneath porch structures and into crawl spaces in order to peer up through cracks and other apertures to witness the world from a distance and within secure confines, the reduced field of vision paradoxically effecting a wider view by way of a tightening sensation around the eyeballs and eyelids. Clinical interviewees support that these moments of reverie, sometimes lasting as long as an entire afternoon, often include delusional historical memories. Stiller's disease in older teens can lead to wayward tendencies, antisocial ideation, and profound spiritual visions leading to a desire for artificially induced visions. Evidence in the case of Allen includes the following: he spent a great deal of time in his grandfather's vast attic space, most often in the northwestern corner, facing Stewart Avenue (one photograph shows him seated in a Hitchcock chair, knees pressed together, his chin slightly raised, and his eyes subdued). An interview with Harold B. Allen, age ninety, is here quoted in full:

He was a good kid, somewhat quiet, and of course he had to suffer through a great deal of turmoil related to his sister Meg. He was a splendid boy until he reached the age of sixteen and grew somewhat morose. One afternoon I heard footsteps in the attic. Our gardener and handyman, Rodney, was downstairs trimming the hedge. I went into the yard to talk to him, and when I looked up I saw Eugene in the attic window, which wasn't unusual because he liked to go up there with one of his books—he was reading Dickens that summer. I didn't think of him again until a few hours later when I returned home and looked again and he was still there. So I went up to the attic and said, What are you doing? And he remained silent. It was baking hot up there. You could hear Rodney downstairs, clipping the lawn, and down the street some kids playing, and so I said something to the effect of You should be out enjoying this beautiful summer day. And Eugene looked up at me and said, in an extremely formal voice, I'd rather not. There was something in his tone that shook me. Something weighty and cold in the way he said it, and I said, Well, you'd better come downstairs anyway and sit in the kitchen while your grandmother cooks supper, or watch the news with me, and he said, I'd rather not, and I said something like, Well, I'm going to have to give you a grandfatherly order and insist you come down, and he stayed quiet for a minute and then said, in the same formal voice, Well, Grandfather, we're all subjugated to someone, somehow, and I suppose in this instant I'm subjugated to you, and then he stood up, his knees cracking, and wiped the sweat from his eyes, and we walked down to my bedroom and I gave him a fresh shirt, told him to clean up, and then went down to the kitchen, where Ethel and I had a laugh over the vagaries of teenage behavior. In any case, the boy didn't come down, and I went back to the attic and found him in the chair, already sweating through my shirt, and I said, Come down, son, right now, and I suspect—I wasn't certain— that his propensity for odd behavior was directly connected with his sister. Don't get me wrong. I had my suspicions, but I told myself that the boy was enjoying some quiet time alone. The view from the window was splendid, looking out on the street— and I might add that it was and still is a beautiful street, a bit worn around the edges now, and zoned as a historical area (it was protected during the riots, one of the ringed blocks, and it survived the looting and so forth). There's a large oak out front that survived the blight—at any rate, I didn't see his behavior as out of the ordinary, at least not the first time. He was always a boy who would wander off on his own. I'd find him between our garage and the neighbor's, or in the little plot of grass back behind the breezeway, sitting alone. I didn't see anything unusual in it at the time and I'm still not sure I do.

Maudsley's report went on to conclude that it was highly probable that a connection existed between the holing-up syndrome (Stiller's disease) and Allen's suicide, years later, although the exact factors were indeterminate and open to speculation.

EDITOR'S NOTE

Suicide is an act around which we construct an assortment of potential causal conditions, none of which is provable. In his notebooks, Allen proposed a number of ways to commit the act. Here, below, is a list, transcribed as it appeared in his early notebooks:

- Go to the top of the new parking structure on Howard Street and toss myself off. But first spend some time tightrope-walking along the edge; make birdlike gestures and attract attention from those down below until a crowd gathers. Wave back at them and establish a rapport of some kind until someone yells, Jump, jump.

- Dig deep hole in Sleeping Bear sand dunes and then somehow rig sand slide to bury self if p— [illegible pencil scrawl].

- Get Billy Thompson angry enough to kill me when he comes back—if he comes back . . . [illegible pencil scrawl].

- Immolation in the style of monk, pour accelerants and ignite self outside the library—or in Bronson Park; make sure it's done in an off-the-cuff manner and sit still during the raging fire, as stately still as possible.

- Jump straight into an ice fishing hole on King Lake, with feet pointed—during daytime—and then come up under the ice to the side and stare up through ice until blackout and suffocation transpire.

- Locate and join group of Wayward Tendency fuckups—full regalia, Harley cycles and etc.—and get self into some police/wayward battle.

- Start riot fire—anywhere in town, in a circular pattern so that fires converge and eventually entrap me. [Indiscernible scribble] . . . fire somehow guided by forces back to my body. No gasoline. None of that.

- Hold on to lightning rod wire—along the side of the house out at East Lake—and pray deeply for a bolt to strike, and when it does, hold on tight. Remember that time you were sleeping out there [illegible scrawl] and the cottage was hit; the wire going bright blue and then red and glowing while the ground turned to glass and . . . [illegible ink scrawl].

- Spontaneous-human-combustion-type fire, self-willed, urging my own cells to fuel themselves into a giant conflagration.

EDITOR'S NOTE

A fragment from Allen's journals:

> We drove over to Ann Arbor last night to hear the Stooges play at the Fifth Forum theater. Billy Thompson drove and we smoked a joint and shot the shit about Meg, mostly. Iggy was fantastic. Woke up in parking lot. Head against parking bumper. Iggy nudging my head with his boot. I woke to Iggy and Iggy seemed to wake to me. He told me to get the fuck up and to shake it off. That's what he said. Shake it off, man, he said, and then he laughed and walked away before I could get up. Then Billy said the same thing. Shake it off, he said.

EDITOR'S NOTE

The manuscript was found in the drawer in Allen's room by his mother, Mary Ann Allen, who gave it to Byron Riggs, professor of English at the University of Michigan, who in turn passed it on to his good friend, the writer Fran Johnson, who subsequently sent the manuscript to her agent, who, with the permission of the Allen family, submitted it to publishers, who, as they say, went into a frenzied bidding war that had little to do with the so-called marketability of the novel itself because, as most admitted, openly, the book was hardly fit for the fiction market at the time (or any time) but was publishable because of the marketability of the so-called backstory: a twenty-two-year-old Vietnam vet sits at his desk and composes a fictive world that is—as the critic Harold R. Ross stated—"bent double upon itself, as violent and destabilized as our own times, as pregnant and nonsensical."

Hystopia was written during the hot summer a year after the Detroit/Flint riots. Allen continued his work on the novel into the fall, devoting all his time to it. The reader might take the liberty of picturing a slender man leaning down over a typewriter in the upstairs window of a house in Kalamazoo, Michigan, trying to concentrate while, downstairs, perhaps, a fight takes place. What is known about the family is somewhat limited; files on Meg Allen are, of course, sealed, but it is generally acknowledged that his sister suffered from adult-onset schizophrenia. (Later her diagnosis—confused by shifting categories—was changed to borderline.) It is also general knowledge that she had relations with a young man named Billy Thompson, who died in Vietnam.

EDITOR'S NOTE

Evidence from Allen's journals and notes suggests that his fictional Grid zone, a safe, controlled area in which treated patients were released from treatment, was based on the proposed Unleashed Wayward Program of 1969, which was part of the Mental Health Corps Program (Psych Corps), part of the Kennedy administration's initiative to solve the mental illness "problem" in general and the returning Vietnam vet problem in particular. Certain geographical specifics—the so-called Gleel Glen, where the Saginaw River cuts into Michigan—can be assumed to be products of the author's imagination.

EDITOR'S NOTE

Below is an edited selection of interviews with friends and relatives of Allen who, upon reading the manuscript of *Hystopia* (rough text, unedited), offered responses.

Stanley Crop

Well, yeah, gangs of marauding motorcycle riders like the Black Flag group, the Summer of Hate, and Kennedy keeping the meat grinder in Vietnam up to full speed . . . all correct. Don't accuse the kid of bending history. Accuse history of bending the kid. And the war, the war bent him, too. Like so many, he came back changed.

Markus Decourt

Maybe the treatment process wasn't called enfolding, but the process I went through was similar to what he describes. As far as I knew, it was top-secret shit, so I suppose he got wind of it from Billy Thompson when he came home on leave, or he heard about it during his tour of duty. All the same, man, he got it right, mostly, and there were reenactment facilities where they messed you up. And the drug called Tripizoid. He gets that right, too, mostly. Little greenies, we called them, no bigger than a saccharine tablet. Pop one of those suckers, go through the reenactment of your original trauma—we're talking controlled, man, scripted, staged right down to the gestures, the whole show run by these Shakespearian motherfuckers—and you'd come out cured. We were doing scenes from the *Iliad*, Hector and all that, and anyway he got it right and how he got it right in his book is a wonder to me, man, except to say he did.

Gerald McCarthy

You'd think it's crazy that three buddies would go from Benton Harbor, Michigan, to Nam—all laughing and joking way over there—but it happened all the time and the Buddy Program was the reason. That Rake character is fucking real. I mean really real. You get home and aren't really home and you're charged up anyway. That guy was a psychopath to start. I believe him. I see his ghost all over the place.

Norman Joseph

I came home from Nam and went back to school. As a scholar of Vietnam literature I can say, with all frankness, that *Hystopia* is one of the strangest documents to come out of the war years. I can't say it's the most honest. A parataxic construct of sorts.

Buddy Anderson

That character named Singleton is a lot like me, man, and I take that as a compliment because I was Eugene's best friend. Hell, my tour was only two years ago. When I sleep, which isn't often, I have the same kind of dreams and I wish I'd've been treated, enfolded myself. Enfold me, man, I keep thinking, but then I guess a man has to carry what he has to carry. But let me tell you this, all the books I've read get it wrong, except for the ones where the main character is KIAed, or goes AWOL, or whatever; but the gung-ho ones are off, each time; too clean, too neat and tidy, even when you get a few killed—you're stuck knowing that the dude telling the story, the writer, man, lived to tell it, and for me that always makes it unrealistic.

Jason Smith

Look, the guy had more than Stiller's (or holing-up syndrome). That guy was wacko. I'm sorry he killed himself, but after trying to read this I'd say it was all for the best.

Tanner Bradfield

Reminded me of my great-uncle Lester, at least in the stories my family used to tell. He came home with a bad case of wind-up from the Great War, the story goes, shell-shocked to all hell, and used to sit out in the yard at night. Well, one night there a new car lot was opening and had hired a search-light to get attention, and, the story goes, when he saw the light up in the clouds he went completely nuts and ran naked through the streets of town and had to be put up there in the state hospital, where Meg Allen was treated for a while.

Reginald (Shaky Jake) Jackson
Detroit burning. He got that right. Only thing he got wrong is that he saved some parts of Flint. The rest of Flint's gonna be gone in a year. Bet on it.

Stan White
My brother, Drew, knew the guy Billy-T was based on. They were in the same unit together. Drew told me he was one of those sweet, down-home motherfuckers, always high on something, shooting at ghosts, is what he said. If anyone would've saw an angel, it would've been Billy Thompson, a.k.a. Billy-T. I believe him. He was there.

Kurt Bronson
Yeah, there was the Buddy Program. You'd enlist with a friend or two and they'd assure you that you'd end up in the same unit; same platoon, same squad, usually. Remember all three: Singleton, quiet, had his act together; Billy Thompson, or Beachboy, we called him. Big-eyed and sweet as cherry pie until he saw action and then he got those dark eyes. Not too bad but bad enough. Met him in Saigon early in the war. We were watching some rich chicks having a séance. He was into that supernatural stuff, man, Billy-T was, and he said some-thing, I can't recall exactly what, but it was along the lines of: I'm gonna have some visions, too, something like that. Maybe that explains something. Maybe not. Rake I don't want to talk about. He was crazy from the start.

Dr. Brent Walk
Friendship under the pressure of war forms bonds like no other. It's easy to say that, but it's hard to really recognize unless you've been in the field of battle; strange bonds that would never form in the so-called real world: Jekyll-and-Hyde bonds, I call them. For instance, you'll have some large black man from pre-riot Detroit paired up with a runty kid from Willard, Ohio; there's a kind of alchemical connection between them, catalyzed by their shared fear of death. Death is the context in which these bonds form. There is a lot of signification; a lot of language play, a lot of jest. I'd venture to say it's a form of love as deep as that between any married couple: in both cases, it's precisely the differences between the two individuals that creates the deep and mysterious attraction.

Lucy Allen
The thing about our city is that it was just big enough and just small enough. Meg was mentally ill, they say. She was sick before she met Billy. Billy didn't make her crazy. His death put her over the edge, they say, but I know a little better than that.

Richard Allen
[Static. Wooden-sounding fumbling with microphone. Street noise.]
    No comment. I'd appreciate if you'd stay away from me. My son is dead.

Margaret Allen
Eugene was a good boy. When he came back from the war he went up there and began writing, and we knew he was writing because we could hear the typewriter, day and night, and

the bell at the end of each line. That bell tinkling. He'd come down and sit and have breakfast after writing all night. He went to visit Meg a few times at the hospital and came back and wrote more. I'd rather not say anything else.

Lucy Allen
I was the tagalong, you know, the kid sister who wanted to hang out and was sometimes allowed to go with them. I went to the beach with them a few times. Billy-T smoked a joint, I remember that, back in the dunes. Meg wouldn't smoke when I was around. [Indecipherable.] Yeah, there's a lot of denial. All that. After Eugene killed himself, the family balled itself up tighter than ever.

Reverend Dudney Breeze
Thomas Merton said hell is hatred. Murder comes out of hatred. Only through hatred can you murder, at least in theory, so one would, most certainly, say that war is hell, because war is murder. There's a sermon in there, for certain.

John Frank
They called me Chaplain, man, because I'd pray over the dead, and I meant it when I did it. I'd do it again. I'd pray over every KIAed in the squad. I'd give them a quick version of the last rites, not the full viaticum, of course, but I'd bless them best I could.

Billy Morton
We were at China Beach on a five-day leave, and this guy named Franklin—I think it was—and I were in the water. He was a big believer, all full of God this, God that, and Christ this, Christ that, and he said, You want me to baptize you, and I said, What's in it for me, and he said, It might tighten

your luck, man. You're a short-timer. You've got to do what you can, and I said, OK, and he did it, right there, pushed me under and said whatever you say. Did I feel different? Did my luck get better? I'll never know.

Stewart Dunbar
History has always had a hard time allying itself to the novel. The young man's creative effort, disturbed though it might be, is realistic to the extent that it captures the tension of history meeting the present moment. Is it not possible that someone looking back at the past, even the very recent past, and bending it this way and that (e.g., Kennedy in this third term, not his second) might actually rearrange the— No, I can't express the thought without getting Einsteinian and saying that retelling the past, as the young man does in his novel, might actually change the past. But perhaps that is exactly what I mean.

Randall Allen
Screw Nam. Screw the novel he was writing. Screw white history. Above all, screw Michigan. And screw my cousin. He didn't know the state at all. He lived in a bubble. He imagined the entire thing. He was freaked out about being drafted. That's my theory. He just couldn't handle it.

Jamakie Lowwater
There are too many moose on Isle Royal. It's impractical to imagine that a group of vets would be able to reenact night battles up there without having moose wandering in and out of their fights; water buffalo stand-ins, perhaps. He didn't put that in the novel but he told me about it as an idea, a concept.

Gracie Howard
They were a quiet and rather formal family, actually. Did we have an idea that the daughter was troubled? Yes, we did. Did

we know that the son was troubled, too? No, I'd say we didn't. Eugene was a quiet boy. When he died we were stunned, just stunned.

Randall Allen
My cousin was hot. Meg was one hot girl. That much is for sure. I used to go to the lake with her. The whole family would go and she'd be in this bikini and I'd be like, man, why does she have to be my cousin? Of course if she wasn't my cousin I never would've been that close to her, because she was that hot. But she was crazy, too. But that kicked in later.

Janice Allen
Kissing cousins. I saw Randall trying to kiss Meg. She shoved him. We were having a fire on the beach and they were just out of the light, but I could see it clearly. She was going with Billy around then. At least she mentioned his name to me. Then when he came home they took off to California. They say he kidnapped her, but I think she was duplicitous—is that the word?—yeah, she was ready and willing, at least some part of her, to take off with him—not to say he didn't force her to go, in his own way. When she was gone all we could do was speculate.

Dr. Ralph Stein
Early indications of schizophrenia? I'd say the temporal lobe seizure suffered by the patient [Meg Allen] was an early indication. Hospitalization for that condition, at her age [15] is rare but not unheard of.

AUTHOR'S NOTE

A Compact Primer on the Theory of Enfolding
by Eugene Allen

1

The process of reenacting particulars of the causal/trauma events turns (enfolds) the drama/trauma inward. Confusion is undoubtedly an element of the curative process: a mysterious blurring of the line between what happened and what is reenacted. One folds into the other, and during the period of adjustment the patient typically experiences disjunction and bewilderment. He or she may vehemently reject the curative process, making statements to the effect of "This is pure bullshit. I remember everything. Nothing has been tucked away. I'm the same old screwup. You can't just yank me in here, make me reenact a bunch of the shit I went through, in a lame-assed way, not even close to what it was really like, and expect me to forget about it." But in most cases, the patient does forget about it, becoming fully immersed in the reenacted trauma's nullification of the real trauma. (Editor's note: The author John Horgan has coined a term—Ironic Science—to define a brand of science that "does not advance hypothesis that can be either confirmed or invalidated empirically." The enfolding process may be Ironic Science at its worst, or it may be visionary science at its best.)

2

General theory: objective cure to a subjective illness. Enfolding rejects etiological description of the specific illness and instead simply objectifies it *into* itself.

3

Avoid diagnosis. Submit to the fashionableness of the cure. Pure theater above all.

4

Inherent in drama and reenactment is a blurring of the distinction between the originating causal events and the apex events—"the moment." Creating an artificial apex calls the originating events into question.

5

Replication alone isn't sufficient to enfold the illness into itself. Asklepios must be invoked by way of communal rants, articulated gesture exercises, and ecstatic submission to pure chance.

6

All cures are bogus.

7

Without the drug Tripizoid the enfolding process doesn't work and the reenactment of the trauma isn't properly confused with reality. Tripizoid somehow incites a doubling-back of memory, a mnemonic riptide—the great drawback of water before the tsunami of pure memory arrives, except that it never arrives but is simply conjoined with the withdrawing currents. Conversely, in cases of *unfolding*, liquid memory returns to its original stasis, although, as has been noted, there may be slight "frustrations" in the form of alterations wrought by older, pre-traumatic memories, which may be discerned in the jumbling of proper nouns and subtle deviations in spoken syntax.

8

Theorists like to cite, by way of illustration, the example of two waves of identical amplitude but opposite phases, which cancel each other out when they coincide.

9

Enfolded memory can be *unfolded* in two ways:

> Immersion in cold water. (Extremely cold.)
> Fantastic, beautiful, orgasmic sex.

Original research on the processing of enfolding was funded by Kennedy Grid Project initiation grants at the University of Michigan. It was presumed that a state shaped like a hand capable of holding itself was superior to other states as a venue for enfolding projects. Florida was rejected on account of its unfavorable climate and its lack of clearly defined seasons. Extremely high humidity, it was found, early on, fosters too keen an awareness of the skin/mind division.

Although reenactment was initially tested in New Mexico and at a cavernous Chicago complex, these tests were both top secret. Michigan quickly became known as the Psych Project state. The process of enfolding was perfected in its lower peninsula with funding from Kennedy's initiative.

EDITOR'S NOTE

Most historians of the curative technique commonly known as enfolding agree that its widely acknowledged bogusness was a necessary correlative of a bureaucratic structure created well in advance of the cure, just as the Eisenhower freeway project created a new cartography of driving needs. Most authorities now agree that the beauty of the enfolding cure lies precisely in the fact that its practitioners, inspired by the vastness of the project and by the excitement of Kennedy's post-assassination survival, bravely admitted, early on, that the cure was a dreamy and even absurd concept, and that therein lay its wild effectiveness. The paradox was that the cure was actually often effective, so that the claim of its bogus nature was itself partly bogus.

EDITOR'S NOTE

Historians have speculated at great length about the concentration of veterans in the state of Michigan. Most have resorted to a geographical theory, in which its peninsular shape acted as a lure. (The same theory can be applied to other end points, Provincetown, Key West, etc.) Wayward souls find themselves longing for some terminus.

A smaller group of historians has argued that the Black Flag motorcycle gang, originally twenty or so in number, helped spark the mass migration of vets to the state. Others simply argue that a large number of vets, particularly those who served the second big escalation after the first assassination attempt, originally came from the Rust Belt region and were simply returning home. Whatever the reason, a decision was made to establish a transitional Grid stretching from the southeastern shore of Lake Michigan, north to Benton Harbor, east to Kalamazoo, and then straight down highway 131 to the southern border. A year later, the Grid was extended to include Battle Creek and the area west of Route 69. The extension area remained rebellious, with some farmers and townspeople refusing to evacuate.

As the designated Psych State, and with hospitals, reenactment chambers, and a release Grid area in place, Michigan received a vast share of federal Psych Corps funding. Before there was an established cure rate, or true understanding of the nature of enfolding, the great hospital boom was in full swing. Magnificent edifices of mental care sprang up in the countryside in every architectural style, from retro castles to immense geodesic dome structures. Grid signs sprouted in equal numbers. The Grid symbol appeared on handbags, paper dresses, and tattoo parlor walls. The idea appears to have been to systemize the unholdable.

AUTHOR'S NOTE

The fires began in two places, the outskirts of Flint and the center of Detroit, before spreading house to house and across fields and uniting near Auburn Hills. All sparked by the raid on the Blind Pig in Detroit that night by the police, who were steeped in the dialectic of revolution and keyed into the idea that a revolt might start at any time. It was on the 266th anniversary of the day that Cadillac stepped ashore on what became known as *de trois*. The National Guard came in to shoot up at the "snipers" after the police were repelled. Soon the Detroit streets were ringing with the chants of "Motown, if you don't come around, we are going to burn you down." An aide to the mayor came up with the idea of burn squads. They would get ahead of the riots with Molotov cocktails and flamethrowers. Let it burn, the governor reportedly said. But the dynamics were simply too intricate to sort out accurately. The big map in police headquarters couldn't handle the information that was being teletyped in—squad cars akimbo, nobody sure where anybody was, rumors spreading even faster than the fire. The governor had begged Kennedy for federal troops, telling him the whole state was at risk, and the federal troops were mustering along the Ohio border—the rumble of tanks could be heard in Toledo. The rumors had had a head start on the fires, anyway: a revolution was at hand. The Negro was going to avenge three hundred years of slavery. The uncured vets would join in; the vagabonds, the waywards. Already the structure of the Grid area was in negotiation; eminent-domain strictures were being argued in the

Supreme Court that summer. Several thousand farmers and home owners were bracing for the order to move. Some had taken the offer and moved down to Indiana, where state law forbade the construction of Grid zones. If the wayward want to be wayward, let them do it in Michigan, Senator Clam of Indiana said. Senator Holly, of Michigan, led the fight for the creation of a Grid zone for Michigan, allowing for a safe place—not wilderness, but not urbane—in which certain patients, after treatment, might go to have a controlled transitional experience before being released into the general society.

HYSTOPIA

By Eugene Allen

BIG AND GRAND RAPIDS

April's the cruelest month, they say, but I wouldn't go that far. At least not yet. I'm going to do my best to make it the cruelest, she heard him say, and then she slipped into darkness and woke, hours later, to the murmur of the engine, the power thrumming under the hood, the hood ornament far out, pointing the way. He had gone in and taken her out of the post-treatment Grid, slipping in, using his words and drugs. His hand was on her leg. Fingers spread. Above everything his talk, his voice ragged and deep, and then as she came up and out of it, his voice and radio static were all she had.

Something was close behind, a spiral of police sirens, the hospital's clean simplicity, the sedation of the treatment, pre and post, that stayed with her when it was over, and she had to command herself to open her eyes and to look out the windows at the devouring slip of the road into itself . . .

Groggy, she found her mouth and made it speak, and she was telling him, Find the Ann Arbor channel, the one from the university, Stooges all the time.

Stooges all the time, he muttered.

Then he began coughing and clearing his throat until he

had something to spit, and he told her his throat was sore from screaming in Grand Rapids.

It had been a confusing couple of hours before they'd split that scene. The houses had been old, once dignified and fine, now slipping into decrepitude, uncomfortable beneath the trees arching over the wide streets. The trees were tired of shading structures of grandeur, optimistically huge Victorians. Slate shingles gone, hauled away by the looters after the riots.

Shaky had been asleep when they entered his bedroom, treading softly. Rake put the gun to his forehead and told him what he had to give them and how he was to do it and with what kind of movement, slowly, and how much shit he was in, deep, deep unbelievable shit, and Shaky did what they ordered him to do, but when he was doing it he stumbled or made a quick move. He was a tall dark man with knobby knees. One of the tallest motherfuckers you're gonna see in the Middle West, Rake said.

Rake shot him point-blank, producing a spongy, wet sound, and an outbound spew of bone and blood hit the wall, making another sound that she heard and reheard and heard again.

That's that, Rake said, kicking the body.

Then they ransacked the house, pulling drawers, spilling underwear, unfurling panties, frilly things that she held for a moment and dropped to the floor.

The feel of silk was still on her fingertips. She could still see the look in his eyes as he stared at the gun. The black barrel in the black pupil.

You're gonna come out of it, the look said. *You're gonna survive this. I'm dead but you're going to live. I'm just one more in the wrong place at the wrong time. One more who wakes up into a nightmare. I'm not going to plead with you too hard, no girl, but I'm gonna give you this last little glance to carry with you when you go*, the look said before the gun took it away.

In the kitchen he removed a loaf of Wonder from the bread box, a glass bottle of milk with a paper cap, and some cheese, and then they headed off into the morning light.

I'm afraid we didn't leave a single print, he said. We're on the lam. That's part of the deal. We've got to mix it up. Sometimes I leave prints, other times I don't. Got to give the Psych Corps something to think about, got to leave some tracks they can obsessively follow. He talked and talked as they drove the Grand Rapids streets, turning now and then to make sure she was listening or at least awake, poking her with his long fingers, gripping her thigh.

Do I talk too much? He said.

Do I ramble on, the king of non sequitur? He said.

Do you listen to me? He said.

Do you listen to me going on and on? You most certainly do. He said. Said. Said. He said. He said. He said.

If you're good for anything you're good as a listener, set to let me ramble while you nod into it. That first time back there, when I finally got to you, I tried that classic dosage, a big 400-microgram dose, the king of all tabs. You get a girl tripping on that and you're free to do what you want depending on the structures you've set up for yourself and I'll admit that I have set some up for myself. I've got my codes and credos just like the rest of them. That's all we had over in Indochina. All we had to live with were the rules and regulations.

Them. It's us against *them* and they know it, and the thing about *them* is that the only thing they really know, if you get my drift, is that they failed me. They failed me big-time by not taking care of me when I returned from the war. They took me down to Texas and put me into one of their reenactments and pumped me full of Tripizoid, and then all they did was double it down, increase what they were trying to decrease. If they knew how bad I was feeling, they'd never sleep at night. They'd lock the doors and nail the windows. They'd put me in their prayers and ask for protection specifically against me. They'd walk faster and glance back more often. If they had even the slightest idea that I was wandering their streets they'd unlock their gun cabinets and get their rifles cleaned and make sure the ammo was dry. Some of them have a vague premonition, an ill-formed vision comprised of Vetdock escapees, Black Flag wannabes, trigger-happy acid freaks, and Year of Hate troublemakers. Guys with bad scars, he said. Then he ran his fingers across the scar that ran from his scalp—the part where the hair wouldn't grow—down his neck to where it disappeared under his collar. He touched it, pulled his shirt open, and stared down as if seeing for the first time the way the scar tissue radiated across his chest in weird formations that had once been his nipples, and into his belly button, where the splash had pooled. (That fiery goop spread over me while I watched—and yeah, I did watch it because I was hit such a blast of dopamine that I flew out of myself and stood there on the battlefield resisting the temptation to pound my chest like Tarzan.)

In Grand Rapids, before going into the house, he had pulled over to the curb, letting the car murmur and hum, the long hood shuddering, waxed, a glistening tongue touching the trees in reflection.

You want to know what my credo is? he said. And without waiting for her to answer he continued:

My credo's: never kill for a *good* reason. If you're going to be a failed enfold, then do it wholeheartedly and with all the gusto you can muster. When you kill, do it quickly so that you pluck the proper method from the situation itself. But never ever, ever be efficient. I mean don't go for the easy kill.

At the same time don't stretch it out too much. If there's a scream I want it to be the brutal, loud, quick kind that it goes in one ear and out the other. You can blame that on Nam or you can blame it on the way my mind works. The one thing I hated over there was hearing a fellow grunt crying, stuck out in the fire zone while we gave the Marine credo a workout (never leave the dead buddy behind and all that). He looked at her and examined her eyes and then reached up to touch her face. For a second there was a softening in his features. He had a lean, sharp chin and a gaunt jawbone that led up to an unusual fat brow. Then he gave her a swat on the top of the head and said, Shit, man. We've got to go in, take care of this Shaky character, and leave a calling card for the police, who will give it to the authorities, and then eventually it'll go up the chain to some poor Psych Corps agent. Their job is to find some semblance of order in all this madness, and mine, as I see it, is to give them something to think about . . .

You're oblivious to the facts, Meg, he said. His fingers moved along her thigh. She stayed silent and looked out at the streets passing, Grand Rapids in the early morning light, nothing but television aerials, the stars, dew on roofs, lights on in a few windows as folks got up to face a day of work. She tried not to listen, let him keep going, as they moved through the cloverleaf.

Let me explain. When I heard your name a lightbulb went off and the word *bingo* came to mind. Bingo, I said. I've got to get her out of there and take her on the road. She's the one for me. She has a story that somehow ties to mine.

Anyway, he said, pulling the car to the curb and cutting the engine. I have a picture in my head of the man who caused your trauma from everything you've told me.

I haven't told you anything.

You've told me plenty. In so many words.

So tell me what you know, she said.

I know he died in your typical big-time snafu, all sparkle and glimmer and flash.

You're sure about that.

I'm certain of it.

Then how come I don't think so. How come I can't even speculate.

I'm not the one to ask, he said. Then he got out, opened the rear door, and began loading his weapons in the backseat, snapping them open and shut, filling the car with the smell of oil while she gazed out at the house and examined the beach towels someone had carefully hung over the railing, lining them up neatly: one with the Detroit Tigers emblem: the roaring tiger and the baseball bat. Another had a map of the state of Michigan adorned with symbols: cherries and automobiles and rolls of papers. Next to it was a towel with a peace symbol. She read them from right to left and then from left to right and thought: the Tigers were playing the night of the first Detroit riot, and then the state burned, and then the peace movement—then the peace movement fell apart. A fourth towel was missing, she thought. The statement wasn't complete. There has to be a fourth towel in the house somewhere, still wet and smelling of lake water and suntan lotion, and on that towel there has to be some symbol of hell.

Rake's face appeared in her window. Get out of the car, he said, and she did.

She could remember the nurse's big, lovely brown hands and the way he had soothed and assured, but she couldn't remember his name or his face. She could remember the med center and the start-off point, a room with long countertops and forms to fill out and secretaries with slightly bemused expressions, tired from processing in-patients who came in a great never-ending cycle, and then the rest—the Tripizoid injections, the hippy encampment with a Buckminster Fuller geodesic dome and campfires—became a blur.

Let me quote myself, Rake was saying in the car. This was later, moving along a road through the darkness, the engine rumbling under her feet, in her legs.

You're driving on some forsaken road like this one, and then some bloke, yeah, that's the word, some bloke appears with his thumb out, and he wonders if you're going to pick him up or not, and he has that desperation in his eyes because he's hoping for some blind luck, some kind of happenstance out of the blue, and you slow down to get a look at him, and fucking bingo, he's some long-lost comrade-in-arms, a guy you knew back in the fray. So you stop and wave him over to get a better look and see that, yeah, he's a buddy you were sure was KIAed. You were sure of it but there he is, looking loopy, his eyes weary and lost, and he leans forward a little bit and says, Hey, can I get a lift? And you say, Where you heading? And he says, Anywhere. And you tell him to get in, wanting to probe a bit, thinking maybe he's not the guy. And he gets in and sits beside you and you drive a few miles without saying much, just idle chitchat, and then you say, Hey, man, you ever see action in Nam? And he says, Yeah, as a matter of fact, I did, and you say, Hey, me too, and he gives you that kind of reaction you've heard a million times, flat and non-committal, full of avoidance—because you get either that or the other thing, the full-on meeting-of-two-souls-in-the-desert vibe, as if to say, and this is usually in just a word or two, How could it be possible that two souls bump into each other? Two souls who were over there and are now over here? As if it were some fantastic impossibility, for Christ's sake, when in truth it's as likely as anything else in this state. And because he's noncommittal you wait it out, saying, Fuck, man, and you wait, maybe putting the radio on, figuring the music might lure more out of him but not caring too much because to want his history isn't healthy.

Outside the city there was nothing much along the roadside

except dead fields with purple skunk cabbage, old billboards advertising truck stops, restaurants long shut down, houses in shambles. In the center of one field a man stood, staring mutely as they passed, resting his weight against an implement. The Indiana border exerted its own unique pull down and down into the great heart of the country, past demarcation signs; past the dullard state of Ohio. They'd get to the border and head west toward Chicago and feel her pull but not venture too far because that would go against what some vets liked to call the Covenant of the Mitten. You got to keep it in the Mitten, you've got to rage against one thing or you'll never get it done, and it does no good to go wildly out into an entire continent, Rake explained. Fucking state's enough to take care of. There's enough drugs in the state to keep a man busy for a lifetime, not to mention Detroit, not to mention the Grid itself, not to mention the riot zones.

He located—in the haze of static—the Ann Arbor station playing the Stooges, Iggy's voice writhing in little hoots, angry, tinny. It was easy to imagine his shiny torso twisting around and his ribs sticking out as he crucified himself on his own tune. He's the one I turn to when I need a hit of salvation, Rake said. I go to Iggy and begin to worship. I'd kill him if I got close enough. And he'd thank me for it, he added. Then he went on talking while she listened with her head back and her eyes closed and just a sliver of white noise coming through the window crack and another bit of air coming up from a hole in the floorboard. The air smelled sweet through the smoke of his cigarettes and hints of mint weed, spring . . .

Oncoming in the distance was a big car, a Lincoln or Olds, with smoke pouring out around the hood.

Fear manifesting itself. The air tarnished with it. Her skin with hives. Everything reduced to her forearms, her skin with hives. Behind them far off a siren unspooling. The look Shaky had given—the moon whites of his eyes, the sadness touching sadness.

I believe that man's drinking under the influence of driving, Rake was saying, pulling the car over to the shoulder. Through the windshield she watched as he stepped out of the car, entrapped in silence, the sun on his neck, the fields behind him empty, the road still and quiet as he pointed, aimed, following the car in the opposite lane, following, following until the smoke of the shot hovered and he squinted, gazed, shot again, catching the Olds in a tire, running across the median (all quickly) and ordering the driver out, a tall elderly man in a black suit coat and tie with his arms up high. The hat on his head was black, with a narrow brim. (For a second she thought: That's my grandfather.) There was something about the break of his trouser around his shoes and the way his shirt was tucked in tight that spoke of a gentleman, a man who had made his mark in the world and was now succumbing to loss. She slid down and waited for one more shot, or two, the sharp hole the sound would inevitably produce, startling the starlings and sparrows that had settled again in the fields (and it did) into a gust of wing flap she'd catch out of the corner of her eye when she'd look up and out the window and see the man sprawled on the road, making electric jerks that lifted his heels up and down while a stub of blood shot from his chest.

He was breathing hard when he got back to the car.

The road blazed in the setting sunlight. A trooper car passed, going the other way, dome light flashing, and then he spoke, saying, I'm going over the border to Indiana for a few miles and then up again even though it's not my style to go out of state even to make the odds better against being caught. You're probably wondering why I shot that one back there, and I'm inclined to tell you, although I have doubts that you'll understand what I'm going to say, he said, adjusting the radio dial, holding on to the wheel with his knees while lighting a cigarette, taking a deep draw and then another deeper one and glancing at her. I shot that guy because he reminded me of my uncle Lester, and my uncle Lester used to remind me of my father, and my father used to remind me of my uncle Lester, and Lester was a crazy son of a bitch who did things to kids that he should've done to adults because he had what my mother liked to call wandering hands, hands that were cut loose from his mind. My mother said Lester couldn't help what he did but she still sent me over to his sign shop to learn the trade, in Detroit. He had a good little operation going as a vendor and he made shingles for dealerships and for the floors—warning signs and the like, things that said Careful Workers Make Better Cars, that kind of shit, and I got to his shop and began to learn to make stencils, cutting them out— I was handy with my own hands, you see—and I was a natural. That's what the old geezer said. He said, You're a natural at this, boy, holding my hand with his hand while he guided the brush, using that as pretext to handle and fondle my fingers, I see now, but I didn't at the time because I was a kid and pure and clean and unseeing of those things, as most kids are, and that went on until a few weeks later he was trying to get his hands on other parts of me and finally, well, to cut this short and give you the whole story, I gave him a blast of paint in the face from a spray gun, and then I cut his throat and then I joined up, I enlisted, and the rest, as they say, is history, but that's what made me kill that man out there, the fact that there was a likeness in the man to the man named Lester, although I have to say it wasn't as good as killing uncle Lester himself, but I can't do that again, can I, so all I can do is keep trying to find a way to get as close to doing it again as I can, he said madly, going on for at least twenty minutes, circling around on the story again to tweeze out more details; the little shacklike building that was the shop, the smell of paint and paper and turpentine.

He said. He said, and he said, and she closed her eyes and slid back down into the darkness, into the murmur of the engine and what felt like time itself at the center of her mind. (She could feel it. She could feel the wall the drugs made between the inner and outer, apparent in the stretch her mind made to locate the missing parts: the enfolded memories sat like a nut, like some seed of potential, tucked away to the side, hiding.) From time to time she came up and opened her eyes to watch the road, a single line drawing into the headlights as they fanned out to the edge of darkness on both sides, and then she went back down while he talked, his voice within a narrow range, the words pristine and sharp—*enfolded, Mexico, gunplay, gunmetal, blood*—but unattached, and then he was nudging her hard in the shoulder until she was up again to see a town passing in dim streetlight, the road dusky with ash, the boarded storefronts, and then she was back down again into the darkness while his words, again, floated—*hideout, cops, tracking systems*—until she awoke suddenly, startled by the sealed silence of the empty car, to see the stretch of bleak parking lot and the single-story hotel, fifteen units, with a brightly lit office in which Rake stood, his silhouette tall and angular, his head big and round, as he turned to look out through the window at her, lifting his arm and his hand and his finger in a sign, as if to say "one minute," while the clerk handed him a clipboard. Then he came bounding out, with a slightly bowlegged walk, his hands jammed into his pockets, his face firm and grim, and he took her from the car, told her to stretch her legs, and led her into the room—wood paneled and smelling of lemon polish and bleach and stale cigarette smoke, with two grimy bedspreads, a television set against the wall, a Bible in red artificial leather on each nightstand. After she used the bathroom, he told her to sit in a chair.

When she came up and out again, Rake was counting and

sorting tabs and baggies on the bedspread while she watched television, the picture unsteady, an old family drama with a clean-cut father and a runty, troubled kid with a crew cut who kept making wisecracks when they asked him to do something around the house. The mother had a beehive hairdo and wore an apron over her dress as she moved through the scenes with devotion to the tasks at hand. The show came in and out, bits of dialogue leading to laugh-track hilarity, the sound of waves hitting a shore. When she opened her eyes she saw, in a quivering black-and-white image, a father with his briefcase at his side, receiving a highball from the mother's hand, holding it up like a chalice and saying something inaudible that sparked another, bigger laugh-track roar that sounded like a wave hitting a shore hard and then leaving with a long, slow, receding hiss, and then more waves to punch lines she didn't hear because, on the bed, she was trying to remember and to reconstruct her own family tableau: father, mother, brother, the house, Colonial, the fat maple trees out front . . .

. . . she woke to the sound of Rake snoring and got up and went to the bathroom to pee and sat on the seat and stared at her knees, which were ruddy and brushed and scabbed. Then she went back into the bedroom and went to the window and lifted a blind and stared out at the parking lot. Two cars. Their own and an old G.T.O. grainy, sandpapery in the moonlight, and the playground, the spaceship monkey bars, the swing with the rotting seat, cordoned off with chain link. She watched a police cruiser, old-style, with a single dome, deliberately slow, blink, turn in, and sit.

Rake, she whispered. He rolled over beneath the sheets and snored again and seemed to settle even deeper into sleep. The room stank. The pills glinted.

There was a thump of doors and when she peeked again the cops were outside, adjusting their belts. One removed his hat. He slid his hand a couple of times up and over his scalp in a habitual motion and then slapped the brim of his hat against his thigh, as if to shake the dust from it, cowboy-style.

Rake, she said again. She went and gave him a nudge and stood back as he snorted and rolled over and settled back into sleep. So she nudged him again and he finally turned over and said, What the fuck do you want?

Cops, she said.

He sprang up, pulling on his boxers, and went to the window, lifting the slat with his thumb.

What were you doing up?

I was just up.

You were just up?

I was just up.

You use the phone?

No.

Out front, the cops seemed to be in surveillance mode, thumbs in their belts, turning one way and another. A car passed on the road and they turned to watch it.

Cops don't just appear out of the blue like this. They're onto something. They sniffed us out, he whispered. This is perfect, exactly. This is hoped-for shit. It can't get any better than this.

Pulling his shirt on, tucking it neatly, he went to his rucksack and found his gun, held it up, spun the cylinder, opened it for a check, snapped it shut, and said, Take a peek and tell me if they're coming to the door.

She looked out and saw them moving around Rake's car, leaning in to the windows, and then standing behind it and reading the plates. One of them held a pad and jotted something down and then went to the cruiser and sat inside, lifting the microphone to his mouth.

He's calling something in, she said.

Rake pushed her away from the window, lifted the slat,

and looked out. Put that stuff in the bag. Pack everything up. We're in one of those situations. We're gonna have the pleasure of blasting them both, he said. They're gonna face something they knew they'd have to face. They just didn't know they'd have to face it tonight. It's that simple, he said.

Words tight and sweet. The relief of putting them together. He would start speaking and she'd gather each phrase, take in the scroll of meaning. They moved together with conspiratorial unity. She felt that much. That much was sure. She was with him, at least for now. In her ears a siren still spun, but softer, subdued. This is how it is, a voice said, far off. This is how it's gonna be. Another voice said: Give in to this and you give in forever. Don't give in. Another part speaking in the clear logic of survival mode. Lockstep into the formation, the grid of the moment. She had been enfolded in a routine stage set. That part is gone, they said. That part of you's gonna be there, you'll feel it, and you'll want to pick at it like a scab, but don't pick. You pick, you open it back up and the blood'll flow. In the dark she felt this. Lockstep to survive. Do what they say to do and you'll be all right, it's that simple, really. They were in folding chairs in a group facing each other, going through the routine motions, the Corps Credo on the wall, the windows open slightly and the breeze coming in. Move around it, work around it, and you'll be fine, a voice said.

Keep an eye on them, he said, reaching under the bed. The double-barrel shotgun was blunt and stupid-looking in the dim light, sawed off, like something carved from a log. He cracked it, loaded two shells, thumbed them tight, and then jerked it shut. All snap and tightness. Old monster, he called it.

The charges hovered: kidnapping a minor out of the Grid and statutory rape to begin with; murder; narcotics, dealing and using, robbery, burglary—he could speak at length about these old-school cops, small-timers like his old man, shifty fuckers who moved with a deliberation you didn't see in city cops, shrouded in a nonchalance that was highly deceptive. All that tedium of speed-trap stakeouts, parked deep in the brambles, clocking with their eyes, trying to find some semblance of drama in a few streets and a lot of land. His old man had come home from work with a dull gaze in his eyes, laying his firearm on the table.

This'll kill both of them if we're lucky. If we're not, I'm going to have to be quick with this one here, he said, tapping his belt.

I've got to use the bathroom, she said.

He turned and gave her a long gaze. *She could feel it. His eyes looking. His eyes boring into her.*

Make it quick, he said. You're gonna answer the door when they knock. They won't be able to get their eyes off you because they're not used to seeing flesh like yours, and that's going to be their death warrant.

The tiles were moldy, the grout gray around the toilet, which was little more than a grim hole gurgling softly to itself. She pulled the shower curtains back, trying not to rattle the hooks, and gazed at the window. It was small, but not too small. She climbed into the tub and pushed it up and looked out behind the hotel. A field opened up into rubble and trash with a shaggy old fence that dipped invitingly in the middle. About twenty yards past the field was a weathered clapboard house with shaded windows. Everything was starting to emerge in the first dawn light.

Into the logic of it. Words clearly spoken. Structure around everything, the lines graphed and solid. Eyes still slightly blurry. As if rising up out of deep water into the fresh light suddenly, but it's still dark in the hotel room. You can run, but then, that wouldn't be in the nature of the program, so to speak, someone said. In any case, running goes against the nature of your rehabilitation. You run and you run

toward that which was enfolded, so to speak. Or you run
around it. You feel it and want to know it and also know that
to know it would be to know way too much, so to speak,
someone said.

Hurry it up in there, he said.

I just have to wipe.

Wipe fast. They're down by the office right now.

There's nothing in my dreams, just some ugly memories, a
voice said from behind her. *The restrictions of a drugged*
state, someone had said. Tripizoid with enfolding is salva-
tion. You can't say that for most of them. You can say it, but
it wouldn't be true.

Get out there, he said.

She went and stood where he told her, in her nightie, shiver-
ing, her nipples rough against the lace.

Just stand like that and tell them something sweet and
nice. Give them the works. I'll let you improvise this time.
You'll be the first thing they see. They'll be dazed and dazzled
small-time pokes. They'll reach up to rub their unshaven
chins and that's when I'll step out and give them a blast of
pure reality.

He braced the shotgun against his leg while from outside
came the distinct clumpy sound of cops who weren't trying to
hide their own presence; cops with an upfront style that reflected the tedium of their lives. At the door they stopped,
knocked, and said, Open up, police. One or two beats, and
then she sang out, One minute, and then waited another few
beats and then said, Hold on, and then another beat and she
went and unchained the lock and gazed out at faces leaning in
to catch sight of her—she felt it, the light and their gaze force-
fully upon her hips and the flat of her belly. One cop had baby
fat on his cheeks and small lips and even smaller eyes and a
complacent look. He was starting to smile, shifting his weight

slightly while behind him the second cop was older, lean, with deep-set eyes, picking his teeth.

Unchain the door, the younger cop said. We have a few questions to ask you.

She took two steps back to give them another view, pirouetting slightly as more light came through and revealed the lines of her body—she could feel it, the cheap silk that had been rubbing against her skin for a week now, beneath her jeans and T-shirts.

We're not going to bring you in or nothing, the young cop said. His voice passed through his nasal passages, barely making it, and came out squeaking like the air through a balloon and then seemed to loosen as it passed his glossy wet lips. While he waited for her to answer she could hear the calls of sparrows in the fields on the other side of the road and the sound of sunrise striking the bare bones of Big Rapids. The older cop brought himself around and in front of the young one and spoke with a husky voice, his hand down low near his gun.

Now, please open up, he said.

Then the door opened with the blast of a well-placed kick, landing hard against Rake, who was up and around it anyway, his gun aimed high to catch them in the face, and the blast of buckshot fanned against the cheap walls with a muted thump, turning them both into a fury of blood and gore that extinguished the sight of her forever: the sight of her standing there was the last they saw before the blast erased all. One for you, and one for you, Rake said.

A high shrieking in her ears that she recognized from other times, a sense of airlessness as if she'd been sucker punched, and then she was breathing hard, collecting her things, while Rake fingerprinted, marked up the blood on the wall with cryptic designs, a pentagram (sometimes) and a cross (most of the time), and even his name (every time), writing into the furrowed carpet around the men's legs and then cursing because spreading blood pooled over it.

Get me a fucking towel, he said, and she came and he swabbed the blood, pulling up the carpet and the padding to give him room, and then he smoothed it down quickly and made more designs while she filled the duffel and got the rucksack.

Go as deep into the strangeness of it and leave clear-cut indicators and be certain that what was left behind each time was a record. That was his modus operandi.

Anyone passing on the road, looking carefully, would've noticed a crime in progress. They would've seen the heels of the two dead men on the walkway, in front of the shabby hotel. They would've seen Rake doing a little dance, leaving bloody footprints all the way to the office. They might've seen—if they passed a moment later—Rake shooting the night clerk. The bright flash.

PSYCH CORPS BUILDING, FLINT

Singleton and Klein had gone over the map that morning, the long strings and the short strings: red ones marking a murder, blues a possible sighting. The target, Rake, was on a rampage, or had been on a rampage, and he had gone and taken a girl named Meg. One more Grid-breaker going in and taking a girl out of post-treatment, Klein had explained over and over for at least a week.

Now Klein leaned forward with his hands flat on the desk, arching his neck to look up at Singleton.

"You know what I did before I joined this outfit?"

"No, sir."

Light coming in from the windows—the smoky morning air taking the sun and diffusing it—or the fluorescent fixture overhead talking to itself. The world buzzed in Singleton's ear.

"I fought in the big one and then I became a historian. You can't fight in that war—I mean really fight, be in the shit, so to speak, and not become some kind of historian. Let me tell you, history misses the point. Take the Somme, for example. The Big Fuck-up. I mean it was called that when it was happening. You had something like sixty thousand lads—and they were lads—die in the first day of battle. That battle cut the world in two. It introduced pure irony into the world, but do historians mention it? Hell no. Are we willing to call Nam the Little Fuck-up? Christ no. The president keeps her rolling and decides to make a repository for irony, and do you know where it is, Singleton? You're sitting in it. And I feel duty bound to dissipate some of the excess irony. And do you know how I'm going to do it? I'm gonna terminate this Rake character first chance I get. Now, you might think that's against the Credo, but the way I see it, he's going around taking perfectly cured individuals and returning them to their traumatized states, and when we tried to enfold him, to treat him, he became one more in a line of failed enfolds, and the only way to make the wider problem—with the treatment, I mean—disappear, the only realistic way is to terminate him. If you're gonna build a big repository for the remnants of Nam, if you're gonna go around believing in the structure of your endeavor, you have to be willing to go out and solve the problem so it doesn't exist anymore—proof of the problem, I mean. So that's why I'm going to eliminate him."

Klein moved back to the map on the wall, touched the pins, plucked the strings gently. "That's just between the two of us, confidential," he said. His voice softened and his jaw slackened for a second and then tightened up. He'd be lighting a pipe in a few minutes.

"I don't really want to go against the regulations," Klein said. "Or the mission, for that matter. But the way I see it, a situational reality must be faced. We've been tracking down these failed enfolds for two years now, and we have cops up north sending the law enforcement liaison down asking for help. They're sure we know more than we say we know, of course. I'm here to train you, so I feel an obligation to speak the truth. But you should feel an obligation—no, scratch that. You've taken an oath to keep this case to yourself. Anything I say in here can be used against you, so to speak. It would've saved me a hell of a lot of time and pain if I'd been trained to see that we're not a perfect organization. The vision we have as an organization, even our building might seem close to perfect, and certainly we've come a long way toward fulfilling our mission, but, again, truth to power, there are points at which the means of war, the problem itself, must be tapped to solve a difficult problem. A man like Rake escapes off into a fury of social nonstructure. He comes to us, his file sealed, as per regulations, and then when we try to enfold him, to give him the best treatment possible—although I'll be the first to admit that he was one of the early test cases, and his reenactment was down in New Mexico—he doubles his trauma, and as I'm sure you know, from reading your manuals and your early training, a failed enfold simply takes the Causal Events Package and amplifies it. Tripizoid, in the case of a failed enfold, doesn't allow for the proper state of redress. It's just a drug, and like all drugs it's still partly—no, scratch that—it's still a mystery. You'd know about drugs, I assume. You could tell me plenty."

Singleton looked over Klein's shoulder and out the window and thought about the agent Wendy, who was probably, right now, listening and nodding and making gestures to indicate she was listening. He thought of her up in Relations, hands in her lap, her eyes fixed on her boss. Meanwhile, the building gave off bad vibes that came of its having been endowed by Kennedy in his third term, when secured by his martyrdom (or whatever the fuck you wanted to call it), as part of his Great Hope initiative. Originally built to serve as a transfer point for veterans coming back into the Vetdock programs, the offices consisted of shoddy government-issue wallboard in preconstructed frames, with flickering fluorescent lights and broad windows facing the front of the building. A sense of mission gone haywire inherent in the walls.

Klein's bearing had changed little in the last few weeks. He leaned forward and seemed to aim his words at a target down-range. He spoke to his own sense of himself as it related to his own history. He spoke in broad strokes and then tightened—with a slight vibrato—to the details of the case.

"We think Rake has a history of finding recently treated patients and kidnapping them. We've already covered that." Klein reached out to align the pipes on his rack again, fingering the bowls. "She was released into the Grid with a tacking band and he somehow knew she was coming out of treatment, knew she'd be freshly enfolded, and he showed up there— most likely hiked his way in—around day two after her arrival. He must've found his way to a list. The lists are going on the black market, and you know, well, we've been through all of this but it won't hurt to repeat it. You might hear something that triggers an idea, Singleton." (Klein lifted a pipe from the rack—an absurdly long meerschaum, broken in, tobacco colored—and twiddled it between his fingers. His mouth puckered and he sucked the stem and then put it back and took another pipe, holding it up, explaining that it was a Dublin, beautiful bird's-eye briar. Then he fixed it, packing, poking, lighting, puffing.) "Her record—I mean the enfolded material—is officially sealed to us, of course. But what we do know is that she was fixed and released with tag."

"Yes, sir, tagged."

"No, not tagged. *With* tag."

"Yes, sir. With tag."

Klein stood up again and moved to the window. Overhead, the building thrummed. Files were held somewhere off facility, locked away, bending against clips, rubber banded and color coded. His own was out there somewhere, Singleton thought, stored in some secure location, loaded with the facts and figures and the basic stage directions of what had to be replicated—a mass shooting, a booby trap, he didn't really know anymore—during the enfold, reenacted into memory with the help of the go-to drug, Tripizoid, and doubled back on itself hopefully forever. One peek in a file—it was said—and the memories would rush back and the fuzzball in the head would explode and you'd be back in the shit again. Treatment failed if the treated knew, or even suspected, that the treated material, the information, could be accessed again. Without a sense of privacy, reenactment failed. Klein went on about Rake's noir tendencies and how it was clear in his actions, in the blood paintings, in the traces he left behind, that he had an inclination to instill his actions with drama, and that this was key—this might be *the* key.

"Brando," Singleton said.

"Yes, Brando syndrome. I've thought of that. And Dean. Most of the dramatic types imagine themselves as inheritors of a great rebellious tradition and see no need to find a cause for their rebellions, so they lean toward Dean. Auden said, 'It's the insane will of the insane to suffer insanely.' Something like that. It's the same with actors. The line between what they're presenting and their own inner life thins, if they're weak of will, and the character they're embodying becomes the body they're presenting, something like that. When you consider the fact that Rake is a failed enfold *and* he has dramatic inclinations . . . I hope you're listening to me, Singleton. We're talking about grunt-level thinking, and to get to that you have to go to the random particulars, or the particulars that seem to map out the random. Like I said, it seems to me—and this is an example of trusting your gut—that it bears repeating that Rake came back from Vietnam and was enfolded in the early experimental station down in New Mexico, most likely at the Las Vegas facility, which I'm sure you know was considered substandard, although there wasn't a standard at that time because it was the only facility. Not the gambling Nevada Vegas, but the New Mexico Vegas.

Then he escaped to Amarillo and, as is typical for these men, made his way here to Michigan."

"Yes, sir. Then we lost his trail," Singleton told himself to say, and said. He had learned over the last two weeks to beat the dead horse, and keep beating it. Kick the can down the road. Fill up these training sessions with as much of his own verbiage as possible.

"Then he popped back in April, made his mark. Now every random killing up north, every psycho killing, every gang-related draw-and-quarter gets pinned on him whether he did it or not. We've got these dinky, small-town cops, these half-assed sheriff deputies flashing badges, talking to the liaison, who comes here with his pleas, his missives that imply that we must know where the guy is. Cops want to shoot him dead. Command wants to get him back in for another round of treatment."

He plucked the string—a shooting in Petoskey on April 5 to a shooting near the Indiana border, an old man shot in the head on April 6.

"There was something in her file about a man named Billy Thompson, a.k.a. Billy-T, a vet who was killed in the war," Singleton told himself to say, and said.

Klein went to his desk and opened a file. "Here it is: Billy Thompson, a.k.a. Billy-T, came back out of rotation for a stateside visit, fell in love with a girl—name redacted, but we can assume it's Meg—took her away to California on a wild road trip, was AWOL for ten weeks and then got sent back with limited disciplinary charges on account of his sharp-shooting abilities, or something. He was KIAed on his second rotation and his trail ended. Whereas her trail ends in this shit." Klein pointed at the map, the pins, the strings.

"He came home in a bag," Singleton said.

"A casket with a flag, as simple as that."

"Then the girl cracked."

"One can only assume. The file is sealed, of course."

Klein closed the meeting with a handshake and a command to take the afternoon off. That was how it worked. You spent the morning in so-called briefings and then were given the afternoon to wander and think and absorb and, in the parlance of the Corps, go Internal.

The last of the industrial surge, cars partly formed, their frames and skeletal strutwork floating down the line, bucking slightly from the conveyor jerk, surrounded by the pop of pneumatic guns and bolt drivers as he punched the rivets quickly and then stood back, looking sadly down the line at the other men who seemed caught in a perplexity of automated movement, waiting for the next door to arrive. That's what she looked like standing in the lobby—another incognito worker, another cog having a smoke after a hard shift on the line, gazing around as if looking for an opportune moment to escape, dressed in her regulation stretch pants and white blouse.

But her face brightened and she gave him a second glance and he knew they were going to join each other for lunch against regulations because that's what they did—they went out onto the sidewalk after being briefed, zoned out on data, and then they let their instincts take over.

She glanced at him again and then went ahead through the revolving door while he stayed in the lobby and tried to look casual. A guard was staring at her as she stood with her face up to the sun, the noontime breeze ruffling her blouse. Singleton waited until two more agents had passed through the door before he went out into the glare.

"Hey," she said. "We'd better stand here a second and pretend to have a friendly face-to-face, agent-to-agent greeting, and then I'll go ahead and you follow."

"How's your case going?" he said. He liked her eyes. They were the blue of faded denim, and they didn't look at all enfolded.

"Same old case," she said.

The guard inside was still watching, for sure.

"Well, good to see you," he said, and she shook his hand.

"Just give me a half-block lead," she whispered, and then she turned on her heels and headed down the street. He lit a cigarette and checked his watch.

A half block ahead she turned and made a come-along gesture, and then turned and continued walking, all shift and sway with the breeze tousling her hair and her beautiful (fucking beautiful, he thought) hips and ass perfectly restricted in her regulation stretch pants. You either wore pencil skirts with a wide belt and a white blouse, or you wore the pants and a white blouse.

He liked the way she waited for him by the cash register, standing with her hip cocked and gesturing with her hands out, as if to say, Here you are, finally. It was a classic coffee joint, somehow saved from the ravages of the original riots; the kind of place that most Corps workers avoided not only because it was old-fashioned, nothing like the canteen with its plastic modern chairs, but also because it was full of vets or men who looked like vets, and if there was one place you could meet without being noticed by other members of the Corps it would be full of potential clients, of patients waiting to be treated, or already treated, leaning into the counter in their old fatigues and sweating nervously into their soup.

A waitress in a yellow skirt and a yellow blouse with white ruffles and a name tag led them to a booth by the window.

"Well, here we are, breaking regulations again," he said.

"That seems to be true," she said. "In theory we should exchange bullshit information, no mention of the cases beyond the fact that we're both bored and tired, that kind of thing." They raised menus and looked them over and went into an exchange that began with "By the way, where are you from?"

She was from Flint. He was from Benton Harbor, not far from Lake Michigan. She was a Lake Huron girl, whatever that meant, and he was a Lake Michigan guy. (They agreed that you were either one or the other.) Huron girls contended with topographical tedium and high pollution levels. Michigan guys—she insisted—stared wistfully out at what they imagined was Chicago's coast. They both agreed that Lake Superior types were cold and stoic in a good way, clean and pure like the water.

There was a moment of tension after he mentioned, offhandedly, that he would really enjoy—that it might even help him with the Internal afternoon—getting his hands on some good drugs, nothing too serious or against regulations, just something to spark his thought systems, to ease up the tension of his repetitious briefings with a punitively old-school agent. She didn't say anything, just raised her brows and touched her nose. She had a birthmark, hardly visible, a small red-purple mark, and the second button of her blouse had come undone (or perhaps she'd unbuttoned it) and he could make out the sprinkle of freckles leading down to the shadow of cleavage. He looked away out the window and then back. She took a sip of her drink and then suddenly threw her head down and let her hair spread over the table and then, just as quickly, tossed her head up, so that it fell back into place.

"Oh, God," she said. "We're already in trouble."

"How so?" he said. But she widened her eyes as if with mischief. He could get lost in those eyes, he thought. He looked away out the window—a vet, or at least someone who looked like one, lurked on the other side of the street, running his hands though his hair, staring in their direction—and then back. Her eyes widened again, the same way, and a tingle moved up from his toes to his groin. The birthmark saved him, drawing his attention away, and then the coffee arrived.

"I've heard things about your agent in charge," she said.

"What have you heard?"

"Nothing that isn't probably common knowledge, or whatever. He's a bozo, a nut job, an old-schooler with his head stuck in the past, a fake, a phony, blah blah blah. I'm sure if you asked anybody they'd say the same about mine. But I heard something else, some rumor, and it made me a little sorry for you. I mean I'm jumping here. I'm taking a leap. I don't even know you. I'm not going to pry. I wouldn't do that anyway. You know, regulations. I just heard the guy's an asshole. That's basically it. Might've been more stuff to it, but that's the gist."

"That's the gist? That's it?"

"There's more gist, but then, again, you know, regulations."

"I can't say much without risk of compromising. You know what they say: It's not what you know it's what you know and don't let others know you know, something like that. I have that wrong, don't I? It's more like: if you know something and know it, then why not know it without letting others know . . ."

"This is when I'm supposed to laugh," she said. She scanned the restaurant.

"I can say this much and not compromise. He says he was a historian. I mean he's been in battle and knows what he's talking about at the field level. It's a little unclear if he was actually some kind of historian, but he talks like one when he's in a bombastic mode, and then he quotes poets, things like that. He hasn't had the treatment, of course—you know, wrong war, too old."

When the food arrived there was a sudden sense of seriousness. He watched her eat, holding her fork and knife in the European manner, cutting with swift strokes.

"We shouldn't meet here," he said. "It's too close to the office."

"I thought the number of vets eating here would make us pretty invisible."

"You had wayward tendencies, didn't you?"

"Not really. I mean I do now, clearly." Again she gave him the look. This time she kept her eyes wide and smiled, reaching out to touch his arm, running a finger along his scar, leaving it there for a second.

A busboy came and cleared the dishes into a plastic bucket. Singleton examined a smear of grease on his placemat—a map of pre-riot Michigan with drawings of emblematic crops and products: blueberries in the thumb region; rolls of paper and stacks of lumber and, of course, automobiles. The smear was near a town called Big Rapids, on the southern edge of what some people were starting to call the Zone of Anarchy. (Look, son, Klein had said. I can't stand the lingo. They're just making the lingo up as they go along. In any case, you can't have a bunch of low-level law enforcement officers operating like fascists—which to my mind isn't always such a bad thing—and simply call it anarchy. It's a misuse of a word that is prone to misuse. What we got here is a situation in which the general public is not sure who's doing the protecting. Some are taking the law into their own hands while others are going mad trying to live up to this so-called Year of Hate thing, and then you have the drugs, of course, and the music.)

The waitress returned, tapping the pad with her pencil. Her face was smothered in makeup. Bright blue glittery half-moons spread over her lids and down part of her cheek; her eyelids struggled against globs that clung to her lashes. She'd been through the riots and come out the other end with the same job in the same coffee shop.

"I don't suppose you'd like more coffee. That is, if you want to continue your secret meeting." She pointed over her shoulder. An agent, or someone dressed like one, was eating at the counter.

"We'd better split," Singleton said.

"You folks let me know and I'll find a way to keep him occupied," the waitress said. "That is, if you give me a good tip. If you give me enough of a tip I'll give you a tip. And my tip is to stay away from each other if you can. I don't know much about what goes on over there, but it seems like it's always the ones that come together that never return together, if you know what I mean."

She returned to the counter, lifted a gate, and approached the man who seemed to be an agent. She was asking him if he wanted pie. The word *pie* seemed to float in the air as Singleton and Wendy left the diner and headed away from the Corps campus.

"You think they're keeping an eye on us? I wouldn't put it past Klein to track me when I go out in the afternoons, even though, as far as I can tell, it would violate regulations. You're supposed to feel free. He gives me these so-called Internal leaves, but then he asks me to detail my movements. Usually it's just stuff like: I walked down to the old canal. I smoked a joint and sat around my apartment, reading. I make stuff up because I can hardly remember."

"Well, you know," Wendy said. "You're supposed to be trusted."

This is where we stand for a moment in awkward hesitation, he thought. She was rubbing her arm, as if tense. The street looked unusually clean and bright, full of people going about their daily business. He reminded her again that he was, of course, on an Internal that afternoon. She told him she was, too, and then her voice dropped and she gave him her address. Then they parted in opposite directions. When he passed the coffee shop again, the agent was gone and the counter was empty.

From the window of her apartment he could see heaps of hot cinders, great piles of debris plowed up during the initial clean-up effort, before the stop order was declared and what remained was left to sit and smolder as a monument to the riots. Her building sat on the edge of the debris area. The smoke seemed blue-green, catching the late afternoon light. Everything has a tendency to become framed. You build a frame and put a window in and there you have it. You meet a fellow agent and have a couple of lunches and the frame appears. She says she's going to change into something more comfortable and you turn away and another frame appears.

She had changed out of her work clothes into cut-off jeans and a halter top tied in a big knot above her belly button, which was small, like a flower bud, turned in. As she lifted her arms to make a ponytail in her hair he saw the powder-blue hem of her panties.

"You've got yourself a fine view," he said. "Just looking at it makes me want to change my position on the stop order. Normally, I'm a put-the-fire-out-and-rebuild-right-away kind of guy. Normally, I'm of a mind that it should be all bull-dozed and rebuilt. But right now, looking at this view, I think the governor had it right. It's all going to burn again some-time soon, so why not leave it."

"You can leave it but once the toxins leach out, eventually it's going to green up, fauna's gonna grow."

"You're an optimist," he said.

"Nature wins eventually. At least that's what they say."

All afternoon they'd been moving toward this moment—it was the object of the conspiracy that had started in the street. First they'd analyzed the man at the counter in the coffee shop. The cut of his suit. The way he kept his head down. Then they'd talked about the waitress, who they agreed was an intuitive woman with that strange waitress radar that picked up on the way people moved. She'd seen that they were breaking regulation: two younger folks eating together, one with a scar on his face and that slightly enfolded tense look; the other a young woman who looked not enfolded but perhaps damaged. (You don't look that damaged, Singleton had said. You're young, that's true. You're highly attractive for an agent, that's true, too. You can see right away that I'm a vet. How old do I look? Do I look about twenty-five? You look twenty-six, she'd said.)

Sitting at the little table in her kitchenette, he'd avoided asking deeper personal questions so that she would avoid asking deeper personal questions. There had been a sweet feeling—with a wedge of afternoon light stretching across the floor—of a mutual standoff. He knew she might be thinking about the dangers of being around an enfolded man. He knew that she was thinking about the risk.

"What's going to grow on the heap, I was told in briefing, is jimsonweed," she was saying at the window. "Which is smokable."

"Speaking of smokable, do you have any pot? You said you had pot?"

"I've got a tin in the freezer."

"Please, get it out," he said.

On the bed it started as newness, the first touch of this, the first touch of that, the whorl of hair at the back of her neck, his thigh, her arm. Pushing away to look and then closing in, losing control and then regaining it, mapping and exploring, high with the first-touch sensations. (And the pot.) She ran her fingers along his scar, starting below his temple, following it to his armpit, across the bridge of undamaged skin that he loved to touch when he was alone, spreading out to his chest—

his one nipple permanently shriveled—and around his side to his back. The scar, tissue where they'd grafted new skin, seemed suddenly charged with a slight electric current that zinged right up to his head and into the enfolded nut up there, as if to confirm what they'd said: After your treatment anything bodily that reminded you of the trauma would remain slightly energized. The high of the Tripizoid left only the nurses' advice, the echo of their warning that sex, really good sex, might unfold you again completely, bringing back your old, traumatized self.

They rolled away from each other and let the charges deplete and the sweat dry, and then they rolled back toward each other. Then it was a matter of heaving and rocking, of attempting to be a neat unit, and he was trying but failing to get hard by releasing himself into mindless memory, as the electric charge began to leak around the fuzzball and he saw a flashbulb negative of a chopper in the air, an old Huey, and he was in it and out of it at the same time, which of course he would've been if he'd died like some of his buddies, but he hadn't died (the flash seemed to say) and before he knew it he was on his back breathing hard, his heart pounding. The sound of street noise, of a siren far off, and the noise of the shitty building, the beat of music through plaster and lath.

"It's OK," she said. "Don't worry about it."

"I'm sorry."

"What were you thinking about?" she said, searching for dilation in his eyes. (She'd been through training. She knew the basics of medical psych, the sweep of the penlight to see if the pupils dilated properly.)

"I was thinking how alive I am because I'm lucky."

He went to the kitchen, poured some gin into tumblers, added ice, and brought them back to the bed. They lit another joint and let it burn and sipped the drinks and leaned shoulder to shoulder. She asked how he ended up in the Corps and he gave her the barest sketch about Nam, about what he couldn't remember, the texture of not knowing but wanting to know, and how after his treatment he had rented a little walk-up over a garage in Bay City where he hung out and read, trying to collect a sense of who he might've been and what he might've seen, finding it in magazines and books and news reports until he felt strong enough and, paradoxically, weak enough and fucked up enough to see himself as someone who might contribute something to the new cause of trying to help other vets like himself. He figured—he explained—that he had had some kind of tracking tendencies that went back to before Nam, and that as a kid he had loved books about animal footprints. That much he could remember. He didn't care so much about animals, per se, but he had loved to track footprints. What about you? he asked. And she explained—her voice suddenly distant—that in the end it had come down to a hospital job, as a nurse, or a Corps job, and she liked the idea of finding a better structure for her desire to care, one that didn't have so much to do with physical suffering. When he pushed her to explain more, to elaborate, she said she'd rather not, and when he asked why, she grew quiet. (It was the first time, he'd later think, that he had seen this state of tense quietude.)

"I made a promise to my mother before she died. I was just nine, so maybe I'm just imagining it, or maybe it's something my dad told me, but I like to think that I really did make a promise to take care of my dad, even though he didn't seem to need my care, not one bit, and maybe I extended that promise out, I don't know. Maybe I just have a thing for vets." And then she shrugged again and spread her hands out as if to say that's it, and she waited until he felt compelled to say something—anything to fill up the quiet—and he explained that in Bay

City, after he had been released from treatment, from the Grid, one afternoon, listening to Kennedy on the radio, he had fallen hook, line, and sinker. It seemed to come, this desire to join, out of a need to help those who couldn't be helped, something like that, he explained. She hugged herself, looking dejected and lonely (he thought), and then, suddenly, she said, her voice deep and confessional: "I don't want to get involved with you, but here I am."

"Jesus," he said. He let the smoke sit inside his head until he could hardly think at all.

"I'm afraid. I don't really want to unfold you. What I said before, it's not that simple."

"If it becomes too good, I'll let you know."

"Ha ha," she said, frowning.

Later, when she got up to make coffee he lay in bed listening to the sound of water running, the scoop digging into the coffee, the tin percolator on the stove ticking as water pushed up through the tube and into the small glass observation bubble. He imagined it brimming past the curved glass, getting one last look at daylight before the plunge into oblivion.

DOWN & UP

Along the Indiana border the road began to yearn north. She dozed against the window, feeling the engine—all eight cylinders firing in a grumbling vapor lock of piston rings and sealed systems. Rake nudged her shoulder. When she opened her eyes it was dark and the fields of dead, unharvested crops had given way to a farmhouse. He pointed to it, cocked his thumb back, made a spoof sound to indicate gunfire and then slowed the car down, and when they got to a mailbox, he began to talk softly about the Jones family, saying, We'll have to pay a visit to the Joneses. You got a name like Jones, a common name, Smith or Jones, and you make a target of yourself. You got all the lights on like that, you're opening yourself up to the potential of someone like me coming your way. You sit in the house and wait. You know I'm coming. You got that sensation under your skin. You build a notion that it's impossible and so forth, you pray to your God to sustain your safety, but he's not listening and you know it, he said, and then he went quiet and she knew what that meant. She was only half-awake. She wiggled her fingers to see if they'd move (they did) and then her toes and pushed back against the seat.

She felt him staring at her in the darkness.

*You move and you have to move somewhere, he'd said.
I'm going light on the substance. I'll learn you, as they like to
say down south. I'll learn you a new way of thinking so long
as you move with me. A new way of moving. I'm gonna hold
the death card close to the vest and then slap it down on the
table when the time comes. I'm kidnapping you for your own
sake. To keep my word of honor made way back. Not that I
want to keep it. You're bound to me by things you don't even
know. If you knew them, you'd know. If you were to know,
you'd understand. Now you see a house here, a house there. A
house passing in the night. It means something, just by itself.
You remove the inhabitants and it means something more.
Smoke coming from a chimney. Down in a valley, covered in
snow. Means one thing. Tucked against another house in a
street burned out, means another.*

On the left side of the house was a tree with pink blossoms
in the window light.

The farmhouse, surrounded by spring mud, was absurdly
neat, with two stories and dormers and black shutters.

The whole package, he said. They've got the whole package here.

He parked the car up the road. Together they walked
down the drive, hunching slightly, until they were at the side
of the house. He pointed at the tree and she knew what he
wanted because he'd made her climb a tree at a rest stop
somewhere, an old one with a stone barbecue pit and a pump
with a broken handle, just to watch her do it. She'd gone up
into the branches, clutching, shaking, until she was caught
like a cat, unable to get down, and then he made her jump
into his arms.

*I'm the bad luck brought home. I'm taking the bad luck
I had and foisting it on somebody else.*

The tree reached as high as the second-story window, and
she got into the middle of it, against the trunk, found a branch

and pulled herself up. (Light as a bird. Your bones are hollow, he'd said at the rest stop. You're high enough to fly high.) In the tree, amid the blossoms, she took a breath. Threading through the floral perfume was the smell of spring grass.

Look forward, move through it, a nurse said, the one with the deeper voice. He looked at her the way you'd want to be looked at, with a calm and steady nonjudgmental gaze. You'll feel it in there and at some point you'll take comfort in knowing it's there, the ball of old memories.

Through the window was an oriental rug and a big easy chair with a man reading a paper and smoking a cigar. Smoke roiled over his head and caught light from a television set. He seemed to be hiding behind the paper from his kids, who were at his feet with their legs crossed, looking forward.

She adjusted her grip and held still, feeling the serenity of the tree, the rustle of leaves in the breeze. From the window, which was open, came the smell of tobacco smoke along with the canned TV laughter and the giggle of the kids. The man lowered his paper and looked at them, tapped his cigar in an ashtray, and then he raised the paper, hiding again.

Rake was whispering, his voice weirdly gentle. Stay up there and look and I'll give you something to see.

She looked out across the yard. The moon was rising and the light frosted the grass.

When she looked back inside, the man still had his paper up. Rake was in the kitchen by now, she knew. He went into back hallways and kitchens first, and there must've been a sound from the kitchen, because the man lowered his paper and tilted his head, and the kids, who were crawl-walking backward toward his knees, giggling again, also turned. For a moment all three of them sat still.

The cat, the man said. He lifted the paper again.

The desire to say something, to shout out a warning, to terminate the scene. Fear, fear, fear was something material.

Hold still and you'll live. Move softly and you'll survive. Take it easy and you'll make it, the nurse had said. If you feel yourself falling look down into the fall. Something like that.

The bloodbath that followed seemed distant. She was seeing it and not seeing it. (You saw it all, Rake would say. You might not've been looking but you saw it.) Rag dolls acted upon by some distant force. There was an explosion and the two children were dashed to the side, heads opening up while the man's head snapped with the opening of his chest and the woman, who had been hidden from view, revealed herself in a scream. A moment later there was only the sound of the television set and he was looking up through the window glass, shrugging, and then he went from body to body and did what he had to do—that's how he put it. I do what I do. You have to know that—making shapes in the carpet with his fingers, leaving messages.

He got his bag from the trunk and found what he was looking for and made her take it, pushing the canteen to her mouth and making her sip, probing her mouth with his fingers to make sure it was gone, and then there was Kennedy's voice on the radio, Boston locutions from his repaired larynx, speaking of the nation's great vision, outlining another one of his projects, reading out figures that suggested victory's imminence in Vietnam. Rake was slapping the wheel with his palms and talking alongside the voice while she listened. Both worked into each other—she felt Kennedy's more, she could catch each of his words and see the way he stood with the damaged shoulder stiffer than the good one and his jaw, repaired, listing as he talked of retreat from the DMZ and a fragmented force left behind in the aftermath of retreat and something about a reckoning at hand (maybe Rake doing an imitation) and the conflagration of battle that would soon collapse into peace as the station bounced in off the higher reaches of the ionosphere and then faded into a preacher's voice, quoting from the book of Isaiah: evil is the torment in the bloodied skies; shy are the defeated; the weak clutch to the stones—and then the Kennedy signal came back in strongly: We're at the apex of the greatest experiment in our history, he said, and Rake said, Yeah, that's what we're doing. We're heading into a big national experiment, and then he snapped the radio off and opened up the acceleration, faster and faster—as the acuteness of her attention increased, each word available to hear again and again, the road coming in under the headlights (she could feel it, she could feel the road). And then, hours later, a lonely gas station with long, narrow pumps and haloed lamps overhead.

The car stretched out to the chrome ornament, crosshairs aiming into the night.

Then they were passing through Big Rapids again, unnoticed, tearing down the main drag.

What goes around comes around again, Rake said.

He pushed another pill into her mouth and made her swallow and poked his fingers, probing.

When you're just about to fall into a dream, you get a sense of it being there.

PSYCH CORPS BUILDING, FLINT

Again behind his desk Klein went through the motions of preparing his pipe, first examining it and running his fingernail around inside, studying the curls of tar on his nail and flicking them onto his desk, and then scraping it out with the tool before filling it up and snapping the match. The tobacco had a sweet, rummy odor. It was packed in a tin that opened with a wonderful hiss when he turned the key.

"You got these folks upstairs wanting to smooth things, talking mission this, mission that, and what they want is what we want, except . . ." He stopped to relight his pipe and leaned back in his chair and puffed. "Those bleeding hearts see the solution as simply a matter of enfolding these wayward types again, even though, clearly, you get a failed enfold like Rake and he's not going to give you another chance. The fact that his trauma has been amplified makes a cure impossible. All you'd do by enfolding him again would be to get him back to his original trauma state," Klein said.

"Yes, sir, sir." Singleton nodded and did his best to look like he was paying attention. Overhead the light fixture continued buzzing. Outside, the wind blew rain against the window, streaming drops along the glass. He leaned back slightly in the chair, kept his hands on his knees, took on the stiffness that Klein expected, hiding his boredom. Klein expected spot-shined boots and clean, pleated trousers and undivided attention all the time, no matter how boring or duplicitous the briefing might be. He took a breath and let the air seep out. The boredom was pure. He relaxed into it and thought of Wendy, the freckles on her breastbone and the tone of her voice, deep alto, resonate.

"I know we went over it, the material about the girl named Meg, but it might help to go over it again. You might go out there with it into the Internal afternoon and think about it in another context. Who knows. Most of her file is sealed, of course. But let me reiterate what we do know, which is that Meg's family was set to inherit part of the Upjack fortune, at least they were until the family lost everything. You familiar with Upjack?"

"Drugs," Singleton told himself to say, and said. "The development of what they called the friable pill, a pill that wouldn't dissolve until it reached the gut. That led to a patent. The patent led to great wealth. Scalp lotion. Ointments. Vitamins. And the serious antidepressants and, finally, Tripizoid, which was originally a veterinary product for horse sedation, a cure for the hoof-kick, for stable-knock, something like that."

"Excellent," Klein said. "It doesn't seem to matter, unless it matters. If it matters, we'll only know in retrospect. Her mother and father met on the train from New York to Michigan, somewhere along the water-level route. Most likely they sat near each other in the parlor car, along the Hudson, and conversed. Then, as I imagine it, they went to her sleeper car and had relations while the nighttime towns passed, little hamlets, houses down in dales, snow falling because it was winter, I'm guessing, and then they conceived a baby, and the baby was Meg. How do we know that they were on that train? Because one of the facts that was not redacted from her file

was that she has a fear of trains. Is there a connection between Upjack and her trauma? Not likely. You get some
strange connection, a link like the Tripizoid, but it has no
meaning unless you try to make up the story to fit the facts,
and we're not in that business here. It's in the Credo. All cures
are bogus. Which I take to mean all stories are bogus. It's impossible to find a causal connection between the end product,
a cured patient, and the events that led to the originating
trauma. In other words, the trauma seems to stand apart from
the initial trauma when you look back in retrospect, after
treatment. When you cure, you eliminate the cause. And when
you eliminate the cause, you eliminate the sequence of events
up to the trauma. The Corps has its own term for everything
eliminated—which is?"

"The Causal Events Package. When you enfold the trauma,
you must make sure you enfold the entire Causal Events Package," Singleton said. He put his hands on his knees and leaned
forward. Klein's pipe hung from his clenched teeth. Behind his
aviator-style glasses his eyes looked dazed with tedium. They'd
been saying basically the same thing to each other for weeks.

"You're not really paying attention," Klein said. "You said
to me that it was a Causal Events Package, and that wasn't
necessary. Even though I asked, I expected something more.
Look, it's late June and the cops are passing the buck, pinning
every little shit-can murder on our target, which is only natural. You get some family scared shitless because they live—or
think they live—in something called a Zone of Anarchy, and
a Black Flag gang arrives one night revving engines, calling,
waiting, until the man of the house comes out—because he
has to come out eventually—and tries to sweet-talk his way
out of what he knows is coming, or else he's one of those guys
with a lot of ammo but no luck who comes out shooting, and
then one of the Black Flag men, fresh from one of those absurd
battle reenactments up on Isle Royal, trying to relocate the

glory and pissed off because reliving the glory has only made him want *more* glory, puts a bullet in the man's head and kicks his skull in and leaves him to the local cops, a bunch of Barney Fifes who have no way to solve the case and don't want to see it for what it really is—because why would they want to mess with the Black Flags?—so they wait until there are a few more killings. When they imagine a pattern, they pass word of a failed enfold to the liaison, and he comes up to my office with his briefcase and puts the pressure on me because that's his job, and when I see his information I do a gut check and fail to find a pattern because there isn't one. That's how it works, again and again."

"Yes, sir," Singleton said. There was something in the hang of Klein's jaw, a new tension. He fiddled with his pipes and then looked up, his eyes steely blue, fixed.

"Have you been fraternizing outside? That's what I've been meaning to ask you."

"Sir, I'm not fraternizing with another agent," Singleton said.

"I didn't think you were," Klein said.

"Thank you, sir."

"I was sure you were fraternizing."

"Well, I'm not, sir."

"When I was in Korea, I saw a man like me, I mean who I am right here, now, an officer in charge, and thought it was absurd that my life was in his hands. You don't remember what you used to feel about your command over in Nam but I can assure you that when you saw a man with a West Point ring on his finger, some fresh change of command come walking up the trail in the Mekong with his spit-polished boots and his fresh shave and his baby face, you felt something akin to what you're feeling about me right now."

"Yes, sir. I thought you were in the big one, sir."

"I said the big one, and for me the big one was Korea. It

was just part of the Second, as a matter of fact. It was just an extension of the Second."

"I see, sir," Singleton said.

"When I start to feel the urge to recite poetry, I know we're about done for the day. And I feel that urge. In that war you had a superabundance of highly educated men in the trenches carrying a working knowledge of Greek and Latin, reading Hardy and Dickens, filled with a desire to capture in words the way a sunrise or sunset looked from the bottom of the trench, or the way it felt to do a stand-to at dusk or twilight. All we're getting from this war is the desire to write rock-and-roll lyrics."

As he continued talking, tamping and lighting a second pipe, the sky in the window behind him seemed to clear (a perfect day to head to the beach with Wendy). Singleton continued doing his best to look like a trainee who still held the purest belief in Kennedy's original vision of a Corps that would solve the problem of mental illness in general and the vast horde of returning vets in particular; a vision that honored the president's sister, who sat somewhere alone and quiet with her brain lobotomized; a vision fueled by a man who had been shot in the shoulder and jaw (if a third term was good enough for Roosevelt, it's good enough for Kennedy, the ads said).

Klein was rambling on about men who dragged Japanese heads on grappling hooks behind a ship, let the sharks clean flesh from bone, and brought them home as trophies. (There's a photo in *Life* magazine, if you'd like to see it, he said.)

Singleton kept nodding as his mind drifted, and he imagined what it would be like to go downstairs into the lobby and openly embrace Wendy. She would kick up her heel and throw back her head and open her mouth and, for a moment, they would strike the pose of a sailor and a lover on V-J day in Times Square, dancing (he imagined) on the seal of the Kennedy Psych Corps.

Klein was still talking, something about the photograph, the one with the skulls—was he offering it to him, a kind of gift?—and again Singleton drifted, remembering—what?— remembering how it felt to run with his arms waving in the air, leaving the schoolhouse, out into the freedom of after- noon, wrapped in the sound of kids shouting around him, free for the rest of the day (no, for the rest of the summer) until he got back to the house, back to his old man, home from the mill, shoulders sagging. It was the only memory he had, every- thing after that moment—leaving school—came up blank and here was Klein, he was still talking, pressing, asking him what he was thinking about, so Singleton said, "The Credo, sir, I was thinking about the Credo," while in his mind he was running out of the Corps building and Wendy was waiting, arms wide, and then he was on the beach with her, applying lotion as an excuse to touch her back, two fingers pressed to- gether tracing the lovely line of her spine to where the taut band of her bikini bottom stretched over a slight gap that ab- sorbed sunlight like antimatter. The shimmer of sand and water and light were the backdrop for the only thing in the state worth looking at, worth pondering, that bit of darkness showing beneath her bikini's band—its cavelike perfection leading to the rest of her body—and his own ardor in relation to boredom (maybe the right word was *freedom*), the two combining in the afternoon light, and the fact that all he wanted—Klein was giving him a cold stare—was for ardor to win.

If I told you what I'm thinking it would make your head explode, you old coot. Fingering your medals as if they meant something when they don't even mean a thing to you, Singleton thought.

"Go out into the world and let your mind go where it has to go," Klein said.

"Yes, sir."

"And you might want to trim those sideburns. They're not regulation. Clean faces, clean hearts, is what they say. Mental health is our business. Or, rather, mental freedom is our business. Pax Americana, son," he said, guiding him to the door.

"Sir?"

"Pax Americana begins at home, son."

"I'm a million miles from headquarters," she murmured, lying back in the moss and opening herself, it seemed, to his scrutiny, allowing him to observe that she was beautiful in a tense way. Her legs had a slight knock-kneed bend in just the right place. They were smoking a joint down by the old canal, on a spot across from the towpath. She'd taken off her work clothes in the car, ordering him (in a new voice, brusque) not to look while she slid her skirt off and wiggled into a pair of jean shorts. Now, on the grass, she seemed to be offering him a good, long look. He explained that he was sure—he touched his head—that the madman in his mind had some relation to the madman's target, something like that, and that he had a running theory that all agents, at least enfolded, treated ones, must be thinking the same thing, because they're burdened with the facts that they can't remember and have to reach out to stories and make them their own.

He paused and looked out across the canal. The trees on the other side were deep green, quivering slightly in the breeze, and beyond them the sky was milky with heat. Weedy brambles rose sharply from the dark water—thick as tar—and the line between the two colors looked bluish brown. "We reach out to stories and can't help but make them our own. I'm thinking that's what they like about us. We can be used that way. They tap our desire to connect, and of course the desire comes from the fact that if we hit a connection, if we link to someone who's in our Causal Events Package, we can start tweezing out the truth."

As she stood, reaching back to band her hair, pulling her elbows up, tilting her head, she again seemed astonishingly beautiful to him in an edgy, new way. The attraction seemed mutual and strong and for a few seconds as he looked into her eyes—blue washed away by sunlight, speculative, searching his face for something—he felt a deep sense of danger. She turned from him suddenly, said something about needing to move, and led him down the towpath, striding quickly, past backyards cluttered with riot wreckage. The burn had reached the far side of the canal, an open vista of ash and char reclaimed, along the edge of the water, by green brush. Eventually, to their left, a neighborhood of spared bungalows appeared, ragged but structurally sound, with yards full of Queen Anne's lace and, from one house, a faint pulse of music.

Wendy stopped and looked at the house and began to explain that she loved the Stones and hated the Beatles because the Beatles were what you get when you're enfolded, treated with Trip, a song with just a formation built around old, unknown memories; whereas (she said "whereas") the Stones are what you get when you allow it all to play out, when you come back fucked up. He resisted the urge to disagree, to say that the lads were slightly boring but seemed to be channeling trauma in their own way, working through the misery of their Liverpool boyhoods, the ration-ticket bleakness of a postwar landscape not that different from this one. It was too early for a petty squabble about rock bands, or anything that might hint at future arguments to come.

She was listening to the music, dancing slightly, swinging her hips, lean, not skinny, but slim. There was something wiry in the way she moved, and it thrilled him. She began to dance go-go style, smiling at him in a coy way at first, and then twisting her arms over her head and closing her eyes. He looked around and lit a cigarette. Then he motioned to a split-rail fence and told her to sit down on it. "Sit on the fence," he said. "I want to see you sit on that fence."

She gave him a look and called him a control freak and then smiled and went over and sat down. The yard behind her, with the Queen Anne's lace and weeds and the house in the backdrop, seemed elemental and part of a package: Wendy sitting on a fence. That's how it seemed to work. They'd said, You'll find yourself weirding out about the way you see things, and you'll be aware not only of your enfolded material, the sensation of it in your head but also the blind spot you have, the blank area.

He admitted that he was feeling turned on, seeing her sit there.

"As a Psych Corps member I have an obligation to remind you of the Credo," she said. She got up and took his hand and led him back to the towpath.

"Fuck the Credo."

He walked to the edge of the canal and looked down into the water. All of the creosote and tar had washed into it, along with whatever the mills had added, and it moved sluggishly along the weeds. It was easy, looking at it, to imagine that in a million years the fossils of small mammals and fuck-ups like himself would be chiseled from the ossified mass of gunk.

He placed his palms together and extended his elbows, a diving gesture.

"Once you're in that you never get out," she said. There was an edge around her words, a fear he hadn't heard before.

"You don't think I'd do it?"

"I hope you wouldn't do it," she said.

"I'd do it, but life is looking up and I'm trying to live the Psych Corps Credo."

"I love a man who recites the Credo in his sleep," she said, kissing him.

"You sounded, for just a second, like a hippie."

"I've never been enfolded, so I can't sound like pre-enfoldment," she said.

"You can take the hippie out of the man, via enfolding, but you can't take the wayward out, or the deeper tendencies."

"Don't quote me that shit. Not now."

Later they drove to the beach and laid out their towels and smoked, looking out at Lake Huron, pollution levels down slightly but still a queer gloss over the surface, a fresh glaze of rainwater over the tension and a few sad birds in the resin, unable to pull free, yanking their wings. On the transistor radio (Nothing like transistor on sand, Singleton thought) a reporter was explaining that Kennedy was on one of his so-called wave-by swings, this time in South Bend, weighing his popularity and the love of the public against the evil elements out there, doing his *PT 109* thing, except in a limo instead of a boat.

"You can ask me more about Klein if you want," Singleton said. "You can say something like, What's Klein doing? Something along those lines."

"You could stop directing me to ask you certain questions," she said. She leaned back and put her face to the sun. "What's Klein doing, something along those lines?" she said, hunching over to form a windbreak, rolling another joint with her long fingers, pressing the papers expertly.

"He puffs his chest out," Singleton said. "Fingers his medals and pretends he's in charge. It's starting to make me sick, to tell you the truth. All I'm hearing now is repeated information, modulation this, formations that."

She shrugged, sighed, looked away down the beach. "I think he's doing the right thing, going about his life as if it wasn't threatened, upholding democracy and the like," she said.

"Who, Klein?"

"I'm talking about Kennedy," she said.

"I'm not going to get into a Kennedy drive-and-wave debate with you, baby, not when I'm this stoned. But you and I both know he's got a death wish that has a lot to do with his back condition. All that pain is an inducement to push the envelope. Take it from someone who knows. I like to imagine I was bivouacked out of Nam, looking down at the canopy, saying, 'I'm flying, man, I'm flying and this is cool, groovy, groovy.' That kind of thing."

He took another deep toke and then a short one and held it, holding, holding.

He passed the joint and watched as she nimbly took a hit, letting the smoke trickle.

"I lost my train of thought," she said.

"I never had a train. Who wants a train when you can have this shit?"

They lay in the sand for a while and he looked at her through the glare, over the top of his arm, and tried to imagine the kind of letters they would've written back and forth, from the war on his side to the States on her side. Her letters would've been chatty, full of nursing stories, patients who were demanding in one way or another, doctors with their know-it-all attitudes, full of authority, the long, lonely night shifts at the desk, sorting files, the small minutiae of everyday life; his would be filled with urgency, written in a crabby longhand, giving faint details and avoiding the truth as much as possible.

•

When a storm began brewing to the west, a dark line over the parking lot, they ran to the car and drove a few miles down to the next beach, concrete car bumpers and spaces delineated by faded yellow lines, reminders of a better era when crowds had picnicked and barbecued and made use of the grills and the quaint stone hut and the fact that the state of Michigan had the funds to keep the water pump working. A sense of common destiny that had been lost in the last few years. They parked in a far corner and watched long curtains of rain steaming when they hit the hot asphalt. The sky darkened while lightning stabbed at the lake, sending up spumes of fire. Even before they started kissing it seemed like a sure thing that they'd have visionary sex, that a memory would surface—two souls sealed in a car by the lake—and then they were kissing, and she was sliding down, unbuckling his belt, he felt her lips on his belly and there was a flash, a quick image along with the lightning *Klein with a pipe between his teeth, closing his lips and making the fish-suck and then opening them again* he lifted his hips and shifted his weight against the seat, her fingers worked the waistband, two seconds of quivering, empty air until her mouth—a faint brush of breath—was close enough to feel. He slid into the open space of it, her tongue rolling softly. *So this is*, her tongue seemed to say, *this is how it's going to be*. She kept at it while another flash of lightning pulsed against his closed eyelids, leaving a purple blot, thunder shook the car and the blot disappeared, *Wendy on the fence, with the Queen Anne's lace moving gently in the air, the smell of her herbal shampoo and the faint patchouli of her skin*, he felt her mouth and he filled it, filled and filled and slipped out as she lifted herself above him, taking his palms and putting them flat on her hips, a sensation of guidance *the tip nothing but the tip the tip just the tip of his cock* a last flicker of fire and then he came, *Rake's face in black and white, a photograph on a file folder, mug-shot grimness and eyes furious, the paradox of being remote and captured at the same time.*

When they were finished, the desire to be dressed and warm seemed to be all that was left.

He turned on the heater and the windshield wipers, the lake outside a fury of dark chop.

"I unfolded for a second again, I think."

She was silent.

"You're supposed to ask what I saw," he said, but she didn't ask. He buckled his belt while she fiddled with the radio dial, trying to find a signal strong enough to cut through the static, and he thought of Rake's photograph in the vision, the look on his face, a look he recognized, he thought (though he couldn't be sure); one Marine to another just before a snafu. Or maybe, he thought, kissing Wendy and reaching into the glove box to get a fresh joint—an apocalypse between each swipe of the wiper blades, fire waves rolling in toward shore, on the horizon bolts of lightning and small geysers rising, falling, devoured by immolation—maybe it was an orgasmic look. Blank and blissful. Tight, angry, happy. Filled to the brim but still wanting.

"It's beyond weird out there," Wendy was saying. "We're living where water burns."

"Where souls are enfolded," he said.

"And then unfold," she said, taking a deep hit.

"Unions are busted. Deals are made."

"Deaths are avenged."

"The good ones."

"The ones that need to be," she said, taking another hit.

STRANGE HOUSE

Meg woke in a strange room, splintery, beaverboard walls, an old side table with a jug of water, a straight-backed chair with an embroidered cushion, a lamp with a tattered shade. She lay in bed and tried to orient herself, trying to remember. The shooting on the highway. The shooting in Elk Rapids. The farmhouse on the edge of nowhere, another shooting, the noise of the car engine and the endless unwinding of the road all slightly blurry in a way that told her time wasn't at a stand-still, exactly. The press of a tree branch against her arches as she stood in a tree looking down at a window. The weirdly soft pop pop of gunfire through window glass. The snort-sniff of Rake clearing gunk from his throat before launching into another soliloquy about the nature of his own violent tendencies.

A man with a big moon face came into the bedroom, pulled the shade, and asked again and again if she was awake until she said she was awake. He had a beard and wore a leather vest over a bare chest, hair thick and curly. He went back to the window and made a comment about the big Gitchi Gumi and then came back to her and sat on the bed and asked if she was hungry.

She clutched the sheet against her chin and looked up at him. He looked kindly, somehow, but mean, too. She waited until he spoke again. He said she had nothing to fear and that he wasn't there to hurt her or anything like that. He said he'd leave her to get dressed and suggested that she go to the window to take a look, that she'd be able to see a bit of the water through the trees at this time of the morning, with the light, and then he went out and closed the door gently and she got dressed and, smelling bacon and eggs, went down a narrow, steep stairway and found the kitchen.

An old lady in a calico apron was tending the stove, and the burly man was at the table eating. He asked her to join him, said it gently, and she did.

As he ate he explained that his father was probably out on a ship, most likely making passage from Duluth to Toledo, and she listened as he talked about the lake, about the men who worked the ships, and then he seemed to catch himself and without being asked, he said, I'm not like Rake, not at all, at least not now.

The lady brought her a plate of pancakes. While she ate, the man explained, speaking slowly, that he had enfolded himself with some black-market Tripizoid from Port Huron, after reading a few leaflets about the subject, and that the old lady, whom he called MomMom, had helped by tying him up. The treatment had worked and the trauma was gone, at least for now, he said. Then he said again that he was not like Rake, not anymore, although Rake didn't know it, hadn't caught wind of it. He was biding his time, unwilling to leave his mother behind, unwilling to kill again, not sure how to get out of the tangle, he said. Then he got up and went out the back door, leaving her alone with the woman named Mom-Mom. She finished her food and felt quiet for the first time in a long time, for a few minutes at least, sitting at the table, warm and safe, and then he came back in with an arm full of

wood and put a few pieces in the stove and poked it. He said
she should go back up and rest if she wanted, and she did,
going back up the stairs, lying down in the bed, pulling the
covers up to her chin and listening for a while, afraid again
suddenly but also extremely tired, and she fell back asleep.

That afternoon the man drove her down a narrow fire road,
two ruts in the overgrowth, deep into boreal forest until the
road ended in burned-out pines.

This here is most likely controlled burn, he said. Most
likely the Department of Natural Resources flame took the
whole fucking acreage as a firebreak line. Least I can do is
teach you about the forest. That's the least. See all those green
shoots? That's nature taking her course. Spring awakening
and all that. No matter how bad it gets you're gonna have
green coming up.

As he led her on a hike he told her to keep an eye out for
the big one, the queen tree. There were trees that had escaped
felling during the previous logging boom.

There's a rumor of a big pine around here. The way I like
to work is to follow my nose, catching the pollen, he said.

The smell of the lake drifted in through the trees, wet
stone and dead flies, with the hint of cold. She clutched the
coat he had loaned her, leather with fringe, and followed him
out of the woods and along a swell of grass and sand. At the
top of the rise, the lake appeared, grand and glossy flat. He
explained how just about every day he took a look—even
when the waves came all the way up to the trees. He had to
see it and tempt himself with the intensity of upheaval, its
hugeness and brutal cold. His heart told him in no uncertain
terms to keep sniffing for trees and listening to the lake as
much as he could. So when I go out to look for trees I make
a habit of stopping like this, he said. Smeary green copper

deposits jutted into the water. A ship sat on the horizon, a supertanker from Duluth on a run to the locks at Sault Ste. Marie (he explained) and then from there out to the St. Lawrence and into the embrace of the wide ocean. His old man had worked his way up from deckhand, captained several ships and made countless runs without sinking. Maybe it's enough to give you hope, he said. I like to think so.

On the beach he had her sit on a rock. He stood for a minute, blocking the sunlight, and then went down to the shore and, with his hands jammed in his pockets, watched the water. He came back and hunched down, plucked his beard, and looked at her with steady eyes.

I'm gonna do my best to help you. Rake's out on a run. The lake is still cold, bitter cold. But the air is starting to warm up. That's something, at least. It's not all you could ask for. But it's something.

That night, in bed, she went over memories. Everything beyond a certain point was a fuzzy abstract feeling in her head. The Causal Events Package, as the nurse had called it, started at an early memory point. She could remember being in her mother's arms, the coolness of a glass of water held up to her little-girl lips, but after that things vanished into a perplexing blankness until she got to the Grid and Rake's appearance—even that was fuzzy—and then her days on the road with him.

THE ZOMBOID

Wendy's father lived in a Sears house, an original kit that had been delivered on a boxcar complete, ready to be constructed, amid row after row of factory homes. On the way over they had passed houses with melted siding, a yard with the cyclopean eye of an old dryer. Dirty and forlorn, a kid stood in the yard chewing something. As they passed, he stuck one arm out, as if thrusting a sword, his leg bent at a right angle, still chewing as he posed (lead paint, Singleton thought). Then they arrived at her father's house, exuding a working man's pride, with a picket fence freshly painted and the only living oak tree on the block. In the yard next door a man in a wheelchair lifted his beer in a gesture of greeting. His legs seemed to have been amputated at the thighs. He had a folded bandana around his long blond hair. He had a face that was ravaged but still beautiful.

"Please don't pay him any mind," she said. "It pains me to call him the Zomboid, but that's what he calls himself and wants us to call him. That's part of what pains me."

"Another veteran sitting out his days in his chair," Singleton said. He returned the salute and then, against his better judgment, went over to say hello.

Freckled and pale, with his arms firmly on the chair's handles, the man called Zomboid struck the pose of a port gunner and said, "Hey, partner. Rank and fucking serial number."

"Can't remember," Singleton said. There was a worn path—two ruts—around the perimeter of his yard.

"Got anything in the way of a cigarette?"

Singleton held out his pack. Around from the side of the house, a dog barked, choked-sounding, as if pulling against a chain. Down the street, another dog responded, full-throated, and then, barely audible, another one, far away and completely free.

"Arms are shot, too, cowboy."

Singleton took a cigarette from the pack and placed it between the man's lips.

"You wanna know what I'm seeing?" The guy's voice was tight and flat, and seemed to come from somewhere else, ventriloquisticly. "I'm seeing nuclear conflagration after the next, the real Kennedy assassination, which is gonna happen soon, for sure. The ghost of Oswald is at hand, my man, and he's gonna get it right this time. No fucking maladjusted scope. No blurry vision or submerged subconscious patriotic bullshit making him quiver; no heartbeat interference on the shot because he had too much coffee or whatever. Next guy's gonna hold his breath and do the backward sniper count thing."

"OK, buddy, I got you on that," Singleton said.

"'Bout that light?"

Singleton pulled the Zippo out and scratched a flame.

"Yeah, Oswald's just the fucking tip, man, of the largest iceberg this country's gonna hit, man, and I'm not talking the riots and so forth, or any of that shit, man," the guy in the wheelchair said. "I'm talking about a debasement of the largest kind."

(Now's the moment, Singleton thought; there's going to be

a glint of something like recognition and then he'll pop into the questioning mode: What's your unit and where were you stationed and how long were you in and all of that.)

"Hold that fucking thing up here." For all of his limitations—his lack of legs and fully functioning arms—the guy had tremendous agility in his torso. (But how, Singleton thought, did he wheel around without the use of his arms? And didn't he lift a salute to me?)

"Light me another one so when this one goes out I'll have something to sustain me."

He put another cigarette to the guy's lips and brought out the lighter again.

"I know that lighter, man. I know it. We might've seen some action together somewhere. I know you think I'm one more crazy fucker, rambling about my visions and so forth. Give me your story. Give me the whole fucking narrative."

Singleton resorted to making the enfolded gesture: he made a fist and held it against his temple and took a couple of steps back and did it again.

"Ah, man. I thought so. I saw it right off. Saw it in the way you were standing there like you never saw a guy in a wheelchair before. Said to myself, there's a guy who saw some bad shit. There's a man who had the good fortune of having it all tucked inside while I sit here with my body too damaged to qualify for the treatment. When I tried to sign up they told me that if your physical damage is bad enough the mental can't be worked on. You get a chair and a yard and a dog on a chain. That's all you get."

"What'd you see over there?" Singleton said. All I can do, he thought, is kick the can down the road. When you have contact, avoid having to be precise about your own story.

"I saw the five-by-six view from a gunner port and everything else in between. Gooks running through the grass with that squat waddle," he said. He'd seen water buffalo stampeding under the blade wash. He'd seen the men in hats running under the ribbons of tracer fire. He'd seen the beautiful spin of dust-off smoke pouring up from the canopy. He'd rehabbed in South Haven, the fucking VA unable to secure for him a decent set of wheels. Then—with seething insects, the cicada in the weeds and up in the trees starting to talk directly to each other—he began making a clucking sound with his tongue and Singleton felt the sadness that came from hearing those who were way, way, way beyond help, the ones who turned to vocal tones instead of words.

"You got a day and I'll tell you the details," he said, finally.

"I'd like that," Singleton said.

"Now you'd better go to your old lady."

"You know her?"

"Like a sister."

Wendy's father greeted him with a meaty handshake, saying, "Come on in. Don't listen to anything that guy has to say. Wendy's told me all about you."

Singleton paused at the screen door. The man—his long hair flaxen in the sunlight—was popping wheelies in his yard, his arms jerking, the metal foot-grills dipping up and down.

"I should've warned you about him."

"I saw him coming a hundred years ago."

The house had a small parlor with two easy chairs, a plush green couch, and a large television console on which two batters were up to bat, the image of one slightly on the side of the other. Singleton resisted his desire to go and fiddle with the rabbit ears and followed Wendy down the hall and into a clean, well-lit kitchen where her father was preparing coffee. The old guy held the pot with his arthritically clawed hands, all pain, nothing but pain up the arm to the tattoos, smeared with age.

From the start a grunt-to-grunt tension was there, both men sensing, and maybe Wendy, too, the weight of the *approaching topic*.

"I'm going to go get us a nip," the old man said when the coffee was gone. He got a bottle of bourbon and poured three shot glasses as tight to the rim as possible, said *salud*, and drank his down before they could touch glasses. If he had been a different kind of man he would've toasted his regiment, or the Black Forest, but instead he'd kept it clean and simple. The old man wasn't ready yet to go into that and instead circled the conversation back to the Psych Corps and to the system and to the hospitals, saying, "So you're each on a different case and you can't talk about it, is that it? You're sworn not to talk about it, as I understand it. But you're allowed to speak in generalities. Most of the men I fought with came home and took the weight onto their own shoulders."

"Yeah, we're allowed to speak about generalities. And in theory we're not even supposed to be together," Singleton said.

In the half-light of late day, Wendy's face seemed to glow. She arched her brows, grimaced, and then smiled. Her face said: You're an old man and can't be expected to grasp the vision behind this huge national project.

"OK, OK, maybe I'm just out of the loop on this enfolding treatment, but there's something fishy about it, and something even fishier about the fact that the administration admits it's bogus and it is written into the creed or whatever it is that you went around the house practicing for weeks when you were studying for your exam." Here the old man turned his attention fully to Singleton and, sounding much older, said, "You should've seen her studying day and night in her room." Suddenly Wendy was repositioned by the kitchen table of her youth. She seemed like a teenager in her father's eyes, and even in Singleton's. He felt the urge to lead her out of the kitchen and fuck her on her single bed. He could imagine her room upstairs, the small bed with a comforter and a pink dust ruffle, and the posters of the Stones trying to look like the Beatles, and her desk with her pencil can and her old school books.

The old man opened up the subject of war by nodding to the shelves and saying, I got the idea for this setup from looking at a sub galley. A buddy served on a sub and got me on board and showed me around and the one thing that I was impressed with was the fact that the galley had the finest bone-white china, and the best silverware. You had to spend half a year breathing shit air in a tin can and sleeping ass to ass, but at least you got good food and fine dinnerware as part of the deal. My buddy joined the Navy and I joined the Army. He went under and I went over the top.

Singleton knew the old man would use the mention of his friend in the Navy to begin his confession. And he did. The Bulge. The Black Forest silence during those woozy first few weeks when the war seemed to be winding itself down, one city after another liberated. Cold snowy days filled with the camaraderie of newly formed units: boys fresh off the boat, struggling to understand that they were on the front edge of the great push toward the bunkered-down Hitler (rumored to be dead). A few weeks in the Black Forest, and the gung-ho vibe was replaced by fear. The old man paused, trying to find a way to describe the way it had felt. He muttered to himself. He wanted to find a way to say it. He mentioned the snow, of course, and the fresh-faced innocence of his buddies. He talked about the wind through the pines, foxholes, plans for movement when the word came down. Just a bunch of ignorant doughboys, he said. We got there, dug in, and waited. The old man's words had an offhandedness from countless retellings. Nothing he said sounded doubtful. The story was a block of stone with the following contents: they waited in the

Black Forest. Scouts were sent ahead on recon missions. Scouts spotted the German reinforcements. Scouts sent information behind the lines. Brass gave a fuck. Men waited in trepidation. Germans attacked. At this point—again predictably—the story took a personal twist. Singleton already knew from what Wendy had said that the old man had been captured by the Germans. He was a lieutenant and had command of his unit and was captured. He was one of the men who'd let the Germans, dressed as Americans, through the line.

Singleton listened while Wendy, having heard the stories a hundred times (no wonder she'd joined the Corps!), tried to locate something new. There was nothing but lies, Singleton thought, when a man began talking about combat. The truth of what had really happened was beyond words. In the truly mad, like wheelchair guy out there in the yard, the haze of lies was thick and serene. Amputees had a hard time with their stories. The listener knew the story would end with a blast of some sort, a flying sensation through the air, a gaping disbelief as the man groped around to locate his missing legs. The listener was always ahead of the game when it came to a wheelchair guy. (And maybe that was why enfolding didn't work on them. Maybe the story they had was trapped in the missing arms, lost like some shadow memory of feeling that kept coming back again and again, mirroring the leg, or arm, or hand.)

What bothered Singleton, as Wendy's father spoke on about his internment, the forced march to Dresden, the escape during the bombings in a firestorm unleashed by his own troops, was the old man's voice. It seemed to say: I'm going to go deep into the memory and give you my war and my experience and then I'm going to come to a full stop, maybe dab away the tears, and you're going to say, Man, sir, that's heavy, and then in turn, as part of the deal, you're going to have to tell me *your* story. You're going to ante up with some words, and the words must convey a sense, at least, that you're down there in the memory of some hidden truth you'll never divulge: but you'll give me a chance to find it, because we went over and saw something that no one else has seen except for other grunts.

In the old man's voice was the older-vet-talks-to-younger-vet tone, and it occurred to Singleton that there was a generation gap that he might put to use. Maybe, when it was his turn to speak, he could signal to Wendy to say they had to go.

Now the old man was speaking in tight phrases. He was running away. He made a run for it. The guards were lost in the chase. He somehow got out of Berlin. Then he was in the countryside. He hid out. He burgled a few homes. He slept in haylofts. He met friendly peasant types. A month he spent on the lam until he came upon an American unit . . .

Singleton had his foot on Wendy's leg and was moving it up along her shin. He couldn't see much of her face. She had her elbows on the table and was running her spoon around the rim of her empty cup.

The story would end, Singleton guessed, just as suddenly as it began. It would come to a dead stop. The poetry would flutter away and the old man would sit silently, shaking his head at the enormity of his memory. (There was always a head-shake at the end of a war story.) Then he'd say, Jesus Christ, didn't mean to go on like that. At which point protocol would require that Singleton ask some question that would direct the story back to the Black Forest.

How many were in your unit?

Did you go on a recon?

What's your theory on the weak link in the chain of command? Or something else that felt detailed, a baton into the hand of a sprinter, so that the old guy would go back around and get closer to the truth of the matter, the big fuckup. No matter what, every grunt had the sensation of having made a grievous error. Maybe it came from being too gung-ho in the moment. Perhaps the error was a misreading of the landscape due to low light. A quick reaction, putting a round through the forehead of your buddy, who had been coming through the dark night to share a cigarette. Maybe it was a fear so deep that it sent you raging into a village to decapitate an old man who had simply been harvesting rice . . .

What had brought this example to mind from the myriad of possible examples? Jesus Christ, had he gone in there himself? Had he done such a thing? Was that the evil bullshit enfolded in him? The fuzzball in his head, free-floating. Theory had it they wouldn't enfold the fantastically evil shit. The evil shit had to be presented to the law, or left external (no treatment!). Reenacting truly evil shit (they said) would only leave you with more shit, so it was unlikely that in some secret facility they were making men reenact atrocities in rigged villages with actors leaning over rice bags, or babies stabbed like Christmas hams on the end of bayonets in the Korean War style; no, no, one had to trust that at some level the web of institutional presumption wouldn't go that far.

Wendy was nudging him gently in the shin, and her father was now finishing up, saying, Christ, did I go on like that? He was rubbing tears from his eyes. The kitchen was nearly dark, a window of lavender light over the sink. Time wasn't exactly still. But it was stiller than usual and both men felt the weight of the story pushing against the one that Singleton might tell, if he could. The old man's story sat like the giant boulder of copper that had been found in the Kewana Peninsula and was shipped at great cost down to the St. Lawrence Seaway. It sank to the bottom of the lake. That's what seemed to be sitting between them, a large mass of some metal alloyed in the heat of history, now gone.

But the universal laws of shared war stories were abrogated

when Wendy got up and turned on the lights and the mood shifted and she and her father could see that Singleton was under too much of a burden to speak. Her father understood. For every man in the VFW who told his story fully—albeit according to the rules, waiting for the baton to be passed in the form of a question—there was another man who sat mute.

Singleton gazed into his shot glass and said, "You know, my shit was a different kind of shit, and well, gee, sir, I wouldn't even know exactly where to begin if I could recall it. I suppose I might start with Tet—and that's just a guess—and take it from there, but all I can tell you is I was in for a tour of duty." And then he choked up and let his throat clear, a few tears blurring his eyes. He was conjuring up images he had from news clips and the photos from *Life* magazine.

"Don't worry, son," the old man said, putting his hands on Singleton's shoulders. "We should eat something, right now, pronto, before the rotgut starts to rot the gut." And that was it. They were all back in the present moment and facing hunger they had put aside to listen to the old man's story. He scurried around the kitchen, removing a string of franks from the refrigerator, cutting them apart, oiling up a pan and getting them sizzling and then bringing out a bowl of potato salad he had made that afternoon, and Wendy set the table. He said a prayer over the food, and they ate for a few minutes without a word, just the clink of silverware. Then he turned and said, "At least we weren't yellow-streaked slackers. At least we weren't that, son. We might've had our troubles but we weren't hiding out in the Red Cross or home at the YMCA, or none of that."

"No, sir, we weren't yellow, not at all," Singleton said.

Pulling out of the driveway, they spotted the Zomboid, moonlight glinting off the spokes of his chair, a cigarette glowing in his mouth. "You'd think he was put there just for us," Single-ton said. "For me and your father. You'd think God would think: Man, I'm not going to put a Nam guy like that next to a Second World War grunt, because it would be too obvious. But God says, Hey, man, it's just statistically there, man. I had nothing to do with it. You get fifty or whatever vets living in the same area, it's gonna happen. Don't blame me, God says. You send them over from Flint and they're gonna come back to Flint."

"So long," the Zomboid was calling. His hand, waving, was clearly visible. Wendy was at the wheel—he was too drunk to drive—and they slipped into the dark streets, past the moldering houses. The little boy was still in the yard, stand-ing in attack mode, pointing his finger into the charge. Every-thing was navigable thanks to the glow in the east. On the radio Iggy was hollering against the fury of noise in a way that somehow seemed to match the stench of charred wood as it mixed with the faint benzene smell from the canal.

"We have a history," Wendy said. She turned the radio down. "The guy in the wheelchair and I have a history."

"What kind of history?"

"We were close when I was in high school. Then his num-ber came up and he went over and came back and we were even closer and then he went back for a second tour."

"How close," Singleton said. His heart was pounding, the nut in his head beginning to throb. To go from an old vet, all that talk, everything that wasn't said and was said, and then to hear this.

"Too close to talk about right now."

If he had learned anything, it was that she made confes-sions when she was high. She'd hint at a fact, put something out there between them and let it fester until she was ready to talk. He'd have to be more patient, he thought. But he couldn't resist and he asked again, how close was close, and as he'd expected, she remained quiet, her fingers curled around the wheel, until she was at her place, parking, and they went upstairs into the apartment and licked a tab and sat, waiting for the high to kick.

Even before she spoke—because she did, finally, when she was tripping—he understood that she had loved the guy in a carnal way. (No other word, he thought. He hated that word but it was the right one.) He imagined a puppy-dog teenage love, fumbling at first but then smoothed out to delicious first touches and then an understanding. He imagined Old Spice cologne on his shoulder blade, her nose down in there as he kissed the smooth skin behind her ear and then the nape of her neck in the backseat of a car. A young man whose draft number came up, went over and served and came back with his legs gone and his arms not working and a smart-ass new language and a new way of thinking. The new language was the biggest change, he imagined. She had had to confront that vacant look in his eyes and his physical infirmities but those were nothing next to the aberration of his language, the defeat that hovered between his phrases, the tight, edgy bark. Taking advantage of a temporarily clear mind—the kick hadn't kicked yet—he tried to imagine it from her point of view, as a young woman, seeing him off, maybe even throwing a small party on the beach with a few friends, drinking beer, somber with the fact that in the morning he would be in boot camp. A beautiful young man with long cornsilk hair, almost girlish, and a smile (it was still there) that was loose and sloppy, who came back damaged. When he got back she was finished with nursing school and working at the hospital during the days, hours and hours of serving up medication—not drugs, she had explained, but medicines—and hanging out with the other nurses, smoking in the break room, listening to them gripe, worrying because they had the patients' lives in their hands (the doctors were blunt, well tanned, always talking about their golf games). One wrong dose, one forgotten IV change, one wrong mark on a clipboard and death might be at hand. But when her boy was discharged from the VA he had stumps where his legs had been, still glossy and wetlooking, and she had tried to nurse him, helping him change the bandages, listening to the pure postwar silence between ranting and raving. Then a line had appeared and that line was a choice, to take care of him and live up to her obligations, the promises she had made to herself and her God (she mentioned that she used to believe, that her mother had been a devout Catholic), in honor of her father (she had mentioned that her father had instilled in her a sense of honor and a sense of humor), or find a way to let him go. It was easy to imagine the whole setup. His high was starting up, but he had a chance to hear himself ask if she wanted to talk about it.

"You want to talk about it?" he said.

Now the ceiling was sparkling with starlight and the moonlight streaming through the window became a rhombus changing shapes and texture, smooth marble one second—he got up and went over to touch—and then quivering and liquid the next. He went back to the bed, navigating through his high, still in control, he thought. When he looked again the moonlight was smoking, steaming. He'd seen that kind of moonlight in Nam. Maybe, maybe not. High or not high.

"I loved him," she said, touching his shoulder, running her finger along his scar. "He was a sweet boy, just a kid, and then he went and came back and I tried, for a little while, to take care of him. I nursed him until I couldn't handle it. I wanted him enfolded but of course you know they couldn't do that. I began to think about men and war, about stupid men and stupid wars, about getting inside somehow and fighting for change . . ."

"Wow, will you look at that," he said. The moonlight was striking the floor, vibrating the floorboards, which looked a yard wide, old barn-floor boards, and he heard a mooing sound and the cackle of chickens feeding and smelled the sweet hay as he got up and got his lighter and held it, monolithic in his fingers, with the eagle and etched words: Tet, Tet, Tet. On the bottom of the lighter was the stamp he had studied (he liked to imagine) countless times during the rage of firefights, to keep his mind steadied (he could hear the *churchunk* of the stamping tool machine at some factory in Pennsylvania) while Wendy, for her part, in her own high, also looked at it as he rolled it in his fingers, and said, Wow, wow, and studied it in her own way. For an hour, maybe more, they passed the Zippo back and forth.

Zomboid's real name was Steve Williams.

She remembered his downy lip and his smooth hairless chest.

His fingers along the waistband of her jeans.

A pulse between her legs.

Williams rocking gently. His boy body against her girl body.

His body back from Nam, washboard stomach, wiry arms.

Getting up to make her father breakfast. Her hair in curlers.

Her father's black lunchbox on the counter, ready to go.

TREE HUNTING

Lumber runners raced to put their claims in. Still do. It was said there were men who could hear a queen pine from a mile away and identify it by the sound of the wind through its needles. I'm one of them, he said.

The man's name was Hank. He spoke of races to the land office through virgin forest. Tracts so brambly that men came out bleeding. The hardships of the lumber business, the corruption and the glory, stripping an entire state from top to bottom in a few years.

I'd just as soon be out here amid them than with just about anybody.

He turned and looked at her with eyes intense and icy blue. At any moment he'd put his big hands on her, she thought. But it was good to be out in the forest. The trees—a second regrowth after the great scalping harvest of the last century, when the small-gauge lines fed the logs down into the mills, and in turn onto the steamers, and in turn to Chicago, where they went to market. The rails were gone but you could still find traces of their tie work, trails in the deep woods, and you still stumbled upon old encampments that were now nothing more than stone foundations and, when you dug with your trench shovel, the charcoal remains of saw-dust fires.

He questioned her. What was it like when you were released into the Grid after being treated, and how the hell did Rake lure you out? What was his technique? Do you think you had something to do with Rake, some connection in the past? Did he grab you and force-feed one of his fucking concoctions into your mouth? She yielded up nothing more than a few grunts. (*Make a story up if you have to give a story, if some-one asks you for one, a nurse in the Grid had said, his voice soothing. If it comes down to it, you just have to dig deep and put two and two together and spin something out. It won't be hard unless you let it be hard. If all else fails, remain silent. If that fails, give the enfolded sign. When you're done with your rehab in the Grid area, you'll feel strong enough to take the questions. Here in the Grid, you'll find a mutual under-standing. They won't ask. The enfolded respect the enfolded, that kind of thing.*)

Deep inside a grove of pines, he got the tent poles in place and unfolded the canvas and pegged it down.

We'll camp here, he said.

She sat down and watched as he gathered kindling and used his hatchet to sliver bark and carefully built a cone for-mation, sprinkled dry needles on it and lit it with a match and then blew lightly and then harder as the fire burst, threading a dark trail of smoke up into the higher reaches of the trees where there was still sunlight, and then he stretched out, with his legs tight together, and patted the ground and told her to come up close, to sit.

Thanks, she said, and she went to him and sat. Whatever trust she had once had was gone, but she could imagine a time when she could trust. A guy would introduce her to a guy on a Harley-Davidson, who would offer her a ride upstate, and she'd get on and go.

She had a fragment memory of a hippie encampment sur-
rounded by a biker gang, the leather on their chaps squeak-
ing. The memory had the quality of being dreamed, a false
creation. That's what they said. You'll make stuff up, draw-
ing from images you've seen recently. The rest was in the
so-called terminal confusion, the faint memories of the reen-
actment, residual aspects that formed a shell around the cen-
tral trauma, the real trauma, that was buried and gone in her
memory. A nurse had explained that. His voice was deep. He
was gentle.

A mother lode tree, Hank was saying. The queen of the
forest. You feel the lure of a giant tree. Catch the sound of
needles singing in Canadian wind. I mean even toothpicks
have tripled in price. Those lovely dispensers you see behind
the cash register at your mom-and-pop. They've been moved
behind the counter.

He lit a cigarette and dug through his pack and came out
with a can of beer.

Do you think I could go with you? she said. Do you think
you could take me up there?

He wiped his lips on the back of his hand and stared into
the flames and waited a moment.

We're in a weird moment in history. I know that's not an
answer to your question, but that's what came to my mind
when you asked.

But you'd take me with you?

I've promised not to touch you. I gave Rake my word. It
might sound strange to say, but it's a matter of honor. Mine,
not his. If he has a sense of honor, and my gut says he still
does, it's linked with the past. I like to think he still has it.

That's not an answer, she said, standing up.

You're getting your lucidity back.

If you heard that queen pine somewhere. If you picked up
the sound of it, or the feeling, would you take me with you?

He stared at the fire some more and then went to his pack and took out a pan, a can of beans, some potatoes, and he began to prepare a meal, taking his time, working carefully, opening up the can and then peeling the potatoes with his knife while the sun set and the wind picked up. He was still talking about trees as he worked. His fingers were long and nimble and the care he took made him look less heavy. From time to time he stopped and rubbed his beard and looked at her and shook his head and then returned to his work, stirring the pot with a spoon, adjusting it on the fire.

Would you take me along? she said.

I suppose if I got a sense that the tree was anywhere near here, and I'm talking a proximity of about a hundred miles, because that's what I think my range is for picking up a scent, then yeah, I'd take you along, but only because I'm governed by larger impulses.

When the potatoes were almost done he took the pan off, holding the handle with a stick, and put it to the side. Then he put a smaller pot on and poured the beans in and began to stir.

When I was a kid my old man took me up here a couple of times a year and we fished and hiked. A couple of weeks in the woods and the rest of the time up on the bridge welding, or out in New York with his Iroquois buddies. He worked high steel until he signed up as a deckhand on a ship. He slipped and almost died on a project in New York, and he used to say, "I almost slipped and went to the ship." That's what he used to say. Maybe that's what he still says. I wouldn't know because the truth is I don't see him much, not really at all, and I'm not even sure where he is out there, except to say he's on the water, I'm sure of that, from spring thaw to winter freeze, and when he's not on a ship he's living somewhere down in Toledo or up in Duluth. He's in Duluth when he's not in Toledo, but I'd guess he favors Duluth because like me—

and I'm guessing here, again—he's a man who likes the glimmer of northern light and the solitude and—guessing even more—a proximity to good forest of the sort you only get up here, or farther north.

He chewed his food and stared across the fire. The tin plate in her hands felt soft and smooth on the edges. The food was simple and good. She could smell the way the pine sap and smoke mixed in the air, and taste the way the butter melted into the potatoes and then, when she sipped, the whiskey on her tongue.

My taste is coming back, she said.

That's a good sign. That's the first step, he said, and then he began to clean his plate with dead leaves. She watched the muscle on his arms and the care he took. She removed her socks, put her feet close to the fire, and enjoyed the feeling of the cold night behind her, against her back.

At one time, he said. At one time the forest could've gone on forever, struggling to find light, the small saplings dying off so that the mighty could prevail—over time. That's what I love about the forest, man, he said.

The bones of his face looked fine in the firelight. He continued talking about lumber barons. He talked about how there were men who went into old houses and took core samples from main beams and dated them and how they could read history from an old stump and see back to the age of Christ, the plagues of bark rot and forest fires, the dry years and the flood years that the tree had survived while humans in their fucking folly marched off to one war and then another and saw their supposedly eternal civilizations fall. He spoke of his time out west, learning a trade, studying the western species, and how one night he had slept in the crook of a beastly old tree, not far from Santa Cruz. He spoke of how it took three men to properly run a cut from one end to the other, taking a beautiful thing, a trunk, and turning it into something even more beautiful—good board feet that could be used to build the west, man—and then he talked about the wastage, the way mills used to dump it until they began to use it to fuel the steam engines themselves, so that the whole thing became cyclical, and the trees were shorn into lumber while they fed the fire with their own sawdust.

The trees might've understood what was happening. I might sound crazy saying that, but I'm saying it. You see, if I want to understand something I eventually have to talk about trees. If I don't talk trees, I don't really hear the words. If you know what I mean, Meg, he said. The thing is, the stuff I enfolded when I treated myself with the Trip must include a lot of what I once knew about Rake, or maybe I should say know, I can't remember all the bad shit he did to me and I did with him as his sidekick, the real trauma, and so I have to make a guess that a lot of it was war trauma and not just the shit we did when we got back, because I know we were in the same unit together, he mentioned that, and I think it's connected somehow with the way I feel about trees, which I can admit have become an obsession, do you get me?

She remained silent for a few minutes—listening to the hiss of wind through pine needles—and then, finally, said, I think so.

If I talk enough I can figure out how to think about something, and if I can think about it, then I can begin finding the right way to talk about it, like the sawdust feeding the mill saws, he said, and then he laughed and took another sip of beer.

A steady breeze was coming in from the lake. He was another male fury of verbiage, and all she could do was listen, to really, really listen, using what seemed to be a newfound ability, because she was starting to hear what this man said, keying into the words, his musical voice, and before she knew it he was onto the subject of Rake.

You know how I think he got his name? He got his name when he took a garden rake and raked this kid's face. I didn't see it because I wasn't with him. This was when he was running with a cluster of vets who had formed a coalition, the one that became the Black Flag gang, and were doing reenactments of battles up at Isle Royal, that island in the middle of Superior. Some kid crossed him the wrong way and he took what was at hand, an old hay rake, and struck him across the face with it. No, not *struck*, that's not the word—is there another word? He cut three deep paths in the guy's face, taking out his eyes, is what I was told, and that's how he got the name Rake.

He dug around for the bottle, found it, held it up to the light, and tipped back a long slug.

She moved around the fire, closer to him, and asked for another drink.

Easy now, he said, passing the bottle.

Why did you enfold yourself? she finally asked. The bottle had gone back and forth a few times and she had taken small sips. It felt good to ask an honest question. She watched as he stared into the fire and thought.

Well, of course I can't remember. An educated guess would be that I took a lot of drugs and Tripizoid. Let me say it was an unorthodox thing to do, but then whatever they do to you is pretty unorthodox, too, I guess from what I've heard. I only know the theories from hearsay. I can only imagine I did it the old-fashioned way. I just reached this point. MomMom, bless her heart, did the tying up. She got a couple of the old man's belts from the dresser and secured me that way, I think. I told her to tie me up with more rope. Then I told her to prop me in the old barn shed we've got at the back of the property and to leave me there for a few days. I knew I'd have to go through the raving bullshit. With all the old hay and nothing much else I wasn't likely to hurt myself. So after a couple of days in that hell I had the guys come in and we painted our faces—or someone else painted mine, I should say—and I guess they took me out into the field and shot at me, live rounds, and made me dog-crawl my ass for hours: tracer rounds and one of them popped an old claymore—all this ammo left over from the Isle Royale reenactment, he said, and then he paused to catch his breath and to see if she was listening, waiting for an indication, and she nodded and said, Then what, and he said, I like to imagine the fuckers shot each other up they were so into it, and I imagine they came back in Vietcong gear they'd captured, or bartered, and they captured me, or pretended to, and gave me a light torture, nothing too bad, because that's what might've happened to me over there, I guess. On the other hand, for all I know, it was just me and MomMom. For all I know, it was MomMom's idea in the first place. Right now, I'm not even sure I was in Nam. Not sure at all. If I once knew, I no longer know. The bliss of the Tripizoid high and all that. The mystery of treatment. I had a passion for nature, for trees and for fishing, for the feel of water against my waders and all of that, long before I had a passion for killing, or for being mean. At least I think I did, he said, and then he stopped talking and began to sob, and she went and put her arm around him as he rocked, and then, later, they found themselves going into the tent to sleep, lying foot to head in their blankets until he said, Meg, Meg, are you awake, and shifted around so she could feel his breath as he spoke, and he said, I wasn't entirely truthful back there, and you were good to listen to me ramble on like that, and when she asked, When weren't you truthful? He said: Not the stuff about enfolding, but before that, when I told you about Rake and how he got his name, because I imagine, of course it's enfolded so I don't really know, that I was there with him and

I was the one who gave him the nickname, and I was the one who laughed at the kid with his bleeding face. That's the kind of guy I was before I had the treatment.

The next morning Hank was up the trail, moving in his swayback motion against the weight of the pack.

She watched as he scraped a trunk with his hatchet and brought her a long sliver of bark with a pale scab of disease, and he held it to her and said, This here is the white pine blister rust. It'll kill that branch and maybe most of the good lumber in the tree if I don't amputate. I'll get the saw out and amputate that limb and maybe, a hundred years from now, somebody will come along and thank me for it. They won't know who they're thanking, but they'll thank me anyway. If there is a future, that is, he said. He went on to explain how easy it was to damage a tree forever. You scrape the bark off a tree with your car. The tree sits there for twenty years slowly dying. Insects bore in, blight, beetles, and then it gives in and dies. The guy with the car died years before that. He went to his grave without knowing what he did, but he did it. That's what bothers me. It doesn't bother him because he don't know about it, but it bothers something. It has to bother something.

On the beach—cold stones, small tendrils of black sand—they sat on a tarp and ate cheese and a loaf of bread. Then they lolled and he pulled off his shirt and she pulled hers up, letting the wind blow across their skin, not too cold but cool, counteracted by the sunlight, which came through the thin, late spring clouds. The blackflies that would pester in June stayed hidden in the crux of rocks, and the waves, barely a foot high, came in and carved themselves into the shoreline and receded in long stretches of foam. Along the horizon, almost out of sight, as if a decorative afterthought, another supertanker gave the lake a deeper, more horrific beauty, because during the last few years, ships were sinking (he explained) at an alarming rate: the *Fitzgerald*, the *Hoover*, the *Drake*, the *Sam Johnson*.

Last winter the *Drake* sank, ten hours out of Duluth on a run to Mexico, loaded with copper ore, the bow low, icing up. The hatches weren't bolted correctly is one theory.

Deadly cold but fucking beautiful, Hank said. He got up and stretched his arms and then sat back down. You had a dream last night, didn't you?

What makes you say that?

You seem like a girl who had a dream.

You want to hear it, she said.

No, dreams are boring. As soon as they hit the air, they become meaningless. I'd rather hear a lie. I'd rather hear a falsehood than a dream. I'd rather listen to MomMom rant about God.

Then why'd you ask? she said.

Because I wanted to know.

So I'm telling you. Yeah, I had a dream. I was with a boy, and we were at a beach—South Haven, I think it was—one summer afternoon in the dunes, hidden from the crowd, surrounded by grass, a safe place, and the boy's draft number was up, I remember that, and he said that he was going to war, and the rest, well, the rest you really don't want to hear because the rest felt like a dream, not a vision, she said. *Much more lucid; the taste of his lips on hers, the razor grass making a dry, husky hiss as the wind blew outside the cove; the sensation of being touched gently—with love—and also the desperate falling away, the sensation of seeing him lean against his car, legs out slightly, cocky, posing for her with his arms back and his chest thrust forward; the last day together before he shipped out, somehow knowing that exactly.*

Chances keep growing that my old man'll land on a sinking

ship eventually. That's the truth, he said, abstractedly. That's what I have to dream about. He works coal burners, and then he works a new oil burner, and then he goes back to a coal like that one way out there, he said, pointing at the ship trailing a thin curl of black smoke along the horizon.

She watched as he pried his shoes off, cuffed his jeans, straightened his jacket, an old army fatigue, and walked down to the shore to dip his toes in, making a loud, joyful hoot. He waded in and hopped around with his arms up. Then he began kicking long, beaded arches of water curling off his toes in her direction.

It was, she thought, one of the most joyous sights she'd ever seen. At least that she could remember seeing, and for a split second, with her head back, exposed to the sunlight, while he continued to kick the water (she could hear the splash), she felt for the first time in what seemed to be an eternity an ability to fully enjoy a particular moment, with only a little breath of fear on the back of her neck.

OLD SCHOOLERS

In mid-July, the Soviets adjusted their nuclear coordinates and Kennedy continued his wave-by tours, visiting South Bend again, and then Lincoln's birthplace in Springfield, where he gave another long speech justifying the war effort. He had given up providing logical reasoning. The fight was about the fight. National honor was at stake. Photos of him on the front pages in early July showed his hand in the air, his face aged, with Jackie in the car beside him looking frightened but beautiful. War reports: The siege of Hue dragged on as the Marines struggled once again to take what was left of the Citadel. Jason Williamson—a.k.a. the stoned reporter—filed nightly radio reports in a drug-dreary voice that was oddly comforting. His modus operandi, which had won him a Pulitzer, was to be on the ground as stoned as possible and to catch a new perspective, to offer up reports steeped in the language of visions. He was on the so-called wire, or outside the wire, or near the wire, filing from a microphone attached to the lapel of his flak jacket, pausing to let the pop of gunfire punctuate his whispery narrative, which seemed at an odd remove from reality, peppered with phraseology that could only come from tripping, describing the way the tracer fire wrapped long ribbony bands over the Vietcong, a sweep of galloping ghosts.

Singleton listened with his feet up on the sill, looking at the view of the ash piles in the distance. Wendy was sleeping soundly on the bed. Dog days of Flint. Two weeks in a holding pattern of nonsense from Klein, who was using the word *modality* a lot, talking about a holding modality—and the fact that the Rake killings had stopped, or had stopped being reported. We have to sustain an understanding of the modality, Klein said, going over to the map again and again, touching the pins, returning to his desk to light another pipe.

"You're going to confess that you're fraternizing and I'm going to listen to you confess and then I'm going to tell you that in this case, because I think it fits the modality it's not reportable, because in this case, and I'm trusting my own instincts, such as they are, my own gut, I sense that you might—and I have to go to the lingo again—be caught in some type of retrospective harmonious conversion. So you're going to admit it to me now, son, and I'm going to listen and let you off the hook."

"I'm sorry, sir, I won't admit it," Singleton said. In the past few weeks Klein had become somewhat disheveled, the knot in his tie was often improperly dimpled, and there was a small stain on his lapel. Today he was wearing his G-man outfit for the second day in a row; he'd been rotating between his old Korea dress uniform and his suit. (I'm both an ex-soldier and an agent, he explained, and I don't see a problem with splitting the difference between the two, do you?)

"You will admit it, son. I've had some reports coming down that put you and another agent together at the beach. A man down in Relations made a report that put you at the canal with another agent. Now, normally, I'd see this as a deep betrayal of the organization because we have our rules, and our rules are there for a reason. For example, if two agents meet secretly there might be some residual sense of needing to unfold each other. Or the two agents start to copulate and in doing so begin to feel at ease, and in that ease, in bed I assume, they might share case information and in sharing it compromise the program dynamic. I don't need to state the obvious fact that if you reach some kind of unlimited ecstatic state, as in a massive orgasm, you risk unfolding."

"No, sir."

Klein got up from his chair and walked around his desk and put his hands on Singleton's shoulders. "Now go ahead and admit it."

"I'm sorry, sir. I can't do that."

He and Wendy had then met in the lobby. Standing on the Kennedy Psych Corps seal, under the scrutiny of the guard who had a shit-eating grin and seemed to know what was coming, they'd embraced and struck the poise of the sailor and lover on V-J day in Times Square, holding the kiss, fulfilling the vision he'd had weeks ago. And when Wendy asked, What are we doing? he told her they were letting the Corps know that they didn't give a shit.

Out in the street that afternoon Singleton stopped for cigarettes and glanced at the newspapers. Ships were sinking out in the Great Lakes; headlines read SAGANAW SINKS, DEATH SHIP, and KEWANAA TRIANGLE. On the front page of the *Detroit Free Press* a Chinook hovered in a freak midsummer storm, dangling a net into raging waters. The teardrop shape of the net in relation to the spray and the chopper—fucking Chinook—gave him pause. The exuberance of a few minutes ago, the sense of rebellion, dancing in the lobby and then strutting down the street, leading her away from the building, had disappeared. He went back to the newsstand and took another look at the photograph. There were rumors that intense feelings like the jubilation he'd felt in the lobby could make you susceptible to the reintroduction of memory fragments. Odd bits of hearsay, usually about how treatment might fail, gathered around the hard facts: cold water immersion and orgasmic sex were the only proven methods of unfolding, and even those were often haphazard and might, or might not, actually reintroduce the trauma.

He told her he needed to get to the beach again, to get near water, to get away, and then he watched as she walked ahead. She had a slight pronation to one side that threw her off balance, and it made his groin tingle. If there is a God, he thought, I'll speak directly to him when the time comes, and if there isn't a God I'll have to invent one, and I'll find a way to thank him for the way I feel when I watch her move.

Then he caught up with her and took her hand, and when she asked what he was thinking he told her he was thinking he'd have to invent God so he could explain to him how he was feeling right now, and then she said, No, you weren't.

Lakeport was an old beach town of boarded storefronts and a single beach-ball-and-towel emporium with sorry-looking, half-inflated figures hanging from poles and lifesaving rings deflated and faded to pastel colors. They took the cooler and the towels and went to the shore to examine the water quality. A snake of sludge stretched the entire length of the beach. A few kids tiptoed into the water while their parents looked away. Near the water, a boy, working with secretive intensity, dug into the sludge with a blue plastic shovel, molding the sand into animal shapes, whistling to himself.

Singleton sat on the towel and took out a weathered copy of *A Farewell to Arms*, opened it, and began to read the neat, clear sentences. The war was around the two main characters and they spoke in a pidgin English, using pet names, in a dialogue that was snappy and efficient and false-sounding in a way that was true-sounding at the same time because it was spoken rapid-fire, without intrusions, and it was spoken in isolation, he thought. Hemingway's war had produced a certain kind of character, a new way of thinking and speaking that came from what was left out, from the things war had demolished and pushed away forever.

Wendy was putting lotion on her palms and rubbing it into his shoulders and on his legs and face, touching the scar, running her finger along it again, retracing, asking him—at least he imagined she was asking—with her touch instead of her voice, but she knew he didn't have the answers and would only resort to conjecture. In Vietnam, was all he could say, all he did say when she asked, and then there was a silence full of the wash of waves and the hiss of sand.

On the drive back to Flint, listening to a broadcast of the Stooges from the Grande Ballroom in Detroit, the sound of the crowd roaring as Iggy sang "I Wanna Be Your Dog," they discussed the old man they had seen on the beach, walking along the water, dressed in a black suit and an elegant hat, shuffling along out of place and oddly removed from the scene, one of many such men, nicknamed Old Schoolers, who were rumored to be spies for the Corps. That's how a rumor gets started, Singleton explained. It's absurd to think that an old man who happens to be walking along the beach in a suit would be a spy of any kind, and yet the desire to fit him into a specific story is stronger than reason, and if you're going to fit him into something that is absurd, or at least partly absurd, it might as well be a vision President Kennedy happened to have during his recovery from the assassination attempt, with his poor sister as a focal point of his deep meditation. If you're going to find a story for that man, who maybe just happens to like to walk on the beach dressed to the nines, cold the way old people are always cold, then you're going to have to find a tool to force fit him into a conspiracy, or at least some complex social system, and that tool is going to be the idea that he's a spy. And then Wendy took the other side, saying it was highly possible that he really was a spy and just so happened to disguise himself as a rumor, making use of the dynamic you just described (she said), taking advantage of the weird mix of belief and disbelief in the program. Then they both fell into a quiet perplexity while the old mills passed again, on the other side of the car, with a different light—late-day, subdued, smothering the thickets of the pipework in shadow, because they were both thinking, they'd later admit, that the argument was somehow applicable to the concept of God, in that he would be walking in plain sight disguised as a rumor.

Back at her apartment Wendy came out of the shower rubbing her hair with a towel, smelling fresh and clean, her eyes free of makeup, watching him as he tapped his head and told her he'd been thinking that his CEP had to stretch back a long way, far back, because he couldn't remember much about being a kid, not much at all. She scrutinized him, up and down with what he was beginning to think of as her nursing gaze, looking for indications of his condition, and then asked, in a sarcastic voice, if they hadn't informed him that he'd lose everything up to a certain point—blah, blah, blah.

"In cases of close friends with shared history, the war trauma will be enfolded along with other residual memories that are attendant to the loss, so that a man who has lost a good buddy from a small town, for example, will also enfold the small details of his life—playing ball, fishing, hijinks, drag races down forlorn streets, going out on dates together, anything linked to the loss," Singleton said. "Some say, technically, that all of the memories related to the trauma repress themselves in a kind of sequential reaction, each one falling in relation to the next, so that in the case of grand trauma, the loss not only of a battlefield buddy but also a beloved friend from prewar, the subject—me, for fuck's sake—will lose, in theory, a great deal of memory from the past." He reached and took her cigarette.

"That sounds about right. Bullshit, but right."

"The twin-brother incident."

"Yes, exactly. What were they called? Pseudonym, I'm sure. The Lawson brothers."

"Yeah, Kit Lawson lost his twin brother, Drew, in a firefight and so on and so forth . . ."

". . . and after undergoing treatment in the New Mexico facility . . ."

". . . Lawson lost his entire childhood to the enfold . . ."

"All of it enfolded," Wendy said. She knotted the towel around her head and stood naked and dry. He remembered the bikini, the oil, the little kid playing in the sand in his field of vision, and he felt his hard-on coming on with force, the blood pulsing in his underwear. They would fuck again and he'd hold that image—the way he'd held the image of her surrounded by Queen Anne's lace—because otherwise his desire would disappear into the fuzz of his enfolded memories.

That evening, as they cooked together, he stood at the sink and shook the lettuce dry in a clean dish towel, feeling the teardrop shape of dripping vegetable weight in his fist. He put the lettuce down on the counter. (Skulls in bags, men being hoisted up in nets, bodies in bags, he thought.) In the living room he turned on the television, fiddled the antenna to bring the signal. Then he went to the bedroom, found her stash, and lit a joint and took a deep hit. Wendy was whistling to herself as she cooked in the kitchen, and on the television a man hunched in the bush with a foam-ball microphone, whispering his report to the wire. His hair was slicked back and combed with a neat part and he gave the location of the fighting as if it were his hometown, his voice lulling, as safe as any man on Madison Avenue, one more con man packaging the goods to sell to the public, unaware, as he spoke, that his image was slipping as the vertical hold wavered, and he was passing up over himself with a small ribbon of fuzzy gray between him and his repli-cated self, until Singleton went over and pushed the button and watched the screen sweep itself into a small pinpoint of light that seemed to eye the world with incredulous judgment before it—the light—dashed up to the edge of the set and disappeared.

All he had was the sound of her whistling in the kitchen.

"Yes, sir," Singleton said to the dark screen.

OUT OF THE WOODS

Those are Rake's, Hank was saying. There's no other reason she'd be washing those sheets. Not for me at least.

They had come in along the beach trail and stopped to watch MomMom hanging fresh sheets from the line.

We're going to step right in there as if nothing in the world happened, aren't we? Just like we rehearsed. We're going to walk right back into Rake's scene and he's not going to detect a thing in the way we move or talk. Not a clue. I've handled him before and I think I can handle him now. He doesn't know the side of me you saw out there in the woods—doesn't know I've enfolded all that shit. I'd kill him and end all this but then, like I explained, that would go against everything that I've enfolded. I just don't have the will to do it. I have the desire, because it would solve everything, but if I went and killed him, everything might come back. I'm not sure I'd know how to do it. You think it's easy killing someone, but it's not, not at all, he said.

On the way back to the house they had stopped in a small inland clearing to rehearse, standing together in the dappled sunlight.

I want this deep inside you, planted there. We'll go through the motions until it becomes secondhand. You're gonna have to go blurry-eyed, to persuade yourself that I've beaten you back into submission.

Imagine we're in the kitchen now. That's where he'll be when we get back, if I know Rake, because the first thing he does when he comes back from an excursion is to start eating, so we're gonna pretend we're in the kitchen. I'll play the role of Rake and you play the role of Old Meg. Not New Meg. I want you to go inside yourself and find the voice of Old Meg. New Meg has a natural voice. New Meg speaks easy and honest. Old Meg speaks in a song, like she's trying to get her daddy to buy her a lollipop.

Say: Hey, Hank, how's it going?

Hey, Hank, how's it going?

No, that's too sure, too flat. If he hears that he'll hear New Meg and he'll sense you're feeling better. Too easy, too precise, and too sure. Singsong it now like a baby girl wanting a lollipop, he said, and he took two steps back and watched her.

Hey, Hank, how's it going.

Perfect, he said, and he took two more steps back and said, Now I'm Rake, I'm going to say, Where the fuck have you been? in my best Rake voice, and you're gonna say, Hank took me with him to look for a tree, and remember, we're in the kitchen and Rake is fixing you with his eyes; he has you in his eyes, even if he's not looking; he's totally got you under his gaze, even if he's directing his look out the window. Now say what I told you to say after I say what I said I was going to say, he said, and he said, Where the fuck have you been? and she said, Hey, Rake, Hank took me with him looking for a tree. Her voice rose slightly but not enough and had too much in the way of assurance and Hank told her so and told her to try it again and she did, saying, Hank took me with him into the woods to look for the Mother Tree, tightening her words up into that part of her that was lost and sad and wanted to survive.

That was better, he said, but not good enough. He'll hear it in there. He'll sense the firmness in the way you're landing on your words. Try it again, but this time pretend you're trying hard to pick up each word; pretend each word weighs a ton, but as soon as you pick one up and start lifting, it deceives you and is lighter than you thought and you're startled. Do it that way—think of it that way, he said, and she did and her voice lilted, became airy and thin, and Hank said, That was great, perfect, and she said, I'm scared, and then she began to cry. You're a great actress. You're brilliant, he told her. You're gonna win an Academy Award when you're through with this. Being afraid of Rake is good. The fear's going to lend your voice the right tenor, so long as you remind yourself to lift each one and then allow yourself to be surprised as the word comes up.

Stay behind me when we cross the yard. Hang your shoulders like I told you and before we go in try not to blink so your eyes are nice and glassy.

Hey, ho, anybody home? he said, striding across the yard. The house baked in the sunlight, and in the corner of the yard the dog lay in the shadows, draped in chains. The car trunk was open, full of pills wrapped like mummies and a few new pieces for his arsenal.

In the kitchen, at the stove, Rake stood holding a long spatula, lifting the edge of a pork chop. A kid sat at the table. He was albino white and skeletal thin. A real mountain freak, Hank thought. One of those junkies of the old school, with a certain delicacy to his posture. He made a motion to stand in greeting, but then, glancing over at Rake, he thought better of it.

Where you been? Rake said, tending the meat.

Lumber running.

Took her along?

Thought it would be the safe thing to do, Hank said. He

stood easily on the balls of his feet, with his hands in his pockets. Then he took two steps into the room.

Why'd you take her along?

Like I said, thought it would be the safe thing to do. She's a handful, in a weird way, and I didn't trust MomMom to keep an eye, and I caught scent of a big one out there and had to go for it.

I'm pretty sure I told you to stay put. I'm pretty sure I told you not to take her out. No, I'm certain I ordered you to keep her in the house, out of sight. I said it just like that. I said, Keep her here out of sight and don't go chasing after any trees, my friend.

Hank chuckled, found a respectful hesitancy, and watched Rake lift the chop with the spatula with an easing of the sizzle sound, letting oil gather heat, and then flip it in a roar of hot fat.

Name's Haze Hall, the guy at the table said, putting out his hand.

Shut up, Haze, Rake said. You talk when I tell you to talk and keep your yap shut the rest of the time if you know what's good for you. He lifted the meat again and again the sizzle died down. Visible in the window over the sink, MomMom was in the backyard with clothespins in her mouth, lifting her sagging arms up and down.

I said no taking her anywhere, Hank. I said it in the clearest fucking terms.

I understood you to be saying, stay put in this part of the state.

Out the window, the wind twisted the white sheets against the blue sky while MomMom stood examining her handiwork. Rake adjusted a burner and let the meat sit, singeing around the edges, giving off smoke.

Meg, is he telling the truth?

He's telling the truth, she sang.

I didn't ask you if he was telling the truth, he said. I asked you, is that the way it happened? He lifted the meat out of the oil and threw it sidearm.

Haze screamed and held his face.

Move, you die, simple as that, Hank said, aiming his gun. Die if you move. Make me do it. Make me blow your head off. He held the gun steady, waited a few beats, and then said, Now put the pan down and greet me in a friendly manner, for Christ's sake. Then he aimed the gun just to the right of Rake's head, waited another few beats, and unleashed a shot that shattered the window over the kitchen sink. The concussion seemed delayed, muted by the thick linoleum. The room seemed to flinch. Haze cowered and Meg, who was used to gunshots, gave a voluntary shout, for effect, and said, Don't kill him, for God's sake, don't do it. Her voice was full-bodied. She was inhabiting her character.

With the pan steady, Rake didn't even flinch. One more gunshot in a year of gunshots. Near misses came and went. He kept his legs apart and didn't even blink. Long ago his shell shock had mutated into something else: he was well versed in the workings of this kind of fear. The room took on a knowing glow. The fridge kicked on with an energetic hum. Outside, far in the distance, a dog gave an expectant bark. (You had to have that bark, Hank thought. Always that bark.) At the same time, a trickle of blood appeared along Rake's temple.

The next shot's going to be between your eyes if you don't put that pan down and shut the burner off.

You'll laugh it off when we're equally armed, Rake said. You let me have a gun so we're on equal terms and then I'll know I can trust you, he said.

You think I'd trust you with a gun right now?

I think you let me have a gun, you trust me, I trust you, and we're on equal terms, Rake said.

You want a gun? Hank said.

That's right. Let me reach behind and get mine, and I'll hold it on you and you hold yours on me and we'll be back where we were before all this started.

Man, Hank said. If I didn't know you so long I'd think you were crazy. But knowing you as I do, I'll let you get your gun, he said.

Rake reached around and pulled out his gun and pointed it and said, There. Now we're both men. Now we're each facing the same shit.

Both men held and held and went into locked eyes as MomMom appeared in the doorway and sighed loudly. It was the sigh of a mother whose kids were in trouble again. It was an old, weary sigh.

Let's lower them at the same time, Rake said.

Fine by me, Hank said.

Together the men lowered the guns and then, stepping forward, laughed and gave each other a hug. Man, shit, man, they said, going into a backslap routine, two old buddies reuniting, until Rake cranked his knee up into Hank's crotch and he doubled over in pain.

That's for old times' sake. You'd damn well better be telling me the truth, Rake said. On the floor Hank lay for a few minutes, keeping his eyes closed, while MomMom prayed over his body, saying: Dear Lord our Host, come down here now and take charge of my son's body and resurrect him, dear Lord. Bring his strength back fully if it be your will. Show him your mercy, oh Lord.

Hank stayed still and enjoyed the sound because it was, as far as he could remember, the most attentive and loving his mother had been in years. Fate or luck had arranged gunplay as a testing point, a way to make sure he wouldn't kill again, not ever again, even if it seemed to be the most logical thing to do. A few inches to the left and it would've been done.

Rake led Meg out of the house to the car and stood with her examining the booty in the trunk, reaching down to pick up a packet or two, holding them out and saying, You're going to be the test subject on a couple of these. Primo Canadian shit. I had to go over the border for these. I thought I was going on a distribution run but ended up on a collection run. I saw and I collected. There are bodies up in Canada, believe me. A few more than there were before I got there.

He turned her around—she allowed him to move her and fell into the role of submission easily—and said, You're not fooling me, are you? You're not going to get the tree-hunting bug and run off with Hank?

No, she said, letting her eyes stray around to the dog, who was barking now at the edge of the yard, pulling his chain. His barks were hard and wooden and came in staccato formations that seemed coded. It was the bark of a dog violent in nature, hungry, covered with burrs and scabs. The bark of a dog on a chain in the woods far from help. He was rearing into an attack stance and barked a few more times until Rake swung around and with one fluid motion took quick aim and fired a single shot.

You're gonna lose the sight in that eye, Rake said. They were playing blackjack at the kitchen table. Night. Cool air through the broken window over the sink, the sound of crickets, an occasional far-off animal sound.

I don't think so, Haze said.

I'm pretty sure of it. You're gonna have monocular vision.

Lighten up, Rake, Hank said.

Sooner he admits it, the better, Rake said, fanning his cards neatly and examining his hand.

My eye's gonna be fine, Haze said.

I'm gonna take a piss right now, Rake said, And when I get back we'll settle this argument.

Hank turned to the kid and said, You'd better admit that you'll never see again from that eye.

Why should I do that?

Because if you continue the argument I know what's going to happen. If you insist that you're right and Rake insists that he's right, he's going to make sure he's right by taking the nearest sharp implement and jabbing it through your head. Maybe he won't do it now, but when you least expect it, he'll make sure you don't see from that eye.

And how do you know that? Haze said.

You're a guy still living in a world devoid of Rake, Hank said. You're a pimple-faced kid who hasn't learned the lesson of Rake. If you don't learn the lessons of Rake, you end up dead. Sometimes folks learn the rules by dying. Lesson number one: Never blink if you can help it. Lesson number two: Rake is always right. Never correct Rake or argue. Keep disagreement safely tucked away and don't brood or even ponder the counterargument. Keep your face clean of emotion. Lesson number three: Join in with him in mayhem. Lesson number four: See the world from his eyes. Lesson number five: Submit to the idea that his history is your own when you're around him. Lesson number six: No lesson can prepare you for one of Rake's sudden, impulsive mood shifts. You can learn the other five lessons but it won't do you any good, no matter how ready you think you are, when, out of the blue, for no viable reason, some past incident causes him to move in a direction that is not only unexpected but absurdly disconnected from his present reality, Hank said.

Because I've seen him stick guys in the eye a few times, he added. It gives him great satisfaction. He'll give you a lobotomy before you know what hit you.

He wouldn't do that to me.

You really believe that? Hank said, sipping his drink, trying to remain in the zone.

I don't believe he would.

Then you're a fool, Hank said. And anyway, if he doesn't put a shiv through your eyeball, I'll have to do it for him.

Do what for me? Rake said, coming back in, hitching up his pants.

Kick this little runt's ass, Hank said.

How's that eye, Haze? What do you have to say about that eye?

Whatever was meant to be seen out of that eye, Haze said, touching the gauze pad, has already been seen.

You said the right thing, son, Rake said. He looked at his cards and then put his hand down and said, Fold. Meg looked her cards over and folded, and Hank presented his hand. Nobody could ever raise Rake. If you had a great hand, you folded it and put it away. Rake had to win.

You want to hear some news from out there, Rake said. A gang of bikers took over a lock at the Soo, jammed it up. A Black Flag–sponsored firefight in the streets of Marquette went haywire. A splinter group joined the fray. All hell broke loose. Some hillbilly types joined in to spice up the mix. The standoff lasted a day—a siege, someone called it. The Marines were called. A Marine is never under siege. The Marines were driven all the way back to Copper City before reinforcements came in. Now it's what's being called a stalemate, a draw. No mention of siege anymore.

Rake talked deep into the night, driven by speed, with an intensity that excluded the others, with the exception of Hank, who added to the talk by describing what he knew of the last big Black Flag battle. (Speedboats playing the role of Swift Boats.) There was a new maniacal element in Rake's voice

(Hank thought) and the way he pounded the table and, on occasion to underscore a point, swatted Haze on the side of the head. Haze claimed he had been a member of Black Flag. Couldn't get the war out of my system, he said. Couldn't get all the way home. Came up here with the rest. Fuckers tried to enfold me but I escaped and hitched up here.

At the table he absorbed the blows until the pain meds eased and he let out a howl that made Rake laugh long enough to forget his point in the first place, slapping his knees and saying, Man, shit, man, that's funny, funny as all hell.

Then it began again, Rake coming in at night, feeding her Canadian pills, forcing them into her throat until she swallowed them, saying, That's a good girl, that's just fine, drink them down, and handing her a glass of water—the glass cool and damp—Drink them down, drink them down, and he said something was amiss in her eyes, something off (his mouth close to her ear, his fingers gripping her thigh), and she told him she was tired and wanted to sleep. I'm tired, she said, I'm tired, and he handed her a glass of water and another pill, another night; one night that was different from another, with the smell of the trees and the breeze and the sound of waves or the deep silence of no waves. He didn't touch her, aside from gripping her thigh, or her arm, and she felt fear in the fact that he was withholding something. Stay up all night, he said, exhaustion brings a clarity to a new day, and then he reached over and held the back of her neck with one hand and brought her to him and forced her mouth against his own. Night sounds and smells, not only the lake itself—she could feel it, sense it, the great, massive body—but jasmine sweetness, the smell of honeysuckle.

•

For days Haze lurked around the edges of action. He stood out in the old barn smoking while Hank sat in a lawn chair and studied his tree guides, his maps, his histories of Michigan forestry. Early dog days. An early summer heat wave. Now and then, finding themselves alone, Hank and Meg whispered to each other words of encouragement.

He'll be going away again soon, Hank said. He'll be back on the road. He can't sit still for long. I'll persuade him to leave you here. He'll want to take Haze as a sidekick. Haze is the new Meg, you see, he said, and then he lifted his hand up as if to touch her and moved it away, looking out over the yard at MomMom, who, in a lawn chair, was making the sign of the cross and whispering prayers.

When Hank asked she said no, no, he hadn't done that, no, not that she could remember, and it was true. He fed her the pills and went off with Haze and left her alone, and then Hank looked at her, his eyes soft but careful, and when he asked her again—in a whisper—she gave him the same answer and he looked at the sky and let out a deep sigh. What is he doing to you at night, he asked, and she said she couldn't remember.

The fact that so far he hasn't done it again to you must mean something. (He wanted to say it, to say the word *fuck* to her, but he couldn't.) I'm not sure what, exactly, but if he's keeping his hands off you there must be a reason, Hank said the next day, out alongside the old shed. The eaves were full of nests. Wasps dipped down and flew off while others came swooping back in. The furious industry of it. Bees don't do that, Hank explained. Bees have style and grace and only sting—I don't need to tell you this—if they have to sting, but wasps have a destiny that comes from their form; they're segmented with that narrow little band and they feel, well, they feel a sensation that at any moment they might break apart; they're locked into the brutal logic that has been passed on to them and don't even know it, but bees are a little like trees. They have a greater sense of their fate in relation to the work they put into time itself. He paused and then took a deep breath of the smell, the dusty bake of the shingles and a moist scent of fern drifting in from the woods. He stood over Meg as she dug a hole for the dog, which was nothing but rib bones and maggots and a sag where the ground met the decaying body and the body the ground, the two sides of the coin, after weeks in the warm spring sun, woven into each other. Let the dog sit until I tell you to do something with it, Rake had said days ago. You don't go burying that dog until it has to be buried, or else you might forget what I did to it.

Hank slapped her back once with his palm, swinging his arm back and making a show of force, because he knew that Rake was inside, watching.

We'll figure something out to get him to do himself in somehow, Hank said. Then he ordered her to dig harder.

It has to be his idea. Stay in the role of Old Meg. Stay as deep as you can.

What makes you think I'm acting? Meg said. What makes you think there even was a New Meg?

Just keep digging. He can't hear you but he can see you.

Quiet static days of summer. One day slipping into the next as Rake seemed to be recharging his anger batteries for another killing spree. I'm trying to catch a new technique, he explained. I'm tired of just popping people. I'm getting sick of the whole thing, he said one night. Another night he said he didn't give a shit. He wasn't tired of it, not at all.

Whatever there was to know about Haze stayed hidden. He leaned against the kitchen wall and prodded the floor with his toes. He lurked around, just a shadow figure, waiting to be tested. Hank kept him in his line of sight and tried to probe, to figure it out. One afternoon he cornered him near the shed, loomed over him.

Say something, Hank said. Tell me about your war.

Something, Haze said. Tell me about your war.

No, fucker, say something meaningful, make your presence known.

Something meaningful, Haze said. There, I said it.

You were in Nam. Did you fight with Rake?

You'd know if I did, right. No, man. I fought all around, man. I got gooks anywhere I could. All shapes and sizes. I saw the guy they like to call the Phantom Blooper. I tried to kill him but he slipped away. And I understood the villages, man, and all that ancestor shit. See, I understood it. They were building those tunnels a long time before we got there, man. They were ready for us. They saw us coming long before we knew we were going.

So you think you know who the Phantom Blooper is?

Everyone knows the Blooper, Haze said.

Not everyone.

Everyone who saw action knows. He went over to join the other side, the Cong, the winning fucking side, the side that's looking back into history, to the ancestors, man, to the worship of those who came before you.

So you're saying you saw him? Hank looked away over the yard. Rake had Meg tied up in a chair and was sitting across from her talking, smoking a cigarette, sipping a beer. The wind was high and the sound of waves came through the trees.

I'm saying I was him, Haze said, and he bent forward

slightly with his chin up as if to offer his face to a fist, his eyes wide open, a dapple of sweat on his brow. It was a face waiting to be struck. It was a testing position—his arms dropped to his side, his tiny hands open, not clenched. High winds were coming in from the west and the sound of the surf came and went, came and went, milky white against his eardrums. You must not fight, Hank told himself. His internal voice was sullen and sad-sounding, coming through the continual buzz of his own treatment. What had just happened with Haze was a skirting around the issue at hand, the sense that if he had been asked the question about where he fought he wouldn't have been able to answer. Had Haze sensed this? All the cocky, bullshit wordplay, the twisting around of his questions.

MomMom began throwing visionary fits with wholehearted vigor. One afternoon, she went to the yard, tossed herself into the weeds, convulsed, and spoke in tongues. Go do something, Rake said. Stop your old lady, man. I'm having a bad enough trip without having to watch her freak out and talk God this and God that. I'll do what I can, Hank said. He went and said, Mom, Mom, MomMom, you've got to stop. He listened and located a vague syntax in her nonsense phrases, a logic in the way she went on about the torment of vanquished peoples, a fiery end, as she heaved her calico chest into the air. Eventually, he dragged her deep into the brush near the barn where the sound would be buffered by the rotting wood structure.

How'd you get her to stop, Rake said. He was at the kitchen table cutting up some product, chopping with quick, efficient strokes.

I talked to her in her own tongue as much as I could, Hank said. I just said back to her what she was saying to me and that calmed her down.

Rake prepared his product like a prep cook, moving from task to task.

I hope you don't do that with me? He looked up with glazed eyes. In his right hand, shaking slightly, he held a box cutter.

Do what? Hank said.

Say back to me what I'm saying to you to calm me down.

THE BLUE PILLS

In the last few days of June they had started to arrive, more and more of them, coming down from the U.P. and up from the south, attracted by a rumor that was passing from vet to vet, from the VFW Hall in Hell, Michigan, to the streets of Detroit—a rumor that the original treatment had been twisted into something better than an acid trip, and that it included not only free grub and a place to hang out but also a chance to pay back command, to frag the guy who messed up your life forever. In a meeting, Singleton was briefed that the rumor's originator was a man named Stan Newhope, who suffered from acute delusions and shell shock in addition to a run-of-the-mill schizophrenia that gave him visions of lumbering ships in the sky—not aircraft, but pirate ships. Newhope was throwing out a good rap, blowing it way out of proportion, saying: "Man, what I hear is they give you AK-47s, not some shitcan M16, but a Ruskie weapon that actually works, and you're free to kill the officers who screwed you in the first place." The weird specificity of the AK-47—the agent giving the brief had explained—was the vital element that had fueled the rumor. The key concept of the rumor was that you could do anything you wanted so long as you came out of a reenactment firefight a winner, on top, alive. By the time the rumor reached the hills of Kentucky, the briefer said, it had been put to music and was being sung like a ballad from the porches of backwoods shacks; by the time it got to Virginia, where only a few vets lived, after the great migration north, it had solidified into what seemed to be a solid slice of the truth. Now, thanks to the rumor, Flint had become a beacon of hope for those who hadn't already come north, luring in the non-enfolded (the briefer said). Most didn't qualify for the program. Some were too old, like Korean War vets, or too physically damaged. The Tripizoid simply wouldn't work on subjects too far—in years, or in memory—away from the actual combat trauma. They were, as some of the vets liked to put it, those who had been back home so long they would never get home.

Singleton held the plastic baggie of bright blue pills and thought about the stunning sensations they might induce when ingested; no holding back, a bright sense of portent had led them to the window where they stood watching the ash heaps smoldering with a new intensity. A sliver of moon hung far out in the haze. The pills had come to Singleton via an intricate series of events—at least it seemed that way, passed from palm to palm secretly through old connections he hadn't known existed, ending with the man who had approached him on the street with big, Howdy Doody ears, produced a snappy salute, and said, "Hey, Captain Singleton? Fucking A. That you? I'd know you anywhere. It's me, man. It's me, re-member? Used to call me Chaplain because, well, basically I was the chaplain and all that. I had a feeling I'd bump into you soon."

The stranger was dressed in full regalia, old army-issue jacket, helmet liner with ballpointed peace symbols. Vets lurked around. "I'm over here to get into the program, sir," the man on the street said to Singleton. "I'm gonna go sign up for the treatment and kill me some of those fresh-faced West Point fucks. Not men like you, sir. You didn't act like a ring wearer. No West Point bullshit from you. It's Wilson I want to kill for making us walk the middle of the roads when we told him we'd be sitting ducks. How are you doing, Sing?"

"OK," Singleton said.

"Man, Captain Sing, I've been wondering what happened to you. I had a feeling if I bumped into you anywhere it would be here, man, because I've seen half the men in these streets."

Singleton took a step back and put his arm out as if to say, "Here I am." "What do you do now?" he said.

"I'm not doing God's work, if that's what you're thinking. Left that behind me, too. Got all that preaching out of my system in Hue. But I didn't forget, sir. I didn't forget the promise I made. I promised to get you some good shit when we got home, and I got it for you."

"Then the guy took this from his pocket and went through the motions, bowing and presenting, one survivor to another," Singleton said at the window. "The magic shit I told you I could score, he said to me. I told you I'd get it for you, I promised, and I'm good on my word, he said. Then he gave it to me and before I could thank him he walked away."

Singleton handed her the bag and watched her hold it, fingering the pills. She took one out and sniffed it and dropped it back into the bag and then handed it gently back to him and shook her head.

"I don't think I'm describing him correctly. He had this helmet liner on, and a flack jacket, and his eyes were spooky but also made up a little bit, with eyeliner or glitter or something."

"So if this guy's for real you might've been an officer, a West Pointer," she said, pulling him away from the window. "That doesn't make a whole lot of sense to me."

"If I was an officer, I was laid-back about it, or maybe it was a nickname. It might make sense that he was a chaplain and might've called everybody Captain, because that's what we did. We took a big word and made it small, got control of it, maybe messing with the real captain by calling everybody the same."

He closed his eyes. Perhaps he did remember a chaplain praying over the body of one of his buddies, ministering the last rites. Perhaps not. He went to the freezer and hid the bag in the back. Then he opened the freezer door again and made sure the bag was hidden completely, behind bags of frozen peas and corn coated in snowy fuzz. Wendy smoked a cigarette as he sat across from her and explained that they wouldn't take them unless he could remember something—anything—about a man nicknamed Chaplain, something that confirmed he was for real, and they wouldn't take them when they were already high—for sure—and he waited for her to say something and she did, speaking in a low, husky voice, asking him if he wanted her to say she thought maybe she could help him out with that, and he said yes, he wanted her to say that, and she said it, and then she took his hand and led him to the bedroom and made him sit on the end of the bed.

A sensation of going out and then returning was part of it, he'd think. She had sighed the word *easy*. Take it *easy*.

When he came, he'd later think, it was weirdly a sensation deep inside himself and a white flash that vaporized all time and hollowed his mind and brought everything to a halt at the tip of his cock, deep in an open zone (he thought the word *zone*) of nonflesh surrounded by flesh, an airy free zone. He moved down into that zone and let his soul leave via that route. Just before he came he had a sharp awareness of being in the room and of touching her and of the fact that the future had been nullified and that the riots had left behind not only ash but something else: a consistent foreboding sense that the future might or might not exist. He felt, pushing forward, feeling the tightness as his scrotum drew itself up, that along with history and the end of the future any number of other things might terminate the mutual feeling they were sharing, the secretive, all-knowing bond of their two beings. She drove her pelvis forward as if to reduce the possibility of such an end, and then, when he didn't think he'd be able to go further, he lost it and gave way and grew light and flew up with his thoughts; then, it seemed, he came again, grunting, while she did, too, her cries short, musical, and he was out of it, back in the world, and could smell her scent, slightly metallic, along with the smoke in the air.

He fell to the side and admitted that he had unfolded. "We called him Chaplain, I think, because he was so pious, always praying and had this little family Bible that his father had carried in the Second World War and his father's father in the First. I saw him going from one body to the next, making the sign of the cross, fingering rosary beads and saying a prayer. I'm sure we gave him shit about it all the time, but he fit with the unit, and I imagine he was probably a source of drugs, always connected in Saigon, a real hustler: God's hustler. He talked Jesus. He talked his boyhood in Oklahoma. He talked a farm, with a real windmill and other Wizard of Oz shit."

She remained silent. All that conveniently in an unfolded vision? her silence said. How convenient that you'd have this particular vision at this particular time, giving us permission to take the pills, it said.

"All that conveniently in your unfold." There was a worried edge in her voice.

"He grew up on a farm and had all of those farm-boy ways of thinking that came from putting in hard work during the spring and then kicking back when summer came to watch the crops grow; so this guy was incredibly patient and didn't mind waiting out the enemy . . ."

He explained the battle for the Citadel and she sat listening, not moving. The five-day stalemate, mortar rounds and tank shells pounding what remained of the structure—thinking it was clear and then, a few hours later, receiving sniper fire. The weather had been heavy and air support couldn't strike, so they dug in and held position and during the long, tense hours and days Chaplain told his life story; he told tales of Cain and Abel–style wrestling matches in the barn loft that started out playfully but then took on epic qualities: getting his brother, Pete, in a half nelson. He told stories of growing corn only to burn it in the fall to collect the no-grow subsidies. He talked for hours of barn construction—the placement of the barn in relation to the sun to maximize the heat in winter and the coolness in summer; talked about the storms that came charging across the flatness, a thin line of dark far off producing tiny, toylike lightning bolts (no thunder); he talked about the long evenings watching the storms approach, slowly at first, or at least seemingly so, and then raging down on them.

"Truthfully, I don't know if he told those exact stories, now that I think about it," Singleton said. "Except for the battles with his brother. His brother was the one who got him to enlist. His brother went over to Nam, came back clean and bright. That must've been in '67, or thereabouts. His brother had been a member of Tiger Force and probably committed as many atrocities as the next guy but still came back in fine shape. That was the only story he told, and the rest, like I've been saying, might've been landscape details. But then I guess he probably told us about his belief in God and how much he admired King David; he told us stories about King David all the time," he said, trying to see her face in the dark, making out her lips, set tight. Her eyes were hidden. Night sounds came through the walls, deep, muffled television voices and the thumbed thump of a funky bass line. In the window across the room the curtains swirled and fell. She wasn't buying it, he sensed, and when he asked, she told him she wasn't. He was simply trying to fish around to find something true, to find a confirmation so they could pop the pills—which she wanted to pop, too, she admitted—and when he told her that he *had* seen the guy, Chaplain, in his vision, crossing the bodies, and that when the time came to take the pills they should feel free to do so, she nodded and touched his scar and then gave a soft, dismissive laugh. He told her it was fate that brought the pills, and as if in response, the bass line fell silent downstairs and there was, for a second, a lull in the noise level, an opening up of a deeper, speculative, judgmental silence, and then he heard himself explaining that fate was whatever you see when luck begins to make sense. It's a retroactive thing, yeah, but it starts to speak and you listen to it and then it seems to have a shape, he said.

"So you're not finding it strange that we're together when you happen upon these blue pills? You're just chalking it up to fate and leaving it at that."

"What do you mean?"

"I mean the chances of us being together like this and you having this flash that helps clarify for you that it'll be safe to take the pills. And you know if we take the pills you'll unfold more, for sure. That's all I mean. I'm sick of feeling this way."

"Sounds to me like you're talking about a conspiracy. The Corps sets this all up, this guy from my unit appearing?" he said, and then they went back and forth for a few minutes, arguing the possibility that somehow the Corps had set all this up. It's simply strange the way the world works, she argued. Things play out along lines of love, along desires, needs, touch. She kissed him and then said, still whispering, that conspiracy was a male thing. Men had a need to find structures in encounters that arrived out of desire. They longed for string-pulling at the highest level.

The next morning they got out of bed and readied themselves for the day, hungover, feeling sluggish, keeping away from each other as they moved around the apartment. Then they headed out to have breakfast, leaving the apartment separately, meeting up at the diner, taking a booth by the window and ordering coffee, sipping before they spoke.

"Everything feels out of balance now," she said. Across the street a man in fatigues stood, glaring in their direction. "There are two sides. I still wonder how much of that story you told me about Hue was true? When I'm high I just take in what you say and let it flow but this morning I woke seriously wondering what I'm supposed to make of the fact that we're together. I mean, when I'm lectured about having to go out and be Intuitive, and we break a major regulation and no one seems to care, if they know about it, and I think they do know, and then we make love and you unfold something that immediately confirms that the pills you got from some street guy are authentic and then we just wake up and pretend that nothing really happened."

There were tears in her eyes when she turned back from the window.

"Wendy, you know I can't really confirm that all the stuff I said last night was completely true," he said. "And I'm not sure I know what you mean by two sides, except maybe to say that the other side might be your feelings, your gut feeling, your intuition."

She looked up at him and smiled. "Jesus, that's not what I'm talking about at all. Not even close. I'm trying to say I didn't sign up for this shit. I signed up for some kind of structure, not to nurse a guy into unfolding, bit by bit. I think we kind of owe it to ourselves to figure out what our function might be as members of the organization."

"How do you propose to do that?" he said.

"Well, if they're aware that we're together and haven't stepped in, my guess would be we're supposed to be talking openly to each other about our cases. My guess would be we're actually here to exchange information on our cases."

The waitress came over with the coffee. "You two want anything else? I've seen agents come in like you, paired up, and I've seen them go away and never come back, but I've never seen them come in and go out and come in again like you two."

"What does that mean?" Wendy said.

"It means you'd better work this out, whatever it is."

"Who sent you to talk to us?" Singleton said. "Did Klein send you here?"

"Don't get conspiratorial on me," the waitress said. "I get enough of that around here. I just saw the two of you, and I saw her crying, and I came over to give you a word. Take it or leave it. I've seen the likes of you come and go. I've seen you crying. I've seen folks come in with clean-cut uniforms, enfolded and cured, and then come back a few months later looking like rejects from the reject pile."

She ripped the check off the pad and slapped it on the table.

"What was that?" Wendy said when she was gone.

"That was the voice of wisdom, or else the voice of a secret operative who is trying to nudge us into a certain modality."

"Don't you think it's obvious?" Wendy said.

"In what way?"

"In the way of all of these things. If she's not part of some grand conspiracy denying she's in a conspiracy, at least she knows something we don't know."

"Everyone knows something we don't know."

"You know what I mean."

"Look," Singleton said. "Again, I'm sure that the flash I got of the Chaplain had to do with Hue. I got a taste of dust—and I don't think I'm making it up—of city dust. I can only say that it's an educated guess."

Music came on the jukebox, and the noise of the diner seemed to lower to let it in. The man across the street was gone.

"I think we both know that we're on the same case," she said. "I think that's been this unspoken thing between us for weeks now and that we've been gaming each other—and enjoying it—from about the second or third day, at least until that time you unfolded Rake's image and saw the look on my face in the car, because I remember you gave me a wink, or maybe not a wink but you indicated that you saw me respond to Rake's name."

"You're projecting, Wendy. I didn't see you respond to me when I said his name, but I remember you didn't seem to respond at all and that was weird, so yeah, yeah, yeah, OK, I think we can both agree that we're making this big revelation. I mean talking here, speaking what has been unspoken and all of that, but to hear you say you're on Rake's case shines a light on the fact that we're both now articulating the fact out loud, right here in the old fucking coffee joint."

"We've been working together and knowing it but not openly admitting it. Keeping that tension tense."

"And when I mentioned Rake to you in the car, when I let that out, you knew for sure but I didn't really know for sure, so for the last few weeks it's been a listing ship of intuitive blah blah blah," he said. "For the last few weeks I've been trying to stay within the bounds of the Credo, or whatever, for your sake, thinking you were staying in the bounds—verbally, I mean—for my sake. You were waiting for me to break, and I was following your lead, waiting for you."

"So if we're on the same case, then you have to ponder why Klein wouldn't care, or at least act like he doesn't know, or if he does know and knows I know, then at least put on a pretense of not knowing," Wendy said. "I'd say they knew all along, from the start. I'd say they have some theory that makes sense, some idea of mirroring two trainees after an assessment of their histories—mine with my father, listening to him go on about the war, and then the fact that my boyfriend came back with his legs missing."

She lit a cigarette, nodded at the waitress, and sat back. "She's seen couples like us come in and out over the last two years."

MAPS

The air-conditioning was down, the vents quiet, and Klein, sweating, paused to wipe his face with a handkerchief, holding it by the corners in an unusually dainty gesture, dabbing his brow first and then his cheeks and finally his chin as he briefed Singleton on new sightings: a man found dead in a ditch north of the bridge, up along the straits, with smears of blood similar to ones Rake liked to leave but different enough, he stressed, to know, if you knew these things, that it was fraudulent. Another couple murdered, in their farmhouse near Alpena, and again the cops called the Liaison and said they were sure as all hell it was the mark of a failed enfold because there was blood on the walls, smeared finger painting, and again a residual smell of a young woman's perfume. But Klein insisted that they had it wrong, they were simply overflowing with cases and were passing the buck.

"I have a feeling," he said, "that you think my passing the buck back to the local law enforcement on these new cases might have something to do with the rumor that you might've heard about Rake being dead. But I want you to know that even if the rumor is confirmed by Intelligence—and I assure you it will be—I'm not going to buy it. I've seen too many fakes, and there's nobody better at faking than a soldier like Rake, who from what we do know saw a lot of action—of course we aren't privy to the facts, the report that came from upstairs is heavily redacted—and is versed in the art of deception, particularly a type of self-deception. Let me give you an example," he said. He packed his pipe, took a few draws, wiped his brow on his sleeve, and then began to talk about an old friend of his at West Point who had made a study of the shooting habits of men in combat in Korea and found that in a huge number of cases men shot *away* from the target, because killing another human isn't all that easy. He had concluded that many soldiers deluded themselves into thinking they aimed for and struck the target, whereas their internal governing systems—he stressed that he abhorred the word *subconscious*—guided them *away* from the target.

"So what do you think happens at the external level?" he asked. His eyes were unusually steady, glinting. He drummed his fingers on his desk and waited while Singleton took a guess and suggested more self-deception and he grunted and said, No, not self-deception, but honest, up-front deception, and Singleton muttered another "Yes, sir," and watched Klein make his fish-mouth suck again around the pipe stem, even though it was on his desk, far away from his lips, and then Klein went on to explain that Rake wasn't dead until he saw his body, bore witness to it himself, because it was easy to disfigure a body, or cut up a face, and then dangle dog tags around a neck to make it look like it was Rake. When he asked if Singleton was with him, Singleton muttered another "Yes, sir," and Klein explained that he wanted to segue—Jesus, I hate that word, he said—into something that had to do with Singleton, and Singleton, again, said "Yes, sir," and listened to Klein as he explained that self-deception, no, make that up-front deception, includes—and this is the segue, he said—the fact that someone who has been through the treatment, who has had the CEP enfolded, is going to feel a desire to unfold. He might think he doesn't have that desire, and his internal governing systems might trick him into feeling assured that he is no longer feeling the desire, that he's over the hump, but in truth it's only natural to want to know the story. "You feel good and clean with the trauma put away, but at the same time you want to know what really happened. I'm sure you were told in post-treatment about the itchy sensation you'd feel, the fuzzball, a neurological dust bunny. But I don't know if you were instructed, if they told you in clear terms that you'll want to know what's up there in your head and at the same time—and this is the paradox, son—you also don't ever, ever want to know because to know would mean you're back in the horrific state you were in before you got the treatment."

"Yes, sir," Singleton said. Sweat had soaked through his shirt and he could feel it trickling along his back.

"Now let me say something they probably didn't tell you in post-treatment, or at least didn't emphasize. They don't tell you how destructive the desire to know can be. How you might turn to drugs. How you might have a desire for orgasmic states. How you might find yourself wanting to wade into cold water, and so on and so forth," he said. He paused and dabbed at the sweat on his face again. Then he went on to explain that trainees were looking for indirect knowledge, a newspaper photo with themselves in it, or a television news report in which they appear, or better yet contact with someone who was a part of their initial trauma, the CEP, in a way that provides a little bit of information but not too much. Then they feel relieved. To find what they knew but didn't know they knew, he said. Singleton nodded and said, "Yes, sir."

"On the other hand," he said. "You might be tempted to test the water, to take a dip in an ice bath, or, in the parlance of a foot soldier, get laid in the best way, usually with drugs, and then unfold. Your internal governor pushes the idea that you can catch a flash here, a flash there, and be done with it. Are you with me?"

Maintain eye contact, Singleton said to himself. He was thinking about Wendy, her strange mix of kindness and care and wildness.

Klein was saying he believed that he, Singleton, would take his advice to heart. He didn't want him to end up like his last trainee, bluer than his balls in Korea, on the rocks, like an olive in a cocktail, dead in a bathtub full of ice, just because he wanted to know what he had been through. Klein lifted a pipe and lit it and then stared across the desk. He furrowed his brow and puffed and asked if they were good, if the message had been received, and Singleton nodded and said, "Yes, sir. We're good."

The question came out to fill the silence. He asked it without thinking, in a sudden jerking sensation. His voice came ahead of him into the silence. Klein had said he was free to go, to head out and have an Internal afternoon. The question had been floating from day to day, in all of the secretive afternoon motions, together on the beach, in bed, in her apartment. He wanted some sort of explanation to straighten out the sense that everything—from the walls of the apartment, to the strange fate that seemed to arrange a meeting with an old buddy—was shrouded in hidden meaning. So he asked it straight out, saying, "Why don't you just send us up there to track him down, to see what's going on?"

Klein waited a few beats before answering, the sweat growing on his brow, his eyes shifting slightly, interrogative, swinging around from Singleton's mouth and up to his brow and then to his neckline, looking for some betraying twitch. Then he asked who "us" was, and Singleton, catching himself, explained that he meant us as in me, as in the two selves, the enfolded part and the part of himself here, now, as someone functioning inside the structure of the Corps, of his work, the part that had been trained so far. Klein stood up and looked, for a second, unusually frail. He had thin legs and his trousers were cut wide, bagging around them, and he shook slightly. He put one hand on his desk, leaning back to assume a casual stance, and ordered Singleton to stand. Then he reached out—it was a gesture that was fatherly—and put his hands on Singleton's shoulders. The buzz in his ears increased. He was experiencing, he'd later think, a boot camp sensation, a feeling he might've had (he could only speculate) when some drill sergeant ordered him to get down and give me fifty. Klein's voice shifted, grew tender—his gullet throbbed like a turkey.

"If I had my way I'd send you on a mission immediately, but I don't have my way, son, because I'm following orders, and even a man in my position has to follow orders. Even Haig was following orders as supreme commander. I'll resist the urge to pontificate again about MacArthur."

"Yes, sir," Singleton said.

"I'm giving you an order, and that order is to get out of my sight and stay out of my sight for the afternoon. If you stop thinking about yourself in the collective 'we,' it might help you locate intuitive material for the mission."

Walking back behind his desk he stumbled again and fell into his chair.

BILLY-T

The dank smell of the lake drifted through the window. Rake was downstairs. The radio in the kitchen poured out lyrics steeped in blood and vengeance. The house's frame was cracking in the first real heat of the year, under the weight of the slate roof. The smell of attic dust seeped down from the cracks in the ceiling. Steadily, day by day, Hank had drawn himself into the role of Old Hank until she began to wonder if he had slipped into his old ways completely. Lying in bed one morning she imagined that Rake would take her away one of these mornings, before dawn, when the rest of the house was asleep, shaking her awake and telling her not to say a word. The gun he waved around when the evening card games didn't go his way would be against her forehead, a cold kiss to her brow as she rose up from her dream. She'd be only half-surprised, because she had woken before to that feeling, down in Alpena, in other places. It was a game he played, to see her startled eyes going from side to side. Rake said he liked her when she slept, but he'd warned her never to sleep too deeply. *I want you to feel what I felt and what I feel now. I want you to learn to sleep with your eyes wide open. I want my ex-*

haustion to become yours. He'd wave the gun and she'd think, Go ahead, shoot me, get it over with, it would be the best thing you could do, but she'd keep moving because she would think about Hank and feel that feeling she knew was love; a small warm place near her breastbone (because it had to be compartmentalized), and then she'd think: Just move and do as he says, and then he'd make her go ahead of him, down the stairs, after whispering: Don't make a noise, and avoid that second-to-the-last step, that one's a squawker, because if you wake them I'll have to kill them all, Hank first; and you don't want to let Hank die, I know that because I saw you two out there behind the barn and I saw him kiss you; you think I wasn't home but I was home, I'm always home; my eyes are always here. I might be out and about, but my eyes stay on this house.

Then they'd go to a car and drive into a morning silent except for the birds singing and the wind in the trees. The trees, she'd think, casting a single glance back at the house in its disrepair, its abjectness and sadness, and then he'd dog-feed her another pill. This one she'd have to take, and she'd fall into the stupor of her former self, curling up on the seat and listening as the car roared to life and he fishtailed out, sending a cloud of dust toward the front porch. That was as far as she could imagine. Subdued by the drugs, she'd see the rest from a place she knew well but couldn't locate, even in her imagination.

I'm going on a distribution run, Rake announced later that morning. I'm taking Haze with me. We'll give out some freebies to entice future buyers. No need to charge. Want to avoid exchanges of funds.

He stood on the porch and winked at Hank. I'm going to have to ask you for a pledge again. You're not to touch her. No running, either.

You have my word, Hank said, glancing out across the yard. I'm just going to clear some of the dead wood out there, not far from the shore, or do a little scouting around.

Take her with you. Tie her up. Don't let her anywhere near the water.

He had a valise, stuffed with product. All night he'd been in the kitchen, sorting and chopping, testing the product. His eyes were glazed.

The Lord will be with you, MomMom said from the doorway. Or else he won't, she added.

I'd bet on him not being with us, Rake said. I'd bet God's gonna take a rain check.

Haze stood quietly by the car with his hands deep in his pockets.

They stood on the porch and watched them drive off. The dust lifted into the trees. Hank put his finger to his lips and said, Don't quote scripture to me now, Mom.

Outside the birds were quiet, or dead, or gone to more cheerful places. Meg showered after Hank, stepping shyly into the bathroom. He touched her on the shoulder, gave her a quick kiss, told her to take as long as she wanted, and went downstairs to brew a thermos of coffee. Out in the yard, MomMom was on the ground again, twisting in a fit. He ran water into a galvanized bucket and then went out to where she lay with her hips upthrust and her back arched. The voice is a pliant thing; the voice can do amazing things, he thought. The air hissed through her teeth. Her stockinged knees looked crooked and sad in the unforgiving sunlight. He doused her in the face with water and watched her sputter and spit. As he helped her up, she muttered, Goddamn it, what the hell you doing, Hank? and he said, I'm waking you up, you're having another fit. I'm heading out and I'm taking Meg with me. I'd like you to watch us leave and take note that I took her with me. I'm going to tie her up and I want you to see that, too, and when Rake comes back you're going to say, Yes, Hank had her tied, and then he asked her to repeat it and she said, What? And he said, You'll tell Rake she was tied. Now say it to me, and she said, Tell Rake she was tied. And he said, No, that's not what I mean. I mean when Rake interrogates me, which he's going to do, about my handling of Meg, and when he asks you what happened, I want you to say, He had Meg tied, and she said, I don't know what you mean, and he said, Forget it, Ma. He brushed the dirt off her back and walked her into the kitchen.

Why'd you do that, splash me awake like that? I was speaking to him directly.

In the mudroom he got two lengths of rope and then went upstairs. Meg was squeezing her hair in a towel.

I've got to tie your hands, he said. We're going to march you in front of MomMom and make her practice her lines. I'm going to tie you and I'll wheelbarrow you through the yard while you scream, and we'll make sure MomMom sees that. We'll make sure she remembers. Ideally she'll forget minor details, which will make it sound even more horrific when Rake interrogates her.

When she was dressed, he sat her down on the bed and gently tied her wrists, keeping the rope loose, using a slipknot.

If you want to get out of these, just pull hard and you'll be free. You can let yourself free anytime you want, even in the yard, even in front of Ma. If you don't want to play the part don't play it and I'll figure something else out.

She went down the stairs ahead of him into the kitchen. Look, Ma, Hank said. I want you to take note of this. I'm leading her out tied up. Can you say that for me? he said. Why should I say that for you? she said. Because I want to make sure you remember. I want you to say to Rake: He had her tied up. Can you say that for me? He crossed his arms and waited.

You got her tied up, she said.

Good, Mom, that's fine. Just remember that when Rake asks you, because he'll come back and he'll be suspicious. This is a test. For all I know, he's out there in the trees right now waiting and watching.

I'm not saying I believe it anymore, he was saying. They were about a mile up the trail, moving along a barely discernible path, a faint trace in the pine needles, close enough to shore to see the water through the trees. Hank made slow, deliberate steps, stopping often to smell the air and scout with his hand up to his forehead. The trees thinned where the rocky berm began, showing shards of slate-colored lake. I'm not saying I even believe in the vision of the Corps, or the treatment, that it works in the long run, or any of that. What matters right now is that Haze and Rake are paired up, tight. They're a new pair. They were loading the car with gas cans and old rags, so I guess the truth is they're going on another burning and killing spree, not a distribution run. They had fuses and a few sticks of old dynamite from the shed.

Then he stopped and turned her around and untied her wrists and rubbed them lovingly.

I'm sorry I had to do that. I was just acting the part as much as I could but didn't feel it, not at all. You know that, right? You knew that. And of course I know some of the New Meg is still there. What we want to do is get more of you back, to take you into the water and get you in the cold—not much, just a bit—and start to get some of your memories back.

He looked around the woods. I've got some Potawatomi blood in me, most certainly, and I would've heard him on this part of the trail if he were scouting parallel to us.

He kissed her and touched her face and looked into her eyes. She was still slightly stoned from whatever Rake had fed her. A lollygag motion in the eyes, disconnected from her thoughts. When she spoke, the words seemed to take a trip to the moon and back, the same kind of delay. He glanced one more time back into the woods, the sunlight streaming through the high branches—the disorder of an unplanted forest—and then once more out toward the lake, at the scrubby little jack pines that hung on for dear life in the steady wind, stunted and short, most of them young because older trees died a quick wintery death in the storms. Everything seemed quiet. They were as alone as they could get.

Another supertanker slid along the horizon on its way to Duluth. He led her down to the water and put his hands on her shoulders and held her for a moment.

Now, this is how it's going to happen, he said. You're going to go into the water and I'm going to go with you. You'll go up to your ankles and feel how cold it is and then you'll want to dash out, or else you'll want to submerge yourself totally right away, one or the other depending on how much you want to unfold, and I'll help you but you might not think I'm helping. I'm not going to force you but I'm going to make sure you don't kill yourself. Holding her by the shoulder, feeling her shivers, he walked with her into the water. Before he could say anything more she wrenched free and ran leaping through the shallows and then, with a small cry, she slipped over the shelf—the drop-off was quick—and sank with her arms straight up and was gone. He dove and swam to find her, reaching out with broad strokes, resisting his impulse to shut his eyes against the cold. When he came back up, she was up, too, finding the edge of the shelf with her feet, gasping. Then she sank back down, and he had his arms around her and brought her in so he could touch the bottom with his feet. He cupped her head with his palm and held her down in the water, feeling her relax. He counted the seconds and then let her up again, spitting water from her lips, and when he asked if she wanted him to push her down again, to go the full count, she said, Yes, yes, and before he could think, before she could think, he pushed her back under and counted again, going as long as he dared, waiting for her to struggle against him, going all the way to the limit, as close as he could, watching the bubbles rise in the clean gloss of the wavelets, and when he finally let her back up he could see in her eyes right away that she had gone through a change; her eyes were sad, bright, frightened, but relieved.

Down under the water she heard a voice speak and the voice said:

I wonder who's going to tell the story, Meg? Nothing else to say. You see, you had to be here and you weren't. You know the one that goes: How many Vietnam vets does it take to screw in a lightbulb? How many? You fucking don't know because you weren't there, man! You weren't fucking there! The texture of history; the rubbery material it's made out of—say, latex. No. Something stronger than latex that can stretch out to a pure translucence until it's nothing but a molecule thick, man, not even that. You had to be high to be there. Listen up, man, let me tell you, they can't reproduce the shit I went through; Tripizoid or no Tripizoid, it isn't going to work for me. No confusion (some guy said, raising his fingers up in the V sign). Don't give me that Walter Cronkite that's-the-way-it-is bullshit, man; I don't care who's directing the reenactment chamber, I'm gonna out-Hector Hector, man, and there ain't nothing to be said. I won't go on, I won't go on with it. They're going to have to drag me in to Vetdock. They'll have to shove the Tripizoid down my throat. There is the buzz in the ear; the buzz in the ear's as close as you'll get. That's what this friend tells me, likes to say that, as if it means something. Just can't get it right, what a friend says to me. Piece it together, dude, put two and two next to each other and figure this . . . shit . . . out. Elephant grass. Man, journalists always mention the elephant grass. And rice paddies— and the Mekong Delta—always the rich beauty of the mountains and the Mekong Delta, man; always that to set up the contrast; and jungle rot, always that rot, man, along with slogging through this and slogging through that; always point man this and point man that and ambush this and ambush that: look close, you noticed the line; the line is late 1967, when the crewcuts grew out and the love beads grew down and the shirts were unbuttoned wide and the refusal of orders became routine and the air mattresses began to sag. Back home the line was pot and acid to speed and meth and coke. You had to be there. You weren't there. You should've been there. Should've been you. Reporters put fear in your eyes. Put fear in your mouth. The grimace. Reporters tell the story: take the hill, lose the hill. Take a hill. Lose a hill. Story has to rotate on an axis, has to spin around the Polaris of fear; story has to make some kind of sense, dissasembled and reassembled: all ticker-tape bullshit and journalese code wired back. The steel cases for the film reels arriving in New York days late: old news is better than no news—so by the time it gets on the tube we're long gone from that shit, man, and the dead have been hoisted up, the net sagging, the chopper struggling to get the heave-ho going, pressing the grass down in the wash, and the men left behind waddle back into the bush; then the chopper does that little dip to one side and swings herself skyward under a barrage of flack—always flack— while the door gunner sprays wildly, his haphazard aim still tuned to water buffalo, and then that profound silence when the dust-off—always the dust-off—has gone out of range, not even the murmur of it anymore, and there's just the silence of foliage and rice, man, that nobody—no writer, no miked-up Morley Safer—has ever caught, bottled up, and taken back to the States: the world, always *the world*, as if we really called it that and maybe we did but not to you, motherfucker; always the helmet graffiti quote, the totems and good luck charms reductio ad absurdum with their meaning couched, that said: these suckers will be offed, retroactively lending those charms the meaning you want; the terrible gist you already got in your living room easy chairs watching Uncle Walter while the vertical barely holds and the image threatens to turn itself into what it is, just so many radio waves coming off a tower for your viewing pleasure; the stately eye of the network, or the peacock tail metamorphosing into color plumage—another line; black and white/color: the browns and greens of the marijuana going to bright blue pills and tabs with psychedelic decoration—the fine bubbling fix gnarly and many-hued; don't go there, man, don't even try to get the combat in: never seen it work, man; only good story is a dead story . . . all that free-formed fear becoming nullified at the brain tip, with dark pure dark, so you sit inside your head for that split second and say: shit, ain't no heaven or nothing but just this terminal darkness while some guy says, far off, in a trickle of audible sound itching the last viable neurons—gonna be all right, Hank, gonna be just fine. Fuck Asklepios, fuck that nonsense: Where was he when we needed him? Just one more bleeder falling into the nonsense of his pain, the gung-ho posture dissipating while he holds his chin up, prone on the stretcher, with the plastic cigar tip in his mouth and says he's going to get the gook that sent the bullet, going to get him—while the camera, immoral and unjust, moves down to the shredded legs. He holds himself off from the pure shot and stays steady in the endorphin high and keeps the pose as long as he can until the morphine drip shoves the endorphins aside so that the pain can come in and you see it in his face, which goes from square-jawed, à la George Patton, Jr., to a prune of pain just before the film is cut and the story terminated: he was the biggest and the bravest motherfucker until he stepped on our own claymore out there, along the line, and then—always along the line, always out there—the faint distant explosion, the small cloud, the camera drawing itself along the tree line, and then (cut in) the medic hustling himself to work, elevating. (There's this place, someone tells me, called the Gleel; some nice little glen down in a grove of trees with the babbling brook and the moss and the microclimate of coolness; place of curative powers, the guy tells me, and then he goes on to explain, getting professorial—in that way of the ex-junkie—that it's where Saint Dymphna exercises her singular healing powers, and I tell him, Fuck off, and then go to it in my mind and imagine myself there.) Never used the word *Bedlam*; never heard the word once. This is Morley Safer, reporting from outside Hue, in the hamlet that can only be called Bedlam, South Vietnam. No tell of the grunt Hogarth—that silly little fuck, skinny as a whip, from Ellison, South Dakota, riding point—yeah, point—that afternoon (always through the head); and after the day was done, after the men took Hill #21, the cost was a high one, five dead, ten wounded. This is Morley Safer, somewhere—Christ knows where, exactly—outside Hue, in Vietnam. Hovercrafts: giant bulldozers to clear the jungle, carving the symbol for the Engineer Battalions into the countryside; sensors that can sniff out the smell of piss ammonia and campfire smoke from a thousand feet up; all kinds of shit to compose the nightly newscast and usually cast into the bright shiny emotion of battle: bric-a-brac, man, was the main thing—a thousand hours of footage filled with that shit—preset images: men with their boots off trying to cool their feet—the skin moon-white and swollen; men lying back smoking kif; boys fingering their love beads—bearded, long-haired (because, man, we knew that the fact that we knew what was up back home was a big kick to the viewing audience and milked the irony and turned it into itself, man, all pose and acting; man, you gotta think: the whole enfolding gig came out of that, the double duplicity of it, actors on the big jungle stage mugging for the lens, even the Hanoi Hilton guys doing their Christmas card home, slump shouldered, singing their hearts out, amazingly in harmony, a barbershop quartet of vocal entwining; hanging bulbs on the tree—the whole thing, staged and restaged and then staged again until the final product had the humility of fine acting, souls embodying characters who, in turn, embodied the words: Say it, man, you bent-back double-elbowed motherfucker—that one guy bowing down too far—early footage, one of the first POW films, making a big show of it, all secret signals to the outside world, lips a bit too high around the edges in the smile department, frowns deeper than normal, fingers crabbing signals. Even the secret gestures were part of the show, man; and later when I got home and tried to really get home there was that, too, in the way I hung the streets of town in the jacket: don't get me wrong, I'm not saying it was a farce, I'm just saying we came back to the bit roles and took the parts that were available partly because our reentry was quick—into the great cargo transports and then, bingo, home sweet home (guys enacted the routine: fell before native soil and kissed the tarmac. Did I? I most certainly did. The grit and dust of Detroit Metro never tasted so good, as sweet as Tang). But the flight went from Saigon to Germany to home in the flick of the Zippo: all brilliant American sky beneath which the pompous Army band played their Sousa (which reminds me: look up the old footage of Air Cav. Band playing their brains out for CBS while the jets drop load after load on the Vietcong for the sake of villager morale). No long rearrangement of reality à la the *Odyssey*; not for us, man: we went in and out of the combat zones, lickety split and just as quick got stateside, back to the World; stumbling the streets in our derangement and grandeur; knocking on home-sweet-home doors and stepping into living rooms with the Namscape still etched on the backside of our eyeballs; Dad in his armchair with a drink and Mom beside him waiting for me to speak; and, Meg, let me say their questions came out of the pages of the ladies' magazines where the articles went, "How to Talk with a Vietnam Veteran," and suggested avoidance of the topic of death. Well, madam, I'd say, and I did say, I don't know *what* to say. Certainly no mention of the war. Not a word. Not one single word the first five weeks I was in the house. Days fell into routine: sleep in as late as possible with the shades drawn until the hot day got too hot and I dragged myself up and went downstairs to face their eyes— not judgmental, I wouldn't call them that: expectant, knowing. Fuck plot and fuck story and fuck the way one thing fits to another and fuck cause and effect, because there wasn't none, and if there was we didn't see much of it. Maybe history was moving forward back in the States. Hell, it most certainly was grinding. The Year of Love was turning itself over to the Year of Hate. There was a purgative thing happening. Ideals were falling neatly to the wayside, one at a time, and giving over to violence. Nam was seeping home. One man at a time it was coming back, talking the talk. We felt it there. Like I said, our crewcuts were giving way to long hair. The men went home and the music came back and we listened to it from tinny transistor speakers. On a fulcrum the whole thing shifted when Soldier #1 put his weight down, stepped off the transport to kiss the soil, the whole thing went down on one side and up on the other. Soldier #1 was Rake. When that boy got home the whole show went from rehearsal to opening night. Number 1 got to Michigan and began the beginning; started it all up. I'd be dead and gone by the time that moment came along, but I could feel it in the wind—that hot jungle wind, the stench of burning hootches (ain't nothing like the smell of burning jungle roof, ain't nothing like the thick smoke coming off a hootch that's been Zippoed to flame). Just conjecture and speculation on how it would go down when the crazy fuck got to the world. Billy-T, he'd say to me: We'd be hunkered down against the bomb blasts called in to some coordinates, scared shitless, naturally, that we'd be a Close Air Support casualty ourselves (needless to say we hated and loved CAS; loved 'em for coming in to save our asses and hated them for coming in to save our asses). Hunched down waiting and Rake would be saying, Billy-T, man, when I get back I'm gonna take the state by fucking storm; I'm gonna haunt that place like a motherfucker. I'm gonna be their worse nightmare, etc., etc., etc. Ah, shut up, man, Singleton said, just to tighten the triangle, to make it right, and Rake said, Fuck you, man, and Singleton said, You'd like to, but I'm corn hole sore, and Rake said, in that seriously real, tight, nasty voice he could get, I'm not kidding, shut up, grunt boy, or I'll frag your ass right here and now. (No, he wouldn't've said it that way; he would've said, simply, Singleton, shut up, in *the voice*, and for the sake of peace between us Singleton would've shut up, and he did shut up; I remember that much, leaving behind just the tension, wordless, that was then, a few seconds later, demolished when the fighters came screaming in just over the trees and unleashed their bombs mercifully and the percussion was enough, just then, to wash it away while we plugged our ears and got as close to the dirt as we could and prayed (at least I did). Being dead doesn't sanctify the living, or the memory of what the living went through. My word is only half good. The truth of what I'm saying might be nil, Meg, or it might be perfect. It's not for me to pick apart and I'm not gonna do it. Forget heaven. Forget eternity. Some sorry-ass shit has been laid down under the guise of the eternal. Don't even ask the question: don't get into the pearly gate shit with me. Don't try to get me going on the intimate particulars of what transpires down in the so-called living world when in truth I don't have the slightest inkling; you go into the pinhole of death, sit there, and sit some more until your eyes adjust to the perpetual cave dark and, in doing so, allow yourself to imagine, now and then, that you're starting to see some light, some glint of it at least, but then you come to realize that it's just a variation on black and nothing more or less. All those neurons; all that memory, zapped. Maybe it hangs on as long as it can in some eternal place, maybe not: all that hangdog belief put in the afterlife becomes so much hokum, one way or another, anyway; to inhabit another, to walk the earth in the form of a dog or a cat, to reform yourself into some Hindu spirit dervish—roiling and forming before some bewildered farmer's eyes as he looks up from his toil behind the mule and plow, reins in his hands—all that's just one more way of trying to imagine yourself into my shoes, and it doesn't work and it isn't real. Truth is there's nothing more than a zip closing the body bag—personal containment unit—and you're gone, flag-draped (eventually) and shipped home like a hunk of cheese, refrigerated—naturally, by the high altitude—flushed by some Army mortician, powdered up, and, if you're in shape for it, put on display for all to see. Do I remember the funeral? Hell, yes. What I remember is the way you clutched yourself, Meg, as if holding your own guts in—and I've seen that, believe me—and the way you quaked and sobbed, and the way the tears popped from your eyes and strung themselves down your cheeks. Did I stare at you? You were thin then, and sallow-skinned, but still beautiful, your hair fine and yellower than I remembered in Nam, during those furtive long jack-off sessions when I imagined myself in deep. Did I imagine the way your lips would move over the hymns that were sung, the voices lifting through the church (First Congregational) with a bit too much gusto, reverberating in the high arched reaches while the organ tried to outdo the voices but failed? Hell yeah, I did. I imagined your lips moving out of sync—like they would later, drugged up by Rake—into formations that were meant to look like utterances but really weren't, because you weren't looking down at the hymnal that your father held open in front of you. Did I scan the faces, seeing my mother and father and brother and the neighbors in anguish, and the minister (believe it or not, his name was Breeze, Dudney Breeze) in his vestments? You bet I did. Did I have that Huckleberry Finn groove going that came from attending your own funeral when in truth I was alive and well, albeit hunched down in a hole trying to survive a friendly ambush—for lack of a better phrase. Hell yeah. Did I imagine your face a couple of hundred times, pained, twisted in front of your loss, blooming like a flower with grief over the death of your boyfriend in Nam, taking in the fact that you would go on with the rest of your life without me? You bet. You see, death isn't much more than an imagining of death in the face of the end itself as it came when you were trying to feel as alive as possible but were having trouble doing so because you were, at that moment, under heavy fire, or riding point through some bad-vibe part of the Mekong, tired but trying to stay alert, hot alert, but faltering because you were by nature a kid who liked to go off into reveries: by nature you'd deviate from all of your training and boot-camp conditioning at exactly the wrong moment. That was your way of rebelling against existence. That was how you got around the truth of your situation. You started to imagine the life you (if you survived) might have and then along the way you got to the possibility of your own death and then, naturally, casually, laughing about it, you got to your own funeral and then really zeroed in on the details. Asleep at the wheel, so to speak. Was I the only guy in the unit who slept on his feet and found himself dreaming, not some half-ass daydream thing but vivid and spatially detailed dreams? Hell no, I wasn't. We all did the same thing, except maybe Rake, who had very little to go back to and couldn't foresee his death the way he could foresee the death of others. Rake drew a blank in the dream department. He could only conjure nightmares, and we all know that nightmares don't stand the test of time. So let me go back and reiterate what I'm saying here, right now: the dead can look back in time and look down at the world in that way live folks like to imagine, but they do so only as living souls dreaming their way forward to death and, in doing so, looking back. Otherwise it's just black with some deceptive hints of light that aren't really light but tricks of the dark and after that an eternal nothingness, etc. etc. etc. Was I having strange visions that summer in Vietnam? Was I spotting angels in the trees and hearing music coming out of the ether? Did I say to Rake and to Singleton: Man, did you see that figure up there in the trees, man? Did you see the angel in the trees? I most certainly did. Was I the only one? Hell no. Was I the only guy who, in the stress and fear and weariness, saw spectral formations of light or whatever that took the shape of human figures with white robes and wings attached to their backs? I'd say not. Were these delirious mind-fuck creations of a mind so wasted—not just from the shit we were in on recon, but from some of the shit I took in Saigon— hallucinatory creations of my own gratefully dead mind? I'd say not. Was I the only guy who saw a vision of Saint Jerome up in the trees outside Hue; a striking re-creation of the da Vinci painting, beating himself senseless to mortify his flesh? Most likely. Did I come up with this image because my old man had a book, and in that book was a replica of the Leonardo painting—not a bad one, either—and I drew upon it when I saw my own vision up there in the trees? Most certainly.

Would it be possible to come up with the original vision without making use of something seen before? I'm sure it would, but I didn't. When we went out on recon patrol, I had to rely on what I'd seen before, and in so doing took the shortest route to my visions because I wasn't strong enough (who is, really?) to rise to the task of creating something from whole cloth. When it came to conjuring up an angel in the trees of Vietnam I had to lean on what I knew, and I drew inspiration from a Christmas card I had picked up one sunny afternoon at the Upjack house; an angel with wings, a pouty face, pointy breasts—somewhat alluring—through a thin, almost translucent robe; the wings sparkled with glitter that came off on my fingers. Was I illegally in the Upjack house? Did I break into the house in search of funds? I most certainly did. Did I—to use a word I love—burgle the house? I did indeed. Am I being regressive in my approach to this part of my story? Yes. Is there any other way to get at it? No. You see, only through posing concise questions to myself—walking point; taking the flack, trying to sleep through a shelling—could I find the story, or at least part of it. My own, that is. Did I love this girl, Meg Allen, one summer? I suppose you might say I did. I mean, what is love but a retrospective bliss seen from afar— even the next day, or the next second. I loved her and she loved me. I went AWOL and we headed to California. Was she seventeen at the time, a girl whose mother drank herself into afternoon fits, if she drank, or shook with delirium if she didn't? Did she have the finger marks of a slap on her cheek as she stood barefoot in my doorway? Was she immediately enamored by the figure I cut—striking, I like to think, with my long black hair, my ragged old leather vest with fringe? I'd say yes to all of the above. Did this girl—and the vision I had of her, a vision that shape-shifted as my second tour of duty went into its fifth month, after I'd seen friends killed—become something more, in my mind? She most certainly did. What did she become? She became nothing less than an angelic vision from my past that represented, I like to think, some potential future, frozen in time, unchanged and still seventeen (or eighteen) upon my return to the States—maybe nineteen. But let me stop here. The dead don't speak. For Christ's sake, the dead don't riff on the living. The dead are silent and entangled in the past. The dead, with me as an exception, can't say a word. Anything said by them is the pure fiction of the living and nothing more. For the sake of illumination, to draw some strings together, to fill in some blanks, because if I don't do it, alive or dead, who will? Let's just say I was dreaming this up on point, or riding shotgun, during the weary patrols, exhausted from the fear involved. Just say I made all this up in my own manner, foreshadowing, tightening the neck of the sack that would close in upon me eventually. In that light, let me regress, floating from one possibility to another, Ebenezer Scrooge–style. Early on, when we were on patrol, I imagined it: the state of Michigan itself, in the shape of a mitten, and the world back home as it would be upon my death; but like I said that's about it, terminus; the only way into me is through the end point and then through whatever visions I might or might not have had before that point—all projection, all outward yearning, the hope and gist of the imagination, also known, in common parlance, as the dream. That's what love is, as far as I can see, an outward forward projection of the self, and that's what we had those few weeks that summer; just pure dreaminess. Her sweet little body— and let me tell you it was sweet and young, youthful, all downy skin, fine hairs and that never-been-touched tingle, charged and electric.

But let me reiterate. The dead can't speak.

All this before the end. All this with the rot in my crotch. The imaginings that come with fear. The step-by-step movement through the jungle. What else could we do to fill the time?

But the thing is, and here I might digress a little bit, we really didn't dream when we were out there; one didn't dream on point. Too much to look for. You were charged up, fired into an acute and exhaustive attentiveness to the things around you, ears perked up, eyes as wide as you could get them, just looking for a hint, a sign, a glint of flash in the treetops, a trip wire at the feet. You began to find a way intuitively; you trusted the sense that you had of seeing what was before you, which was why, when we were ordered to go down the road by the new guy, the one who came in on his West Point high horse, Singleton said no fucking way. We're not going to obey that order, send us home, lock us up, whatever you want, man, but we're not going down the road.

That's how we found ourselves in the place I met my death.

All this is a cop-out. What I mean is I can't speak from this vantage, not honestly, and not without sifting it all through the retrospection of someone who is, or might be, as I said, gone. That terminal point came and went. That's what death is. You're taken away and a point is made—a pinpoint of anti-matter, if there is such a thing—until people forget you (I mean really forget) and your life as it was dissipates and evaporates, and then it becomes more of a fuzzy remnant of that terminal moment, and then eventually it's gone, a mossy tombstone, if you're lucky, that someone clears the weeds away to read the words of it, and then later not even that; just an overgrown field outside of Benton Harbor, Michigan, in my case—and then, of course, nothing. Yet theoretically that terminal point is still there. Anyway, the cop-out is that I bring myself up in the first place. After all, I'm gone. Trapped in that moment. That's how I imagine it—not on point, or even in the middle—the safe spot; the safest spot on recon, in the middle where you're not at the end or at the beginning but hunched down in a hole calling in coordinates for an air strike—I'll be this terminal memory for a while, as hard and cold as

anything in your mind, and then it'll get subsumed by the rest
of your life until it's smeared out and bloblike, if even that,
and then it'll be nothing much to you, a sliver of pain you carried through your life from one place to the other. All I could
do—weary, humping my weight in shit on my shoulders,
my feet caved in, the itch of jungle beyond annoying—was
imagine that point, make it up, and see what might transpire
as I tried to imagine it. We paused and stopped to catch our
breath in the middle of the jungle. How many clicks outside
Hue? I couldn't tell you. That battle was just a memory of
streets. A real vintage Second World War street fight; we'd
created what we could in the way of language around it, taking sips from the end of a rifle, good long hits of the best dope
we could fine, passing the peace pipe, until it was nothing but
a tangle: Frank praying over the bodies until his hips were
tired from genuflecting; he'd lean over and say his prayer and
then come up hollow-eyed and spiritless and say, Fuck God,
fuck him into the ground. I'd like to see him come down and
kiss my ass, I would. Where's Jesus when you need him? he'd
say. I'd take his cloak or shawl and yank it and say, Save us,
and he'd give me his shit and I'd say, Don't fuck with me,
man, just save me, and he'd say, Do you believe, and I'd say,
No, man, and he'd say, How much don't you believe, and I'd
say, Not at all, not much at all, not even much, not even at all,
and he'd smite me with his jagged bolt of energy, man, and
the fucker would fry us all with that bolt of energy he would
shoot out, and then Frank would lean over and spew vomit
and cry with shame and collect himself, going into the her-
mitage of his tent or foxhole tarp, and then he'd come out
cleaned up, refreshed, ready to disbelieve again, because he
was circular that way, and he'd start the routine over again
and did so until that day when Deek Johanson got zipped—
he was fresh meat, most certainly, but not that fresh, a month
in, and he and Frank were buddies, and when he got to Deek

he gave it all he got, did his cross and prayed, and then came up with his gun firing into the woods, drawing more fire, that fucker, until we were pinned down for a night because of his faith—before that we'd been slithery and quiet until Deek took a phantom shot, out of the blue, just some gook popping them randomly to keep us awake; took it by sheer chance in the head, a skull opened like a hardboiled egg in a cup (not the first one, I might add), so that what Frank was praying to was a skull spilling the cauliflower brain matter in the moonlight; did I mention it was moonlit that night, all glorious bright, so that movements could be easily detected? Everything in that hallowed colorless light, visible in texture and quality but not with colors; senseless in a way but completely sensible. The fire that Frank drew lasted for what seemed like an hour and sent us scrambling to reposition. Phantom gooks who could pass through trees. Amid all of it Frank crab-walked and then did a belly crawl back to us and, while we yelled at him to get fucking moving, he curled up, still in the fire zone, and buried his hands in his face and did that snort-gag-cry—the one a guy does when his buddy is killed, the one I'd do in the morning, at dawn light, when I lost Kingston, my buddy; the one they'd do for me—I could only imagine—when, in Hue, I was offed in the big fire bloom of misplaced napalm. (Don't get me wrong; not that I could foresee that exactly. I'll leave the fore-seeing to Eugene Allen. I'll let him conjure my life.) The napalm rounds came in halfheartedly, adrift on indeterminate axes, tumbling to the earth without the precision of a finned bomb; no careful target at hand; they just fell down from the sky tossed like coins, one after another, to spill fire into rect-angular zones of death and destruction and so on. There was an arrangement to the fire they produced, but it came only after the fire raged, one bomb into another, to form a mass that could and would be driven into form by the wind, if there was some wind, Vietnam wind.

What else could you do in a firefight but imagine the pos-sibilities at hand, just ahead?

Did I imagine my fate was just ahead of me? You bet I did. Did I stand there at dawn, a Nam dawn creeping across our weary faces and fleshing out the colors in the jungle, and imagine my death? You bet. Because what else could we do between firefights but try to foresee the possibilities at hand, all of them, including our own deaths? What else could we do? Along with imagining what it would be like to take you, Meg, into my arms and to nuzzle up against your warm sweet neck, to take your earlobe in my mouth.

Hank led her to the shore and went and got a towel from his ruck and dried her. Then he held her from behind as she leaned back into his arms. Then told her to rest and went for cigarettes. The beach seemed emptier than before, beneath the smoky white sky. It was a late spring, early summer beach with dark stones and black sand before a vast body of water, with a lone young woman hunching in a towel. Hank wanted to lift her out of her solitude, but he knew that he couldn't. His duty was to continue to protect her from Rake. It was that simple. He lifted his head, blew out smoke, and sniffed the air. The wind was coming down from the Canadian Shield and he could catch the scent of the boreal forest, the long, lonely, isolated strands of untouched forest, the last remain-ing purity. He had things he wanted to say, things that might make her feel better. He'd tell her that she reminded him of a balsam willow. It wouldn't mean much to her, but it would mean something to him. He felt limited in his ability to make metaphors beyond trees. He'd say a balsam willow. They make good smoke, they have uses if you know what they are. He'd tell her that maybe she was like a sandbar willow, because they were slightly forsaken, no board feet in the species, but they had good uses, made sweet smoke, great charcoal from the bark. Or maybe he'd go with the crack willow, because it was for baskets, for weaving, and even, if you worked the fibers the right way, pounded them down, for blankets.

When he got back to her she was crying into her open hands. She looked up and he could see in her gaze—the firmness of it—that she had unfolded something and that something had changed in her. She stood up and pulled him into an embrace. She felt firmer, stronger, and when she looked at him again her mouth was also set in a different way, not grim, not slack with sadness, but firm.

That felt good, she said. That felt really, really good. Someone spoke to me, and I know who he was and I think I understood most of what he was saying. Rake was part of it, and I'll explain it if I can, once I figure it out. I was part of something in the past—obviously—and it's up here, she said, touching her head. Her hair was tangled and beautiful, and the gooseflesh on her neck seemed to bring out the hidden paleness of her skin. A breeze was picking up now, and they just stood holding each other. Yes, a tree was calling to him from far up in Canada. He could taste the yellow pollen along with the dry residue of the shore. It wasn't that he knew exactly what she was going to say or do. She'd come out of the water, walking over the hard stones, bracing herself against the cold. It would not be enough to say she had awoken from the dream or terror that she had been moving through. There was more to it than that. When they finally let go of each other she was smiling, the freckles on her face around her eyes and on her cheeks, and he was smiling, too. Released from the embrace, she looked radiant, lovely, as perfect as anything nature had ever cooked up.

THE BLUE PILL KICKS

It was gonna happen, man. It was gonna happen because he was out there, testing the odds, making public appearances, driving around in an open limo, with Jackie at his side, doing the hand-wave, the little movement, halfhearted, just a flick of the wrist, all slo-mo, the way the motorcade moved—with the cops on choppers out front, clearing the way, checking the crowd for a sign of disgruntled vets, or Black Flag members in their jackets and colors; the president with his bright white smile, his shoulder sagging on the side where he had been hit the first time, a hunk missing, the bone gone. In retrospect, looking back—if they ever had time—they'd remember the tension in the air that day, the sky over Flint blazing with heat. When he got to her apartment, after hearing the news from someone in the Corps headquarters lobby, she was in the doorway waiting.

"I got the news and left right away. You must've been stuck in a meeting. They're saying the shot might've killed him this time," she said, pulling him into the living room. Her face was flushed from crying, but her eyes were angry, not sad, and as they held each other she kept saying, "Men kill fucking men."

"It's not that simple."

"Yeah, it's that simple now. Without something to enfold there's no enfolding. Men go out and make sure they have something to treat."

Outside, in the streets, there were shouts. The sound of breaking glass, far off. The phrase "national mourning" on the television, something about a dark day in a tone that seemed unbecoming in relation to the figure on the screen, the great Walter Cronkite, father of all authority, the most trusted man in America, as he took off his glasses, held them to the side, stared watery-eyed into the camera and, with his voice cracking, made the announcement that Kennedy had been shot again not far from Springfield, Lincoln's birthplace.

"We can't say we didn't see it coming," Singleton said. He went to the window and looked out. Below, a few people milled. Someone carried a bouquet of flowers, bright white, and someone else was placing another bouquet onto the edge of the ash heap. "We can't say we're horrifically sad."

"Well, I'm horrifically sad. And I want to do something about it," she said.

"He threw men into the fire and then felt guilty and had to face fear himself," Singleton said. He went into the kitchen, got a beer, checked the freezer for the pills and decided not to take them out—not yet, not until they'd been through some kind of tense deliberation, because the pills, whatever they were, seemed destined to be a point of contention. Back in the living room, she was in front of the television set, listening attentively.

"OK, I am sad," he said. It seemed like the right thing to say. If he didn't say it, he was one more soul dead to history. The buzz in his ears sang from one side of his head to the other. He went to the window and looked down and the street was now empty. The flowers, even brighter now, in the fading twilight, were piled on the edge of the heap. A few people leaned from their windows, looking out. When he turned she was gone, and he heard the freezer door open and shut, and when she came out she had the bag in her hands and was holding it out like an offering, or something tainted.

Twenty minutes later they lay in bed. He fingered the pills. They had talked it out, the sense that Kennedy had simply pushed it too far, the weird day, the way the streets had felt before the news came in, the tension in the air that they knew came only out of retrospect. It didn't seem to matter. She reached over and opened the drawer to her night table and took out a photograph, an old photo of the Zomboid, and held it up for him to examine: same sloppy smile, same long blond hair, but an eager and youthful face. He was standing straight and tall with his arm around Wendy. Does it matter if I see this and know what happened later; I mean, am I seeing what was or what was in relation to what happened? (She didn't say that, not exactly. In getting the photograph out, it seemed to be said. The photo was saying it.) The day had been weird, and maybe looking back, knowing that Kennedy would be shot is what made it weird, but that doesn't mean it wasn't weird, she explained, and he agreed, and they kissed. A deal was being sealed, he thought. From now on, this moment would be held between them, forever, even if they didn't stay together. There was a sense of intense deliberation, he thought. It was a pre-drug thing. It was what you felt when you were about to pop a mystery pill.

She put the photo back in the drawer and rolled over on the bed and took one of the pills from him and held it to her lips. Walter was still speaking on the television, his voice firm and resolute, talking about the need for calm, for a sense of national unity. Smoke drifted in from the window, and now and then there was, far off, the crackle of gunfire and sirens across the night. He held one of the pills to his own lips. The apartment seemed grimy and dank. He could feel the history of the place seeping through the cracked plaster, the old, worn-out millworkers who had come back to the rooms deranged from their suffering, broken-backed men who had worked to earn money to get out of this dump, for a future they might never see. It went unspoken between them, this sense of a shared past. They had both had fathers who worked the assembly lines.

"Here's to those who worked the lines," he said. "To our fathers and their fathers. To our mothers, too," he said, and then they counted to three and took the pills at the same time and sat in silence waiting for the kick. It was the pre-trip silence, the ticking of time measured in the potential of the high that would be coming, and he held her hand and twisted her fingers and stared forward into the darkening room while she did the same, and when, after five minutes, nothing happened, he said, Nothing, and she said, Nothing at all, not even a buzz, and they agreed that they had been duped, that Frank wasn't Frank.

The pills kicked as a field reporter outside some Illinois emergency room with his collar up around his trench coat, a drizzling rain collecting in droplets on his brow, claimed on the TV that Kennedy was dead. Side by side, like two teenage kids, they kissed each other and felt the immensity of the new situation, the taste of it, the long stretch of nerves to the surface of fingers and leg. He felt hard against the empty air. He could feel her tongue and her fingers, and at the same time he wasn't there at all, feeling nothing except the charge of energy from the pill, and then she was whispering nonsense to him, right into the buzz. She got on top of him—he was lifting, pushing his palms to receive her weight, and then there was a zero-gravity sensation, her motion matching his motion on what seemed to be totally equal terms. (His cock searched the wetness for a space of nothingness where love seemed to

reside—and his mind, oh Jesus Christ, his mind was in a glorious sustained suspension, no thought, nothing but a blank.)
She slid away to one side and he rolled with her and got behind
her with his hands holding on, as if holding the gunwales of a
rocking boat, and then, as she tossed her head and hair, he
began to come and to see the vision, and to smell a familiar
smell, ashen and chalky, limestone and mortar; he was inside
the vision and the vision was of a man, a soldier named Billy-T,
with a radiophone to his mouth, calling in coordinates, his
voice lisping as he shouted the numbers, and the man named
Rake (again), his face intense, and then the flash of heat and
fire and a far-off scream and the word *Hue*, and from Wendy a
coo that sounded like water over stones.

After a while, she said, fearfully, "Oh, God, God, I hope
that wasn't too much, too far."

"Vision not complete but vision beautiful, man, beautiful.
Rake and a man named Billy-T and fieldphone and flame. A
battle. In Hue, for sure. He called in an air strike and it hit
too close. A ball of fire and then a fizzle. A fizzle out."

"I'd like to do it again."

"But I can't," he said. He located an ability to reason inside his high, a rip current countering the tidal pull of the
drug. (Later, when he went back and tried to imagine how it
had felt on the blue pill, he found himself thinking of the easy,
persistent flow of water, following the easiest path.) He had
an awareness of the fuzzball of lost memory smoothed and
spread from ear to ear. He was still hard. If they did it again it
would be even better. He'd go double and unfold the unfolded
until a chain reaction began. Already he could see the blue
flashes in the pleasure of touching her neck—small sparkles
out of his fingers. She was saying she was sorry, sorry. He
heaved himself up out of bed, pushing through the high, and
then she was behind him, kneading his shoulders. They were

both in a zone of mutual pleasure beyond anything they had felt before, but it dissipated almost as quickly as it had arrived, with a kind of pop of the eardrums and a quick return to reality: the smelly room in a cheap boardinghouse and, outside, the firecracker snap of gunfire, the spiral of sirens, and the cellophane crackle of fire.

THE PLAN

It'll be even harder now that you have a better sense of your real self, now that you have some sense of your past. Harder to go back and act like Old Meg, because I'm seeing you right now and what I'm seeing isn't just New Meg but a new New Meg, he was saying, poking the fire. They had hiked a few miles along a footpath through the pine needles and a grove of trees planted in a neat formation, with the light shafting through the rows. On the beach, when she had cried in her hands, he had resisted the urge to question. When she looked up, Hank knew, just seeing her face, her teary eyes, that she had had a vision, caught sight of something that had been enfolded in her, the source of her trauma, and he could see it in the way she was walking, the shift of her gait, her toes pointed differently—with more assurance, he thought, a nimbleness on the trail, a sense of how to walk in the woods. The waves had seemed indrawn when he glanced back one last time, a looming quality in relation to the ones that hit the shore, shoving the stones in with a roar.

When a tree is damaged it forms a knot. You'll do the same, he told her. Not the old adage about a broken bone being stronger, but something different than that. Up the path, she led the way, as if they had a plan, but they'd didn't. Behind them clouds were gathering in the west and the wind was rising and the undersides of leaves were showing. The canopy overhead was shuddering, making long beautiful sighs, lifting and falling. She led the way to their old campfire—dead, a blank eye of coals surrounded by stones—and the flattened spot where the tent had been and, without a word, she began to roll out the tarp.

We'll stay here tonight and then we'll head back, he said. Rake's going to return soon.

He was shaking out the canvas, sweeping it clean with his palm, and he stopped and watched as she got a tent stake out of the canvas bag and held it the way you'd hold a knife.

Back on the beach, she said, I became aware of the sound of a wave. Did you hear it, too?

I'm sure I did, he said. Her statement was strange but not that unusual. Her senses would be improved with each unfolding, until, if she went too far, she went over some edge into an acuteness that was beyond normal. Then she'd be raging around like Rake, seeing portents and signs in the way a dog shook his leg when he pissed, of the angle of a doorjamb, or whatever . . . it didn't really matter, he thought, looking at her.

Well, I mean I was aware of the sound it made, coming in low in a shush from one side and then sliding to the other.

They built the fire together, gathering wood and piling it neatly. He showed her the best way to get the kindling, small curls of bark, not too much to hurt the tree. It has a desire to burn because the tree has a desire to help, is the way I see it, he said.

You're weird, she said. I mean you're really, really weird.

You're getting better, he said. That's a good sign, hearing you say that.

So you're not going to deny it?

What you have with me is a man who has given himself the treatment but who was probably weird before he had it. Which is to say, before I treated myself I was still able to smell trees and to lumber run with the best of them, but I was too busy with violence of one kind or another to properly attend to my obligation to nature herself. I hate to put it that way, but that's the way I put it.

They boiled some water and cooked pasta and he found a can of sauce in his bag and pulled it out and they heated it. When they were finished eating, they waded through the brambles down to the stream and cleaned the pot and plates.

This used to be a famous fly-fishing river, he said. No one really fished in it, but a writer used it in a story and made it into something it wasn't, so for a few years people would come and give it a try, but it was too brambly, too rough, and you couldn't cast far enough without getting snagged unless you knew the exact right spot.

He resisted mentioning the balsam willow until later that night, when they were holding each other, drinking whiskey, watching the fire and listening to the flames. Then he told her—clearing his throat, taking a deep gulp of whiskey—that he had wanted to say it back on the beach, right after she came out of the water, that she was like a balsam willow, or maybe a sandbar willow, or better yet, a tree that you can't even find here in Michigan, but the guys—the grunts, or whatever you want to call them—have in Nam a tree called *sao den*, or better, its nickname, "black star," because that's a tree that somehow resists termites, he said.

What are you saying? she said.

I'm just saying you're going to be strong enough to resist, Rake. You know it now more than before. It's going to be a very fine line—the act you'll have to perform when we get back there.

You're really weird, she said again.

Maybe I am. But I'm not the first. In India, some folks marry trees. They go through a ceremony and hitch for life. Anyway, you seeing me as weird only means you're getting better.

If seeing that you're weird means I'm better, then I'm much better, she said. Then she began to talk about the vision. Her voice was a whisper. She said she'd heard a young man speaking, and as soon as she heard him speaking she saw his face. He'd been in Nam.

He leaned back and waited for her to say more. She spoke now clearly, with assurance and in a voice that was, he thought, much more musical. The guy in her vision was someone she had been in love with—she left that vague—and he had gone to fight. Something had happened and Rake had been involved.

Rake was involved, he repeated.

Rake in my unfolded vision, yes.

So this guy must've been with Rake, over in Nam. Maybe Rake knows that so he goes into the Grid and gets you and brings you out. He doesn't know what he's going to do with you, but he knows you have a connection with something in his past, with some little residual shred of honor he still feels, or a sense of mission. If he knew exactly what it was he would've dunked you in ice, or worse, unless he's done worse and I don't know about it. Maybe there's another factor involved, something else, a promise to somebody he made over there that he has to fulfill. He might not even know because when they tried to treat him they just doubled his trauma and made it so intense.

Rake knows something, she said. The wind was lifting again and, far off, thunder. She was beginning to weep.

The rumor, he thought, was that if you unfold a little bit, the right amount, you could take what you saw and work back from it and very carefully—without all of the trauma coming at once in a rush that would make you sick again— tweeze it out, gently, the way you'd peel an onion, or remove a splinter. If you want to live a life that is stable and decent and good, you maybe go in and let a little bit come and then do it only that once and that's it.

Don't say any more, he said gently. He had his arm around her shoulder and felt her easing against him. He would have to resist all he could not to touch her any more than this, he thought.

Later, as they lay in the tent listening to the rain, he explained that they needed storms to cull the dead growth but also to sway them so they'd dig deeper with roots. He explained that nothing was meaningless when it came to trees because they were too smart to play games; they had a resolve that came from a blunt, brutal, natural being. That's what I am, Meg. You'll see that more and more as you see more and more, he said, and she put her finger to his lips and whispered shut up and kissed him gently.

I still don't understand. Why don't you leave, or do something? she said.

Like I said, I can't kill him because to kill him I'd risk becoming who I was before. Not that I don't want to. I mean I have the impulse, believe me, but if I do it it'll be a betrayal of my new self. I'm biding my time, I'll admit, partly because MomMom won't leave the house because the house is her house. It's the house my father will return to—if he ever returns.

She kissed him again and had a flash—lightning—and saw Billy-T, his face in the sun, the bright shadow-lit beach sun, just a few inches from her own. They were on the beach on Lake Michigan, up in a cove, with the razor grass all around.

In the morning I'll have a better plan, he said, his voice far-off, sleepy. The storm had passed and the thunder was to the east, bouncing off the copper deposits and the cold stone coves of the lake, and then it was gone and she was drifting against him, and together, amid his beloved pines, they slept.

TERMINATION REPORT

Outside, the streets were tense; small pockets of violence had already broken out in response to the news about Kennedy. Police were posted on corners and powder-blue sawhorse barricades were in place—a shit-storm was coming, it all said—but the Corps, determined to maintain decorum, had called a meeting. So far, official word of the president's death hadn't come down. His body had been whisked away to another hospital: the only images afloat were of an ambulance backed into a loading bay, a gurney being removed, men in suits guarding the way. Singleton sat with Klein at the wide conference table on the second floor listening to an agent named Hogarth, an expert on rumor formation, reading from an index card, giving a brief about a rumor that had started in Kentucky.

Hogarth had the demeanor of an FBI agent, a quality of knowing more than he needed to know about things that he'd be better off not knowing. Also at the table was a trainee named Ambrose, who, according to Wendy, had published a book or two before his number came up. He wore Ben Franklin–type glasses and looked too delicate for fighting.

Probably a 3A who'd worked as a dental assistant or stared at fuzzy U-2 photos.

The new rumors, Hogarth said, had started in Kentucky and then moved up the Ohio River basin before somehow making a big skip all the way to northern Michigan. He snapped his phrases as if to combat the stultifying buzz of the fluorescent lights. Klein, dressed in full uniform, fiddled with his pencil and nodded. Vets were tripping and dropping double doses and unfolding beyond the fold point—to put it in layman's terms, Hogarth said. Some of them hadn't been in combat; some of them were playing out delusional fantasies of traumas they hadn't experienced.

He packed up his file and left the room.

"Philpot, you're up," Klein said. The room tightened in anticipation of another long-winded report, and as if in response a pop of gunfire came in through the window glass. Philpot, with his sweet-sounding Harvard voice, was known as a blowhard with a wide-spanning jargon vocabulary. But there was an uptick of attention as he shuffled his papers. Across the table, the agent named Ambrose yawned, patted his mouth dramatically, caught Singleton's eyes, and winked.

Philpot said that there had been no further sightings—killings—by the failed enfold Rake (last name: unknown) since the report, dubiously pinned to him, of a mass murder near Alpena. The problem was that the public seemed to need to blame the Corps for these failed status problems, and that many of the untreated renegades out there were leaving clues clearly meant to indicate that the crime had been committed by someone who had been through the treatment.

Philpot went on to explain that not only was the public pinning random acts of violence on failed enfolds, but failed enfolds were figuring out that they could get their own acts of violence—and he admitted that this was pure speculation—

pinned on fake failed enfolds, and thereby cast doubt in the minds of the Corps. In other words, it was starting to become impossible, unless you were acutely attuned to the nuances, to identify acts committed by honest failed enfolds.

"Nice work," Klein said, cutting him off. "Before we go, I'd like to brief you on Rake. These are internal rumors, of course, but some people say a body has been found and that the body was identified as Rake, and that his name, his real name, was Ron Martin, at least according to his dog tag. I want to bring this rumor to your attention because that's all it is. If there's a file on it somewhere, I don't know about it, and if there's a file I don't know about, it can't be a real file but rather one of those generated in order to make sure someone out there maintains enfolded status; in other words, I know we don't talk about this openly—at least they don't in Relations, and I'm sure they don't in other departments—but from time to time we have to fictionalize a background report in order to make sure the patient is never at risk of exposure.

"I want you all to know," he continued, his voice booming, his medals swinging. "I believe the rumors to be unfounded. We're going to continue on course and go after failed enfolds as mandated. Until I see Rake's body for myself, I'm going to operate as if he's still alive. And if I say he's alive, he's alive."

Out in the hall, after the meeting, Ambrose approached Singleton. "Come with me. I've got some information for you."

They went into the bathroom. The sinks were dripping and the toilet valves gargled. The bathroom had inlaid tiles and fixtures that seemed absurdly out of keeping with the rest of the building.

Ambrose put a briefcase on the edge of the sink and began unbelting it.

"I've got the information you asked for," he said.

"I didn't ask for information."

"You don't know you asked for this, but you did, if you know what I mean. I'm a trainee like you, so I know you'd ask me for this if you knew I had it. I mean, if you knew what I know, you'd want to know."

Ambrose bent down to peer under the doors of the stalls. "You go in that one," he whispered. "And I'll go in that one, and I'll pass it under to you and you look at it and then give it back," he whispered.

"Are you kidding?" Singleton said.

"No funny business," Ambrose said. "I'll save the funny business for another day."

Ambrose's voice rose slightly into a sweet register and Singleton had another flash: a young man, dressed in a billowing white shirt and high-waisted pants, lounging on a bench in Central Park, posed for a photo on the back of a book, a book he had read just after treatment, on the back porch of his apartment.

"Are you the guy who wrote the book?"

"Yeah, I'm that guy. I'm the one who wrote the book Kennedy had on his bedside table around the time he was shot the first time. Now let's get back to business. Go in that stall and I'll go in the other and when the coast is clear you'll see why I made you come in here."

"Jesus, just give it to me."

"Get in the stall," he said.

In the stall there was the kind of shit smell you could taste, the kind that stayed with you forever—beyond microbial, some residual cosmic aftermath emanating from deep space.

A dainty hand curled up under the partition. It clutched and opened and then disappeared again.

"You OK over there?" Singleton said.

"Shush, we have to make sure the coast is clear."

"If you say that again it's not going to be clear. We've been in here for about five minutes."

The file was taupe-colored, with the TOP SECRET stamp. It was coded TERMINATED. It had the blue label of an operation report.

"Open it, look, and give it right back while I do my business," Ambrose whispered.

"Christ," Singleton said.

He opened the file and read the report quickly. The target, Rake (a.k.a. name unknown. Speculation as to Ron Martin), had been located (see photo) dead in Mackinaw City.

"Where'd you get this?" Singleton whispered.

"When you work in Terminations, you tend to have access to termination files, my friend. That's Rake."

Clipped to the upper-right-hand corner of the top document—the case outline—was a small photo, taken in a photo booth somewhere. The face was thin and reminded Singleton of Vincent Price, a Vandyke beard and beady eyes and a ten-thousand-mile gaze. It was a face to go with the stench. This was a guy who maintained the same expression day after day, until his very skin conformed to it. Deeper in the file was a larger photo with a termination stamp, smeared slightly, and a note scrawled on the back: target Rake (Ron Martin), see note on dog tag located; body discovered in Mackinaw City, Michigan.

"Hand it back," Ambrose said. "Got to get back to the post-briefing. Just wanted you to see this," he said.

"Hold on," Singleton said. He stared at the photograph and began to skim the report—body positioned against a tree . . . Suicidal ideation . . . Near Ft. Michilimackinac . . . Terminated case . . .

Someone came into the bathroom—a throat clearing, the heel-toe click of dress shoes. The hand flashed under the wall of the stall and Singleton gently put the report in it. He heard

Ambrose close the briefcase and flush the toilet. He heard Ambrose leave his stall.

"Hello, sir," Ambrose said.

"You didn't have anything to add at the meeting?" Klein said. "I didn't expect someone from Terminations to contribute, but you might want to think—and this is advice, son, man to man, about making a pretense of giving a shit. When I mentioned that Rake wasn't terminated, you could've at least given your two cents, argued your case, or given me a nod. That's my advice, man to man."

"Sir, yes, sir."

In the lobby she was waiting, silent and alone, by the revolving door. The lobby was full of energy, more movement than usual. He fought the urge to grab her hand, but he risked a nod and a look that said: Follow me, you're not going to believe what I have to say. When the moment was right, he'd give her the news. As far as the Corps was concerned, they were tracking a dead man. The face in the file, at least the one clipped to the file, and the face in his unfolding flashbacks were the same, a perfect match with a memory from a dream.

Outside, in the blunt, brutal light of day, her face looked pale and frightened. She wanted to get to her father as fast as possible, to get him and get out of town. They made their way past a police barricade—the cops nodding them through checkpoints.

"It's time to get out of here, Sing. Time to get to my father and head north."

"We'll be AWOL, we'll be in deep shit."

"This is deep shit," she said. She had his hand and was pulling him down the street. There was smoke to the east where fire trucks dodged sniper fire and the police and the National Guard were taking control-march formation. The lower part of the state had been fueling up with riot potential for months: one spark, everyone had been whispering, one single spark was all it would take. Even Klein had mentioned it weeks ago—he thought, getting behind the wheel—saying something about Franz Ferdinand, an alignment of forces set to explode. Maybe we don't have a man like Franz Ferdinand, but we've got Kennedy. He was standing at the window, staring out. It's going to explode when the president explodes, he added. But our job here is not to pay attention to the external political or social factors but to keep our eye on the certain targets.

CONG

Vietcong put heads on sticks, cutting them not neat and guillotine-style but in a way that leaves the necks shaggy, Rake was saying. He was at the kitchen table and MomMom was cooking and there was a claustrophobia that seemed to come from the smell of the frying food and his intensity, his fists balled, his eyes shifting from Meg to Hank and then to Haze and then to Meg and Hank again as they tried not to listen, to remain calm. They sat across from him at the table, hands folded in their laps, listening as he explained how he and Haze had taken out an entire picnic, done the head-on-stick thing. He asked them to imagine four or five kids playing in the grass away from the picnic blanket, away from the parents. Then he asked them to imagine the folks with a thermos bottle, a wicker basket—people who should know better than to let their kids run with butterfly nets, people who have suspended their fear for the sake of hope.

He was probing, it seemed to Hank, testing for a reaction, but some of his jitteriness seemed directed at Haze, whose hair seemed longer now, hanging down into his eyes, parted like curtains to reveal shriveled eyes that had trouble focusing, drifting slightly. Whatever had happened on this run had taken some toll on the young kid, sapped whatever little strength he had before, and there was a new scar up in his scalp, a patch of missing hair as white as chalk. Rake was saying that it would be easy to imagine the Corps seeing the heads on sticks and knowing it was him for sure, and then he pounded his fists on the table—the silverware jumped, MomMom jumped, Haze blinked, Meg stayed perfectly still, staring straight ahead. MomMom came over with a pan and served him cabbage. He took a bite and spat it out and was at the stove before Hank could get up. She fell to the floor and began to kick her feet. Lord, Lord, she said. Rake kicked her and she began to speak in a crazed tongue, her words half-formed, and she began quoting fragments of the Bible at random, senselessly drawing from the book, saying, Go forth and blow the trumpets into the fortified cities! A lion has come from his thicket to waste your land!

Get her up and out of here. Put her in the yard, do whatever you do to shut her up. If she's going to speak in tongues, let her do it tied up out there, Rake said. He picked a pot from the stove and held it over MomMom's head and said, Get up, old lady. Get up or you'll get some of this slop you call food in the face.

I'll take care of her, Hank said. He spoke calmly, with deliberation. There was a sudden tense silence in the kitchen—the drip of the faucet, the sound of birds far off in the trees. MomMom grew still, hardly breathing, her big gray eyes staring straight up.

You do that, Rake said. You be a good son and tend to your loving mother. But before you do that you look me in the eye and say you're not on her side. You show me that in your eyes so I can see, he said, and they looked at each other and to keep his focus Hank thought of a man chopping into a thousand-year-old sequoia. Then he envisioned two men and a long saw working back and forth while the tree cried and sprayed phonemes that would catch the breeze and ride across the Great Plains, touching the goldenrod and the quack grass until it reached Wisconsin, where the other trees, tasting it, gave out their own anguished cry and released a blast of pollen that, on the same breeze, rode to the shore of the Atlantic Ocean. He put into his eyes his hatred of the men who cut that particular tree. It allowed him to forget his mother.

Out in the yard MomMom was babbling about the mercy of the Lord, about Jesus on the cross, about the wounds and the blood and the pain of the crown; something about a cave, about pissing in the wind, about King David, and then she was crying in the chair, her hands bound lightly, rocking slightly from side to side.

When they put me in that chamber—we're talking down in New Mexico, in some big aerodrome-type thing that they used to use for war blimps or whatever—this was in that scrubby desert, must've been somewhere near Santa Fe. They put me in chains, really tight because they knew I could pull a Houdini, and they took me on a train from there through the desert, up toward the mountains, and then they put me in with all kinds of half-assed props and such, guns and mortar rounds, but with blanks, Rake said a few nights later. They were in the yard. He stopped speaking and lit his cigar, rolling it in the flame, and Hank watched his face, a primitive death mask in the darkness.

Anyway, they put me in a fake firefight and a double dose of Tripizoid—the guard told me that much—and I just laughed and popped off rounds from the blank gun, and then they tried a tie-and-torture routine, using a Phantom Blooper type, an American over to the other side, who spoke perfect Yankee English but was in NVA gear—and the torture thing wasn't faked; they must've seen in the test they ran—when we took breaks they kept me handcuffed—that they would have to go the extra mile on me to get me properly enfolded. Man, they doubled down, and when I laughed that off they stuck me in a cell and the next day they put me back in the combat reenactment and I began to fake it, made a full-blown art of it. You see, I did all that to earn their trust.

He turned to Hank in the dark and spoke in a low voice, as if sharing a secret.

You'd know about earning trust, wouldn't you, Hank?

Hank stared at the faint outline of trees and brush in the moonless dark.

I'd know about what it's like to make damn sure I look like I give a shit, he said. If that's what you're saying.

I feel like killing something, Rake said. He got up and crossed the yard to the shed, the coal of his cigar an orange point, and when he came back he had the ax.

You feel like killing something?

Sure, I feel like killing, Hank said, resisting the urge to wrest the ax from Rake's hand and put it into his head, to unfold and feel the old primeval rage retroactively. To kill and then locate the impulse to kill in the act itself.

You're thinking this is some kind of test, Rake said.

No. I don't think you're the type to test, Hank said, rubbing his sweaty palms on his pants. I think you're the type to go ahead and make a move. He stood up in front of Rake and waited. He knew that one wrong move and Rake would be upstairs in the house, raising the ax over Meg.

I think you're the kind of man who strikes first and takes a look at the ramifications later. And I'm the same kind of man, Rake. So if what you're saying is you think I'm a different man, or that I betrayed you somehow with Meg, out there on my run, then we might as well kill each other right here, he said. Then Rake had his arm on his shoulder and they were hugging, saying fuck fuck, and Rake was still saying, I want to kill something. He took the ax and went back to the shed, with Hank following beside him, and killed the new dog with one swift chop, a jangle of chain and a single, soft yelp, and then he stepped away and Hank, who felt sorrow akin to a tree sorrow, followed him back to the chair and had another drink. In the false camaraderie, Hank imagined winning an acting award, hoisting the trophy into the air as he thanked his beloved Meg for being with him when he needed it, and MomMom for all her demented wisdom, and the stars in the sky and then, finally, above all, the trees for being such good role models over the years, strong and stable and outside of the human realm, and when he laughed he did it from his belly and Rake joined in.

RUMORS AFLOAT

Summer had begun to push north through tense days. The days seemed long, with the sun coming up early and setting late, but they weren't that deep into the summer. What was it? Late June? Early July? Nights were still cool, but in the middle of the day, in the seething tension and silence, the sun baked the grass in the yard and curled the leaves in the trees. A stench of decay wafted in from the shore, because things were dying in the sun, rotting all around the state. On the beach blackflies were rising into the sky in swarms from the crags along the shore, spinning outward and coming back together like migrating birds. There was the smell of the dog, too.

He was watching her bury a dog again, out by the shed. He leaned down and looked at the hole. It was deep and wide— deep enough for the dog. He needed more time so he told her to keep going. When she took another break he looked into the hole again and spoke softly. Look, Rake's wound up more than usual, and his suspicions are high. I think we can take advantage of his state, channel it back at him somehow.

He gave her a soft swat on her back and watched as she put her heel on the shovel and tried hard not to look at the remains of the dog, sagging but not part of the earth yet, just like the other dog but sadder this time. The smell was fantastic, burning into the nose and staying there.

I'm getting scared of you, she said. Nothing moved on her face and he saw that she was completely serious. Her shoulders were pink from the sun and he longed—more than anything in the world—to touch them, to run his fingers along her back, to pull her up against his chest and feel her looking up at him in a sweet release from fear. He gazed around the yard and saw Haze in the trees, standing as straight and still as a Buckingham Palace guard. His eyes and face were in shadow, but he was watching carefully. Suffering seemed to slip into him and stay there forever; he knew how to hold himself when it came to military-style actions. He had gained back some of the weight he had lost on his last run. On the other side of the yard, MomMom was again taking laundry down and putting it in a basket, wooden pins in her mouth, and then taking the same sheets she'd folded and putting them back up again, pinning them in a long line—standing back and walking along amid them, weaving through them as they sailed in the wind—and then taking them down and repeating the process.

It wasn't true, but he thought he saw this in her eyes, as she looked at him without blinking, anger and fear and something terrible, some judgment: Why don't you do something, or let me do something. To bide time in a strategic manner is foolish beyond a certain point, and if you could remember your war experience you'd know that for a fact. And he wanted to say (but he couldn't, with Haze in the woods, watching) that he was sure that what he was waiting for would come. He was trusting his instincts: a sense, deep, deep inside—tied most likely to his love of trees—that told him that when things got to a terrible climax they would somehow resolve in a plan of action. He lost his train of thought and pushed her away and ordered her to dig deeper, because Rake had shouted something from the upstairs window, not a word, at least not anything discernible, but a barking sound, or a howl.

I'm watching you, he said, to Haze, cornering him in the yard that evening, trying to bore into the kid's eyes, to put the fear in him and make sure he knew where he was situated in the structure of things, but the kid just returned his look and said, Well, I'm watching you watch me, and he got up and stood shirtless, his chest concave and hairless. He was jittery in a way that suggested he was going to try something soon. Inevitability was implicit in his distance, his hanging back on the margins of the yard, hidden in the brush, or in the shed doorway, back far enough to be hidden in shadow.

I see what you're doing, Haze said. I know you and that girl are up to something.

Hank threw an uppercut—he felt good doing this and imagined (but wasn't sure) that he had a memory of boxing somewhere, a club back in Detroit, the swat of leather against a bag, the echoey glove-on-glove slap of men sparring—that struck the kid in the jaw. Then he followed with a jab and watched him as he flopped to the ground and looked up with a smile smeary with pink.

That was a sucker punch, he said. That second one. The first one I saw coming.

You're lucky I didn't hit you in your good eye, and you're lucky I don't kill you right now, Hank said.

Who says I can see out of the eye? Haze said. Who says it's my good eye?

I says, Hank said. And I'm telling you to be careful what you see.

If it sees, it's gonna see what it wants to see.

That's what I'm saying. Everything that eye needs to see

has been seen, he said, and then for good measure he aimed a kick into the kid's chest and left him squirming in the yard to consider his place in the pecking order and how easily it could shift—the same as the wind blowing up the sheets—with a sudden movement of flesh. Exhausted, he walked into the trees so the kid couldn't see how he was sweating. Instilling fear wasn't his way. Old Hank would've felt a surge of joy, he speculated. His ears were buzzing. Through the trees he could sense the lake, beyond, throwing itself urgently into the sky. Out there his old memories rested, waiting to be reclaimed.

They could feel it, a tightening sense of doom in the long afternoons. Rake sorted on the kitchen table, picking the pills up one by one, holding them to the light for inspection, placing them in bags, and then he sat in the yard drinking, expounding on his need for speed and the rumors he'd been picking up (or so he claimed) on his drives in the morning to connect (so he claimed) with Black Flag members. One of the rumors concerned a duel up on Isle Royale, a formal confrontation between two grunts who had fought in the same unit and had betrayed each other during a reenactment, the same way they had betrayed each other when they were deployed. They'd shot each other dead, and their seconds, the guys who helped coordinate the duel, got into it and offed each other, too, but the cops or some investigative agents from the Corps had found the setup, the handkerchief that one of the seconds used to start the duel and the rope that was the line between them, and there'd been witnesses, too, he explained, his eyes bright with excitement. Rumors of the double-enfold, double-dose of Tripizoid that Black Flag members used as they reenacted battles so intense they went insane and had to fight them over and over again. Rumors that Canada was trying to establish a new kind of Corps, something to counter Kennedy's vision, a group that would reenact with a different, better drug, something that didn't leave even a trace, a fuzzball. The rumors went in and out of mouths until they somehow reached Rake, who went out—random times, random modes, random ways—and came back to fill the air with talk, his voice gleeful as he described Oswald's twin, who was making a final salute and taking aim, following the president as he toured the Midwest again. Don't fuck it up this time, Rake shouted. We're counting on you to do what the rumor fucking says you're gonna do.

Whenever she arose out of the stupor of the drugs, it came to her that she had been in love with the guy in her vision when she was seventeen or eighteen. She remembered that sadness of knowing he would be gone and lost forever, one way or another.

From the vision she'd had underwater, she connected to another memory she had, a boy on the beach, in the dunes on Lake Michigan, his body young and lean in the sun, his eyes liquid blue and squinting, the sweet smile with which he'd closed in for a kiss, a breeze blowing over them and shifting the razor grass, the salty taste of his kisses, and she knew—in bed, alone, trying to extract meaning from the voice she'd heard—that he was, in the memory, heading soon to Vietnam. His number had been called, and this was one of the last days they'd spend together.

Billy-T, Hank said, when she mentioned his name. That rings a bell. I feel like I know that name for sure although I have to admit I don't know it the way I should know it except I do somehow—and I'll admit that maybe I'm just imagining that there's a connection, Meg, maybe I'm just taking a hopeful spark that doesn't exist and turning it into a lament that has something to do with something I've lost. It's a name stuck in whatever I enfolded when I treated myself. That's what I like to think.

Hank, she said softly. You're long-winded. Did you know that?

I do know that, he said.

They were on the porch. He had her hands tied and they knew that Rake would appear at any moment. He went out and came back at random intervals, but there was still a rhythm to his movement, and his car had a bad muffler and, if the wind was right, was audible from a half mile away.

It bothers me that I think I know the name, he added. But if I know it, it's likely that Rake knows it, too. There must be a connection. It tempts me to try to unfold a little bit of myself, to get in there and poke around.

He comes at night to my room and when he's touching me I want to scream because I'm sure he wants to kill me. He talks to me and he talks to me and I can tell he's wondering if something in me unfolded, and he wants to know what it is and he's fishing around for it. We have to do something.

We'll take action soon.

He led her down the trail toward the water. The afternoon air was sweet and soft. They stopped for a moment and listened for footsteps behind them. At the fork he took her to the right, a path that ran through forest to a clearing—he left her hands tied just in case. In the clearing a small brook bubbled up to the surface. He scanned around again and then hunched down to scoop some water, washing his face, and he loosened her ropes, let them hang, and told her to take a drink. She drank and splashed her face and when she came back up she was smiling. He nodded and retied her hands and they continued along the trail for about half a mile, cutting down to the soft, sandy soil, along the low-growing shrubs and razor grass and then along rockier ground until they got to a cut in the headland, a path in the embankment, a natural way to the shore. He stopped her and smelled the air, listening to the sigh of the surf, and then took her by the hand—gently, softly twisting his fingers against hers, holding her so their arms were touching—down to the beach, where he loosened the ropes and then pulled them away. The stones on the beach were dried white, coated with powder, except where breakers had come in, forming black tongues, and when they walked they kicked them over and blackflies swirled. There was a strong fishy odor drifting from the west—he took a deep breath—where alewives had died en masse, washed up in clots, a stench, when it drifted in, so persuasive it seemed to be saying something.

There might be something in the rumor about men having duels, she said, swiping the flies off her arm, shaking them out of her hair. He's mentioned it a few times, so he's thinking a lot about it.

Hank looked out at the water, his voice low and weary. Well, a duel is an arrangement, a formality, an unnatural structure around death. It's a way to solve disputes. It's a way to make sure two men shoot at each other no matter what. It doesn't make sense that men up there, trying to reclaim their glory days, would resort to duels. It seems too orderly. Too pat. But then maybe that's why it's a rumor and not necessarily true. Maybe it's something hoped for, deep down. Not by Rake but by whoever's out there dreaming. Someone thought about duels and then they imagined a story behind it, or they were delusional and believed what they imagined, something like that.

He knew what he was feeling—a chill went through him and he shivered. He was resisting the urge to unfold himself, to reverse the treatment he had given himself, to go back to the water, to put his feet in the lake, to dive all the way in and hold himself under. He sat next to her and looked at the sky, at the pearly whites and heavy grays and deeper silvers out to the horizon, gripping the water as it reached up—close in color, not too different—and the sky reached down to form a slice of deeper dark where the two met, and the heavy waves, closer in, lumbering slowly with large gaps between as if avoiding each other, and he could hear—in the sound of the waves, in the lift of the wind—the way it spoke to the trees behind them, and the trees were speaking back, with a deep sigh, carrying the far-off scent of wide, boreal forests in the high reaches of the Canadian Shield, where an answer to the eternal question was forming.

RETURN

It takes two to fight and five to riot, Singleton thought, struggling to keep his attention on the road as they drove to her father's house. Kids were throwing rocks, darting out of yards with their arms raised, aiming at whatever was moving. The trick was to keep to a moderate speed, not too fast to kill someone if they ran out, but fast enough to scare, and it was important to stay on the side streets—empty, sad-looking, arched over with trees.

"Didn't your old man have some kind of escape plan?"

Wendy stared ahead and said, "He said he'd stick it out. We'll have to drag him out. It's going to take force."

"Good old force," Singleton said, abstractly.

The horizon was a rubber gasket of dark clouds. Looters were gathering.

"He's incredibly stubborn. He's been through a lot. He'll see this as one more thing to go through."

She spun the radio dial through static and signals of the Emergency Broadcast System. Finally she found Iggy All the Time, another spin of *Fun House*, the beat quicker than usual because the turntable was fast. Iggy's voice had a fresh manic edge. Two blocks from Wendy's house, they passed kids lugging cans of gasoline. A block later, they passed the kid in the yard, the one who had been striking the charge pose, and he turned with his middle finger raised.

"L.A. Blues" ended but the needle stayed skipping and popping into the runout groove.

Her father's house sat serenely amid the unusually green trees. The Zomboid sat in his wheelchair with a rifle on his lap, the wind ruffling his long blond hair. As they pulled to the curb he raised one hand, slowly, and made a victory sign. Wendy put her hands over her face and sighed, sliding down.

"Peace," he shouted. "It's good to see the Cav arrive to save the day. Never too late, never on time." He wheeled himself forward, pressing his foot supports against the chain link.

"Guess he got the use of his hands back," Singleton said. They watched him back up and shove against the fence again.

"He's always had the use of his hands. Believe me, he knew how to use his hands." Her voice was low and sad. "I should go and say how sorry I am that we can't take him along with us. I should reconcile with him somehow. But I can't do it."

"Man, the sound of a skipping needle," Singleton said. "You go in and talk with your father. Tell him we're heading north and we need him with us for support, armed support. Make sure he understands we're heading on a mission. Throw him a bone. Make him feel he'll be part of something big."

She got out of the car walked up the path. He dragged his duffel into the front seat, unzipped it, and took the gun out from beneath a pair of pants. He snapped open the chamber, checked it, snapped it shut, and sighed because his hand felt a kinship with the crosshatch, no-slip surface of the grip, the heft. He thought of Rake's face in the file, the face in the dream. He tucked the gun into his pants and pulled his shirt down and got out of the car and stood in the evening light. There was a faint tannic smell in the air. In the yard the Zomboid, his hands lax on his gun, called out, "Wait, man, wait. Come over here, man, and help a fellow out."

At the fence he saw that the Zomboid's eyes were slightly off in some kind of high.

"You're packing, man. I saw your gun."

"I'm not packing."

"You can't fool me. My own eyes saw you in the car."

"What do you want?"

"You see these hands? They're of no use to me. On occasion they come to life, but for the most part they're attached to my arms, and my arms are dead. Maybe my hands are fine and the arms are dead so my hands won't work. Or maybe it's the other way around. How would I know?"

"You got ahold of that gun, somehow."

"My old lady put it there for me and told me to guard the fort."

"Where is she?" Singleton scanned the lot—the same accumulation of garbage, old bed springs, a car chassis (on blocks), and a double set of ruts from one corner of the yard to the other and then from the house to the fence, forming a cross.

"She split to Port Huron to pick something up. Then she's going to truck her ass over to Sarnia, Canada, where her folks are from."

"You're alone?"

"I'm alone, partner. I need a hand. If you could just position the gun higher, I'd appreciate. Lean it on my shoulder so it looks menacing. I've done it before. Scared the fuckers off. Nothing scarier than a guy in a wheelchair with a gun."

Singleton went through the gate and gently shook the Zomboid's hand. It felt dead.

"Up against my right shoulder," he said. "Lift my arm up slightly and I'll use the dead weight to hold it in position. Then when they come I'll heave my ribs—because I can at least do that much, for Christ's sake—and the gun'll fall into position. I'll depend on the luck of gravity to make it look like I have the complete and full control of my faculties." His eyes, two dried-up beads in a sea of tears, were set deep below the dirt and grime of his brows.

"You sure you can't will those hands to work?" Singleton said.

"I was sure the hands were dead the second that RPG hit my ass, man. The minute I was in the air, I knew. Legless slash handless. Right up there, spinning head over heels, I knew what was coming."

Singleton backed away a few steps, gave a salute, and then went back around to Wendy's house while the Zomboid shouted, "You're going to at least back me up, right? You're gonna help a fellow out, enfolded or not . . ."

The picture on the television was in disarray, not only riding the vertical but also twisting around an invisible pole, as if trying to straighten itself out but failing because the main towers were down and the station was on backup. The old man was sitting in a massive easy chair, a rifle on his knees. A cigarette was burning in the ashtray next to a glass of something—it looked like scotch—with ice. He had a grim look, working his jaw side to side.

"Don't explain why you're here," he said, glancing at Wendy. "Wendy, you go upstairs and check through your room to see if there's anything you want to save. I've got a good plan and I'm sure we can hold out here for a while, and maybe save the place."

"I don't think there's anything I want," Wendy said.

"Just do it for me. It'll make me feel better knowing that you went and took one last look. Look in my room, too, and see if there might be something of your mother's you want."

He waved her away and reached for his drink. "This is just a precautionary measure. I don't mean to scare her, but you can't go fooling yourself in these situations." He lifted the rifle and sighted through the scope and held aim on the television.

"I can see that you're thinking this old man's crazy to think he might have a chance. You're standing there—and this isn't a friendly visit, we aren't going to sit at the table again and trade stories—thinking I want one last hurrah. But let me tell you, you're wrong. I'm just helping out that kid next door, with his wheelchair and his gun and his delusions. He thinks I'm going to go up into the attic and snipe while he lures them in. They'll hesitate to kill a vet in a wheelchair, he thinks."

"Well, sir, we're going to take you with us." Singleton sat down. From outside came a pop of gunfire and the sound of the Zomboid laughing. On the television, Cronkite's voice was reporting calmly that riots had broken out in Detroit, New York, and Los Angeles. The Year of Hate was back in swing. It was unclear if Kennedy was officially dead. Had it been confirmed? The voice was steady, avuncular, calm, and dissociated from the reality at hand.

"Wendy wants to help you, and she needs your help. It has nothing to do with me."

"I'd like to go with you but I've got my honor and like I said I've got to take care of that kid out there, even if it's the last thing I do. You know, I worked the line at Ford and made a living and put her through nursing school." The old man pointed to the ceiling, there was a thump of footsteps and drawers opening and closing. For a second, Singleton again felt an urge to go up and to throw her down on her childhood bed and have a wartime fuck, Graham Greene–style, the way they'd done it during the Blitz, with bombs blasting and walls crumbling and the fear of death. The urge swung through him and dissipated into the buzz in his eardrums, disappearing, one more shameful thought arriving from his primal past.

The old man said, "I did what a man's supposed to do, I tried not burden Wendy with too much of *my* past. Your generation doesn't understand. Which is to say I'm going to go in the style of a man my age and time."

"But we're still going to take you with us," Singleton said flatly, so that he could tell Wendy he'd said it.

The old man shook his head knowingly. "Let's do it like this. I'll tell her you tried. Better yet, when she comes down here we make a show of it. You can even try to take me out to your car by force, but I'm not going with you, no matter what. But, see, if we do it that way we both win her forgiveness. I'm her father, and she knows it's not in my nature to run from this house that I built with my own hands—and the help of Sears—and you did your best to help her out. That'll be your gift to me. It'll be the last thing you do for me until we see each other again, hopefully, and then I'll talk to you not only as a fellow soldier but like a son-in-law."

Singleton stood up and shook his hand. When Wendy came downstairs, carrying her mother's wedding dress (resting on top: a small maroon jewelry box, and a copy of *Little Women*), the two men began the act. Singleton, as a member of the Psych Corps, a direct link to the commander in chief, ordered her father to head out. The old man, standing up, arms on his hips, a fireplug of a torso, countered by arguing that the commander in chief was dead now, so his orders were worthless.

"I'm ordering you, as an outranking officer, a former captain, to come with us," Singleton said.

Wendy's father touched his shoulder and said, "Kid, I outrank you. You must've forgotten. I'm not budging. Wendy, believe me, honey, I'd like to go but I can't cut and run as the last thing I do."

In the neighborhoods on the outskirts, most people had fled ahead of the riots. As soon as Kennedy was shot, or presumed shot, the few remaining millworkers had probably headed to Chicago, which for some reason had a low response to historical upheaval, or to their fishing cabins in Canada.

A new sense of mission seemed inherent in the road as it crossed the Flint line and entered a no-nonsense desolation. They stopped at a gas station with two old pumps and a big orange round Gulf sign. The attendant had a cigarette dangling from his mouth and a holster on his belt. As he came around to the front of the car, he patted the gun and nodded as if to say: no funny business. Singleton said, "Fill her up," and then, "Pay phone?" The attendant pointed at the side of the building. "She's all yours."

"Good luck," Wendy said.

On the phone, Klein's voice was weirdly soft and muted as he explained that they were in lockdown mode. The connection was weak and filled with clicks—they were being monitored—and his voice seemed to struggle through the wire. "You get it, you're getting it," he said. "I sense you have a clear sight line now."

"Yes, sir, I think so, sir," Singleton said.

Done pumping, the attendant was eying him suspiciously, his hand on his gun.

"You don't really get it, do you?" Klein said. "You can't put two and two together. I'm under orders not to say to you what I really want to say right now. You're a good kid. Can you put two and two together now? Can you do that for me, son? Can you think a little bit about whatever you've unfolded? Because I know you've unfolded, and I can't say it, so you'll have to say you've been fraternizing with a young lady, a fellow agent, against orders, against the Credo. From me it's just speculation—you get it, son, speculation—but from you it would be a confession that I could confirm and send up to Command."

Singleton held the receiver out and looked at it—earholes cracked, the handle smeared grimy with grease. Wendy was in the car, waiting. Nothing wanted to make sense except the sky, milky white, holding the world together.

"Say it, Singleton. Say it and I'll respond. I can't say anything until you say it. Say it. Say it."

"Say what, sir?"

"Say what I said you might say, about your fraternization state."

"What about it?"

"You know. Admit it to me is all I ask." Someone else was definitely listening on the line, there was a click and then another click.

"OK, why not?" Singleton said. "I'm with Wendy right now and we've been together all summer, fucking each other senseless, and now we're striking out on our own."

"There," Klein said, "I'll send that statement to Command," his voice lowered. "I'm going to confirm that you're officially wayward, that you've gone AWOL, but I'll use the Corps lingo. Now, if you were to say, I mean if you were to draw a conclusion looking back, accessing all of your actions and everything you learned in your training—if you were to look back, the way I taught you to look back, would you remember our talk about the proper way to write an operations report?"

"Yes, sir," Singleton said. The pop of gunfire came from the distance. A single pop followed by another. Brittle small-arms fire. Another pop—deeper, woody, a different tenor, a rifle—that seemed timed in response. Snap and woof. Another exchange of some kind. Behind that the dry, lonely sizzle of cicadas going about their afternoon business.

"So if you were to write a proper operations report, you might find a pattern . . ." There was a faint wheezing sound, and Klein coughed. He was lighting his pipe, speaking around the stem. "Again, I can't say it because it would be a betrayal of a promise I made to Command, but if *you* were to say something along the lines of, well, along the lines of being suddenly aware that you're tracking Rake, who from your unfoldings—I'm just speculating that you had a vision of Rake, that you're aware that he's in your Causal Events Package, that you might also conclude—and if I were to hear you say it I could confirm or rather, at least, send your understanding to Command—that you are under a form of advanced treatment." He began to cough the way he did when a bit of tobacco somehow traveled up the length of the pipe and got to his throat. The gunfire was getting close.

"I'm unclear, sir. Are you saying that you want me to say to you that I'm aware that Rake is part of my CEP, part of my past, enfolded in treatment, and that I somehow figured out that I'm under a form of advanced treatment?"

"Did you say it, or are you just asking?" Klein snapped.

"I'm saying it, I guess," Singleton said. Wendy was beckoning to him. The man in the station had his gun pointed out at the field.

"There you have it. I'll pass it up to Command. You not only went AWOL, but you also—to put it in the proper lingo—became aware of advanced treatment methods and thereby nullified said treatment. You drew your own conclusions."

"Got to go, sir," Singleton said.

"Take care, Singleton." A paternal urgency had entered his voice. "Shoot and then ask the dead questions. Get to the safe house if you can. Locate Rake. Get up there and terminate him. Don't ever quote me on that."

"Got to go, sir," Singleton said. He left the phone dangling and went to the car.

"Sounds like a firefight," the gas station attendant said. "You folks better get moving."

"Who's fighting?"

"That would be anybody with a gun," the man said.

"Get in the car," Wendy said. She had a look of fear on her face that he had never seen before.

Two more pops—closer this time. The attendant aimed at the sky and fired two shots into the air. Then he waited a few seconds and fired another shot. "They won't bring their firefight into my firefight."

Singleton drove with both hands on the wheel.

"What did Klein say?" Wendy said.

"Let me think through what he said and get back to you. I was distracted by the gunfire."

"You get back to me." She climbed into the backseat and began taking an inventory, lifting one gun and then another, putting them back. There was a kit bag from the Corps with pills. There was a first-aid kit and her mother's wedding dress. When he looked in the rearview her face was shrouded by the veil. When he looked again she had it flipped back over her head and was talking about her mother, who had married when she was eighteen, just before her father went into the service. Then she was explaining that she'd never agree to marry a man who kept secrets. She climbed back over the seat, still wearing the veil, and remained quiet.

"Well, he asked me to say and I said that I'm under some kind of advanced form of treatment. Rake was part of my CEP. He was there with me in Nam."

"An advanced form of treatment," Wendy said. She took

the veil off, folded it, lifted it to her nose, sniffed it, and then put it gently on her lap.

"That's about it. Some form of treatment."

"As if he knew we were together in the afternoons, and that was part of the treatment?"

"I'm thinking, if I'm reading him correctly, they took me out of enfolding, put me into Psych Corps, made damn sure I connected with you, and that's as far as I can go, because it seems virtually impossible. It's like what he was alluding to was not a treatment structured by the Corps, but some kind of impromptu field operation, a seat-of-the-pants thing of his own devising."

"You're saying Klein figured out we were fraternizing together. He saw that and decided it would be good treatment for you?"

"I'm saying he saw that I was breaking the Credo, going off with another agent, and he made note of the reality in the field. That's the kind of thing he was always talking about, the reality in the field."

"You're saying he went renegade. He knows we're heading up on this mission and it's against orders and all that but he is sanctioning it on a personal level?"

"It's one way to figure it," Singleton said.

A half hour later, there was nothing along the roadside to indicate they were in the Year of Hate, or that the riots had bled far out from the urban centers. This part of the state had been desolate to begin with, folks eking out a living from bad tillage, land overused, dejected-looking homesteads spaced far about, yards filled with trash. He wanted to tell her about the face in the file, but he was unsure how to proceed because she'd been quiet for miles, not moving, the veil resting in her lap, and he guessed that she was thinking about her mother, or her past history with the Zomboid. I'm the kind of man who doesn't know how to respond to a woman's deeper silences, at least in the car, he thought. There's only so much you can do in a car. A car has its limits. Yes, he felt her emitting sadness when he glanced over, something in the position of her fingers resting on the faded tulle. Finally, he found a quiet, straight stretch of road and pulled over so they could get out and move their legs, get the blood flowing. They stepped out into the lingering smells of a hot day, tar and dust and a hint of something—lavender, bindweed? It was an inland smell, far away from the lake, although they were only ten or fifteen miles from shore. Together they walked a few yards from the car, keeping an eye out for movement, down a slight decline, through a gully, to a clear spot between two trees, hidden in shadow. He turned and gave her a kiss and felt destabilized, as if they might settle down at that spot, slide to the ground, two young pioneers staking a claim on a barren patch of land, full of hope, the wide expanse of emptiness quivering around them on all sides, full of portent and possibility in a land unsettled but waiting eagerly. Then he told her about the photo in the file, the face of the burned man, the termination stamp, and he watched as she turned away from him and took a few steps toward the field. Her body was tense and it seemed to him that at any moment she might bolt. Then she turned around and walked past him, up the verge, to the car. "Let's get going," she said.

KILLDEER

The world's not gonna end with a whimper but with a bang, Hank said. It was just a thought. It came to mind and he said it, channeling deep into Old Hank, who knew that the best way to cut into the illogic of Rake when he was super high was to throw a non sequitur back at him, pushing him further away from a train of thoughts, because a train of thoughts always led to violence. They'd been exchanging non sequiturs deep into the night.

The only way to die is to kill the death within, Hank said.

You hear a whimper you want to make a bang, Rake said.

A good ship has a captain who doesn't know he's a captain, Hank said.

The only bad war is a war that I haven't started yet, Rake said.

Drugs that really hit hard hit the hardness first and the softness second, Hank said

Meg's a token of something I want to feed to the slot machine of death, Rake said.

A tree that needs to be cut says so before the wind picks up the scent, Hank said.

When I feel a hankering to kill I appreciate the fact that

blood is still flowing from the top of the state to the bottom, Rake said.

If I kill Haze it'll be because he's already close to dead, Rake said. I still have a little bit of honor left, such as it is.

June is the month of killing. April might be cruel, but June is pure murder, Rake said.

The day had been hot and the evening was only a bit cooler and there was a strange, unnatural silence. The lake sat shimmering and quiet, unusually smooth—two days straight of no movement, nothing at all—and in the woods the birds were silent, too, even the chickadees, and because of the airlessness he hadn't caught the scent of a single tree, not one, on which to pin his hopes. Meg was inside resting, tired, her face healing. His father was out there, navigating by starlight or with a compass, reading charts, whatever he did as second mate.

What do you mean by that? I'm going to make damn sure it ends with both a bang and a fucking whimper, Rake said. He gripped the chair and screamed. That's how it was in Nam, not that I want to talk about it, not that I give a shit, that part of me is dead and buried in the best way. You'd hear a little whimper and that meant shoot.

For two days he had been packing his gear, readying himself for another drug run, and then unpacking and repacking, testing everyone. When they could, Hank and Meg whispered assurances to each other, or exchanged meaningful glances. A plan will shape up, Hank assured her when he could. We'll take action soon, but the timing has to be right or we'll be the ones who end up dead.

Haze staggered around the yard with his arms out and practiced being blind because that's what Rake had told him to do. Get used to what it might be like because that other eye of yours has seen almost all it's gonna see, he said.

I'm not sure I'm sensing what I'm sensing, but it might be that one of you is trying to scheme against me, Rake said one afternoon. He held an ax over the kitchen table, swung it around. A sound came from outside, high-pitched, canine.

In the yard, MomMom was throwing another fit. She spoke of God as a friendly presence, as someone right on the edge of the yard, as a deity she knew personally, someone who would come charging to her rescue when the time came. Then she said she was the Alpha and the Omega, the beginning and the end. Seven bowls of angels will be fed the lamb of God.

Tell her to shut up. Make her shut up, Rake said, lifting the ax.

Hank went to her and lifted her off her feet and carried her back to the shed.

Mom, he said. MomMom, please, please, it's me, Hank, you remember Hank, he said, and then he watched her eyes sway, unable to focus, up at the sky and then to the east and then, finally, when he lifted his index finger and waved it, asking her to follow it, she focused.

Sweet Hank, she said. Your mother loves you.

Rake sat in a lawn chair with his ax across his knees.

You get her fixed? If I hear the word *God* again I'm going to remove her head.

She's might continue to mention God, but you know she's crazy so it doesn't mean anything.

Well, it means to me what it means. And I'm on edge.

I'll keep her away, Rake. Whatever works. Or I'll get rid of them both if that's what you want.

Yeah, whatever works, Rake said. Meg was approaching from the house and he fixed his eyes on her and touched the blade and began to explain how it was going to be him first who took care of the girl, if anyone, and that was an order, and that if he wanted both MomMom dead and Meg dead he'd do it himself. To keep himself calm, Hank looked into the sky and tried to catch the scent of a tree. He imagined a group of men tearing into the trunk of an old tree, not cutting with a clean notch on top and then another on the bottom but hacking at all angles, opening a big fat wound, and leaving the tree standing to be invaded by insects. The image forced him deeper into the role. He shook his head in agreement and Rake gave him a brotherly nod, as if to say: We'll both do what we have to do, and we'll do it together as brothers in arms.

If he doesn't kill her I might, Meg said, her voice loose and casual.

That's a good girl, Rake said. That's what I want to hear.

Hank glanced back at the trees and told her to pull away, to make it look as if she wanted to lunge for the water. She did as he asked and he pushed her down, holding her shoulders gently, but pushing hard, and then he gave her a fake kick to the groin and she gave a fake response so that Rake, who was up in the trees, hiding, watching, could rest assured. He had been trailing them daily—his footprints along the path, the feeling of being watched, his eyes in the trees, down in the grass.

Now let me help you up, he whispered.

I really do want to go in the water. I want to hear Billy-T again. I need to hear him.

The lake was shimmering with the last light of the day. It was still cold but would slowly warm up, the sunlight plunging down through the water, searching in vain for something solid.

Don't cry. If you cry, he'll know something's wrong. I'm going to move you over there and I'm going to lecture you on that bird, you see it, the killdeer. He pointed, keeping his hand up so Rake could see if he was still watching. The river came out through the trees and spread in a small delta.

You clear forest and they come to nest, he said. Rake is going to go out on another run because he's like that bird. He has to follow his internal compass, however messed up it might be, he said, pulling her. Now stumble a little bit and resist and let me pull you back again.

They made a show of it. The bird was glancing nervously in their direction, freezing still and then hopping, poking and probing in the rocks for food and glancing back intensely, fearful and yet free. As they moved closer, it hopped out into the flat, hard sand, dragging one of its wings.

It's injured, Meg whispered.

It's an act. They do it to lure predators away from the nest.

He took another step toward the bird and it skittered up the sand, keening loudly, dragging its wing.

Let me try to explain. Living things, all of them, are tied together. A bird is roped in tension, it's beautiful to watch. It's part of what makes a bird beautiful, he said. She'll fake it until it's a reality if she has to, luring a predator away, at the risk of her own demise. Once it gets near enough she'll keep playing and playing until it's close in and then she'll try to scare it. That's about ninety percent of what you need in the natural world; the one with a bigger bark, a display of power, wins.

And you have a big bark. Old Hank has a big bark, she said. She pulled away from him, hard this time, seriously. He yanked her back and got in close and looked down at her face tenderly.

I've got what I hope I need in the way of an idea, he said.

You and the bird.

Killdeer have a fine ability to mimic. I'll say that much. I just said that much. He pulled on her ropes and marched her away from the bird.

Take me back into the water, she said, pulling away. He pulled her back and they continued walking, sticking close to the water. When they looked back the bird had settled down and was returning to her nest. Hank stood still, the wind ruffling his hair, and gazed at the trees to where Rake was hiding, or not hiding, watching them with intense scrutiny.

SURETY IS A THING OF THE PAST

For miles, as they continued north, the needle was still making a shish pop, shish pop, as it rode the eternal runout groove at the end of *Fun House* on the signal out of Flint, strong off the night sky until, finally, it merged with white static and became faint background sizzle while the state unfurled—the same stubbled fields and denuded trees and finless windmills and equipment left to rust—and then, finally, Johnny Cash pushed through, his voice weary and low to the ground as he sang a lament that seemed to match the landscape, speaking from within the prison walls to a train whistle out there. Wendy was driving now, keeping both hands on the wheel, paying close attention, the kind of driver who concentrated on the road and made the conversion slightly one-sided.

Her father's voice had been like Cash's when they left the house, forlorn, suddenly distant, speaking as if through a wall.

"You really didn't fall for that act at your dad's house, did you?" he said. Cash had faded out again. Why bother finding another signal, the white noise said. It was neglected but necessary background noise. Leave me on, it seemed to say as the road swayed inland away from the lake.

"What act?"

"The act your father and I put on," Singleton said.

"I fell for what I had to fall for," she said, tapping the wheel. "And anyway, I knew when I was upstairs that when I came down you two would be in cahoots. I guess I knew it before we even got to the house. And you didn't want him along on this anyway."

Her old man had leaned into the car window as they were pulling away, telling them that he'd get through it, that he had some serious firepower and a lot of grunt experience. And an old Howitzer in the attic, he said, pointing to the muzzle in the little crescent-moon-shaped window, poking out ominously, a little dark disk.

Klein had said that a soldier could fake, or embody a state—was that how he put it?—in order to fool the enemy, or whatever. All of Klein's long-winded briefings, all that chatter, seemed to blend with the sound of the car's engine and the slight aftermath of the mystery pill, and he reached over and dug around in the ashtray and got another joint lit and decided to end further discussions on the topic.

"What do you think's going on in your department?" he said. "Do you think they're in some bunker somewhere trying to figure out a way to spin this fucked historical moment? Sending out bulletins to the cops upstate, making the case that Rake is dead?"

"I think they're doing what they can to spin the unspinnable," she said.

They were running north on the shore road, following the index finger part of the mitten alongside Lake Huron. The safest way was to stay close to water. Inland rage was more intense than shore rage, at least in theory. The road was old concrete, glinting with embedded stone and glued with swirls of tar. A voice was struggling through the static on the radio, a sermon materialized in medias res, an old-time preacher saying: God's mercy is severely limited. He has his doubts, man, about this one. He's lost in the clouds of his own thoughts. Surety is a thing of the past. King David pisses in the wind. God's like the Phantom Blooper, the supposedly kindhearted American who went over to the gook side and began to fight against us, hiding with the Cong, fighting his own beloved.

"I doubt this preacher even knows what surety means," Singleton said. "Surety isn't what he thinks it is."

Wendy remained silent, clutching the wheel, leaning forward slightly. To their left the remains of the Au Sable State Forest fire appeared, carbonized wood stinking of pitch.

"Are you sure you know where this safe house is?"

"We'll make it to the safe house. Klein made damn sure I knew where it was. As if he'd expected this all along. If this is some sort of treatment, or if we're supposed to be thinking this is treatment, he'd want us to be aware that we're aware of our own awareness of the situation."

"All I know is they trained me early on, when we were doing the basics, to think about the idea of north."

"It sounded like bullshit then and it does now," Singleton said.

The road ahead was empty, no sign of Black Flag gangs, no evacuees. The asphalt seams between the long concrete slabs made a rhythmic beat beneath the tires. If there was indeed a lure of north, and if he was feeling it, it had nothing to do with the Corps theory that vets were drawn north into the peninsular formation of the state by some residual attraction to potential enemy action. Nor was it a matter of the polar magnetic field. It had to do with desolation. A sense of the sky being closer to the ground.

"You're thinking it *isn't* pure bullshit," Wendy said. "You're thinking we're both attracted to the idea of north."

"It's anyone's guess how safe this safe house is going to

be," he said. Klein had mentioned it in a briefing on the plan of action in the event—he said—of further upheaval. He'd gone to the map and pointed it out. Something about the operative being a blacksmith.

A few miles later, past the state forest, she pulled the car over, left the engine running, and said she had to pee. He took his gun and stood beside the car, keeping an eye out, watching as she waded through the brush and then, a few minutes later—nothing to fear, just a field and a few trees down the road—she came back out, buttoning her jeans, straightening herself, smiling at him.

"There's a little brook back there. Can you hear it?"

They stood for a moment. The car ticked. When the wind eased, he could hear it, a faint burble threading through the overgrowth. They waited again for the wind to die down again. Nothing moved.

"I wish we could stay here for a while," she said.

"We can if you want, for a few minutes at least."

"Are you afraid?" She pushed slightly with her hip against his hip.

"Well, yeah, a little bit," he said. He touched the gun in his waistband. The safety was on, it was locked up tight.

"I'm not," she said. "I'm fearful, but that's different. Fearful for my father. Once you've been heroic like he has, you want to do it again."

"Your father will be fine," he said. He didn't believe it. Fine for the old man meant upholding a vision of the self that had been created at a young age, in circumstances that were unusual—the Black Forest, snow, youthful cunning and gumption set against huge historical forces. He'd be fighting the wrong war.

Back behind the wheel she drove quietly and carefully and continued thinking, he guessed, about her father's chances. At least the old man *could* remember his combat training.

Some said—and this might just be one more of the countless rumors, of course—that the mechanics, the fighting techniques, the useful stuff could never be lost, because it was somehow entwined into your sense of destiny (something like that). It was all tiresome. Rumors appeared around a context of need; they were nothing but a formation of an idea around a precise desire.

"What are you thinking about," she said later. Darkness had fallen quickly. He listened to the engine, felt it vibrating at his feet, on the floorboards.

"Nothing," he said. She shook her head, letting her hair drift into and remain in her eyes. Then she took one hand from the wheel and swept the hair back into place.

An hour later as they were nearing the safe house, he rooted in the duffel for the Corps kit bag, which contained pills that could light you up when you needed a zip. He took one and she took one and within minutes their eyes were wide open, their night vision enhanced. When the house came into view, a two-story farmhouse with a wide porch, across a wide field, they could make out a strange lean-to structure behind it. A small chimney in the structure was releasing puffs of smoke that looked chalky in the rising moon. Nothing moved. Behind the structure were dark woods.

"It certainly doesn't look safe," Wendy said.

"That smoke in the back's from the forge. Klein said the operative is some kind of blacksmith. We should sit for a few minutes and assess this in a professional manner. You know training. Never think a safe house is safe until you feel safe."

"Never feel safe unless you know you're safe, I think it was," Wendy said.

They waited. The zip pills had given them a good, clean professional edge, an esprit de corps intensified by a sense that they were facing a convergence between what the Corps called Forces of Inherent Evil imported into the culture from abroad (meaning Vietnam) and what the Corps called Trained Moral Positioning. When he mentioned it, she told him to shut up.

In his operations report he'd write about how they got around to the back of the house undetected, on tiptoe, past a mound of cycle parts rusted together—smelling of rust and oil—and then past a pump with a broken handle (every farm in the state had a pump with a broken handle). Discrete puffs of smoke rose from the forge structure, white, signaling to the sky. Singleton put his finger to his lips. Let the scene gather some meaning, he thought. Hearing the absurd pounding of his own heart, he wondered if his ability to sense danger ahead had been enfolded, or simply lost in the war. Wendy watched as he lifted his gun, held it like a divining rod, let it quiver slightly, and then, as if following its advice, moved forward with a sudden assuredness along the side of the house toward the front porch. (Why the front? he might be asked later. *We went to the front because the front was maximally distant from the forge, and the forge was emitting bad vibes, not just smoke—I mean, it was weird smoke, sir. So we went around to the front and I told Agent Wendy Z to wait. I used the recommended hand signals. I did the toe-to-heel walk, as instructed.*)

On the porch he touched the top of his head once with his palm, and then swung one arm in a windmill motion, the old Nam signal to provide cover. He stood and listened. Just the tick of wood contracting in the cool night. Another rotting porch in a state of rotting porches. He moved slowly to the window and then swept a portal in the dust and ash. Wendy came up behind him as he peered inside, trying to make sense of what he was seeing. In the pale light from under a door he could see an old pump organ against one wall. Hanging from the ceiling were six vague shapes, slightly conic, widening as they approach the floor, swaying slightly. He looked out the corner of his eye. The six shapes were bodies hung by their feet, bound tight, with arms extended out to the floor beneath them, some of them moving slightly.

(He knew what he'd have to say when he was being debriefed. He'd say it took him a while to make sense of what he was seeing, those forms hanging down, although for God's sake the truth was he knew right away what he was seeing.)

"He's hanging them by their feet."

Beneath the shapes were oily pools of blood. (No, sir, he'd say. We weren't sure what we were seeing exactly. They were slightly conic in shape and seemed to be swaying—but the light coming from the back room, a bit of light from under a door, was hardly enough to make them visible.)

A voice came from the yard. It was deep, husky, with a French-Canadian accent. "Them is the ones on the edge of oblivion, not quite there yet but on the way."

Singleton and Wendy stopped breathing.

"Give me the passphrase and I'll consider your salvation. Otherwise you'll hang up there with those folks."

"The dominion of the Corps is over memory ceded to terror," Singleton said.

"Non-fucking-sense," the voice said. "That was last month's passphrase. Every man north of Grand Rapids knows that one. Give it one more try and get it right or you're dead. This old buddy of mine is itching to go off. The clip longs to ease the burden of the spring, so to speak."

Singleton visualized the rectangular spring pressing the follower. (Don't remove the follower from the spring when cleaning, he remembered. Jiggle spring follower to install. If the spring comes loose, turn in the pieces. Don't fix in the field.)

"Come out with it, folks," the voice said. "Last chance to give the correct passphrase."

"The stillness within is still within," Wendy said.

"Correct," the voice said. "Now turn around so I can get a look at you."

He was at the foot of the stairs holding his flashlight to his chin. His face was caked with ash. He waved them down with the gun.

"We'd better go around back. You never know who might be watching us out there." He gestured at the woods with the gun. "You two trainees look so out of place I'm surprised you're not dead right now." He staggered in his buckskin chaps, swinging a gimpy leg, motioning for them to follow him around to the back of the house. He opened the forge door and led them into a dark room with a low ceiling. The forge wasn't much, just a small brick structure with a pile of charcoal and a bellows beneath a steel hood. Hanging from the ceiling—Singleton imagined he'd write in his report, if he lived—were all manner of motorcycle parts, chopper bars, along with what looked to be dried animal hides or jerky.

"The name's Merle," he said, bowing slightly. "The gang members, the wayward failed enfolds, whatever you call them down there, catch the scent of the smoke and know I'm working metal. That lures them in here and I do some work on their choppers and gain some trust. I was a biker myself, before the Corps got ahold of me, so to speak. I enjoy orderly flames after seeing so much fire that wasn't controlled, so to speak."

He lifted up his shirt to show a scar that flared out from his belly. (A burn scar, Singleton thought. If I were looking for conspiracy I'd say we're linked.)

"This doesn't look like much, but it produces brilliant heat," he said. He pumped the bellows and stuck a poker in and shifted the coals.

Singleton would put in the report that the fire hurt their eyes because the zip pills made light too light. We were standing there blinking, trying to see in the brightness.

"I'd do some work for you. It's wrong to betray a hot fire by not using it. I mean that's the way I look at it. Out of respect for fire you've got to use it whenever it's hot," he said, leaning down and blowing on the coals.

"We're not here to watch you work," Singleton said. "And I'm sure the fire wouldn't mind if you let it alone for a while."

"The fire minds what it wants to mind. That's why it's a fire."

"Well, then it won't mind if we don't mind it for a few minutes while you explain what the hell is going on here," Singleton said. The man stood back and held himself straight for a moment as if pondering not only fire itself but all of the rest of the elemental aspects of the world.

"It might mind, but you wouldn't know it," he said.

"Well, then you can say we didn't know. You can blame it on us."

"I guess you might be right. You knew the password for the week, and you're both blinking like you're on zip pills. Klein sent a courier a few months ago who said someone might be coming, but the date and time were to be determined later. Said there was a possibility of two agents—trainees—something like that. I don't pay a hell of a lot of attention to what's going on down there. Too busy."

"Did Klein give you a message?"

"I believe it was someone named Klein. Never caught his first name."

"Klein in Status."

"You know I can't confirm that. Have to limit the information flow. Just leave it at that. I knew you two were coming."

"But you said it was Klein?"

"Did I say that?"

"Yes."

"You're hearing the zip pills. I said no such thing." The man ran his palm across his forehead, leaving a smear of char, or ash. "Before I take you in there to see what you saw when you looked through the window, I'd like to say a few things. I'm afraid you might not be so happy when I throw the light switch. It might present itself to be a mite bit, how should I put it? Visceral. Mean to say, it might not cast the best light on me as upholding the standard of the Corps, the Credo and all that, but let me say that you've got to push some of these folks as close as you can to the edge but not over before they'll give up any information, and I've got a logbook of data that will likely prove useful to you. For example, if you tell me who you're looking for, if he isn't hanging up out there, I might be able to provide you with information, because anything that's going on in these parts, from here to north of the Hudson Bay, is in the logbook," he said. "If it isn't in the book, it hasn't happened yet, or I just haven't had a chance to catch and interrogate the targets, although, if I do say so myself, eventually most of the failed enfolds, the waywards, will find their way here, because there's something about the stench of a forge that lures them in. They long for the days when hot metal was worked—by their fathers down in the mills in Gary, or Flint, or Akron."

He went to the bench and pulled out a leather-bound journal. "Now tell me who you're looking for and I'll see if I can find a name that rings a bell and then we can go up front and I'll show you around."

In his report he'd have to play up the effects of the zip pill. The intense light and shadows and the stink not only of metal and fire but of flesh, of burning flesh. He'd leave out that he had been aware of a moral perplexity that he was trying to decide, standing there, whether the Credo allowed him to use whatever information the man named Merle might give them. In theory they should have arrested the man and taken him back to Corps headquarters. Terminated the mission and taken him back to Klein. Singleton looked at Wendy. She gave a curt nod and pointed to the book on the bench.

In the report he'd say they went around to the forge first, knocked the code knock, gave the passphrase, and were given information. Or maybe he'd explain that they'd had to withhold judgment lest it compromise their ability to use the information he provided.

"We're looking for a man named Rake," Wendy said. "That's about all we're authorized to tell you. He's up in these parts."

"Rings a bell." Merle opened the book, wetted his index finger, and flipped pages. Fountain pen ink light and faded in the early pages grew darker as he fingered his way through the months. He snorted and leaned both elbows on the workbench. Everything about him was ponderous and strange.

"I've had about fifty men in here and most of them were willing to give me information as long as I worked carefully and didn't allow them to cross too quickly, as long as I kept some semblance of hope in the air along with the edge of oblivion, if you know what I mean. The French have a better word for the fine work I do, he said. They might use this word *termine*, which means not only the end but to get through. One of the Canuck guys told me that just before he himself terminated."

"Just find some information on Rake," Singleton said.

"Like I said, the name Rake rings a bell and I'm sure there's something of use in here. It was just a week or two ago." He flipped to the last few pages. "Ah, well now, here it is. Here's the bell ringer. Had a man named Udall here and gave him the treatment and he knew about some action, a man named Rake and his partner Hank running a camp some-where in the Upper Peninsula, a few miles east of a place called Grand Marais." He ran his finger along the page. "Said you find the Harbor of Refuge and locate a place called Lonesome Point and then take Sandy Lane all the way to the end. That was all he said before he reached termination." He turned to the forge and pumped the bellows. "All's well that ends with information. You put an end to something the way you have to dip the metal in the sand and harden it. All bad things come to a hardened state."

"Did he say anything else?" Singleton said.

"That's it. Location and then he gave a grunt and died the death of a man who grunts and dies."

The man walked back to the bench and closed the book and put it back. Then he pumped the bellows again, tweezed a bar of metal, thrust it in a shower of sparks. When it was red hot he held it up to his lips and spoke into it the way you'd speak into a microphone. "I'm talking into the heat. I'm telling you that you'd better be sure to let those suits down in Flint know that these lips gave you the tip that helped you out—that is, if you live to tell them about it."

He jabbed the air with the hot bar, waving it wildly.

Singleton took the gun from his waistband and aimed it at the man's head. "Put that down and show us to the front room," he said.

"You put that gun down and I'll put this down."

"Just lead the way," Singleton said. "I'm not going to put this down."

"It's not right to heat up a bar and not work it," the man said. "You betray the metal by not working it."

"Just show us to the front," Singleton said.

"You folks don't need to see any more of what you've already seen up there," he said. "You got what you need and now you should be on your way. It won't do you any good seeing it in full light."

"Take us to the front," Singleton said.

"Well, all right." Merle put the metal bar onto the bench and then led them through the kitchen to the front room. He threw the light switch and moved in among the bodies, nudging them with his palm as he passed. Two of the bodies were leathery, dark blue, clearly dead. Two were seemingly still alive, swaying with a gyroscopic stability. The status of the other two was uncertain. (The breeze lifted the curtains— pale blue—twisting into the room.) Singleton would never be able to put this in his report. Great care had been taken in the securing of wrists.

"You see, all torture seen by the nonparticipant is about creating a spot where death can appear but not appear completely. You want to get 'em as close as possible but not right over the edge. Too far, and you get the natural painkillers going. Not far enough, you get the spirit and will in the way, and then you're in trouble."

"Too far, not far enough?" Singleton said. "That's insane."

"Well, it doesn't matter to me what you think. That one there gave me the location on Rake." He gave a body a tap with his boot and watched it swing. "I pushed him as far as I could and then pushed him a little further, but not too far. You want them moribund. That's the word. You want to keep them in a fresh moribund state. You push 'em too far, they just want to die right there. You've got to hold out some hope. You've got to mix it up. I'm a worker of metal, you see, so I understand just how far you can push it and how hot things have to be to bend."

"Cut them down," Singleton said. "Get a ladder in here and start cutting them down."

"No need for the gun. I've got them rigged so I can just

ease them down. I'll do it as soon as you leave. And feel free to call in a report to headquarters, if it hasn't burned to the ground. Most likely, it's gone with the rest of Flint. Those folks know damn well what I've been doing up here."

"No, now. Take them down," Singleton said.

Wendy kept her eyes averted, cupping her hands and looked out the window into the darkness as Merle got all the bodies down—each one quietly, the ropes slipping through well-oiled grooves—and they lay crumpled, all in unnaturally easeful positions. Singleton now had his gun against the old man's head, pressing it tight to his temple, as he told to him stand still while Wendy tied him up.

"I'm not going to tie him up," she said, softly. "I want to get the fuck out of here and get on with the mission."

The zip pills were wearing thin and everything had a stark, newfound clarity; the grappling hooks in the ceiling and the pulleys—and the old man, his face tight-scrunched, eyeing the gun fearlessly, staring right into it, only a few feet from Singleton, who held it out straight, his arm shaking slightly, his lips set firm, his legs apart, too, in a manner that seemed to indicate that he was resisting all temptation, and he was.

"I should shoot you right here. Save you a trial. A court-martial."

The old man guffawed and then, in a swift swing of his head, spat to the side. "You two are the ones who are going to be up on charges. I know that for a fact. Nobody ordered you up here. If you were supposed to come to me, I would've been informed."

"He's right," Wendy said. "This is a problem for head-quarters, not us."

"Listen to her, son. You walk out that front door and go ahead with your mission and leave me to be the man with the burden of having to push it to the limit to get what you needed in the first place. You walk out that door and don't turn back around and I'll go back to working with my hands. You work with your minds—whatever they call it, that intuitive nonsense—and I go forward in the old traditions. The wonders of the blocks and tackle, the usefulness of know-how."

"Let's go," Wendy said.

"Listen to the lady," the man named Merle said.

Singleton put the gun back in his waistband and spread his arms as if to say, OK, fuck it. It's all yours.

"Nothing personal," the man said. He had the door open and motioned them into the night air. They ran to the car through air sweet with pine and dew-wet grass. If Singleton wrote the report he'd say they left the house at gunpoint, the man unhinged by the dictates of his own mission. He could then discourse on the immorality of certain operations, the way things were actually done in the field in contrast to the vision that Kennedy had set forth.

A few miles down the road he stopped and Wendy stumbled out of the car, staying to the edge of the headlight beam, bowing down and vomiting into the gravel. When she got back in the car she said it wasn't so much the bodies, or the stench, or the old man, or even the fact that they were in deep shit—officially AWOL, as the old man had indicated—that made her sick but something else, something she couldn't pin down exactly, although it might've been the zip pills wearing thin. (Should we have another? Pop one more? It's a great high.)

"No," he said.

"No, what? No, we're not AWOL."

"No to more zip pills. No more drugs. We're going to find a spot to park and hunker down for the night, get some rest, hit the road tomorrow fresh."

Leaves were shimmering on both sides of the road, fresh and living leaves, frosted with moonlight.

He followed the road as it cut toward the shore.

"If I have to write a report, and I mean honestly do it, maybe under closely monitored treatment with further Tripizoid because who knows what the Corps can do to an AWOL agent, I want to be able to say we ran away from the safe house before we could look around, forgot the passphrase, something like that, and then we parked to rest, following procedure." He stopped himself. What she didn't know couldn't be used against him in an interrogation.

"What? What were you going to say?" she said.

"Nothing. It's beautiful here. This might be the place."

They'd entered a small state park and were following a dirt road through a grove of quaking aspens.

"Whatever happens when we find Rake, the Corps is going to write up a report, either in response to our dead bodies or because we nailed the target, and if they interview me I'm going to claim that I had a vision right here, in this location, and that the vision told me where Rake was. I'm going to skip the safe house altogether. I'll say you fucked me into unfolding Rake's location, something like that."

"Or you could tell them the truth," she said. When he kissed her he tasted the forge on her lips, a faint tang of carbon. He thought of the windows on the other side of the room back at the safe house, the hanging bodies, and the dark portal in the window glass where he had cleared the dust.

Later that night, after Wendy was asleep, he opened the door quietly and got out and walked to the top of a dune and looked toward the car. It was hidden by trees shaking in a long sway of sequins as the leaves caught the moonlight.

Search and destroy was what they called it in my day, Klein had said. Now we call it a sweeping operation, or a reconnaissance in force.

Elastic with tar, a wave stretched itself from one end of the beach to the other, roping back as a cleaner wave overtook it, topped it, and spilled down into the sand. From far off came the tenuous whine of an engine downshifting. A gang of bikers riding along the road. The sound grew faint and slipped beneath the shush of waves. No shootout with bikers to end the night. Singleton felt relieved.

Would he use the old phrase in a report—or would he use "sweeping operation," or "reconnaissance in force"? He'd say they had stopped at the beach for a rest and he had got out of the car alone—he'd make a point of saying that Wendy was sleeping soundly—and that he had stood at the top of a dune, whatever it was, and that he had watched the gunky waves coming across the water. He'd say he'd resisted the urge to walk to the water, to test it for coldness. But he'd admit that he'd had that urge.

He'd say that he began thinking about Huron, about the big spills that had presumably gunked it up when he was off in the war. It was enfolded, he'd explain, and it led me to thinking about the unfolded flashes I'd had (maybe he'd admit that he'd seen the photo on both folders, Klein's and Ambrose's). He'd say he was looking at the lake and had a vision—a big flash from the fuzzball—of the man with the phone to his lips, calling in coordinates, and that in the vision the numbers became clear to him, a longitude and a latitude, something like that.

With his fingers on his temples he gave it a try. One of the older rumors had it that if you pressed hard on the temples and really dug in, you could perhaps catch a snag, a bit of memory, in the fuzzball, something like that. He imagined the face of Rake and Chaplain Frank, and the other man, the one who looked up from the radio as he was calling in the numbers and the fireball struck. Another wave was coming in, and with his eyes closed he followed the sound from one end of the beach to the other. He pressed harder with his fingers and then, when his head began to hurt, opened his eyes and walked back to the car to Wendy and was filled with what could only be called love, a sense of destiny that was somehow related to the fact that she could sleep soundly with her legs tucked up awkwardly, and to the fact that they were both on a mission together. His love felt deep, but he knew that only time could reveal how deep. Only when the story is over and the report is written can the truth be known fully, he thought; or perhaps only when the depth of my love for her is fully known can the story end. If I'm debriefed after all of this, I'll have to say the grove of aspens felt like a little island of beauty in a world of hell. I'll have to say I felt a sea of calm. I'll also make sure to include the fact that the offbeat rhythm of the waves had seemed to me like a good jazz beat, and that I'd become aware that the distortion of what is natural is somehow more beautiful than nature itself. He turned things around in his mind until his breathing matched Wendy's own steady breathing. He was half-awake in the alert way of an uptight dog just trying to survive. He stayed that way until he dozed off at dawn and woke to the trees burning with sunlight. A bird was singing with a high, throaty warble. The waves had died. Wendy was just awake beside him, lifting her hair out of her eyes, blinking, looking angry and relieved at the same time.

"I didn't know how exhausted and frightened I was until the last of the zip pill wore off and then I couldn't stay awake, and when I did wake up, you still weren't here, and I asked myself what Training would say, and I said to myself, stay with the car, one agent should stay with the car, and then I felt totally foolish but too tired to move so I fell back asleep, but I was saying a prayer when I fell asleep. That's how worried I was. I thought I'd find you out in the water," she said.

"It's not cold enough to do anything to me anyway. Superior is still cold, but in Huron shallows and the tar absorb heat and warm it up."

"But you were thinking about it."

"Yes, sure, I had the thought."

REUNIFICATION

On the other hand, if they were following the right course of action, and if the riots died down and order was restored, he could simply go back and tell Klein the truth: He and Wendy had silently (it seemed) agreed that they had to follow the lead they got from the man in the so-called safe house. In the report he'd write that they were following the intuition so valued by the Corps, although he'd also have to mention that he felt betrayed: his belief in the Corps, whatever was left of it, had been shattered by those hanging bodies. Klein would light his pipe, and expound about the Corps insignia. The scales are there for a reason, son. We don't have lady justice on the insignia because balance matters more than lady justice, if you know what I mean. When Singleton noted in the report that the man at the safe house had tortured informants, Klein would shrug (probably) and explain that even the Geneva Conventions were retroactive nonsense. They had been written after the First World War. After the fact, son. After the deeds were done. Then they were rewritten yet again when the need came, after the fact, you see. And then again, for God's sake.

Ahead the Mackinac Bridge stretched over the straits in

the late morning sun. The roadbed, partly metal, partly poured concrete, had been damaged and patched.

"Maybe if I write up an operation report I'll have to mention those hanging bodies."

"If you write up an honest report you'll also have to say that I fucked you into orgasmic unfolding," she said. "And I'd appreciate it if you put in there that I acted as a nurse, that I relied on those skills, and you should also put that I feel horrifically conflicted about that fact."

"If this is part of our treatment, then don't you think the point was nullified at the safe house? I don't want to believe the Corps would condone that kind of action. Klein would, but not the Corps, not Command." Singleton guided the car over the rumble strips on the approach. It had been built optimistically and quickly in the teeth of winds roaring between the Upper Peninsula and the Lower, over the conflicting waters of the two Great Lakes, and now it looked thin and reedy. But once they were on the bridge, a tightrope of concrete and steel, they could appreciate its gracefulness and the majestic link it provided between two worlds, one new and connected with the rest of the world, the other separated and primordial.

Wendy had yet another joint going to celebrate the crossing. He slowed down and they took in the view.

"You love the Zomboid and can't say it and it's my duty to get you to say it," Singleton said, suddenly.

"I have said it but not the way you want to hear it."

"What do I want to hear?" Singleton said, taking a toke. Cars were streaming in the southbound lanes. His side of the bridge, with the exception of one car far ahead, was empty.

"You want to hear that I was fantastically in love, in love the way you can be when he's your first and he was beautiful— just perfect—and then came back and his legs were missing and he couldn't really remember who I was, beyond saying to me that I was his girl and that he had carried my picture into battle. You want me to speak of the kind of love that you feel after the object of desire is destroyed and all that's left is a pulse through deep space. That kind of love," she said.

"You might be right," he said. He was feeling disoriented. Had he told her about the exchange of information in the bathroom? Had they talked about that?

The car ahead had stopped, blocking the lane, and two men seemed to be at work prying open a hatch of some kind at the base of one of the towers.

"Those must be jumpers," he said.

"Jumpers?"

"You get your folks who stop on the bridge and leave the car running and leap. Those are East Coast mainly. Then you got West Coast jumpers, the ones who go out to the Golden Gate, climb atop the railing, and swan dive into the bosom of the bay, which is supposed to have something to do with the womblike nature of the formation, or something like that, and up here, well, it's more brutal. The state maintains the elevator and all you have to do is know where to go—in that hatch—and you go up to the top and jump."

They were passing the middle section and began the decline, the two parts of Michigan behind and ahead while far below the straits ran cold and choppy with currents revealed in long, white strings of foam.

His operation plan, attached to his report would be written after the fact, postdated to cover tracks and make it seem preordained. That's how it was done, Klein had explained. Orders in a plan have a snap and zing, a knowingness, a resonance ahead of the curve. Gumption is what you need to be a commander, Klein had explained. The gumption to go back and revise history. The key to planning an operation is to take the facts and then speculate. When you start an operation, all doubts must be put aside. There was a general in the First

World War who understood that. He had to assume that he was one step ahead of the krauts and to make his point, he renamed German trenches ahead of their capture, gave them English names, before the attack. He assumed the win and took it from there, which is what made him a supreme commander even when he lost a battle. And that's what I intend to become, Klein had said, turning away. Win or lose, I'll win.

A clump of cars passed coming the other way, a caravan of station wagons and campers loaded with frightened-looking men in madras shirts and housewives with their hair in scarves. Wendy gave them a wave and they waved back sadly.

"What are you thinking?" Wendy said again.

"You keep asking that."

"I want to know what you're thinking and I can't think of another way to put it," she said.

"I know you want to know, and you know I want to know, so we both know we want to know what we're thinking all of the fucking time."

"It helps me to say it out loud. It's an old nurse thing, if you really want to know. You ask how they're feeling again and again until they finally tell you, or at least give a hint."

"Only when the operation is over, Klein said. Only when it's over can you write a solid operation plan. You write it after the mission and it comes out perfect. That's what I'm thinking."

"Sounds like your department. Mine wouldn't do it that way. We'd tweak it to shed the best light on the Corps, but we would never revise an operation plan after the mission and postdate it," Wendy said. "We'd stamp it top secret and redact everything in it and stash it away for the future."

Only when the story is over and the report is written—or not written—can the truth of my love for you be fully known, Singleton thought.

Then he said it aloud as they approached the end of the bridge, easing down into the Upper Peninsula.

"Are you trying to say you love me?" Wendy said.

"I won't be able to say it until this operation's over. I mean, of course I do love you, but the kind of love I'm thinking about is something I won't know until I write up a report and sort through everything that's happened this summer so that I've honestly done it justice."

"Bullshit, I think you said you love me."

"I think what I'm saying is that before I can really say it, I mean in the way I want to say it, so you hear it the way I want you to hear it, I've got to make sure I know for sure if this entire thing was a fucking setup, something they anticipated, playing matchmaker in a major way, or if it was just a matter of pure chance, the two of us, in the lobby, that first lunch, that second lunch, the whole thing."

"Rake faked his death so that Status would think he was dead but he's really alive and Relations would think he's alive but he's really dead. Is that the way it's working?" she said, flicking the lighter and pinching what was left of the joint, holding it to the flame with shaking hands. "Who cares if they knew we were together early on? They understood that we were two trainees who might work well together and find Rake, but the rest . . ."

"Was set up to fuck with me," he said. "To fuck with us."

"One minute you seem to believe in the goals of the Corps. The next minute—usually when you're high—you say the Corps is just a big structure to hold irony so Kennedy could go on with the war."

"I didn't say that. Klein said that early in the summer. When he still sounded reasonable to me, when he was talking World War this, World War that. I didn't say it. He said it and I told you what he said, and now you quote it back to me."

"That day you came over to my father's house."

"What about it?"

"You seemed pathetic to me."

His throat got tight. When they were only half in love, Singleton thought, the fights had been petty and fun, a prelude to make-up sex. Now they were heading into a storm. It really did seem to matter who was right and who was wrong.

"How so?"

"Well, my father seemed like a *man*. I hate the way that sounds, but it's true."

"Do I seem pathetic?"

"Yes," she said. "Not as pathetic as you seemed that day at my house. Or even at the safe house. You seemed particularly pathetic."

"How so?"

"I knew what you were thinking. You sided with the operative. You took his information and you ran," she said.

"And you ran with me," he said.

They were off the cloverleaf at the end of the bridge, turning west per instructions, following the coast of Lake Michigan.

"I didn't have a choice. I don't have one right now."

"You had a choice. You have one right now. I can stop the car and let you out," he said. His voice was tight and angry. The fuzzball in his head was singing.

"You need me in this operation. You need me, period."

We went over the bridge, made note of some jumpers opening the hatch to a tower. We had a brief, terse exchange about the nature of the Corps, and the nature of our mission. We silently agreed to disagree. Then we relished the cool northern summer air and we felt ourselves committed, agent-to-agent, he would write, if he did write. *Our confusion was acute. A debilitating sense of not understanding our own actions was internal. We understood that the Corps believed Rake was dead and that Klein either didn't believe he was dead or was putting on an act that he didn't believe he was dead.*

"Your father, he was the pathetic one," Singleton said.

"The word is *pitiful*. I felt pity for you. I used to feel pity for my father, but when he talked to you I heard a new tone. He seemed pitiful and pathetic until he talked to you. Next to you, he seemed heroic. You might think he told those stories again and again, but the truth is, Dad kept his mouth shut. He folded it up and went on with his life. I knew he'd been through trauma. I knew he was walking around holding it all in to protect me. But I respect him because he's a fully functioning man."

The whine in his ears was getting higher and louder and the road seemed to flex from side to side. He gripped the wheel tight while Wendy looked him over and told him he looked like he was getting sick, or having a flashback.

"I'm not having a flashback. At least not a pharmaceutically induced one. I'm still thinking about how I'll put this in words, explain this part of the mission."

"The president was finally killed. All hell broke loose. We took off." She frowned. "Why this obsession with the operation report? Why do you feel this need to put everything into a system?"

"How did Ambrose get hold of that file? If they keep them under lock and key, how did he get a copy?"

"They wanted him to have a copy. When they handed it to him they knew he'd hand it to you."

"I need to know. I need to know," he said.

He pulled over to the side of the road, under tall pines clutching sandy soil, the isolated sunlight, dappled, coming down through the branches, and got out. Across the road, empty beach stretched to the west. There was an old grill and a pump with a working handle.

"I came up here as a teenager," he said. "We camped on this beach, or somewhere near it." He sat on a picnic bench carved with old names and dates. He put his face in his hands and suddenly began to sob.

"I feel genuinely sorry for myself. I feel this huge pity for myself."

Wendy spread her arms and took a deep breath. "This is a real place and it's beautiful, and it smells good, too. I say, fuck whatever they're trying to do to us. We're heading up to the target if he's alive or dead, and we have to follow our guts on this."

Looking out at Lake Michigan, across the road, he sensed again that he'd been here as a teenager, and that it had something to do with Rake, and the firebomb, and that scene in Hue. On a hot summer day he might have seen the Chicago mirage, the streets and towers visible high over the water, an optical trick of heat and light fantastic to behold if you were lucky enough to catch it. Whether or not it ever happened, the idea held a place in the hearts of Michiganders, who kept it alive from generation to generation. He felt the urge to cross the street and wade into the lake, which would be cold enough to unfold him completely if he stayed under long enough.

His eye was distracted by a gull riding out on a gust of air, holding wings steady and straight as it floated in a gentle swaying motion.

"Do you have an urge to go into that water?" Wendy said. He studied the freckles on her nose and her eyes. He remained silent.

"I'm sorry about what I said. My dad knew his story. You don't. You know a little bit more now and you're not as pathetic."

"And I'm sorry about what I said. But I meant it. I can't really say how I feel, I mean exactly how I feel, until I know exactly what the deal is."

"Love means saying you're sorry over and over and over again," she said, and they laughed.

"I really don't want to go in the water," he said.

"You looked, sitting there, like a man who wanted to go for a swim."

"Maybe a quick romantic dip? To wash the smoke out of my hair."

"We should get in the car and keep driving. We don't want to arrive at the target in the dark. Not if we can help it."

The guns were out in the backseat, arranged neatly, along with two grenades. Miles and miles of forest were making Singleton's head ache. In his report, he'd describe how the trees had been planted in a straight line that somehow suggested eternity, forcing the eye down long corridors of green, creating a strobe of light on the road when the sun was at the right angle. The only clear signal on the radio was from Canada, a CBN show playing Bach, the notes too pure and clear and precise.

"I'll remember my military training when the time comes," Singleton said. "I did the hand signals, on the porch back at the safe house. They came to me. I remembered details. A diagram of a clip and a spring came to me."

"We don't really have much of a plan, do we?"

"Training says approach target with assurance. Entrapment is the result of not having an exit plan, a detailed map of the stakeout area."

In the report, he'd say the trees in their straight lines seemed to draw him onward toward Rake, either to terminate him or to confirm his status as dead. He'd tweak it as needed.

"Stop with the report," Wendy said. She was eating a C-ration bar. He glanced and saw her tooth marks on it.

They drove until abruptly the trees thinned out and the road passed through a gate in a chain-link fence and the sky opened overhead, a galvanized, post-sunset gray. Right here, he thought. This is where the north begins. This is where at night the sky shimmers with cosmic activity. This is where the imaginations of most folks reach a limit and they draw a blank, like the isolated edge of my Causal Events Package. The beauty of the land disappeared as soon as the first house appeared, a one-story with peeling paint and a yard littered with stone monuments (some kind of private graveyard?), white concrete angels with stubby wings, three crosses, absurdly white, seemingly lit from within. On a wooden pole a black flag was snapping in the wind. Three choppers sat parked in the driveway, lined up side by side, like a chorus line, exactly at the same angle.

Wendy poked through the ashtray and found the half-burned joint. She lit it up.

"Late May the snow finally breaks and then in mid-October the snow begins. Not much of a season for riding a chopper."

"Want a hit?" she said.

"Keep it low, don't let it show. I've got to maintain an edge."

A gas station. A liquor store. A tavern with a cop car—a star on the side panel, faded, gray—parked in front. Past a stoplight (blinking yellow), the lake revealed itself, a vast gray corrugation of waves, an inland sea.

"Give me a hit," he said.

Headed east from the Harbor of Refuge as per instructions, he'd write, if he wrote. Took Deer Park Road. The lake was relatively calm.

They drove through the wind-battered landscape. This part of the state looked completely untarnished, but it was deep into the so-called Zone of Anarchy. At any moment a gang of bikers might appear beyond the bug specks on the windshield.

When they got near Rake's encampment, Singleton pulled over and parked the car in the grass. Wendy kept lookout while he checked the weapons. He handed her a gun and watched as she kissed the barrel for good luck and tucked it into her waistband. The night was getting cool. She put on her leather jacket with fringe. (*In the report, he'd say they were wearing the regimental uniform with badges, as per regulation. Pants clean pressed and shirts neatly tucked. He'd say they made it clear that they were agents from the Corps. He'd say they had assessed the road situation—dead quiet—and assured themselves that no one was coming. He'd say they were keenly aware of the idea of north, remembering, from the manual, that northern climes enhanced the intuitive clarity of agents while increasing the psychotic intensity of failed enfolds.*)

"Hug," she said, pulling him close. He would omit from the report the desire he felt for her. There was a faint smell of smoke in the air.

"Time to reconnoiter," he said.

"I fucking love that word. *Reconnoiter.*"

Approach the perimeter and establish the target in relation to the landscape and make necessary adjustments, he might write in the report. They stopped and listened. A clear intuitive drive. That was the phrase he'd use. What does it mean, he thought, that all I can do is try to frame this in the technical terms of a report I might write. He shook his head. He was feeling lonely, isolated.

There was a single goat in the field to the left. It made a sound like a laugh. Then another.

The gun slung on his shoulder; the grenade hanging from his belt.

Farther down the road they came to a driveway with a mailbox, a sign that said KEEP OUT, and a skull impaled on a stick. The skull was clearly human, not dog or goat. It was missing the jaw and bleached clean and white.

Merle had said the hideout was at the end of the paved road. Two rutty tracks ran through thick weeds and plunged into a dark hole in the woods. To the right, what Singleton would call a windrow in his report. *Windrow* was the word he'd use. *The windrow formed a perimeter of deadfall with a clearing that was visible as a brighter glow of purplish light.* He put up his hand to signal halt. They listened to the faraway sea sound of the surf and the wind rising in the pines, dying away, rising again. Nonspecific vibrations at the coordinates' location, as specified in prior vision. Dangerous vibrations, northern negative lure. This had to be the feeling you got being on point in Nam.

Singleton crouched down and Wendy crouched beside him. You can enfold the trauma but you can't enfold the age and time. In the field you'll be thinking about the war, starting from the moment you stepped onto a Pan Am airline flight and heard the stewardess sweet-talk you, serving coffee, knocking hips, flirting, to the final moment you were lifted up and out of the hellhole to return home, passing fresh grunts on the way in, their assholes clenched, their faces fresh and bright as they went to their destinies. Just can't wash all that away, no matter what, Klein had said. Yes, sir. Yes, sir.

The smell of her patchouli and the glow of her hair beside him. He stood and she stood. They walked forward a few yards and stopped.

"What about the zip pills?" she whispered.

They were in the brush near the edge of a yard. Sheets on a line luffed softly, straining skyward, as if to gather whatever light remained. The house's clapboards were shedding paint. There was a light in the back window, presumably the kitchen, and a thin thread of smoke from the chimney. The breeze lifted, and the sheets stretched out in unison, and then luffed down again.

"We won't need them," he said.

A few minutes later they heard a screen door slam, and an old woman came out onto the back porch huffing, grunting down the steps and shambling into the yard with a basket in her arms. She took down the sheets one by one, folding each one over her arm and then in half and then in quarter before laying it in the basket. Then she began to unfold each one, lifting the corners up to the line, pinning them back into place.

"Sure this is the right place?"

"I'm sure," he said. "You know what they say. Every failed enfold has a hefty old lady tending to his needs, some mother figure who believes he's a pure little angel. The hardened cases are often the most pathetically in need of maternal care."

"OK, but she looks nondangerous in a deep way."

"All the better for us."

The old lady took the sheets down from the line again and stood with her arms at her side and her face to the sky. What happened then was hard to see from their position. She'd fallen to the ground and was partly obscured by the basket. Holy holy, she seemed to be saying.

The subject appeared to be speaking in tongues, he thought. Glory and holy, or holy and glory—the wind rose and covered the words—and then something about the wrath of God being torn away. She seemed to be running in a supine position. The screen door slapped again, and a similarly large man (a son, Singleton thought) with a beard strode across the yard and said, Mom, MomMom, it's OK, go easy.

Wendy took a step forward, her gun out.

"Wait," he said.

The man was helping the woman into his big arms. *Likeness of physique indicated a genetic relationship. No sound from the house. We held our position and assessed the situation. Male subject assisted female subject up the steps to the porch . . .*

The screen door creaked open as they approached. A young woman emerged, wiping her hands on a towel, and let them into the house.

"That might be the one Rake kidnapped out of the Grid."

"Total weirdness," Wendy whispered. "They don't look dangerous. I get a vibe of a loving relationship."

"The closeness of these folks, from what I understand, is even more intense than the closeness of normal folks. They practice violence externally and live in small-group formations, or whatever the Corps calls them, an intense familial groove. A failed enfold often doubles not only his psychotic intensities but his sentimental attachments."

We posited that the familial vibration derived from a projection of mother-son love as he had experienced it in the field of battle heightened by an abnormal dose of Tripizoid to an abnormal intensity.

"I know that. But I don't necessarily see it in front of me."

"When we're sure they're inside we'll get up to the porch and take a look."

Northern darkness fell slowly, and they waited until the yard was dark and the window in the back glowed brighter, throwing bars of light onto the floor of the porch. Over the yard a bowl of stars appeared.

"Now," Singleton said. "Cut around as far as you can to the side of the house and then we'll cross one at a time. Keep me covered. I'll go first. If anyone comes out, give them a warning shot. I don't want an element of surprise in any form but gunfire."

He mentally set aside the report and placed himself in the moment. He felt mosquitoes biting his legs and the heavy pull of the rifle on his shoulder as he moved swiftly around to the driveway, taking the shortest exposed approach between wooded cover and porch, and without thinking, without even saying go, he ran across the gravel and flattened himself against the side of the house. Moving in a side step, he slid to the corner of the house and peered around it—gun first, always gun first. Then, removing his shoes and glancing back to sight his cover, he walked heel and toe up the steps and onto the porch.

He crouched, glanced through the window, and ducked back down with an image in his head: The image might have been called "Domestic Bliss": three people were seated at a table, lit by a lamp hanging down over steaming dishes, and eating together with their bodies relaxed, no sign of a gun, no sign of intensity (and no Rake, no Rake at all). The man with the beard was sitting on one end of the table, the girl named Meg (if this was Meg) was at the other end, the old woman between them, with her back to the window. Singleton briefly raised his head again. The man with the beard was lifting his fork while the girl laughed about something. (Her laugh came through the glass, a flutter, delicate-sounding.) Beyond the table was a dark doorway.

It was possible that Rake was away (or actually dead) and they were holding down the fort. Also possible that the bearded man was Rake with some extra weight after a summer of killing and eating, killing and eating. Target had gained weight. Target had facial hair. Singleton struggled to get an intuitive read on the situation.

He waved Wendy in. She came running silently and crouched down beside him. She indicated the door with her gun. He pointed to the window with his own gun and made a poking motion. "Break the glass and hold them," he whispered. "I'll go through the door."

She spread her fingers, clenched her fist, and spread them again. Count of five. Everything on a count, the manual said. Decide upon a course of action, using hand signals if necessary, and then, on a count, strike.

At the count of five she shattered the window with her gun

and yelled, "Don't move," before they registered her gun and shouted and jerked in terror, for a split second, forks and spoons midair in the warm kitchen. Singleton passed through the mudroom—its smell of rubber boots and tools and mink oil—and burst into the kitchen as they froze.

"Move, I'll shoot."

The old lady heaved up from the table and began to howl.

Wendy went in with her gun raised, moving it from Singleton's target—the big man—to her target, the girl.

Norman Rockwell, he'd write in the report. We approached target in cover formation—Wendy covered—and entered a Norman Rockwell scene. Total element of surprise accomplished. No reactive counterattack in relation to our action in the field.

"Christ, what took you so long," the man at the table said.

HOMECOMING

Jesus Christ. What took you so long. The words came to Hank swiftly, and he said them and felt himself grow still in the brilliant tension of the moment. To project a sense of knowingness, to center the fear, to draw everything into an assurance that it was unexpected. This was his instinctual reaction to the breaking glass and the sudden appearance of two guns. Not sarcasm, but basic survival in the form of nonchalance with a dash of sarcasm as MomMom slid down against the stove, hands up, waving, making an unusual screeching sound, like a wounded animal, her watery, rheumy eyes bulging, a sound that somehow matched the persistent buzz in his ears. The man in the doorway was blinking and lowering his aim slightly. The woman, beautiful, with startling eyes, in a leather jacket, her legs spread, her arms up, looked like she was Psych Corps. Both were, Hank speculated, keeping his elbows on the table, a finger on his chin, scanning the room. It was clear they were Corps from their careful adherence to their training. Or maybe not. The man had scars and was holding his gun in a soldierlike way, in a zone, breathing hard with his eyes pinpointing. But the woman was clearly leaning on her training, with her legs properly apart but her finger off the trigger, down around the guard. An agent for sure. A renegade, one of Rake's old customers, a Black Flag member, would've trigger-fingered and shot the ceiling or hit somebody by now.

Don't move, the male agent was saying. He had a burn scar that ran down from his neck and disappeared under his collar, only to reappear on top of his wrist. It wasn't a stretch to guess it was a combat scar, not at all, and the scruff on his face and his hair, grown out beyond regulation, seemed to tell a story, too.

Who are you? the female agent said, directing her question to Meg. He located a slight, faint quiver in her voice. Before he could speak, Meg answered from her seat at the table, giving her name.

We're agents from the Psych Corps, the male agent said.

There it was in the guy's voice! A tiny trace of a stoner's quiver, leftover desire for Trip, a need for substance and maybe a hint of enfolding around his eyes and in the way he held the gun, as if he half remembered how to maintain his aim in this kind of situation. The scar confirmed it. He'd seen action, been enfolded, taken the treatment, and was out to save the world.

The male agent tightened his grip and steadied his aim. Don't move, he said. His hand was shaking and he didn't sound so sure about what he was doing.

Let me soothe my old lady, Hank said. She's frightened off her rocker, but she's harmless. Keep the gun on me if you want. I won't bolt or move against you. If I were a failed enfold you two would be smeared on that wall there. I would've had a gun at hand, of course, at all times. You know that, I know that.

Go ahead, the man said, following with the gun as he went over to MomMom, who was leaning back against the stove, her mouth wide open, shaking her head but remaining un-usually quiet.

These folks are good folks who are here to take care of

some business that doesn't have a thing to do with God. God's outside the house right now. I'll take you out to see him as soon as we talk a little bit with these people.

Keep her inside, the man said. The woman agent had lowered her gun.

Where's Rake?

So I was right. You're looking for Rake.

That's right.

It's just the three of us—me, Meg, and the old lady. Rake's out of the picture.

Is he in the house? the agent asked. He moved around to the doorway and glanced down the hall.

No, he's gone. Take a look around. You probably don't believe me, I can understand that, but when I get around to explaining it to you, I trust you'll agree that we did what we had to do beyond the law—not that the law means a whole lot up here—and in accordance with the nature of nature, such as it is. I'm a lumber runner, you see, and Meg here is a survivor, an enfold—you probably know, I'm sure you have a file on her, I'm sure you could tell me more about her story than I could.

The two agents seemed to calm down. Window glass covered the sink, and once again a breeze came through the broken window. Hank took a deep breath and smelled a tree, a faint itch of pollen from Canada, and he thought of the roles that he and Meg had played. They'd cast them off in the past weeks, but it might be necessary to revive them now, when they were looking into a gun barrel (no darkness like that of a gun barrel). Meg was totally out of her old role, her face clear and healthy from relaxing in the open air. But there remained a chance that these were rogue agents, acting in bad faith, a couple who had their own dramatic license to play a part.

His muscles had hardened from chopping wood and cleaning around the house. He'd enjoyed relaxing with Meg, but there was still the rumble of motorcycles at night. The locals would keep away, thinking Rake was still around, but others might come flowing in from the Lower Peninsula, now that the fires had started.

I'll go take a look around, the male agent said to the female. You stay down here but keep your gun trained. Get the old lady to sit down at the table.

Hank's telling the truth, Meg said to the female agent. As a matter of fact, he saved my life and I saved his. A few minutes later the man with the gun came back into the kitchen and put it on the counter. No sign of him, he said. He motioned for the woman to put the gun down.

Sit down at the table, Hank said. Join us. We got nothing to hide from you, nothing at all. And we don't have much against the Corps. As a matter of fact, we've both had a form of the treatment. She had the official version and I had my own version. Black market or not, the Trip is Trip. I'd like to exchange names, Hank said, if that's all right with you. I'd like to establish an atmosphere of trust quickly because, in case you haven't heard, all hell is breaking loose downstate and it's heading up this way, the chaos, not that it hasn't been here already. It's not going to take folks out there long to figure out that Rake isn't around. When they do, they're gonna come to extract some revenge for the things he did and the things they imagine he did.

Where is he? the agent said.

Hank leaned back and tweezed his beard. To let them know Rake was out of action would be to open the door to a new place, and that fact would either placate them or, if they were rogue, give them a new sense of freedom and lower their fear level a notch.

In the mission report, he'd describe it as a static scene with a domestic aura. The smell of baked bread. He'd say the girl looked rested and calm, with a small scar on her face. Eyes: blue. Hair: dirty blond, Targets offered hospitality in the form of drink and food. He'd explain that he withheld trust as was warranted in this kind of field situation, assessing for hints, taking as much time as needed, avoiding any kind of interrogative stance until it was proved necessary on account of the fact that it seemed possible that information would be forthcoming if trust could be established. He'd try to describe the old lady, leaning back against the stove and shaking violently, making strange guttural sounds—and the solitude, the sense of seclusion in the kitchen—the exchange in the tension of the guns, the heated delusional space in the fear, and the sense that he had of knowing exactly how to handle it, aiming away from time to time. He'd try to explain how the big one, named Hank, had gone to his mother, kneeled down, kindly, gently, with his big hands on her shoulder, and soothed her, speaking gently, urging her over to the table and pulling the chair out for her, telling her to sit, making her sit down and getting her a glass of water from the sink. The woman was mumbling things, speaking of the end, something about the end, the beginning and the end together. (He'd summarize in the report, explain that the old lady was demented in the way of someone hearing voices that are speaking what seems, to her at least, to be the truth.)

The big burly one was trying to exude a calm. "If you take our point of view, I mean our vantage, if you can do that you'll understand that we can't be totally sure you're not two rogue agents or Black Flaggers in disguise. For all we know, you two are wheeling in here to poke around and see if Rake's really gone or not, and if we tell you he's gone you're gonna play it out to the end, take what you can, get your revenge on us. So I'm not ready yet to say he's not coming back any second. He might be. He might not be."

"We're not rogue agents," Wendy said. She took a sip of her drink, raising her glass as if in a toast.

"Radio reports say it's pretty bad down there. Radio confirmed the Kennedy's genuinely dead this time, no miss, and they say whoever becomes president next is going to walk right along in his footsteps and keep the ball rolling. They say that in theory nothing's really gonna change and that the chain of command has been passed according to the Constitution and all that."

"What's your name?" Wendy said.

"I go simply by Hank and this is Meg Allen. She's the one you're looking for, if you're looking for a girl who was kidnapped by Rake. If that's what you're looking for, that's who you've got right here. And over there is my mother, who got the name MomMom by me when I was a little kid—I could only say things twice, I guess, when I was a certain age—and when she got her dementia she had to be called that or her fits would get worse, so we all just got used to calling her that," he said.

"MomMom's sick," the woman named Meg Allen said.

"She's up and about now, but she's been bedridden since the report came in about the president. It would help us if we see your badges," Hank added.

"They're in the car," Wendy said.

"In case we caught you and held you hostage."

"You could put it that way." Singleton lifted the gun slightly.

"You can put the gun on me as long as you want but I'm not about to tell you what's going on until I'm sure you are who you say you are and doing what you say you should be doing."

"You cover them and I'll go to the car," Singleton said. He felt the exhaustion of the last two days in his arms, holding the gun. The weight of being armed, Klein would've called it. Holding death at your fingertips too long was unbearable.

I had an intuitive recognition of the instability inherent in the scene and an awareness of my own awareness as it related to my enfolded material, he'd write in the report.

What is this sadness? It is the particular sadness that comes at the end of a certain sequence of planned events—an entire summer, in this case. Again, he had a sense that he knew the man at the table and perhaps the girl, too, and it saddened him. Had the entire summer been dedicated to achieving this scene?

"You OK?" he said to Wendy.

"I can hold them," she said.

"How far up the road are you parked?" Hank asked.

"About a quarter mile."

"That's probably fine. Farther away you'd be in trouble because of Black Flag. They come in on recon missions, poke around, look for signs of change, and then leave. They don't dare come up too close, not yet.

"I'll pull into the driveway."

"Make sure no one follows you in."

It was a beautiful night outside. He kept his gun out as he walked up the road to the car. He stood for a second, listening to a distant bike roaring. Assessing, trying to pick up a scent, an awareness. He had—he admitted to himself—been hoping to put a bullet into the skull of the man named Rake, to get it all over in one quick action, to reach an end equal to what he imagined.

He could feel the wild rage of the lake just through the trees, the vast, heavy gravity of its cold depth. This was a land that held on against the forces of wind and raging snow, and the air had a hint of winter and iron. The brutal individuality of the men and women who lived here had been channeled by historical forces, by the anger in the wind, and yet he knew, he was sure standing there, taking another deep breath, lighting a cigarette, that there were also good people, and that it was just as likely, in the scheme of chance and luck, that a soft, warm, cleanly lit kitchen scene would be found in a house hidden from the road.

An hour later they were in the living room, still tense but exhausted. Two old sofas faced a coffee table and, in the corner, a wooden stereo console stood with records piled on each side. Sinatra's youthful face stared out from one, his lips pursed in a smile flushed of irony. Don't fuck with me, the smile said. I'm humorous but only to a certain degree. His hat was cocked to one side and he looked like a man—Singleton thought—who had been enfolded again and again until he lost sight of everything but his body and his voice. On the other side of the console the Rolling Stones sneered at the world, completely unfolded. They jeered and mocked and looked out with twisted lips and a frankness that was clear and brutal but honest.

"You folks go ahead and interrogate us now if that's what you want to do," Hank said. "If you want to start right in, feel free, but I'm not going to be ready to confess all the details until I'm sure you're not just here looking to see if Rake is alive or dead, to confirm the information and pass it on to some gang members out there waiting to know the truth so they can strike as hard and fast as they want, and believe me, that's what they want because Rake called in accounts all over the state, even up into Canada, and made as many enemies as he could."

The subjects struck an assumptive pose of innocence that had a tinge of disguise. The feeling—he'd find a more technical term when the time came—was that Meg and Hank were enfolds partly unfolded, something like that. Search of premises revealed absence of target. Established a friendly cooperative vibe—again, another word?—and a casual rapport via the use of marijuana.

Singleton sat alongside Wendy on the couch, still holding his gun, resting it against his knee but keeping it aimed slightly away from Hank. His hand was tired and his head was starting to pound from the buzz.

"What can we say that will assure you that we're agents?" Wendy said. "We've shown you our badges and the papers and explained that our mission is to come up here to find Rake."

"I'd like to hear something that testifies to your nature," Hank said.

Singleton explained that they were running ahead of the riots downstate, but that they hadn't been sent up ahead of some kind of collapse.

"Anybody can buy a badge and papers on the black market. All we want now is to be left in peace. If I tell you—I mean, really confirm it somehow, although I'm not sure how we'd do that because we don't have something to show you in the way of a body—that he's dead, not lurking out there, or on a run, coming back any moment, are you gonna take that information back to the world and bring every member of Black Flag, every man Rake's ever screwed over in one of his bad deals, not to mention all the men he betrayed in Vietnam. Are they going to swarm our encampment?"

"You can trust us," Wendy said.

"How do I know?"

She leaned in and kissed Singleton and put her hand on his knee.

"That's a good sign. How about we do this? You place the guns on the table and we kick back here and see what happens. You can keep your guns trained if that helps you, but consider the vibe. Truth is, I'm close to believing you are who you say you are, and I don't want to string this out just for the sake of stringing it out, so let's put some music on and see how it goes."

"You're a man of the woods," Singleton said.

"No, I'm a man of the forest. There's a big difference between the two, but I'll spare you the lecture right now."

"Thank God," Meg said with a laugh of newfound happiness.

Deep in the night, they turned the music off and listened to the night sounds, the moan of mufflers down the road. Sometime, near dawn, they drifted asleep—Wendy and Singleton against each other on one couch, Meg and Hank against each other on the other, MomMom upstairs snoring loudly.

Singleton woke first. He'd been dreaming of a cozy, warm house full of love. He'd also been in a train looking out into the dark night at a house down in a hollow, one single light glowing, the roof frosted with moonlight. In the train and the house at the same time. The house, secluded, the train somehow secluded, too, in its transcontinental rush across the dark valley, moving tenderly to some unknown destination.

He'd never mention in his operation report that they had fallen asleep, but he might mention that seeing Hank and Meg curled up together on the couch asleep had given him the sense that they were telling the truth when they said Rake wasn't a threat.

What he really wanted, he realized, was to write a fictionalized report that matched what he'd been hoping for: to be upon the dunes with Wendy, hiding, scoping out the target, aiming, waiting, drawing a deep breath, holding it, and then taking a kill shot to end the matter once and for all. He'd been hoping for a way into violence, for an apex of all narrative lines leading to Rake. He'd imagined that face exploding with the impact of a shell. He'd imagined a beautiful purge of inner tension.

THE FURY UNITES

In the days that followed, as they tried to gain each other's trust, the man named Hank kept stopping to lift his nose to the air, like a dog. He claimed to be able to tell as much from the scent as from the radio reports. Smell was a spectrum to be broken apart and analyzed: lots of burning rubber and cut lumber from buildings in Detroit and Flint and Bay City (Bay City buildings had a spice to them, like oregano, because their lumber was old and seasoned), and then the tires stacked by gang members as barricades (a bitter scent, nothing to ever smell if you could help it), and then of course gasoline and oil and tar, and finally the more natural (and even lovely, in a sick way) smell of forest fires, which according to his nose were moving up the state and would probably hit the top of the mitten in a few weeks.

Wendy gave him pitying looks and told him to stop writing the fucking report. Something had shifted in her demeanor. In bed the second night, she refrained from touching him, rolling away, sleeping on her side. He ran his hand along her hip and she slapped it away.

What? Nothing. What's wrong? Silence. When she fell asleep he put his hand back on her hip and left it there until he drifted off, only to wake deep in the night to the sound of motorcycles down the road, and then, when they were gone, the distant shush of the waves and the buzz in his ear. Wendy was breathing quietly, an almost inaudible shush. *Put something in the report about bonding between Wendy and Meg, some indication that they had found a mutual point of commonality, both of them having lost lovers in Vietnam. Something about the afternoon chat, over tea, at the kitchen table, sharing stories while he listened from the hallway, pressing his back against the cool plaster (no, he'd leave that out), catching words, the name Steve Williams (a.k.a. Zomboid), something about the beach, the clink of the cups against the saucers. In the process of interrogation she and Meg had formed a silent alliance.*

Early one morning, jittery with exhaustion, Singleton drove into town to use a phone outside the tavern. When he left, Wendy was still asleep, far over on her side of the bed, hugging the edge, breathing softly.

"We got to the target," Singleton said to Klein. "We believe, although we're not sure, that he is dead. You were wrong, sir. Or perhaps you were right."

"Son, I want you to envision me deep beneath a mountain, behind a ten-ton door, in a bunker," Klein said. "Because that's where I am right now. We had all incoming calls rerouted out here. I'm deep underground." His voice indeed sounded attenuated by the lines slung from pole to pole across the Great Plains, following the railroad right-of-way. Lines humming in a perpetual wind, twanging against the glass insulator bulbs. "Couldn't hold on in Flint. We not only had too many failed enfolds out there but we also put too much trust in the treatment without understanding that the things we didn't understand were just as important as those we did. Now we're undertaking a review of the entire program, top to bottom."

"I'm formally resigning," Singleton said. "I want to get that in before the connection is cut."

"You can't resign, because I'm having you processed for administrative adjudication, son. Believe me, it's the best thing that ever happened to you. I filled it out yesterday. But the papers are going up this morning."

"Yes, sir, sir," Singleton said. The parking lot at the tavern had a single bike parked near the door. Black streamers hung from the handlebar grips, fluttering.

"And now that you're not my charge, now that you're AWOL and on the run, I can give you an order man to man, from me to you. Father to son, so to speak, although of course I'm only taking a paternal role in theory. I assume you've had some time to think about your own real father," he said. Klein's voice faded for a moment and again Singleton imagined drooping lines along the right-of-way. ". . . hereby order you to interrogate the girl Meg. Get what you can from her. Use any means necessary—"

The connection clicked off with seeming finality. Holding the phone, Singleton watched a man in a leather jacket with Black Flag tags stumble out the tavern door and across the parking lot, singing to himself in an Irish brogue, his voice loud in the morning quiet. Singleton reestablished a dial tone, put some coins into the slot, and read numbers from his palm. The ringing signal, he heard at his end, presumably took the form, on the other end, of a clapper striking a bell in the belly of a black phone. He was about to hang up when Wendy's father answered. The voice of a thousand smoked cigars. A throat that needed to be cleared every few minutes.

"Headquarters," it said.

"It's me, Singleton. How goes it down there? You surviving?"

"We're alive," Wendy's father said. Another man came out

of the tavern drunk. He flopped down on the sidewalk and sat with his legs crossed and his head bowed into his open hands. "We're in the fray but it's looking good. We held off the first wave. Nothing like a man in a wheelchair with a gun to confuse matters, and it didn't hurt that I covered him with the big gun. Mostly kids and a few disgruntled locals but no vets, thank God. The vets aren't in this one, because they came—most of them—for treatment."

"So the violence is dying down?"

"Not at all. All of our scouting reports—and by that I mean what I hear on the radio—indicate that a counterattack is gathering."

"Well, be safe. Please pass word to Steve Williams that we're thinking about him."

"He still prefers to be called the Zomboid."

"OK, pass word to the Zomboid."

"I'm being processed for administrative adjudication, which is a fancy phrase for court-martial," he told Wendy when he got back to the house. Everything was quiet. MomMom was upstairs still sleeping, and Hank and Meg had taken a hike to the beach to look around for signs of Black Flaggers. She was in the kitchen, at the table, smearing jam on a slice of toast, leaning into the task, not looking up, keeping her head down as he explained that her father was OK and things were quieting down.

"They're not quieting," she said, softly. "And there's not going to be a court-martial, because we're not going back there for a long time."

"I'm not sure about that. If this entire thing was meant to be part of our treatment, especially if it was Klein's idea, then maybe we can go back and beat the rap."

"It's pretty clear. It isn't exactly open to interpretation. The safe house wasn't safe. The target isn't a target. Now here we are."

"But he's in a bunker. Who knows what he really meant. He was cryptic."

"Cryptofascist might be what you mean."

"He told me to interrogate Meg."

"I've already done that. It's pretty simple. Rake took her out of the Grid because she probably had some connection with someone in his past—I didn't get that far. She lost her boyfriend over in Nam and had a breakdown and was selected for treatment."

"I know you've done it, but I think I should, too, somehow."

"She won't say much to you," she said.

"Well, maybe not. I'm going to interrogate Hank first anyway. We're building trust, but we have to consider what he said about his acting abilities—that he enfolded himself and then played the role, his words, of someone who was still in there with the derangement. He might be acting now."

"Nobody's acting," she said. "Can't you see that, Sing? Can't you see that you're the only one who's acting?"

"I'm not acting. I'm doing my job."

"See what I mean," she said, and she got up from the table and went out the back door. When he looked out the window, tight in the frames of light gray, she was alone by the shed looking out toward the woods.

Final action reports contain enemy body count, men cured of trauma, proper enfolds, number of failed enfolds, psychological profiles, guns and ammo seized. They were about horseshoe formations closing in on all sides, always ending with a sharp forward thrust. A good report had a subtext of preordained domination. A twisting of failure into success. He would have to make the initial standoff in the kitchen much tenser. He'd have to stress that he in no way intended the action as a form of self-treatment, or a way to gather information about his own trauma. According to the Credo—and leaving aside Klein's transgressions—it was an agent's duty to sustain an enfolded state and relate impersonally with the target (in other words, to become as inhuman as you could, subordinating your impulses to the structure of the Corps). That meant he would have to avoid all mention of his wartime relationship (indeed, if he had had one) with Rake. He'd have to pretend, if he ever went back to Flint, typing it up on the old manual, that his own needs had not played a role in the intuitive decisions he had made. He'd have to pretend that he had not unfolded himself at all.

To establish—as he'd write in his report, or claim at the adjudication—esprit de corps with Hank he agreed to go out on a recon mission to assess the level of gang activity. The two of them hiked through the brambles and then crawled across a field and into woods, weaving between trees until they could see a house behind which two men were sitting in lawn chairs, smoking and looking out in their direction. They crouched and watched for a few minutes before retreating into the woods. Hank said the two men had been sitting like that for most of the summer. He sniffed the air and led Singleton farther south to a second house, which consisted of multiple mobile homes connected by breezeways to the main house. Choppers were neatly parked in a line out front. A man with a rifle slung over his shoulder sat in a chair under an awning. Hank scoped him and made an ID. "That's a guy named Duke, he works a big-shot connection down in Pawpaw. He's been standing guard for about three weeks. There's a few new choppers, so I'd say they're arriving from downstate now. Rake had some kind of agreement with those folks, a truce.

I'd say they're waiting for someone to come riding up with a sweet rumor. They've sensed a lack of activity."

They hiked back into the woods and came out in a clearing about a mile inland from the lake. Hank swished through the grass and then, like a dog, turned around and around to clear a spot, motioning for Singleton to sit down, offering up a hand in a gesture that seemed sweetly out of place.

"You've got to trust me, Singleton. The way you and Wendy have been acting the last three days shows outward trust. You've been acting like you trust us, hanging out, joining me on this mission, and that's a first step. But there's still internal doubt and all of that."

He lit two cigarettes and passed one to Singleton. Then he lay back with his arms crossed behind his head.

"What'd they train you on interrogation? I'll bet they told you to begin with easy banter, establish trust, and then, when a moment like this comes along, hit hard."

"That's about it," Singleton said. The air was filled with late summer chaff and insects. A breeze sifted through the grass and then died away. Singleton thought about how it must've felt to wade through grass with his rifle overhead into a horizon that was brutally open and visible.

"This might be the time," Hank said, "to tell me something, not too intimate, about your journey that might help me trust you a little more."

"I can tell you one thing," Singleton said. "You ever hear of blue pills?"

"*The* blue pills?"

"Or green. Sometime they're gray or green or whatever. We're talking about putting a stress on the 'the.'"

"A story with a pill," Hank said. He closed his eyes and let the sun bathe his face. "I've heard plenty of stories with pills."

"A grunt recognizes a grunt who's been treated and can't

remember a damn thing about the war. There's a strange moment between them. The guy who's been treated racks his brain knowing that he should know the other guy. He digs and digs because he can see, in the way the other guy's looking, a pure connection. All this in a few seconds."

"The man doing the recognizing puts the onus onto the man being recognized," Hank says. "I know that feeling, man. I know it all too fucking well."

Singleton took a deep breath, took a sip from his canteen, and told Hank the story of the blue pills. The Flint streets, the desolation of afternoon, how it felt to leave the Corps building after a briefing session, to pass through the revolving door and bump into Frank. He described the helmet liner. The weird sensation of being recognized by somebody who, presumably, he had once known in battle.

"Folks come out of nowhere, like you and Wendy did the other night, to present themselves as part of your past with no way to prove it," Hank said. "You have all of these folks drifting around with the pivotal point of their lives buried, not sure if they should be digging around, and from time to time someone comes along. It's a fucking strange world, man."

"He came up to me and called me Captain and then said he was going to fulfill a promise he had made to me in Nam, and he handed me a bag of pills and I had to confirm it, had to know for sure before I took them, and when it was confirmed, I mean when I saw that he really was there with my unit, Wendy and I took them."

"You still have some of those left?" Hank said. He looked out across the grass at the trees, mostly jack pines, against the sky.

"I've got exactly four left," Singleton said.

"One for each of us, is what I'd say," Hank said.

"Now it's your turn to tell a story."

"You already know my story," Hank said. "It's a story you know too well. Except instead of getting tagged and put in treatment I partnered with Rake before they could find me. I was so fucked up, I'm guessing, upon getting home that I didn't have a choice. I told you I treated myself. It's all enfolded now," he said, tapping his head. "So you know the deal. I'm making it up based on the backwash I picked up from things Rake told me. He didn't like to talk about that shit, so basically I just have a vague sense that I came out and met up with him and took to the road and played it all out that way, one killing at a time. Was I a psychopath like Rake? No way, man, and I can attest to that, of course, because I'm not a failed enfold. There was part of me that could be saved, otherwise I wouldn't have been saved. I like to think it was my love of MomMom that pulled me through it and created a will to self-treatment, but I'll never know and don't want to know and if I do start wanting to know—heading to the waterline—you do your best to pull me back, and I'll do the same for you, man, if you want me to," he said, and then he lay back down and settled into a silence.

"What happened to Rake?" Singleton said.

Hank laughed. "I knew that was coming. Deeper trust formed and you struck. You've been trained."

"What happened to Rake?"

"Meg and I had to find a way to channel his desire to kill into the little bit of honor he had left—something like that. He had a little bit left, my gut told me. I had to trust my gut. We had to find a way to get him killed without either one of us doing the killing. I thought about getting him to commit suicide, something along those lines, and, again, I thought about killing him myself, risking going back to that old place, reversing the treatment. Believe me, there was nothing I wanted to do more than take him out. I was itching to do it. Meg wanted to do it, too. Then these rumors came in about duels up on Isle Royale and I made use of them in my own way."

"How'd you do that?" Singleton said.

"I'd rather not get into the details right now. But believe me, Rake's dead. He's gone. Nothing to worry about. I get the sense you know that anyway."

A perfect blue-skied end-of-August day with a faint hint of autumn. A front had come through early in the morning and pushed back the southerly smell of burning tires and trees and cleared out the sky. "One last daytime beach excursion," Hank suggested. The night before, the Black Flaggers had approached closer than ever.

Now, on the shore, Hank was on his back with his hands crossed over his chest, his soft belly exposed. He was talking about the good groove that he and Singleton had going, the sense of shared mission that was developing. Wendy and Meg, arm in arm, were sauntering down the sand, staying close to the waterline where the gravel was smooth, stopping on occasion to look out at the water. (Later he'd look back and see that there had been intention in the secretive distance they had kept. Sitting across from Hank, he had felt something, an urge to run to them, to take Wendy by the hand and lead her into the berm—not really a dune—where he would declare his love for her in no uncertain terms. Later he'd understand that he had been locked into an operative task, focused, zeroed in on getting some kind of answer from Hank.)

"I need to know what you did with Rake's body. I need details on how you handled the duel."

Hank sat up and lit a cigarette.

"What difference does it make. If I could enfold *that* story, I'd take fucking Trip right now and do it. That's all in the past. I just want to forget it."

"No. I need it for my report," Singleton said.

"You're not going to write a report. I heard if you go back, you'll be court-martialed."

"Sent up for adjudication," Singleton said. Wendy had turned and was looking back at him with her hands out as if to say: What are you doing, exactly? What are we doing?

"Same thing. You're not going back there and you're not going to write a report," Hank said. He lit a cigarette, blew the smoke to the side. "It's not that I don't want to tell you. It's that if I say it, if I put it in the air, if you hear it, you're not going to want to go back, ever."

"I'm going to write the report."

"Well, Singleton, let me tell you, it was risky and we had to go deep into our roles. To make sure the Black Flaggers wouldn't know he was dead, I took a big risk and drove down to the L.P. Left deep in the night and got down to the bridge at dawn, crossed over it, and then propped the body in front of Fort Michilimackinac. You probably know that the police took over the fort because it is supposedly avoided by failed enfolds, or something like that. Word goes around that failed enfolds like Rake can't stand anything that harkens back to the wars before Nam. There's nothing that screws with the mind like a fake old fort, with all of those logs carved into points, is what they say."

"Why leave the body for the Corps to find?"

"In retrospect, which isn't really fair, I'd say the idea was to get you to come up here so we'd able to leave on friendly terms with the Corps and avoid being tracked. I'll say one thing. We had both reached a limit. If we went deep downstate with Rake's body, we'd be dead meat before we got far. If we went ourselves, we'd never make it alive. Not if word got out—and believe me, it's gonna get out—that Rake was dead. Rake alive was what kept us safe. There must be a catchphrase for someone in a situation that is simply not winnable, for a road that splits into two options that are just as bad. Two roads that lead back to the original option."

"There isn't a catchphrase for that," Singleton said.

"But you at least get the gist," Hank said. "Meaning if we didn't put the body there you wouldn't be here, and if you weren't here, I wouldn't have to come up with a precise explanation for our actions. It wouldn't matter. The fact that I need to explain what we did has everything to do with the fact that it's you who's doing the asking, and you'd never be asking if I hadn't put the body there, you see."

Hank cupped his palm over a match and lit a joint. He inhaled and held and released a cloud and hit again.

"I think I'll have a hit of that," Singleton said, reaching for the joint. He'd have to say the body had been transported downstate to the fort for unknown reasons, if he did write a report. He looked out at Meg and Wendy, who were still arm in arm, down near the water, but turned slightly, looking back at him. The waves were slathering in with long, slow sweeps, arriving at what seemed to be an angle to the beach.

"You're probably thinking it was a neat, clean operation. I imagine that's what you're thinking. But it wasn't clean, man. Not at all. It wasn't neat."

"I wouldn't think it was," Singleton said.

"I took advantage of Meg, in that I discovered that besides being another one of Rake's prisoners, she had another connection to his past, one I couldn't remember because of the Tripizoid, but I sensed it. I guessed it was there. All that is lost to me. Everything before she arrived. But I'm guessing, because I can't remember, that he went gonzo crazy when he saw her name on one of those black-market lists, just as I'm guessing I didn't enlist with him for the Army, I mean we didn't sign up together with the buddy program, because I do have vivid recollections of my boyhood up to the day I was in my bedroom packing up my stuff, heading off to boot camp, along with some residual memories of flying over to Nam, landing, the smell of the trees over there, and things like that. Then everything goes blank. If I'd been friends with Rake before Nam I wouldn't remember all that shit. It would be enfolded. He was a nasty fucker as a kid, I'm sure. He went in with a chip on his shoulder and the war was his feeding ground."

"So you immersed her. You gave her a controlled dunk in the lake?" Singleton said.

"I was careful and told her it was a onetime deal. I kept my own head above water."

"And she came out and told you what she saw?"

"Well, I wouldn't say that. She told me bits and pieces, but eventually she mentioned a name that seemed to trigger a little bit of a spark." He tapped his head. "Enough to hint that her connection with Rake had to do with whatever I'd enfolded in myself and that her connection with Rake in the past was also a connection with me. It made me think, maybe the Trip doesn't get it all enfolded. Maybe we *all* have something that'll spark a memory."

"So you used the name to somehow provoke a duel?"

"Rake had been out on a long run and I enfolded myself with the black-market Tripizoid when he was gone. Then he came back, months later, with Meg. Then he went out again and brought this kid named Haze back. I'm guessing I knew he'd gone into the Grid for Meg specifically, although I didn't figure why until Meg unfolded and had that vision. After that, we had to keep in our roles of Old Meg and Old Hank. But that was wearing thin by late June, early July."

Singleton stared out at the water. Riding atop the horizon, like a block of stone, another tanker headed on course to Duluth, or away, it was impossible to tell. Down the beach, Wendy and Meg were sidearming stones into the water, making them skip.

"I've come to the conclusion, thanks to the Trip, that killing goes against nature in the deepest way, that to kill another no matter what the reason, no matter how justified in war, leaves you coated with some kind of residue. You pay a price, no matter what. Animals don't pay a price because the price has to do with the fact that you know what you did. Trees don't even have the price."

"So you had to find a way to get him into a situation that would result in his death, and to make it his idea, to make him the initiator."

"It makes me sad thinking about it, but knowing a little bit of Rake's story, I wanted him to have the satisfaction in his last moments of thinking that he had somehow resolved things that could not be resolved—because really, Singleton, you and I both know that there is nothing more tragic than a man like Rake, someone who doubled up a trauma so huge that he wants to eat the earth itself."

"You wanted him to initiate it so it would be part of his own story, somehow connected with his own trauma."

"Initiate's exactly right," Hank said. "Haze was dumb as a peg, but he had unusual smarts when it came to his place in the pecking order and knew he had to worry about me as much as he worried about Rake. He put on a front that he didn't give a shit. Meg and I waited as long as we could, and then one night when we were all at the dinner table and things were relatively calm I decided to play the trump card. At least I hoped it was a trump card. Truth is, it was just a shot in the dark because I wasn't sure if I'd made the right connection. I figured that Rake had gone down there and grabbed Meg for a reason. I figured she had some connection with his past, but, again, the rest of the story was lost to me. Bad timing, what have you. A bad twist. Meg didn't tell me that much about her vision, but again she did mention the man's name, the man in the vision, and like I said, it gave me a feeling that he had something to do with Rake, his initial combat trauma situation. I figured our only shot would be to put that name in Haze's mouth."

"What was the man's name?" Singleton said. He had a feeling it would help with his report, snap everything into place. Far down the beach the women held stones, waiting for a breaker to ebb, finishing its journey across hundreds of miles of lake and leave behind a momentarily smooth surface, perfect for stone skipping. Hank was saying he didn't have the slightest idea what the T stood for. Hank said the name that had sparked the duel and he said it again, saying, "Billy-T, Billy-T's the name," and then he kept talking as Singleton tried to process the name, one part of his mind listening while another felt a current dashing around the name itself; one part of his mind clear and engaged with reality (another stone tossed, the two women looking distant and conspiratorial) as the other began to process the name that had been spoken, while the other part was unfurled into an acute, brutal, lonely, isolated desolation in which his mind's eye (no other way to put it, he'd tell Wendy, later) saw his father, dressed in his olive overalls with goggles, at work, car after car, and then sitting during his lunch break with his black bucket between his legs on the windowsill eating a sandwich his mother had made, and worrying over his son in Vietnam, his son becoming a man in the infernal heat of combat.

The next thing he knew, water was closing around him, the cold pounding his temples and his jaws and shoving the air out of his lungs. Even as he sank below the surface, feeling the vise of the cold, he was aware that he was a man who had been flung into direct contact with something huge from his past—and later he'd swear that he was thinking about the report, the name Billy-T expanding in his mind until he could hear it speaking, a slight lisp, and then arms came around him and lifted him up, ordering him not to resist, to stay calm and then for a few seconds he was deep again. He could feel the mighty body, not just the water but the entire lake. *There have been rumors about men who, confirming a specific element of their Causal Events Package, went wild with a desire to be permanently unfolded.* And then he felt arms around him, lifting him up, and he was above the surface and Hank was slapping him softly, speaking into his ear as he pulled him to shore, saying, "You're gonna want to do that again. You'll want to get back into that water but as long as I'm here it won't happen." He pulled him along the sand and wrapped him in the picnic blanket and made him sit down.

Through chattering teeth he said the name Billy-T over and over again, his voice incantatory, as if he were trying to memorize the sound of it, and when Meg came up, breathing hard, she stood and listened and then got down next to him and asked, "What happened?"

"He made the connection I thought he might make. The deal has been sealed."

"What deal is that?" Wendy said. She had her hands on her hips and was staring down at them. "I mean, what deal exactly are you talking about?"

"The deal that started as soon as I saw you walk in the door," Hank said, and Singleton closed his eyes and felt the beach shift beneath him, a sense of complete dissociation and then, a second later, the feeling of being rooted in the sand. Klein had once said that it didn't take much to put two and two together when you're in the field, when you're on the ground making minute-by-minute conclusions, trying to go with the information you're seeing, smelling, instead of orders the staff sends down from Command. Draw your own conclusions. Shoot first and ask the dead questions. Was it really possible that the Corps had set the whole thing up as some kind of re-habilitative structure? It was a sad, simple, clear question.

"So you, Billy-T, and Rake were in a squad together in Nam," Hank explained. "You were buddies with Billy-T. You lost him. You lost your dear buddy, your best friend. The three of you signed up together—at least that's what it looks like. But I didn't enlist with you guys. Like I said before, I have memories that go back to the day I was packing my stuff up before leaving for boot camp, and everything before that—growing up downstate, summer afternoons playing ball, friends and buddies and girlfriends but nobody named Meg, and no Rake, that's for sure, so for me it's clear that what I enfolded started in Vietnam and was finished in Nam. I was drafted clean and simple. I got my notice. But you and Meg share a common past with Rake."

"Is that the way you see it?" Singleton said, turning to Meg. Her face was pale and pinched with pain.

"I knew it as soon as you told us your name," she said. "He talked about you in the vision I had. You two were there together. You were good friends."

"What else?"

"He was in the jungle, in a firefight, and there was some-one named Frank who liked to pray over bodies. Then he was in Hue. Then he was dead. I was in love with him. He was my boyfriend and then he got drafted."

This is the moment he'd heard about, that was rumored to exist, when you came into contact with somebody who had a direct connection to the trauma and shared the grief. Hank had taken Wendy down the beach to give them a little time alone. Space but not too much space was the way he put it, a chance to talk alone.

"He was angry," she said. "And he was dead. He talked to me about going to his own funeral. Were you at the funeral?"

"He was in a casket and I was in combat," Singleton said. "I remember when he was killed. In my vision we were fight-ing in Hue. Obviously, the second siege of Hue. He was calling in for air support and the strike came and it came in too close, and he was at the phone, first calling the coordinates in and then still holding it when the strike came, so it isn't clear to me if he was calling in a second strike or if my vision compressed time, or if he just liked to hold that phone to his mouth, but then there was the fireball."

"He had a slight lisp," Meg said, her voice quivering. "I loved his lisp."

"I don't remember that," Singleton said.

"Now you do," Meg said.

She reached out and touched his face and he did the same and for a few seconds they held their hands there, as if passing thoughts and memories through their fingers.

"We were dating, me and Billy-T. He took me out to California, I think, and we went to the beach out there."

"What did he look like?"

"He had curly hair—wavy, and it was sun blond, bleached, and he had this great smile," she said.

"If I could remember him that's the way I'd picture him," Singleton said. "He had a big smile."

"Yeah, a sweet smile," she said, and then she went on to explain more, to lay it all out, to describe some of the things he already knew and some that were new to him. Down the beach Wendy and Hank had gone as far as they dared and had turned around, facing in their direction, arms down, looking straight ahead as if to wait for something to resolve.

There was an unnatural attraction between two linked by grief. Wendy's awareness of that attraction was apparent in the swing of her arms as she ran down the beach. There was a connective name between us, Billy-T, and when the name was spoken, Agent Singleton (I) had a reflexive response. There were rumors that if two enfolds met and exchanged information a natural unfolding would take place, whereupon the two patients would share enough mutual memory material to counteract the Tripizoid in a natural manner, inducing a natural memory outside of the traumatic material.

.

"Maybe grief has to work itself out like this or something. If it's not felt, if it doesn't happen, it finds a way," Hank said later that night as they sat at the kitchen table. They had returned from the beach, cooked dinner—chicken, potatoes, green beans—together, working alongside MomMom. She seemed aware of the shift, the change, and when she spoke her voice was lower, calmer.

"I don't mean to throw even more disrespect on the Corps, but there's simply no way they knew you coming up here would result in some kind of reunification. If they did know, they're a hell of a lot more organized than I thought. It's better if you don't even consider that as a possibility. Put it aside, man, put it aside," Hank said.

"No, I can't. The best way for me to think about it is to believe that Klein knew," Singleton said. "For my own sense of sanity I'm gonna say that he arranged things, maybe not specific things but the general pattern. He made a point of disregarding the instructions from Command as a way of making damn sure I knew that I had to make decisions in the field, based on the field. The last order he gave me was to interrogate Meg."

"And he said it was a form of treatment," Wendy said. "Don't forget that."

"He made me say it."

"And you said it. Now put it aside," she said, and she pushed her chair back, took Meg by the hand, and they went off into the living room, where they sat talking, their voices coming down the hall and into the kitchen while Hank and Singleton sat in silence, listening.

That night, in their room, they heard the old lady crying out in her delirium, her words coming down the hall. From the window there was the usual sound of surf breaking and, later, the roar of a gang of bikers coming closer and then receding with the pop of a backfire. Then the wind began to pick up, a long, low hissing through the bramble and trees as each gust approached, blowing the shade up into the room as it struck the house broadside, shaking away into a deep quiet (the buzz was completely gone from his ears) again until the next one arrived. That was how his grief felt. It came welling up out of the connection he had with the young woman, Meg, and then it receded into the logic of his assessment of the situation, his desire, for whatever reason, to somehow remain inside something that resembled an operation, a plan of action, a sense of being on a mission. His desire to find a technical way to describe the afternoon seemed to fade and he tried to focus his mind on Meg, her freckled face, her wide eyes, wondering if he had known her at least through a photograph that Billy had passed around to the guys in their unit, because he had carried a photo, for sure, if he was a normal grunt. Then he thought of the structure of the bridge, the long, beautiful arch of it across those brutal currents, and the two parts of the state, and he thought of Wendy's father holding out down in Flint as he let his mind zoom into space to look down at the hand shape that was supposedly part of what drew vets in from all over the country, attracted not only to the shape itself but to the peninsular aspect, the fact that there were so many places in which to find an end point, and he thought about the streets of Flint, and the young man in his wheelchair, smoking a cigarette, his gun aimed at the sky, and he quickly let his mind zoom back down to the house he was in—beneath a roof, comfortable in bed with Wendy, who was letting him rest his hand on her belly, sliding it along the band of her underwear, not responding but not pushing him away. When he asked her if she was awake she said she was wide awake.

"I'm disappointed and relieved at the same time. I thought this would make me feel better. I was hoping to get here, find Rake alive, and take him out."

Another gust of wind gathered in the darkness and the shade sucked back tight against the screen with a snap and the house seemed to grow tense in the rafters. He slipped his fingers along the band of her underwear and lifted it gently.

"I saw the way Meg reached up and touched your face when you were talking on the beach," Wendy said. "You wanted to touch her back, I mean really touch her, and you stopped yourself by keeping your hand on her cheek. You wanted to go deeper, but consciously you drew a line that you really needed, like my father. You just knew that enough had been spoken, revealed. Now you're going to leave it alone," she said.

"What makes you think so?" he said.

"Because I want you to."

"So I didn't seem pathetic?" he said.

"Yes," she said tenderly, pushing against him.

"Yes, I didn't?"

"Yes, you seemed pathetic," she said. Another gust gathered, the sudden stillness, a drawing back not only of air but time, too, it seemed, and then after it had gone through, in the stillness, a complete silence. The old lady down the hall had fallen asleep.

It's impossible for me to think that this entire thing is merely an elaborate form of treatment, he would write in his report. And yet the implausibility of the conspiracy is precisely what makes it plausible. To be AWOL but, in a deeper sense, not AWOL at all . . . Was the intention that I terminate Rake, or that, by confronting him, I effect the cure that the Corps had failed to effect with him? Or was this only about me? That I was supposed to go to Rake and, before killing him, get filled in on what really happened over there, to learn

*about my experience in Vietnam from the horse's mouth?
But the horse was dead.*

Without a word Wendy reached over and turned on the
light and got up and went to the bag on the floor and came to
bed with four zip pills, popping two and swallowing them dry
before he could stop her and then putting her hand out as if to
say: Now you. He popped his and laughed because it was already coming over the edge of his grief, a bright, delusional
sense of being able to see anything and everything, and when
Wendy turned off the light the room was suffused with phos-
phorescence, greenish in hue, trickling through the window
and around the floor and across the sheets, which roiled and
shimmered. She touched his scars and ran her finger down his
arm, leaving a trace of green light where the warmth remained
on his skin, and he traced his name on the soft curve of her
belly and then watched her as she got up, went to the window,
pulled the shade up, and called him over to look as beyond
the trees, in flashbulb bursts, the lightning flared out the yard,
metallic silver—and then she turned to him, offering her
mouth, kissing him with the taste of ash and mint, everything
accentuated by the pills, sharp and acute, her tongue twisting
with his own.

"Not yet," she told him, pushing away. "We've got all
night."

The edge the pill created seemed acute and sharp but with
a wave of sadness pushing behind. He imagined that Billy-T
had felt the same way, just before he was killed, and that the
Zomboid had had a similar feeling, a kind of refinement of
his senses shoved forward by sadness into a precise, particular moment. As if she had read his thoughts, Wendy was quietly crying, her tears bleeding, glistening with sparkles down
her cheeks, and when she rubbed them away there was a violet
bloom of color that faded into green. He could only imagine

that she was thinking about her own loss, or about the mu-tual shared loss she had with Meg. He wanted to ask her, but when he began to speak she put her fingers to his lips and shushed him and got up and began to get dressed, slipping into her pants and then pulling a shirt on and telling him— with a wave of her arms—to do the same, motioning to the door and then leading him down the hallway, past Mom-Mom's room, past Meg and Hank's room, down the stairs, and through the kitchen to the back porch, where they sat watching the yard burst into brightness and then diminish into residual light, pale silver and green, as another gust arrived—the sound raking the air far off, reeding through the dry grass and through a million dying leaves with a low, toothy hiss—and she raised her voice to speak through it, and he lis-tened as she told him that when the Zomboid came home— when Steve came home, she said, softly—he was angry and violent, first at his legs, at what was missing in his body, and then at her, at what was missing in her, because no matter what she did, it wasn't enough, not even close.

"Nothing's missing from you," Singleton said. "Nothing at all."

"Nothing that you can see," she said, taking his hand.

When the rain started they went inside, back through the kitchen, up to the bed. The pills—he'd later think—provided them with the necessary acuity, funneling all sensation into the fingertips and eyes, into the sensations that under normal conditions would simply be erotic.

When she told him to fuck her—that's how she said it, di-rect, no buildup, *fuck me*—he drew himself over her in the bed but she stopped him and turned him onto his back, hold-ing her hands flat on his chest, fanning her fingers over his scars again, leaving a faint handprint when she moved them back. He closed his eyes, and when he opened them a few minutes later he saw that her head was tossed back like a floating swimmer, keeping her head above water for air, her lips parted, her hair sizzling with static. The nearness—a tenseness at the back of his cock, deeper still—caused him to ease up, because he wanted it to last a long, long, long time, but it didn't because he was pushing up into the sweet vacuum, the airless zone somewhere deep inside, the same one he had felt months ago, and he felt himself slipping away not into another unfolded vision but into something much calmer. Then there was the same backdraft as another wind gust gathered far off, and for a few seconds—maybe it was minutes—while the clouds recharged, there was a pause in the lightning and thunder and the house was silent except for her moans, and his, and then she came and he came, a flutter and tightness, and when she was done she collapsed against him and he wrapped his arms around her back and they stayed still for a few minutes, rocking gently.

They talked deep into the night and at some point he heard himself declaring his love for her, and she listened and accepted it. It was that simple. He was not finished with his sense of mission, of being inside something that was larger, a conspiracy or whatever, but the fact that he had admitted it, that he had met someone with a shared memory, had released him, freed him.

"You're full of shit," Wendy said. "But that's OK. I think you meant what you said."

At another point in the night—the zip pills had worn thin and an acute but pleasant exhaustion had taken over, birds were waking each other up in the trees, and the grainy twilight was materializing the dresser, the bed frame, the walls—she went to her bag and got the veil and held it in her hands, flat against her palms, and stood in the center of the room for a few minutes and waited until he got on his knees and kissed her belly and said maybe he would, and she asked would what? And he said betroth himself to her someday, and she asked him where he got such a pretentious word, and he said he didn't know, maybe from a book, it's not a word he would normally use, and he went down the hall to the bathroom to pee and came back and found her in bed, sleeping soundly, and he got in next to her, and in beautiful exhaustion of the diminished pill, cradled in the sounds of dawn, he fell asleep.

THE DUEL

Rake had begun sharpening all the blades in the house one day in early August, starting with the ax, using a file and whetstone, buffing it to a shine before starting on his knife collection—switchblades, his deer-gutting knives, his swords, taking them to the kitchen window to check them in the sunlight, dabbing water and running a cloth along the edge. All action a manifestation of some end point, Hank thought, watching. He went out to find Meg, who was in the yard, chained to a post near the shed.

"It's time, tonight," he whispered. "He's totally charged. He's on edge enough to believe it when I get Haze to say what he has to say. Rake'll hear what he wants to hear and not what's being said. He's so high, so angry that he'll twist anything that he hears into a provocation, and we'll provide that provocation in the form of a name, and then if I'm right, if we're lucky, we've found the right connection, and all we have to do—I should say all I'll have to do, because what *you* have to do is just follow my lead—is to channel that anger into the direction of a duel, which, given how many times I've already planted the idea, he should go for—if we're lucky."

Hank went back to the kitchen, where Rake lifted a sword, ran his fingers along the edge, and pointed it at him.

So you're saying this is about my honor?

I'm saying it's about honor, hell yes. There's a way to kill Haze with honor and then burn his body and make it hard to identify, put it somewhere agents will find it. They'll think it's you and not you. Both at the same time? You'll tap their ineptitude, the fact that the cops, who'll find the body for sure if we put it near the bridge, will send their liaison down there with the news, with snapshots and all that, and they'll open your case even wider and send some agents up looking, he said. Get it, man, they'll speculate that you're fucking with them but they'll wonder, too, and you know, I mean, I've been telling you that Haze has been back-talking you. Just look at his face and tell me he isn't thinking things he can't say aloud, the dumb shit, and like every other sidekick you've ever had, with me as the exception, he's figuring a way to disappoint you. And he's been talking. He's been speaking the unspeakable.

Keep it vague enough to let him fill in the blanks, Hank thought. He took the sword and went across the yard and with wide, dramatic swings began shredding the sheets while MomMom, standing to one side, for the first time that summer somehow seeming to understand the nature of the situation, stayed quiet and watched.

Say it to him, Haze. Say what's on your mind. Say what you said to me in the yard. Say Billy-T betrayed Rake, Hank said at the kitchen table that night. That's what you said to me this afternoon, isn't it? That's what you said?

Said what? Haze said. He was stoked up on a concoction of Rake's, his eyes were dilated into dark seeds of black, his face was pale and glossy with sweat. His voice was fluty, perplexed, full of fear.

Hank whispered to Haze. Say what you said to me the other day about the man named Billy-T.

Haze shifted his fingers on his fork and spoon.

Say what? he said.

Say what you said. Say Billy-T, Hank said.

Say Billy-T, Haze said. He spoke loudly and urgently and he looked at Rake and then back at Hank and then at Rake, who tensed up tight.

Billy-T, Haze said. That's what you want me to say?

There were vast forests waiting, Hank assured himself, trying to stay in character, to remain completely still, drilling the kid with his eyes, ignoring Rake, who was starting to lift himself from the table.

No, I said say it to Rake, right here, right now. Tell to him what you told me. Say it to Rake. Billy-T betrayed you.

Say to Rake Billy-T betrayed you.

No. Billy-T betrayed you.

Billy-T betrayed you, Haze said to Rake. The words sounded flat and solid and sure. Rake turned and seemed to listen for the first time. He made one swing with his head, as if to clear water from his ears, and tossed his hair back. He cut loose, suddenly becoming all bulging muscles and speed as he sprang up and grabbed Haze by the neck, squeezing hard, producing the knife in a sweeping glint, and held the blade to the nape of Haze's neck, pressing it hard.

Kill him the right way, in a duel, and you'll get a payoff, Hank said, and you'll get two birds for one stone because you'll be able to settle the score in an honorable way and send a message. But a knife isn't the right way.

What's to say I can't just cut his throat or shoot him right now and then send them the body? What's to say there's any difference one way or another? Rake said.

He challenged you to a duel, Hank said. You didn't hear him

because you didn't want to, but he said that, too. He said he's gonna challenge you to a duel in honor of Billy-T.

You say that? Rake said. You challenge me to a duel?

I guess so, Haze said.

("I'm saying I played it right but wasn't sure at the time I was playing it right, if you know what I mean, because I never knew what was going on in his head, I had to guess at it, of course, but you could sense it if you payed close attention to the way he blinked—the more he blinked, the more confused he was—and he was blinking like crazy while he held the knife to the kid's throat, so I knew he wasn't sure, wasn't ready to kill yet, and I went over the whole deal again, saying we'd tag the body and put it for the Corps to find, but first we'd have a duel, tapping that rumor. But the clincher, I think, was probably the fact that it was Saturday and I told him we'd have the duel the next day. I talked that up, big time, because I knew he'd appreciate the fact that duels were never supposed to take place on a Sunday. It would be a test of God, I told Rake. I said if there is a God then we'll find out for sure because if there was one he'd be in a rage about dueling on a Sunday, and if there wasn't one we'd know for sure because we'd get no reaction, so to speak, and he looked up at me at that point, man, and I saw that he'd lifted the blade from Haze's neck, and he smiled at me and I knew that we had him, that he was pondering it the way he did. His eyes stopped blinking, you see, and then the plan was in motion and one thing led to another. On the other hand, I get it. I mean I get that it seems preposterous that a psycho like Rake would suddenly give a shit about honor. But I had it figured right—and believe me, it was a guess more than anything—that when he heard the name, the precise name, he'd lock back into the old story, the Nam story; all that terror was coming out of something, a precise story—I mean, you should get that, you had it in there and when you heard the name you freaked, too, started to feel the trauma. Rake was cold-blooded in Nam, so it was a matter of getting his blood cold again. Rage is hot-blooded, is what I figure, but sorrow is cold, and *honor* is a cold word, if you see what I mean.")

("Sunday at noon. A cooler day, the air clear, the sun straight up. High noon was his idea. I had an empty clip up my sleeve and swapped it out after they both made an inspection.")

("No, I'm telling you, I'm telling the truth, man. So it doesn't fit the story line, write it in your report any way you want if you still want to write a report. Some things don't hold up to examination, to the scrutiny of logic; it was out of character only as far as his character was rootless until he heard that name, Billy-T—and maybe he was playing us, man, maybe it was a game he was playing, I don't know, but I do know that what happened, happened. We're not killers. He's the killer.")

Acting as a second to Rake, Hank prepared the duel site on the beach by sweeping the sand smooth and flat and putting one of MomMom's white hankies at the center and pacing each man back. Meg paced Haze and Hank paced Rake, who seemed sober in his seriousness, rock solid and steady.

This is about honor, he said. This is about making amends for a lack of honor on the part of Haze. I've been waiting to do this my entire life.

The switch-out of ammo went smoothly. Hank palmed the empty clip against the inside of his sleeve and let it slip down and put it into Rake's gun, letting him see it slide in, holding it out to him. They presented the guns and watched as the two men stood back to back and then counted paces east and west. Hank waited for the wind to die to pull the string, to move the hankie, to start the duel.

("Had to risk it, man. You see, I thought maybe Rake would freak and demand that they switch guns, become suspicious, something like that. In that case, I figured he'd switch and then freak and switch again, but he was unusually calm. Hearing the name Billy-T did something to him, I think. He was killer-calm, and he put his trust, such as it was, in me as his second. I'd fed him a line about the seconds being the only ones to get the guns ready—that's their job, man, I told him. Seconds are duty-bound to make sure all the conditions are correct. I know how it sounds, hearing it from me. The plan was drawn from my gut, from a sense of whatever it was that had been enfolded, maybe.")

As expected, Haze seemed to open fire first but they'd never know who got the first trigger-squeeze. Maybe there was a hollow click as Rake squeezed in frustration, realizing that his gun wasn't kicking, that his clip was empty. Maybe not. Across the empty space between the two men in that split second everything seemed to freeze up. Haze fired until his clip was empty, stepping forward with the shots until he was over Rake's body aiming down into it and then his clip was empty and he continued to press the trigger, clicking until Hank had his own gun to the back of Haze's head.

Hank held his gun against Haze's neck and told him he'd done the honorable thing, fighting Rake. You're going do the next honorable thing, now. You'll start walking down the beach to the east and you won't stop.

His gun jammed or something, Haze mumbled. What makes you think I'd start walking?

The fact that I'm saying it makes me think you'll do it,

Hank said. The fact that I'll shoot you now and bury you in the sand is another.

Rake owed me some cash, Haze said.

I've killed for the hell of it, but killing you would be for fun. Now, killing you because you mention cash, that would be priceless, but the only reason I'm not going to do it is because I don't feel like digging a hole and I'd rather watch you walk away from me with that good eye working. I'd rather watch you make a run for it, but you'd better be quick because believe you me every single fucking man who was betrayed by Rake will be after you as soon as the word slips out that he's dead. You understand me? They'll start tracking you because they've built up in their minds that he's some kind of figure in history and that's part of the price you pay as his sidekick. Rake's a mythic figure out there and so are you, my friend.

Haze staggered away down the beach. They watched him until he was out of sight.

Now's the hard part, Hank said, holding Meg. Now we have to go into whatever strength we still have and use that part of ourselves that we'd rather not use to burn him and take him downstate. We'll go to the house and get the wheelbarrow and we'll put him in it and then I'll build the fire and I'll put him in while you stay inside and pretend it's not happening. I'm sorry you even had to see this. I'm sorry it had to be done this way.

That night, after the fire—he put the body on it, leaving it to burn—it began to rain and they lay in bed listening.

I'm tired of this, she said.

I'll leave in a few hours. You stay here and take care of MomMom. Nobody will know until the Corps sends someone up here, or word gets here from Flint. They'll see his body and report it and then it'll have to go through a vast network of bureaucratic bullshit before they identify. They'll see what they want to see.

Out in the yard, a few hot coals still hissed. He went down to check it, casting the flashlight beam onto Rake's face. His mouth curled back into a leathery smirk. The rain had passed and clouds scuttled across the moon. He caught the scent of honeysuckle and trees happy in the rain. The body seemed almost weightless as he moved it onto a blanket. He went back to the fire and put the dog tag into the coals and let it sit there for a while. Then he rubbed it with ash and, lifting Rake's head, drew it around his neck. He patted it once, gently. He carried the body to the car, put it in the trunk, and went back to the house for his bag: a gun, some food, a grenade just in case. When he left around three, the trees hung with wetness. Tendrils of fog threaded across the road and through his headlights. He had the radio on, and when the state forest signal came in he scanned for music and, finding none, settled for a talk show out of Canada. They spoke of the spillover riots that had somehow crossed the Freedom Bridge to Sarnia before subsiding into a tense peace. A caller spoke of the potential for long-term peace. There was hope in the air, she said. She had a wonderful Canadian tartness to her voice that reminded Hank of his mother before she had gone mad.

He got to the bridge before dawn and pulled over to scan with his binoculars. The bridge lights were out and in the twenty minutes he sat looking only two sets of headlights went over, both heading from south to north. The water in Lake Michigan sat leaden. He resisted the familiar urge to go down and take a swim. Instead, he thought of Meg lying in bed, her hair pooled around her face. Her beauty seemed to him the only thing that could save him from himself. His mother would be asleep, too, snoring and then snorting and settling into that breathless silence that was near death. The weakness apparent by day in her weirdly unfocused eyes was even more apparent in those silences. He took a deep breath and shook his head and listened to the tense fuzzy hum of blood against the thin membrane of his eardrums.

He crossed the bridge and found the side street leading to Fort Michilimackinac. The body in the trunk, charred to feathery lightness, bones and shrunken skin and the grimace of teeth, shifted slightly, curled fetal in the blanket. He imagined he could feel it.

At the fort he parked on the far side of the lot and scanned with his field glasses. A man was asleep in a folding chair, a glint of badge silver on chest. His head rested against the log wall of the fort, which was a fake, a reconstruction for tourists, but in the predawn darkness looked real. Hank got out of the car, lifted the bundle of blankets from the trunk, and dragged it to the curb. An old oak had been violently pruned away from the entrance driveway. It had a long scab, a scrape on its trunk bleeding down to the roots. He touched the sap and took a sniff. Then he unfolded the blanket.

You're dead now, he said to the corpse. You'll be dead in five years, he said to the tree.

He lifted the body, again noting its lightness, and set it down carefully into a crook at the base of the tree. He silently thanked the tree for providing a nifty seatlike structure. For years the roots had clutched and changed direction, piling up against the concrete curb, bulging and pushing to form what he needed, a place to enshrine the body of a man who had done the same thing in his own way, struggling against forces invisible to him, responding instinctually, cell by cell, seeking nourishment in poor substrate. He adjusted the dog tag, pulling the chain straight, and wiped ash from his hands on his jeans.

The bridge was empty when he headed back. The hanger cables thrummed in the wind above the brutal currents, the contending forces from two huge bodies.

Hours later, back at the house, he found Meg in the kitchen drinking coffee.

They spent the next few days cleaning out the house, getting rid of reminders of Rake and reestablishing a sense of ownership. They built a fire and burned Rake's junk. They hiked down to the river and he taught her how to line-cast in a clearing he knew about—the only one, really, where you wouldn't get snagged. The word eventually would get out that Rake was dead, and then they'd have to make a move. For now they'd bide their time and take care of MomMom.

Those were sweet days, and nights. Hank took her down to the river each afternoon. She caught on quickly, wading barelegged into the icy water, finding her footing on the slippery stones. He spent evenings studying forestry survey maps and making plans. MomMom was growing weak. When she threw a fit, she did it quietly. He held her and tried to read her eyes, to see something of the past, but it was all gone.

News of the assassination came on the radio one morning while they were sitting at the kitchen table. They listened and wept together.

Kennedy pushed his luck as far as he could and I respect him for that, Hank said. We did the same thing but were luckier.

The trees were just beginning to change, not in color but in the tenseness of the leaves, a loosening at the stems. Late summer weeds had bloomed and dried in the sun and were filling the afternoon air with chaff. Hank went out and chopped some wood and at night, when it got cold, he blessed it and fed a fire in the living room and they listened to the Stones and the Beatles and lay together on the couch. He had a loaded gun he kept on the table in case word leaked out about Rake. But the road to the house stayed quiet.

Several days after the assassination, the news reports were of the funeral train transporting the president's body back to Washington, reversing the route of Lincoln's body a century ago, across Ohio and through upstate New York. That night he built another fire and went outside, the grass crunching frost, and saw the northern lights through the trees. He went inside to get Meg and took her down to the beach to look at the long furls of electromagnetic radiation. He sniffed the air and said he was catching something new from the north, way, way up. He said they'd go there as soon as they didn't have to fear being followed by gangs of agents.

That night they made love for the first time. She told him to stop saying he was sorry, that her desires had nothing to do with anything except the fact that she was her old self again, her original self.

DULUTH

The water had taken on a cold, wintery glint. The light had shifted, making the beach look wider, more ominous. The situation was unsafe, but before the four of them took off, they had taken one last hike together, through second-growth forest to the eastern branch of the Two Hearted River. Hank had wanted them to see it. They marched single-file, Hank leading and stopping them on occasion to sniff and listen.

They were still doing a penance for a loss, and it would be that way for a long time. The river snaked through the brambles and deep green beds of fern, hidden from the world, a river that had to be seen at ground level. From the sky it was obscured by a canopy of leaf.

Singleton, at the rear, experienced a sense of recognition. The buzz in his ear was still gone, leaving behind a feeling of having lived through battles. The fuzzball had resolved into concrete thought—images of a boy on a beach with freckles and a loose smile. From Meg he had gathered a sense of who Billy-T might've been, and he saw him through her eyes and she saw him through his eyes and Wendy saw her loss through Meg's eyes and Meg through her eyes.

Hank led them to a mossy open clearing with limited snags. The only good fishing spot for miles and miles. He explained that the reputation of the stream was much greater than the stream itself.

When they got back to the house that night they found MomMom dead in the yard, her laundry basket next to her.

"Natural causes," Hank said. "She must've dragged herself out of bed."

His voice was abstracted. He stood for a moment and then walked over to her body, which looked less weighty, the apron loose around her hips, her chin flattened and her eyes still open.

"I don't believe this," Meg said, crying.

"I never got to know her in a sane state, because I was insane when she was sane," Hank said. "Before that I was a kid and she was just my mom. It was clean and simple back then." He dropped to his knees and kissed her cheek. "I treated her badly before I got the treatment. I was an evil man and I cast her aside, and me and Rake, whatever we did, it had to have been unspeakable."

"Don't blame yourself now," Meg said, holding him.

"I'm blaming the man I was when I came back from Nam. I can't remember it but I'm sure that when I came back she told me something like, 'You're not the boy I knew, not at all,' something like that."

"Blame the old Hank, but don't blame yourself," Meg said.

"When the president was killed I knew it wouldn't be long. She started downhill, I mean physically, when that news came out."

"I'm sorry, Hank," Singleton said.

"I know you are," Hank said.

"Nothing prepares you," Wendy said. "I'll go get a blanket."

MomMom's death was a sign. They all thought, but didn't say, that the timing would ease the burden of travel. What would Klein say? He'd say that sometimes men died in the field to ease the burdens of other men. If they were beyond the reach of a dust-up crew it might look—and he'd stress only look, because he wasn't coldhearted—like an act of God.

They buried her under the clothesline, along with her basket and her Bible.

"Love is the great transition of fury into stability, into the serenity of a mutual shared vibration," Hank said, spreading his arms. "Love is when you see the forest and the trees and have a complete sense of both. Love means saying you're sorry again and again and again."

It was their last night on the beach. Lake Superior. Thirty-two thousand square miles of water producing waves that arrive in a sequence of four or five smaller ones and then a breaker born far out in the fury of a distant storm, where tiny bolts were caught up in the clouds, flickering their underbellies visible and then, a second later, consumed back into darkness. A log shifted and sparks were unleashed into the sky. Smoke from the embers was milky gray against the blackness. They were all aware not only of the fire's warmth but of the dangerous dark beyond its light.

"You know what I hate," Hank was saying.

"What do you hate?" Meg said.

"I hate it when people say something is 'painfully beautiful.' Pain's never beautiful, man, never. The forest is beautiful, but I'd hope I never get to the point where I claim it's painfully beautiful. MomMom used to rub Vicks on my chest when I was sick, and now, when I smell it, I can't figure out why I feel this intense despair. All I can think is that it must have something to do with Nam, that smell. Is that painfully beautiful?"

"Do people really say that?" Wendy said.

"It does have something to do with Nam," Singleton said. "I can't tell you I know this firsthand, but when I got out of treatment and was trying to figure shit out I hung out with a vet for a day or two, and he told me they used to rub that stuff under their noses to mask the smell of death and rotting flesh."

Hank stood and then Singleton stood, reaching down to pull Wendy up. Then Meg stood and they walked away from the fire to the water and stood looking out at the lake. The air smelled autumnal. A trillion leaves changing color and beginning to decay. The fire behind them looked small and insignificant.

They sat by the fire deep into the night, sharing stories, while the wind picked up, shifted, and forced them to change positions to avoid the smoke.

At one point, later, Singleton walked away from the fire and went into the darkness to listen again for Black Flaggers.

The plan was to go back to the house, finish packing up, pray at MomMom's grave, and head to Duluth. Hank knew the way. He stood up and raised his hands and said he could, if necessary, walk the footpaths all the way in his sleep, blindfolded, drunk, high. Then he gave a shout and, his voice preachy and declarative, said that going into nature was the ultimate recourse, a way back into his own soul and the only resolution available in conditions that were, when you got right down to it, considering the state of the supposedly civilized industrial world, unbearable. He pounded his chest and spread his arms to the sky, cried out again, and then, pulling her up to her feet, embraced Meg in his huge arms.

All afternoon they had worked, burning things, burying the arms they wouldn't take, anything they didn't want to leave to Black Flag, or the Corps agents who would inevitably come on a search mission. Singleton sat for a while and composed a final report on a sheet of legal paper. He kept it short and to the point, outlining their original plan of action, describing the trip up, the initial contact with Hank and Meg, and the last contact with Agent Klein. The actual establishment of trust, he reduced to a single sentence: "*We used our guts to establish that the targets were loving.*" To use the word *loving* in an operation report went completely against training. It didn't matter. He was leaving a lot out.

Hank came into the kitchen and sat down. "I'm sorry we didn't keep Rake alive so you could come and save the day the way I'm sure you wanted to," he said. "You were hoping for some kind of gallantry, something symbolic. But symbols are why Rake fell for the trap. He had a hankering for old gestures, so when the duel rumor began floating around he fell for it, because it fulfilled the idea that there was a mission buried in all of his rage. He thought he might land on the moral high ground. He might land on some idea of honor in relation to himself, man, and that's the thing, man, that's the thing that can really mess you up. Nothing is more corrupt than the idea of honor, at least right now, in this day and age. I love trees because they don't bother with honor, because they move slowly through the years—at least from our vantage— and reckon with time in a different way."

The plan was to drive as far as they could, until they didn't feel safe, and from there take backcountry trails to Duluth, where Hank would make a token gesture of searching for his father, moving from tavern to tavern, checking in with the harbormaster, eyeing the lake, which would be shimmering and tense-looking with the winter cold, getting ready to freeze up. Then they'd stay a few days together, take the final four blue pills in one last party, see what transpired, and split up if that seemed the right thing to do. Meg and Hank would head over the border to Canada and spend the winter in Thunder

Bay. When spring came they'd begin searching for the Queen Tree, the mother of all mothers, which Hank guessed was somewhere in Quetico Provincial Park. It was crazy, he admitted, but it kept him going and like all good delusions it was fueled by genuine hope and dedication to the truth. Singleton and Wendy would, perhaps, stay in Duluth into the spring—see how they liked it up there, and then, when the smoke cleared, if it ever cleared, they'd head back down to Michigan to find her father. They'd avoid headquarters, if it still existed.

Singleton left the report on the kitchen table. He left it there for someone to find.

RUMORS

There had been rumors and theories about what were called exchanged memory packets. According to the rumor there was a way to abolish the desire to know what had been enfolded in treatment by meeting up with one or two folks who had a common trauma. It was still just a theory, and had yet to be supported by studies. Back at headquarters, some committee was pondering the question, examining log sheets and intelligence data, speculating about sample cases, men who had accidentally linked up with other men (or women) and shared enough to establish that they had been in the same unit, somewhere in Nam, or in a chopper bay, a medic and his charge, or a pilot looking back to check the baggage and seeing the eyes of a dying boy afraid of death as he pulled back on the joystick and sent the bird skyward, and for some reason the pilot could never forget that particular moment. The pilot meets the guy he thought was dead and together they smoke a joint around a campfire and rehash that scene and in doing so feel the lifting of the chopper and the joy of recognition around their mutually enfolded materials. The eyes hadn't been fading to death after all.

There was another story—rumor or truth, it was impossible to know—about two men who went off the Grid after treatment, hitched rides and hopped trains and ended up deep in the wilds of Mark Twain National Forest down in Tennessee, each on separate journeys that would lead them together, by pure chance, in that strange way that people meet against all odds, straphanging in a crowded subway train amid the multitudes of New York, for example, having just arrived in the city from disparate points, randomly arriving from, say, Los Angeles and Miami, and then suddenly finding themselves side by side on the subway, swaying in a miraculous confounding of mathematical possibility, and there they were, saying hello, laughing it off as one of those things that happened. Those two men had been in a horrendous massacre together and had each returned injured on separate dust-offs and had no contact whatsoever and then, in the Tennessee woods, in a long, beautiful glade of grass, coming in from the northerly side and the southerly, they had approached each other with trepidation until, about halfway across, according to the story, recognition set in and they waved and shouted greetings and danced around each other. It was a scene of requited love, most agreed, because when the love of two buddies in battle was broken apart, it was like the splitting of atoms into pure anguish.

Then there was the hugely improbable rumor about the agent from the Corps, one of three men who had gone over to Nam to fight the second siege of Hue (that point was always made) and been caught in the furious fight for the Citadel. The agent had been enfolded and treated at the facility near Flint, coming out of his reenactment ready to be part of Kennedy's grand vision, not caring one bit about the itch in his head (in most versions), paying it no heed, pairing up with a young female agent whose father was a vet and who had lost her boyfriend to the war. Some versions had him dead, others seriously injured. The two of them went AWOL (in some versions) from the Psych Corps on a mission to the Upper Peninsula of Michigan to find and locate a target, who by chance happened to have been a guy in his unit and not only that but had a girl with him up there, too, along with another guy— this was the amazing part, the part that kept the story riding—who had paired himself up with his buddy after the war, the two of them raging mad, not ready to finish the war, never really home if you know what I mean, and the guy— big burly guy—had enfolded himself behind his buddy's back. So they got up there, the two agents, and began to exchange memory packets, small bits that they had unfolded—the usual way, good fucking and cold dunking—to find overlap, to seal the deal with what had happened, so to speak, and at this point the rumor broke apart and scattered over the hills and mountains. In one version the duel was mentioned and it was explained that the young girl, who had been in love with a grunt who never came back, had a part in it, played a role, and they fooled the psycho grunt into having a formal stand-off with another guy, a twerp (in all versions), and they switched out the ammo and he was blown away, died in a blaze of glory, and in another version they just shot him and burned his body beyond recognition and dog-tagged him (that version got traction ahead of the other version and spread to New York). In all versions the stress was put on the beautiful ending. Four folks up there sharing stories, trading memory packets, finding grace with most of the trauma gone, the horrific parts. In both versions, the four headed out to Canada. In one version it was the Arctic Circle where they lived amid the Inuits, learned the language, helped to build igloos, spending nights in the wonderful heat—no heat like an igloo heat, with ice walls between you and the howling winds—and in another version they built themselves a log cabin, a real one, and shared the household duties together in a communal bliss, growing their own pot and mixing up bark to make new drugs, blissfully wallowing in a mutual love that was far beyond anything you could imagine unless it was on the lips of a man who was telling the story, shaking his head and saying, Man, can you fucking believe it, man, they had the best of both worlds, man, got to share what they could and leave the rest submerged. In still other versions of the story, the four of them performed a sequential dunking, going out into Lake Superior one by one, watching over each other, taking care not to go under too long, coming out of the water with new visions and new information, piecing it together methodologically, carefully, and then drawing a line when it got too close to a complete unfold, stopping when the stopping was good, so to speak, and then one blissful evening—always at a kitchen table, drinking wine, lifting glasses in toasts—they got the story straight and agreed that each of them had lost the same buddy. They toasted his name and then bowed and prayed for him, knowing that he was listening, sure that he could hear each word. Then they left ahead of the violence, slipped away. Most versions of the rumor included Hank's tree-smelling abilities, his woodsman know-how, and the fact that he was key in the long trek out of the hinterlands of northern Michigan to the border. Some versions had them hiking all the way west to Duluth, staying off the main roads, camping on Keweenaw Peninsula, invigorating themselves with talk and drink, and then, thanks to Hank's connections with deckhands and the like, they settled into the town for the winter, where they explained they were waiting to ship out in the spring. In other versions they went east to Sault Ste. Marie and somehow fought their way past the guards there in a glorious Wild West, *High Noon* kind of shootout. (That version was a favorite west of St. Louis.) Early on in the formation of the rumor, allusion was made to a strange document floating around, passed from hand to hand in the form of a final report that had been found in the house up there east of the Harbor of Refuge, written in the jargon of the Corps, on a few sheets of legal pad paper, addressed to a man named Klein, describing in detail how the operation had proceeded up to but not including the final sequential dunking. In another version a blue pill was mentioned, along with the fact—always stated by the one telling the story, to stamp the validity of the narrative—that the pills had been provided by another grunt, back at Corps headquarters, a pill with fantastic powers—better than LSD or STP or QRD or whatever—to produce visions that were clear in the best way. On the Bible, someone would say, I swear, man, this is a true story, and then they'd go on to tell one version or another, east or west, final dunking, no dunking, final blue pill blowout of interwoven visions, no blue pill, but always ending in happiness and glory.

It was the kind of rumor that was necessary in an age when everything else seemed to be spinning deeper and deeper into despair. It was the kind of rumor that tried to speak of love without saying the word *love*, and it was the kind of story, however fragmented and varied it became, that retained a core of validity that its hearers could taste even if they weren't sure what they were tasting, and left an aftertaste of some eternal forward future when that which was lost was regained in the words that were shared. That was it. That was the tale spun from the mouths of hopeful vets, twisted not only by intentional additions and subtractions, subplots that reflected the lives of the tellers, omissions of details found wanting, but also by the weakening signal, the inevitable depletion of the story's punch as it passed from mind to mind through time.

In some versions it would be clear that Singleton and Wendy had been duped by the Corps, sent out as part of a conspiracy, an elaborate form of treatment, a curative solution. Men who believed fully, or wanted to believe fully, in the Corps would tell that version, altering it slightly as they passed it along, until the structure of the conspiracy became tight and believable. But the ones who most cherished the rumor, the ones who passed it on with the greatest care, believed that in the end hope could be found only in the impossible made possible by pure chance. In the version that lasted longest, the blue pill came into play outside the camp, on a beach along the shore of Minnesota, or in a cabin up in the Canadian forest, and the Corps had little or nothing to do with the four hooking up. In this version, Wendy and Singleton fell in love by chance, went AWOL of their own free will, and were saved not by a conspiracy but by the grace of God. The durability of this version lay in the way chance related to landscape and memory—life itself. Chance put them together, necessity emerging only in retrospect, just as soldiers looking back at their lives saw their survival reduced to moments of luck in which one person happened to live and another, no less afraid or skilled or brave, died. A story of chance and grace spared the teller from having to explain the damn thing—hey, it's a fucking rumor, it means what it means and that's all I can say, make of it what you want and pass it along if you see fit. If you don't believe it, don't believe it. If you do, take it with you and share it when the time feels right.

The End

It is sometimes claimed that the second great riots were sparked by the assassination of JFK on September 17, 1970—the Genuine Assassination, as it came to be known. (Even now there is significant confusion over the identity of the real shooter[s]: Identical twins, Utah B. Stanton and Stan B. Stanton, both of Springfield, Illinois, claimed responsibility.) But the third burn of Flint and Detroit, along with the Canada Spillover (in which gasoline cans were hauled across the Freedom Bridge from Port Huron and used to ignite portions of Sarnia, Ontario) and the great Thumb inferno, cannot be definitively linked to Kennedy's death. Anger had reached a boiling point; factors included the devaluation of the blue-collar worker, the destruction of factory infrastructure, and large numbers of wayward vets and minorities seeking justice. (Howard Harper in his study, *Black Despair, New Slavery, the Burning of Detroit (Again) and the Way Talk Has Talked Itself into Talk*, has pointed to an avoidance of clear analytic approaches in the assessment of the so-called riot sparks in the state of Michigan.)

[Author's Note: Accompany the main body of the story with author's notes, editor's notes, and interviews. When writing it go ahead and use real names and change them later if necessary. EA]

FURTHER INTERVIEWS

Ned Bycoff

He went over and served and came back and started right to work on his book. When he came out of the house he was wearing his combat fatigues most of the time. He'd just come out and look around the yard and then up at the sky and shake his head and go back in. We knew he was writing something because you could hear his typewriter going day and night. I'd come home from my shift—I was working the night shift as an electrician at Allied Paper—and he'd be up there typing. His desk was in the window and I could see his head bowed.

Molly Stam

Eugene's sister had a breakdown. I remember that the Allen house got suddenly quiet that summer. You had the sound of his typewriter but otherwise it was silent. The summer before, it was doors banging, shouts, and cars roaring up and down in front of the house. Eugene mentioned something about that. He didn't like these guys who came in to hang with his sister after Billy was gone. He told me once, I mean we were hanging out and he said: At night these guys come and pick her up, or drop her off, and I watch them out the window. That's all he said, but it was the way he said it.

John Burns

Perhaps the true history, without enfolding, without JFK miraculously alive and in his highly improbable third term, was simply too painful for Allen. Not that I care. Like I said, I was weirdly happy to see that he offed himself after he got back from Vietnam. He bugged me. I beat the shit out of him one time when he was a kid. His sister was a slut. I mean, she was a slut when she was about fourteen, starting then, and went around asking for it. You know what I mean? Maybe I shouldn't be saying this. But that's the truth, man. I can say that. [Prison noise in background.] Biggest mistake I made was not killing him before I landed in here. I mean, what difference did it make to me if it was this guy or that guy; I knew if I got caught I'd be in for life. Go ahead. Put it in your tape machine.

Eugene Allen

Billy Thompson came up to my room to talk. He was back from his first tour and came into my room and sat on my bed. He called me "son" that afternoon. He poked around my room and lifted my mattress and found a magazine and gave it a look, flicked through the pages, held up the centerfold, and then put it back and gave me a smirk and said: Good, son, you're a normal guy. Then he sat down again on the bed and began to tell me what he wanted from me. "You gotta let the world know if I don't come back what's what, man," he said. He told me once I'd been over there and finished my tour of duty, I'd understand, and then he left.

Buddy Anderson

His sister had been been missing from state hospital after she cracked up, or whatever. That was the summer girls were found all over the state. A girl was found at Gull Lake, battered and dead. Another girl was found in the sludge pond near the paper mill. It's sick but it's true. As far as I know, her boyfriend, Billy, went back for his second tour. They spent a lot of time together that summer and then he went back. He was AWOL, is what I heard, but they cut him some slack because he was a long-timer and was good at what he did.

Eugene Allen

This car drove up and this officer got out. He had that anxious look of a bearer of bad news. He stopped for a second, wiped his brow, looked up and down the street at the sun coming through the trees. He was wearing white gloves. He had some paper in his hands. I heard him knock on the Thompsons' door across the street and then I heard the screams. Like steel on steel, maybe, or glass on slate, as keen and horrible as anything I'd ever heard—maybe like something being pried apart from something else—and then this new kind of silence that let the wind in, the sound of the leaves, the midsummer afternoon hush and then the abatement of hush and then an even deeper silence through which, far off down the street, you could hear kids playing ball, and then an even deeper silence that I can't describe here but hope to get in at the end of the next revision.

Randall C. Jones

We were treating her with EST and I was the only male nurse on the ward, which seemed to mean something. Just this sweet little girl who'd been into all kinds of shit. We had a lot of those, and this was around the first riots, and there were a lot coming in, most of them lost causes, just wrap and let them rock away the afternoons. We used convulsions as an excuse to pump them full of Nembutal. I remember some of the weird nicknames. We had the Attorney in there. We had the Butler. He was a famous case because Dr. Morris was working him and he thought he was Lord Byron one minute and then went back to his usual state as a tool-and-die man out of Detroit. I remember that. But Meg stuck in my head—

and I guess that's why we're having this interview. [The sound of a cigarette being lit. Coughing. A phone ringing in the background.] I remember Meg Allen because she was one of those rare breakouts. She took off one afternoon, slipped away from the back of the hospital, near the loading dock. She must've gone under the fence, worked her way down the hill behind the facility. It was tough going down there, but she had some skills. From that point it's all conjecture. She was found upstate, from what I heard.

Lee Wolf

The thing was Allen hated it because these guys called his sister a slut. They didn't just say she's a slut. They'd say: There goes the Slut. She was slim, beautiful, unstable. I think we all felt that, as if her fate, if you know what I mean, was in her instability. For a long time Allen was just this quiet little geeky kid brother, and then he was a young man. I don't remember that much. He was in my class in school, and we knew he was smart, and we knew that the older kids gave him a hard time. I don't recall the incident you allude to. I mean I knew that he got picked on. That was the natural order of things back then. You had the bullies, and the tough kids from down the hill, and they just existed and you worked your life around the fear and found ways, if you could, to avoid contact. If they kicked your ass, you simply saw it as part of the way your world worked.

Buddy Anderson

I don't believe the report would've used the phrase "friendly fire." I'm not sure if they were using that phrase during the second phase of Nam, although I might be wrong. Whatever the report said, it alluded to the idea that Billy Thompson was somehow involved with his own death. There must've been something about the coordinates. I don't believe Eugene made that up. That's what he might've said to me when we talked about Billy coming into his room that afternoon and poking around and then saying something along the lines of: If I don't come back it's gonna be up to you, the writer, to tell my story. Have a vision of it, he might've said. Eugene was always talking about having visions. He'd say: I have a vision of myself at the very end, and I'd say, What the fuck are you talking about? and he'd say, Don't you ever think about how it would be, right before you die? Don't you think you'd have some kind of vision as the time compresses in on itself; I mean, you start splitting the seconds until you find eternity, man, he said. We were driving up north looking for a fishing spot, smoking a joint—I mean, I don't really remember, but I kind of assume we were smoking. It was the summer after they found his sister, and he told me he was taking a break from writing his novel until he could figure out how to end the thing.

Dr. Brent Walk

We all know his sister wasn't found up there the way Eugene described it, which for me is just a bunch of bullshit. Yeah, she was killed, most likely. But maybe not. Maybe she got lost or something. Or maybe she overdosed. But it's just as possible that the cop killed her and then tossed her body into the weeds. I've been to that spot, not far from St. Ignace, just over the bridge. There's one of those dunes on the other side of the road, across the beach. Pine needles and all that. Thing is her body was so far gone with decay that it's just speculation, but he had to pin it, I think, on some gang of bikers. That's what he went around telling us. He went around saying she was killed by some Nam vets. Least that's the way I remember it.

Stan White

Here's the thing, man. It's not enough, the way I see it, to change the name Billy Thompson to Billy-T and leave it at that. Billy was more messed up than Allen lets on, and his fuckedupness was combined with Meg's fuckedupness. But one thing Eugene had right about Billy was that he loved Iggy Pop. He said Iggy was Christ, or maybe Christ was Iggy. That's what he said. But even before he went to Nam, is what I'm saying, he was messed up. He was one of those gentle screwups. He had this kind of slippery, lazy way of dealing with reality, and he admitted it. He'd say, Man, reality is too real for me. I'm gonna just take it slow and easy. We've got all the time in the world. He said that again and again until he didn't have all the time in the world.

Capt. Willard Starks

I'm only speculating that Thompson told him about some of the fighting he'd done and Eugene combined that with his own war experience. His old man was in Korea, so he got some of that material from him. But Allen wasn't in intense combat as far as I know. He seems to have had a desk job in a recon outfit in Saigon, although I have to admit that his files myste-riously disappeared.

Buddy Anderson

He wasn't happy with the ending of the thing and said it fooled him. He said he let it play out but was shocked because he wanted the end to have a big shootout. He said his desire to have revenge in the end just didn't work out. I never be-lieved him when he said that.

Gerald McCarthy

You ever hear about Project 100,000? You know, man, the thing was these were all working-class guys and would've been rejected anyhow, at least I'm talking Billy would've been because he wasn't such a bright bulb, not stupid but not exactly educated, if you know what I mean. If you haven't heard about Project 100,000, you'd better look it up.

John Burns
The thing was Billy and Eugene were draft bait and couldn't land a decent job because they were draft bait and they, meaning the managers hiring at the mill, or at the pharmaceutical plant, always asked if you'd fulfilled your service. Why would they train you on the line at Upjack, or in the mill, if you were going to be yanked out? They joined up because they felt it coming, if you know what I mean. Billy's old man could've landed him a job. His old man worked at Ford and could've gotten him something down there, for sure. Eugene's old man was a manager, but he started out on the line, I think, and worked his way up. He hauled a lunch bucket like the rest, though.

Buddy Anderson
I'm thinking his draft notice came right around the time he was just starting to write the first draft, which no one ever really got to see because he burned it and rewrote it when he got back. At least that's what I remember him talking about. He was saying he was closing in on the end. His grandfather had been on the board years back, but from what I know that didn't do no good with pulling strings and his number came up anyway.

Gerald McCarthy
You remember that recruitment ad the Army ran? You'd see it at the post office, or in school. It said, "Make the choice now—join, or we'll make the choice for you." That's the way it was for us kids. I mean, it's not like we had much of an

option, not like the rich kids on the other side of the river who could get a doctor to write up some bullshit crook knee, or someone heading to school full-time. Billy Thompson was part-time in school for a while, but that didn't do the job with the board because you had to be full-time. His old man just couldn't afford it, and he knew he'd be drafted so he figured he'd sign up and make the choice like most of the other guys did.

John Frank

Operation plans during Nam were often written after initial contact. In other words, you'd go in and draw fire and fight and then they'd name an operation after the mess and the mission statement would be backdated to the start of the fight and written after the fact. Singleton and Rake were in Operation George Washington, I think. Singleton must've known at the end, tracking Rake, he was in Operation Duel. The way I read it, the guy knew the entire thing would be rewritten after the fact, after he caught Rake, to look retrospectively like it all fit together. Then it would seem as if there were intuitive—some might say conspiratorial—factors involved. I look at it as that kind of deal. That's what led them into contact—that kind of delusion that was in the air, the delusion you get when what you're going through, maybe you know it, maybe not, is going to be written up to make some kind of sense from an operational standpoint when presented to the bigwigs in Washington as a report. That shit was in the air when Eugene wrote this thing. There was still that shit in the air.

Carrie Anderson

Meg used to hang out at Look Park with the other stoners. It was just across the road from the school, so it was where you went when you skipped a class and then decided to skip the whole day. We were friends, I guess, but not close friends because she was one of those girls who hung around with guys more than anything.

Richard Allen
No comment. I'd rather not say anything in response to that question.

Buddy Anderson
It's like you can't really get your mind around it when it's being thrown at you the way he threw it at me all the time, saying I'm going to kill myself if I get drafted. Then he gets drafted and goes. When he came back he worked hard day in, day out, and when he did come out for a drink he'd just sit with his head in his hands and ask questions: What's the plot, man? he'd say to me. What's the plot? Thing was, around the time he was drafted we thought the war was starting to wind down, or at least it seemed like it might end any day and we figured we'd be shipped to Fort Whatever, somewhere down south, to go through boot camp and all of that and then we'd come back here, like I did, and live out our lives. When his draft notice came he'd already written me a bunch of the suicide notes, and we thought, at least I thought, they were funny, so when he got back—and he was changed, man, of course he was changed like everyone else—and he started to write them again, while he was writing his book, it wasn't so funny anymore. I didn't save those notes. I saved the ones he wrote before he left.

Susan Habb
There was this time these kids beat Eugene. We were walking home and John Burns and some other guys jumped him. They broke his nose and dislocated his shoulder. After that he was different. I mean, this kind of thing happened all the time. It was a tough neighborhood, with a mix of kids from the mills

and kids whose dads were laid off and all of that. I'm not saying I saw he was different but now that I think about it, I mean looking back, I think he was different. He began to stay to himself more after that. He had friends, like the guy named Buddy. But things were different.

Markus Decourt
Yeah, yeah, that guy named Rake is a lot like the guy, Johnny Burns. That was the guy who came around to see Meg after Billy Thompson was killed in Nam. This sleazy snake came knocking, so to speak. Real snake, this guy named Johnny. There weren't really established gangs in our town, but there were loosely associated, you might call them, somewhat organized clumps of young men who liked to fuck things up, and he was one of them. He could exploit her weakness, and I always guessed that he was the one, if there was somebody, who helped her escape the nuthouse and took her up to where they found her body. What would they say in court? I guess they'd say that's all hearsay. But hearsay means something, too, is what I say.

Markus Decourt
It seems important that he wrote his book before they found his sister's body, because he had to guess where she was, and the truth is he guessed pretty close to what really happened, except she wasn't up in Canada safe and sound with some lumberjack like Hank, searching out trees, trying to make a killing in the lumber business. Whatever happened to her up there, she came into contact with some bad elements, rest assured. Actually, those are the words his father used when he could finally speak again, after the funeral. He said, bad elements. She got in with some bad elements, and they took advantage of her. That's what he said.

Carl O'Brian

Allen had one thing right. You'd write an operation report after the fact and backdate the thing and then it would somehow fit the strange, horrific logic of the battle, at least the initial point of contact with the enemy and the charge up the hill and the number of your KIAed and injured in relation to the number of VC KIAed and all of that, all written in a kind of cable-ese that reduced the complexity of battle; even reports that were not written in the field, by some desk jockey in Saigon and meant for secret transmission, were written in that jargon, that reductive nonsensical, staccato mode. I get the feeling that Billy knew, and I mean we used to sort of talk about this stuff, in our own way, that if he was KIAed over there in his second tour, he'd be reduced to just some bullshit lingo on an outgoing report that somehow rat-tat-tatted out on a teletype machine in some deep basement of the Pentagon.

Richard Allen

[Static, fumbling with microphone.] Like I said, I really can't talk about it. My father-in-law died shortly after my daughter was killed and so the grief was double, and I lost my son. So it was three in about two years.

John Burns

I seriously doubt if Billy ever went up to that kid's room and had a man-to-man with him. I know for a fact he wouldn't call him "son."

Chuck Stam

Billy had a lisp; something about his teeth and his tongue. So I can see that he might've called in the wrong coordinates. That mind-flash—or whatever you want to call it—that Meg,

the character Meg, has when she's in the water and he speaks
is about the way he sounded. He was a big questioner. He
asked a hell of a lot of questions and then came up with a lot
of answers. He loved to talk. He would've attended his own
funeral for sure.

VARIOUS SUICIDE NOTES

Dear Buddy. Here's the basic problem as I see it. Now
that I'm back, I'm bored with the mystery of life. Why
did Meg end up dead in a ditch? Why am I still here?
What does it mean that I wake up early in the morning
to hear a mourning dove cooing and listen to it
intensely, as I did one summer morning a few years
back? I lay and listened, knowing that I'd remember
that moment forever. I told myself—in bed, shrouded
in the cool sheets—that I should and would remember.
And the deeper, eternal mysteries that, just a few years
ago, I seemed to care so deeply about. That silence
between Mom and Dad when the conversation,
usually about what to do about Meg, lulled and then
they were looking at each other, for just a second,
fondly. The question of where time goes when it's
finished evoking the present moment. What it means
when history devours a beloved, like Meg, or JFK,
or MLK or whoever. I just can't seem to rise to the
occasion of giving the slightest shit anymore. This isn't
the kind of suicide note I'm sure you expect from me.
But right now, here, on the edge of doing myself in, it's
all I can come up with. I wrote my draft and now I
want to terminate myself before I finish revisions,
partly because the entire mess is obviously built

around the thing I'm avoiding. As Grandpa said to me
years ago, I'm a hider by nature. I'm a loner. I'm sure
I'm abnormally reacting to the fact that my sister was
killed, on one hand. On the other hand, my own
manhood was at stake. Whatever. I'm lonely, sad, and
I've been beaten. That afternoon, the one you know
about already, when I was walking home and jumped
by Larry, and John, and some other assholes. They got
me. I mean, they told me that Meg was a slut, and
then beat the shit out of me. I said a prayer for them,
and it was my last prayer. So let it be recorded here
that Eugene Allen, on his last day on earth, admitted
that he said one last prayer and knew it was going to
be his final attempt. I mean, let it be known that I said
goodbye to my attempts at forgiveness for those guys,
who for me at that time, on the street, walking home,
were emblematic—I can admit this—of certain men
who have an inclination toward violence, that I also
said so long to the inclination to forgive the world
in general. In other words, my friend, where is the
grace in all this? I mean, the war goes on. I see the
photographs. I pay attention. Billy is gone, of course,
but the men like him still go off to fight as I write this.
(Note: Buddy. I know you're gonna see this as yet
another in a long line of relatively lame suicide notes
I've composed this summer. This one might be for
real. I'll put it in your mailbox later tonight and you'll
get it before the lights go off. So I'm sure you're
thinking: Ah, man, Eugene does it again, spells out his
last thoughts.) Anyway, back to my main point, which
is that the deeper mysteries that I used to be able to
feel with such ease, and by feel I mean respect, sense,
and take in but not answer—that's it, man, Buddy, I
can no longer take in the mysteries. And I could do

that a year ago, even when Meg was AWOL, out there
somewhere, and the cops were coming to the door. I
could still feel that delight—yeah, that's the word—in
the strangeness of reality. But that went away and with
it my urge to stay involved with the present moment,
and I have to add here, Buddy, that I have an
unwillingness to look back, so I can't even live in the
past, not really, which would include some pretty
traumatic shit—and you know what I mean—when
we didn't understand that Meg was going crazy, or
was crazy, and before she was, as they said, diagnosed
and treated.

Dear Grandpa,
    I'm writing this first off, ahead of the fact, to say
I'm sorry for whatever pain I've caused you. Please
forgive me and know that I went out believing most, if
not all, of what you taught me about God and about
my place in the world and the importance, as you said
again and again, of looking at the big, big picture, the
one that goes forward in time and backwards and
shows, or as you always said, the vastness of eternity
in relation, as you said, to our small speck of lives.
There are some things I've got to get down in this
letter to let you know that I do remember. First off,
I remember your elegance and the way you dressed—
won't force it in here, but I'll describe a few things: the
way you wore your hat, with your name and address
and a note in the band that said, Reward if found.
Return to Harold B. Allen. (I'll spare you what you
know.) The suits you bought in Chicago, and the time
you took me and let me watch while the tailor chalked
and measured and lifted the bolts of fabric out for me
to finger, treating me, the tailor, like a man instead of

a kid; also the cufflinks you wore along with the sock garters and the shoes. Anyway, your elegance and the house and the time you let me stay there, those days, when things at my house were too chaotic. I'll spare you the narrative here. This note isn't to explain why I'd end my life early. I realize that my desperation, my despair, will be linked directly to my tour of duty in Nam, of course, and also Meg's death and the pain of all of that and the way Mom drinks and so on and so forth, but the truth is I'm simply not equipped for manhood as it is defined in this—I'll spare you the rest [indecipherable scribble] . . . I should type this up because the writer's cramp is killing me, but it seems wrong to type out a note like this on the same machine on which I wrote fiction. I'm slightly obsessive about your hats, to return to that subject. It seems to me that the covering of the head with an elegant object somehow is emblematic of your time and place in the world, and the fact that I've grown my hair long, too long to fit under the kind of hat you wear—although in theory it might work—should stand out as a major indication of the difference between your generation and mine, although I do, as I stand here, with a can of gas in my hand (or a gun, or whatever), have to admit that I side with your comment, and agree wholeheartedly, that the concept of generations is a creation of, as you say, the culture gone haywire, and that between your world and mine there is really only a slight, tweaky difference. I go out now because I can't find a way [indiscernible scribbles] . . . *foothold* might be the right word. My body feels unable to relate to the gravitational pull. I thought of this when Neil Armstrong stepped on the moon and I became obsessed with that footprint more than anything, the

pattern on the sole, the boot prints, and then I began
to wonder if maybe the world would be better if he
had stepped onto the lunar surface in a pair of
Florsheims (can't think of a better brand), or better
yet one of your handmade shoes, the ones with nails
holding the sole. If he'd left a better print perhaps the
whole Year of Hate thing, the riots and so forth . . . I
won't go there. Suffice it to say that a young man who
can only come up with a lame little riff on the nature
of moon footprints deserves, in some way, to stop
existing. Or maybe I should say that a man who has to
resort to a riff on footprints and then resorts to
resorting to mention of that resorting as a lame excuse
and then talks about his desire to end it all deserves to
end it all? Anyway, I know you did your best with the
draft board and pulled whatever strings you could and
were in the uncomfortable position because of your
former service.

Dear Buddy,
    This is it, man. The real deal. Please disregard
other notes and take this one seriously. I've been
typing like a madman and failed to get the following,
not verbatim, but in essence. Here's a last list of
things:
    The time we went fishing up at the Two Hearted,
which we agreed was really a shit stream, and you
caught the hook in my fist when I was watching you
cast from the footbridge, looking down and studying
the riffles, trying to see where the fish might be lurking
from a better vantage. You were wading with your
back to me and made a fantastic cast, just beautiful,
and then another even better cast, and I was watching
the line and the hook—I think it was a muddler—

stuck in my wrist and you thought it was a snag and
before I could yell you began yanking; not that actual
moment but the way we used it later, driving up to
Duluth, smoking, talking, as the butt of a joke,
twisting it and turning it, taking your point of view
and then my point of view. That moment, in the car,
rehashing the snag, is where the glory of my life
stands. I mean it, man. That was the peak, and the
fact that I lived through that moment—I should say
moments, in the car—while back home all hell was
probably breaking loose, with Meg going into the
hospital, is enough for me. In other words, I'm sure
now that I've had my moment of grace and glory.
There's that moment and the other moment. One
night when I was about twelve and Meg was about
fourteen we went out into the snow and hiked around,
just walking, and the streets were buried and the snow
was pouring down and we held hands and she told me
that she didn't care if Johnny Burns called her names,
and I asked her what he called her, and she told
me and it was the first time I heard the word. I listened
and she shrugged it off and that was it, man, the
moment I relish because I didn't know the word and
yet heard the word from her own lips and it didn't
pain me yet the way it would when, for example,
Burns said it when he beat the shit out of me. The
fact that I got all the pain in the thing I'm typing
but couldn't get that tiny, little sliver of grace irks me,
but only insofar as any writer feels irked, and they all
must, over the limitations of story. As I think we
talked about a few days ago, it's impossible, for the
most part, at least for this writer, to get in there and
find a way to show how those tiny little fucking

moments of ignorance provide pure grace. Time, I
think I said, is the only thing [indecipherable scribble].

Love, your buddy

Dear Buddy,

Scratch that last note, if you got it. I'm sure you got
it and I'm sure we'll have a good heart-to-heart about
it if this one doesn't do the trick. I'm off to the blue
yonder. So long. But before I go let me say. Things I'd
Enfold If Tripizoid Really Existed:

Basic image of my sister in brush before her body
was found, as I imagine it. Alone with the hiss of wind
through the pines. The sound of waves breaking down
on the shore. Can't stop seeing that image and would
like very much to find a way to enfold it.

Entire war from start to finish with the exception
of a couple of R&R leaves, one in Saigon, another in
Hong Kong.

[Editor's Note: The following handwritten fragment was
found taped to the back of the manuscript.]

Up in the weedy ditch, not far from the lake, on a
singular fall afternoon—the few trees about a half
mile away flaming bright, astonishingly colorful, and
then beyond them the muted slate clouds against a
tinge of autumnal blue. The cop in the patrol car
just making his usual run down on Route 2, heading
west, trying to catch one more speeder, to write the
last ticket of the day, not so much trying to reach his
quota as wanting to find some way to close it down.
He was thinking of his daughter, Anna, and her play
at school, and he caught sight of the body in the

weeds, a bit of white, could've easily been some
garbage. But his cop gut was at work. The third
wayward girl he'd found that year. They always look
windblown, silent, with speckles of mud and blood on
their cheeks, and almost always the legs akimbo with
a sad kind of entwinement that speaks of being parted
and then moving back together with a kind of resistance, an elastic snapback. A naked torso. He had his
own way of looking at a body; it was a resistance to
the truth that even an officer of the law, seasoned in
those parts, having seen several bodies of young
women in woods, covered half buried in pine needles,
or mourned with leaves. Most of the killers made only
a halfhearted attempt at full burial. They were pressed
for time, or simply didn't care. Most of the killers up
there worked in homicidal haste, not giving much of
a shit if they left evidence or not, always seeming to
assume—it seemed to him—that the onus of the crime
would somehow be cast back into those twilight,
silent, betrayed eyes that stared up out of the skull,
sometimes bones, the flesh almost eaten away; the
crime—drugs, usually, and then abduction and rape
and eventually, using them up, murder—no matter
what, at least in the mind of the killers—he thought—
was a natural outcome of a sequence of events that
began far, far back, starting with a casual pickup, or a
seductive lure, or the usage of pills in various forms,
and then followed a jagged logic of fear. He theorized
a lot about this kind of stuff, as did all of his
colleagues. Anyone who came upon the end result in
the form of a body, at least any law officer, had to
go back through the chain of events, in theory,
and attempt to guess at some kind of motive—in a
mind-flash—and in doing so felt stained and sullied

and implicated somehow in the crime itself, as if by
finding the body you were playing a key role in the
death itself. Any cop will admit—in some secret part
of themselves—that they're just one step away from
the criminal; that the good-cop part is closely
associated with the fact that with ease any one of them
could've gone the other way, into crime, as an
avocation, and in making that deep admission also
saying—again silently—that crime itself is a vocation,
and around any good criminal, even a psychopath,
stood a calm that seemed to hold the realities of life in
acute focus. Psychopaths, the ones who seem to come
about it naturally, worked with a fluidity, a deeper
instinctual, even, some cops (this one included) might
say, artistic flair, and when he saw the body, as he
walked through the weeds, smelling the sweet taint
of lake breeze, he knew right away that this one had
been the work of someone in a certain zone. How
could he tell that? What triggered this sense of all-
knowing understanding in a man who had a young
daughter; in a man who had just two days ago
attended her first performance in a school play? What
part of him understood the killer, or at least told
himself—perhaps later, in retrospect—that he had had
an understanding right away, intuitively, putting two
and two together, knowing that this was some guy who
had been in Nam, or at least been through some
primal trauma—in the parlance of the times—and so
could connect somehow with the man who had killed?
(Nonsense, he'd tell himself years later, when he'd
been through so much more and understood, from the
keen view of wisdom, that what he had been sensing
at that time was just a rookie's vision. A rookie cop—
or a young cop—made up for his deficiencies, and his

fears, by creating an inner narrative that was, above all, coherent: he—or she—saw a causal sense of one thing leading to another; whereas the older, wiser cop, or the retired officer, understood that the terminal result—a dead body—was often of dispirited, random, windblown, senseless events.)

PRAYER FOR POP

Twisted on the gist of Christ
against the beat of *Raw Power*
twisted on the twist of nice
you tore another (a)hole
in the beat blood senseless
Ann Arbor night, right
before "Search and Destroy."
"Somebody's got to save
my soul, somebody's got
to save my soul . . ."

[Eugene Allen, August 20, 1973]

ACKNOWLEDGMENTS

I would like to thank those veterans who, one way or another, shared their stories as I was writing this book—in particular Chet Lubeck and Gerald McCarthy.

And thanks to those who gave me support along the way: The Guggenheim Foundation, Jonathan Franzen, Jamie Quatro, Rebecca Nagel, Andrew Wylie, Mitzi Angel, Will Wolfslau, Donald Antrim, Rodger Stevens, Joanna Goodman, David Patterson, Frank and Holly Bergon, Eric Chinski, and Laird Gallagher.

Finally, I'd like to thank my father, who died before I finished but who—I hope and pray—would've seen that this was written in the spirit of *via negativa*. His belief in the wider cosmology, in the before and the after, in the permanence of grace as the fundamental light in the darkness of existence, is the gift that keeps him alive in me.